Literary Agents Must Die!

A novel by Bo Parker

Literary Agents

Must Die!

by Bo Parker, copyright 2024

This is a literary work of humor and satire. It is a product of the author's imagination; any resemblance to persons living or dead is purely coincidental. Some locations may or may not exist. All are used purely in a fictional context, without accuracy as to their location or existence.

Book design and cover/jacket by Bo Parker

ISBN 979-8-9914709-0-2

First Edition

This book is dedicated to Alfred B. Parker and Jane B. Parker, who came to Vermont with Willie Green to build a house and carve a mountain. And to Mr. Lehman, my ninth-grade American History teacher who would wail at Tyler Rentz and me, "Tell me not in mournful numbers . . . " Now I know what he meant.

TABLE OF CONTENTS

PREFACE

There's nothing funny about mental illness. In our culture, one does not poke fun at those suffering, especially, the mentally ill.

But that's not true in the entertainment world. The mentally ill are most often portrayed in films, novels, or on stage as evil criminals or vicious serial killers. The public has little trouble accepting an insane axe murderer or a satanic character for entertainment.

In film, who can forget Stanley Kubrick's twisted characters in *Dr. Strangelove* in which nuclear war is advanced by comic, yet schizophrenic characters? Or Stanley Kramer's *It's a Mad, Mad, World* where zany characters end up in a hospital with broken bones rather than a mental care facility where they belong? That's accepted because, within this comic genre, the mentally ill are usually outlandish, lovable characters. In novels, one of my favorite Floridian writers, Carl Hiaasen, is a master at creating nutcase characters living in an unhinged world.

In today's apologetic society, there is often an attempt to shroud the sad reality of the functioning mentally ill as suffering from "eccentric behavior." Similarly, the term "crazy" has been sanitized to become "mentally ill." To the layperson, crazy denotes some manic, dangerous behavior. The second carries a broader meaning and in many cases will describe a life of profound sadness and despair.

A central character in *Literary Agents Must Die!* is comically loony and mentally ill. Like those suffering from mental illness, our heroine needs a second chance to find compassion, love, and an opportunity to live out a life in a way best suited for her.

If you'd like to know more about coping with mental illness issues or would like to become involved, a great organization is the National Alliance on Mental Illness (NAMI).

The targets of our skewers are literary agents. Certainly, most literary agents are not self-engrossed prima donnas. But as an esteemed group within the powerful media franchise we call entertainment, they can take this poke.

So, don't get your undies in a bundle and please read with an open mind. It's only a romantic lampoon, and no harm or insult is intended for anyone in particular. Keep an eye out for the next novel in Bo Parker's Revenge Series: *Lawyers and Property Developers Must Die!*

CHAPTER 1

Andy Thornton, you knucklehead!

William B. Thomas screamed, "Andy Thornton, you knucklehead!" and banged his fist against the empty 1,200-gallon sap-holding tank, making the galvanized tin sides vibrate long and loud—and giving Andy an opening to creep toward the darkest corner of the sugar shack.

"I messed up, Mr. Thomas. Anyone could have done it," Andy grumbled, avoiding eye contact.

Next to the arch and finishing tanks in the rustic hand-hewed hut stood the annoyed Vermont Association of Maple Products Board of Directors. They were very unhappy being called to the emergency meeting in William Thomas's sugar shack. Five scruffy businessmen (they hadn't shaved in three days) in traditional hunting gear were most eager to get back out into the brush to bag a buck before the season closed.

Set in a hollow of the northern tongue of the Green Mountains, only forty miles from Lake Champlain, the hut was filled with the massive evaporator (known as the "arch") and equipment ready for the year's sugar run. In another shed was coiled over a mile of wrapped green plastic piping sterilized with Clorox, ready to be plugged into the twelve hundred taps on the six hundred-plus maples of William Thomas's sugarbush. Neatly stacked along the shed's exterior walls were over fifty cords of firewood, ready to feed the arch.

* * * * * *

Not so far away, the headquarters of the Vermont Association of Maple Products, or VAMP, was located in a tidy office park in a three-unit cluster on the outskirts of Burlington. The VAMP cooperative was formed in 2002 to showcase and attract buyers of bulk maple syrup products. To show its members they were doing something with the reasonable quarterly membership dues, the board, led by William B. Thomas, agreed to initiate an aggressive and expensive promotion.

VAMP had commissioned the filling, with member-donated maple syrup, of five thousand 1.7-ounce bottles, similar to the small liquor bottles sold on airplanes. Every case of a hundred samples came with a stack of collapsed cardboard flats designed to unfold and snap together, making a strong enough box to avoid gumming up the sophisticated sorting machines of the central Rutland post office. Included in each box would be an introductory letter urging the recipient to contact VAMP for bulk purchases of their syrup products.

Samples were to be sent to large wholesale channels: grocery store purchasing agents, fast food conglomerates, nationwide restaurant chains, and out-of-state manufacturers of sweet products. Bulk manufacturers typically added a minuscule taste of legitimate maple flavor to their corn syrup-based pancake syrups, usually to create the nugget "made with real maple syrup" for their advertising departments. The bottles were filled with Grade B syrup, the darker, richer brown syrup most recognized as more flavorful and desirable by industrial users. Grade A was clearer in color and surely sweeter, but way too expensive for VAMP's shoestring promotion.

All this would have gone smoothly had the task been assigned to anyone with an iota of intelligence. But it hadn't been.

* * * * * *

Taking an allergy-induced wheezing breath, William, known as Bull to his friends, wasn't finished with Andy. "So, you're telling us, when you did the budget we approved, you added up the cost of filling the bottles, the cartons, the piecework to be done by the gals at the Rotary Hall, and finally, the cost of mailing. Correct? You told us the postage would be around a dollar apiece. So, each sample would be on its merry way for a little over two dollars! Right?"

Andy spoke meekly, causing several board members to draw closer, "Well, that's what the post office guy said."

"What did he . . ."

"When the post office guy in Rutland asked me their weight, I told him they were 1.7 ounces, and I . . ."

"Dammit, don't you interrupt me!" William's cheeky face was reddening and his index finger was pointed with a disturbing amount of quivering.

"When you brought Mr. Postman the boxed, ready-to-go sample, you asked for a postage estimate. Correct?"

"Yes, sir."

William the Bull was ready to strangle. "No, you didn't, did you? You didn't actually have him weigh the bottle and the box, did you?"

"No, sir. I mean yes, sir. Okay, I did forget the sample in my truck. It was way out in the parking lot, and I'd lose my place in line. It was a really long line, too."

"Andy, Andy, Andy. You told him they were 1.7 ounces, didn't you? But something your listless mind didn't stumble on was there's a difference between weight ounces and volume!"

William was so enraged he was turning crimson and shaking. "This is maddening!" he wailed.

One of the board members, Harold "Hal" Lusterchen, stepped forward. A retired sportswear manufacturer from Troy, New York, postwar refugee from Frankfurt, Germany, now-turned gentleman maple syrup producer and owner of 460 acres of prime sugarbush near Jay Peak. One thousand tree taps.

Hal raised his palm, curbing William, who had begun talking to himself while pacing about the room.

"Calm down, Villyam," Hal burst out in his quirky German accent. "Vee don't vant you have zee stroke or, Gott forbid, a hernia like zee last vinter on zee scheemobil."

William justly acknowledged Hal's concern, leaned against the holding tank, and caught his breath.

Hal turned to face Andy, "Andrew, tell us vat's final kosten fur sample to get to zee targets?"

"Well, when a sample was sent to my sister in Baltimore, I was told the postage would be a pig's whisker past five dollars, making it about seven bucks per."

Andy drooped his head, avoiding the board members' stares, which was followed by unanimous, deflating exhales and rolling eyes. William, his coloration returning to normal, glanced around at his associates.

"I don't think you were cut out for this type of work, Andy. Is the board in agreement, we need some new blood to manage this promotion?"

Everyone nodded in total agreement.

Moments later, Andy strutted out of the sugar shack with a final VAMP check in hand. He let the spring-loaded door slam behind him, pulled a Canadian Chesterfield from his vest pocket, and fired up. Relieved to be let go—that fucking job had too, too many details. Too much for him to remember. Too much for him to cope with. Besides, he was a good wood butcher, and his brother-in-law had cash deposits on two chalets to put up near Sugarbush.

Andy climbed into his banged-up Dodge Power Wagon and wheeled briskly out the dirt drive, smiling all the while. He was contemplating a long afternoon perched on a stool at the local slop chute, The Dusty Nailer. Maybe he'd drop a few dollars in the jukebox, listen to *The Highwaymen* a couple of hundred times before going home and announcing to Sally that he had found a new and better job.

Better not quit your shift at Walmart quite yet, honey pie.

Back in the sugar shack, after the contemplating board had had time to shuffle and reshuffle their camouflaged hunting boots on the sugar shack's dirt floor, William finally came up with a solution.

"I kinda think our KC's got time to take on more responsibility. She's been part-time, keeping the office running while her grandson gets out of diapers. She's well-versed with our members, been with us for five years. I suggest we sweet talk her into full-time. She'll do all she's been doin' and do something smart with this promotion gone haywire."

"Bull, vat more vill she kost us?" asked Hal, aware of the tenuous financial crisis they were now swimming in from the promotion catastrophe.

"It's not how much she's gonna cost. We need her. KC's been like family to the association. She'll do what she's gotta do, and honestly, too. She's smart as a whip, nice to look at, happily divorced, and knows how to sweet talk a porcupine from a tree," answered William, skipping the figure question.

Everyone nodded their heads. What's to disagree about? The seasoned, knowledgeable Kirby F. Clark, or KC, would be offered the reins as the new Director of Promotions for VAMP.

CHAPTER 2

Welcome aboard, Director Clark

Previously rock-hard as a hockey forward, in the years since leaving the ice, Kirby "KC" Clark had acquired a pleasing layer of feminine softness. This, her former husband would nibble on and irritatingly pinch during sex right before she climaxed. This would inevitably open an argument of whether the pinch was the trigger encouraging the climax or was more often an impediment to her getting off. The trouble was, when Kirby climaxed, her mind tended to go blank for a millisecond, leaving her unsure as to whether her husband was on to something or just messing with her head.

Endowed with a sharp intelligence she had disguised for years while being a gifted player on the high school's hockey team, Kirby found making As in school and university a breeze. As she was a favorite of the hockey crowd, they would chant: "Ooooooooooh, don't mess with Kirbeeeee!" whenever she pucked a goal. An active outdoorsperson, she used to enjoy jacking deer with her he-man husband who guided hunting trips up into Canada's wild parts. She now believes hunting is unpleasant and enjoys bowling, snowmobiling, and especially fishing. In her late forties and divorced, she'd settled down and bought a new townhouse near Burlington with a community outdoor pool and a used, but cherry condition, red Jeep Cherokee. No reason to remarry, she had a nice part-time job and an alimony check that covered the basics every month.

KC's proposed new responsibilities were officially defined over sausage and eggs two days later at Snap's Restaurant in Bristol.

William "Bull" Thomas, whom she'd only called Bill, explained she was to spread the good word about VAMP and ensure the safety and conformity of member products, which were generally maple syrup, maple candy, and the like. A little behind-the-scenes price fixing was also part of her responsibility, but that wasn't germane until she held the post for a year and knew every major, trustworthy member *very well*.

Kirby liked Bill Thomas. He never hit on her, never tried to sexually compromise her. She later learned from her reckless and loud-mouthed scoundrel husband that it was rumored Bill had a "defective" daughter—like his daughter needed a refit water pump or a new clutch. Apparently, she had some weird mental limitations that kept her isolated in a home across the state. This speculation led Kirby to figure Bill was religious enough that he didn't want to tempt God's further retribution for any past or future misdeeds that stank of unsanctioned procreation.

Bill, having dripped a little yellow yoke onto his wool plaid shirt, dipped his red napkin carefully in his ice water, puffed out his tummy, and stroked the yoke off.

"First and foremost, KC, we got to deal with this damn promotion mess. Your opinion?"

"You guys, the board, may not cherish my recommendation."

"Well, test me."

"First of all, Bill, let's realize this syrup is probably two seasons old and, notwithstanding the scuttlebutt and misinformation, it does age. Maybe not enough yet for anyone to notice."

"Gotcha. It shouldn't sit around much longer."

"What I'm saying best for the association is to quietly unload everything to retail. All fifty cases, along with the mailers, a tad above our cost. Offer them to restaurants, tourist shops, ski boutiques, local ma and pa groceries, and gas station marts. I'm certain they'll get gobbled up in no time."

"That sounds more work intensive," said Bill, making a slurping noise with his hot coffee.

"Not really. We don't have to use the temp agency girls to fold the carton, insert the sample and letter, and attach the preprinted addresses. And you won't have to grease the Rotary Hall."

"I get it. In simple terms, KC, your recommendation is to quietly get rid of everything by going retail."

"Yep, and before membership gets wind of the expensive screwup. We'd break even, and we would be getting our association members into more retail markets. To hell with fighting in the wholesale channels. They're giving us nothin' for our products and buying more from the Canadians, anyway."

Bill stuck his hand across the table, "Welcome aboard, Director Clark."

After sweeping Andy Thornton's promo disaster under the rug, Kirby knew she'd have to be an A-one creative to keep the full-time job. Bookkeeping was currently a two-day-a-week stint at VAMP, but she liked the idea of going full-time. Liked it a lot: medical, paid vacations, all the good stuff.

Gonna have to keep the new money quiet; don't want to upset the alimony cart.

Yes, she'd need to entertain the old buzzards on the board with a nonstop flow of imaginative and captivating solutions—and she already had one up her cozy St. John's Bay sleeve.

What was Kirby's great idea that was sure to take over America? Since the invention of the hotdog, a favorite eat for sugar-shack cookers was to drop a few dogs into the finishing evaporator. When the dog's skin fractured, shriveled fissures were created, and the syrup was quickly absorbed. Maple syrup dogs were irresistible, even to the most zealous weight-conscious and incorruptible vegetarian.

Sadly, Kirby's idea, commercializing the matching up of maple syrup and hotdogs, had been a personal disaster earlier. She used to help out in a neighbor's sugar shack at the finishing evaporator. She'd indulge in the irresistible hot dogs, which unfortunately led to a distressing bulge around her waist and hips. No workout video or trial-month membership taken at the College Street YMCA seemed to remove her "love handles," as her former husband affectionally called them.

Love handles were not Kirby's favorite thing, especially as that plumpness created pressure against her undies, causing the seams to show through her tight slacks or jeans and letting every gawker in the Grand Union know if she was wearing a thong or granny panties. Either way, she wanted her underwear selection to be private or have only privileged access, so she went on a draconian no-carbo diet, finally got rid of the nasty handles, and followed up by ditching the cheating husband.

Led by her persuasive marketing skills, VAMP could partner with Kirkland, the quarter-pound hotdog masters, and conduct a joint national rollout of their dogs infused with real Vermont maple syrup.

Kirby's head reeled with the potential. She'd have to be careful with her epic idea. Those unscrupulous Canadian producers would rip them off in a flash if they got wind of her concept and the size of the market it was sure to open.

* * * * * *

Soon after hiring Kirby, four thousand syrup samples were delivered without fanfare by Bangor's Quick & Reliable Delivery Service minivans to gas stations, mini-markets, diners, and touristy haunts throughout Vermont. Many samples landed on the premier munchie-site counters right next to the cash registers. The balance of the undistributed samples was reserved for members and friends of VAMP for which they were likely destined to become Christmas stocking stuffers.

Unbeknownst to Kirby Clark and Bill Thomas, Kirby's solution, approved by the board to resolve the maple syrup promotion fiasco, would play conveniently into an odd couple's deranged and ghoulish desires.

CHAPTER 3

One sweltering night, needing to urinate . . .

In the late 1930s, Pierre Duclos, a properly mustached French Canadian truck driver, regularly carried stripped spruce and fir logs to be milled in the U.S. for the framing industry. One blustery wet night in 1938, an axle snapped on Pierre's overloaded rig while entering the treacherous Deadman's Gulp near Salisbury. Waiting for a replacement axle from Buffalo, New York, he was forced to spend three nights at The Dewy Drop Inn, a rustic establishment owned by the Willcoxes, a traditional Vermont family with roots of mixed European ancestry.

Like most Americans, the Willcoxes were hard-pressed and still recovering from the Depression. At the time, the Wilcox family consisted of a bosomy thirty-year-old daughter, Rose, and two rambunctious sons, Johnnie and Hanson. Sadly, Johnnie was later vaporized in a fiery explosion when he foolishly used a lighter to inspect the copper spigot that was dripping moonshine in prohibition Vermont. The other son, Hanson, died only weeks later in a freak accident—a ten-point deer leaped in front of his racing jalopy truck, crashed through the windshield, and antlered him to death.

Thus, The Dewy Drop Inn, run by an aging couple and their daughter, was desperately short of masculine help.

In the wee hours of Pierre's second overnight, inspired by warm whiskey hot toddies, his disarming French accent, and a willingness to massage Rose's edematous ankles, they began a passionate sexual relationship. Over the following year, The Dewy Drop Inn became Pierre's stop of choice. On his fourth trip, a tearful Rose informed Pierre that their candlelight romps in the Evergreen Suite had led to her pregnancy.

Surprisingly, instead of a shotgun-wedding threat by old man Wilcox, Rose's practical father offered Pierre full-time employment at a reasonable salary—if he'd wed Rose and stay. Pierre already had an unhappy wife and three children in a backwater hamlet near Toronto. However, convinced he had fathered another child (it was difficult to determine for certain because of Roses' size), one who would have American citizenship, he decided to abandon his Canadian family for the innkeeper's daughter and a less dangerous life in quiet Salisbury.

When Pierre returned to Canada, he parked the rig at the mill, walked home, and told his wife he was leaving her. He said he would send money and write to the kids when they were old enough to read. This coincidentally and conveniently, fit into her aspirations with the neighborhood's widowed butcher who was rumored to have been lifting the scales and giving her an unreasonable discount on his shop specialty, Superior Sausage.

Determined to make something of himself with the fresh start, Pierre hitchhiked back to Vermont, was taken in by the Wilcox family, and began turning around the declining inn.

Ironically, it turned out Rose Wilcox wasn't pregnant. But no matter, Pierre liked the setup at The Dewy Drop Inn, and so Rose Wilcox became Rose W. Duclos. About nine months later, a local midwife tugged Tilda Wilcox Duclos, immediately tagged as "Tilly," out of Rose on the kitchen table while a cantankerous crowd of drunken friends held a birthing vigil in the Candlelight Taproom.

Soon, the inn prospered with the injection of Pierre's brawny help. Not shy about taking on more responsibilities, in addition to being a manager at the inn, he began teaching conversational French at the local junior high school. The thankful school administration not only paid him a staggering one dollar per two classes every week but aided Pierre in becoming a U.S. citizen.

Unfortunately, the fickle nature of that era was to doom the promising future of both Pierre and their infant daughter, Tilly. When the Japanese bombed Pearl Harbor in 1941, newly nationalized citizen Pierre was drafted into the Army Signal Corps. Because of his fluency in a foreign language and a simple clerical blunder, he was shipped to what was then known as Burma. Since Burma had been a British colony, his fluent French was generally useless.

Tragically, while involved in the retaking of Rangoon, Pierre was not only fighting the Japanese but also a mind-numbing, unshakable case of malaria. One sweltering night, needing to urinate, he staggered from the platoon's camp into the tiger-teeming brush and disappeared. Forever.

CHAPTER 4

Tilly had to know what it was all about

Growing up in Salisbury was stressful for Tilda Wilcox Duclos. Not only was she fatherless, but Mama Rose, her mother, was a steely task master when it came to managing the inn. But in the evenings after hours when they were alone and had kicked out the after-hours hangers-on and had closed the taproom, Rose would sit with Tilda and tell her endearing stories about her grandparents and the epic founding of The Dewy Drop Inn.

When not in school, Tilda had to work shifts just like the other four employees. If someone didn't show, Tilda had to fill in whether it was pulling beers in the taproom or maintaining order at the front desk. Steered by her mother, she was industrious like people raised in the hospitality industry often are. Never afraid of long hours in the kitchen or rising in the wee hours of the morning to be the breakfast bar hostess, Tilda was determined to succeed.

But things changed for young Tilda when she began the daily bus ride to Otter Creek High School. As most youngsters approach legal age, sexuality inevitably rears its innocent head. She wanted her love to be deeply treasured and never-ending, as portrayed on the nightly soaps she'd watch on the tiny black-and-white television at the inn's front desk.

Tilda was not unattractive, but not eye-catching either. In a homespun way, she had an obliging look about her, which too often led to being taken advantage of. Her first foray into finding love was with a reprobate high school slacker in the school parking lot while stuck in the snow waiting for the town plow to clear the lot. Attempting the deed on the tattered seat of the freezing Ford truck was jinxed from the start. Instead, it happened the following year, her junior year, in a neighbor's barn. One steamy afternoon on the straw-covered floor of a neighbor's barn and atop an itchy brown saddle blanket, she tossed away her virginity to Billy Winston, Jr., a worthwhile catch and a soon-to-be well-employed plumber's assistant.

Billy was the high school's most sexually active male student, not because of any special romantic talent, but because word got around that he was so large. All the girls from ninth grade to senior year were overcome with wanting to see it—not necessarily to have it in them. Plump and peachy-skinned, Tilda had to know what it was all about. A simple introduction to French kissing with Billy led to a hurried, painful act. As soon as it was over, Tilda knew she was already being discarded.

It was later as a high school senior that Tilda earned the moniker, Dizzy Tilly. This came from her ability to hold massive amounts of Jack Daniels and a willingness to be sexually available with almost any boy who expressed a glimmer of love and affection. With those qualifications, she was soon accepted in the seedier group of upper classmates who were for the most part having a second go-round at their senior year.

Unfortunately, Tilda had only clouded memories of her hero father, Pierre Duclos, whose sole contribution to her well-being was one spermatozoon. His tragic absence left an emptiness no amount of whiskey or beer could repair, although she persistently tried. Eventually, her compensatory activities landed her on the local constables' watch list. But, on account of her father's sacrifice to his adopted nation, her divergences from the already lax standards of the community were reflexively ignored.

At the end of her senior year, Tilda vanished from the local scene. Her few friends were confused as to why she was sent into compulsory isolation and recovery in an upstate New York clinic. Was it because of infectious tuberculous meningitis? No way! Had to have been something else! The magnanimous school principal, Wilford James, graduated her anyway, without her having to take final exams.

* * * * * *

Tilda plodded through an associate's degree from Lyndon State and, after months of searching, obtained a part-time job as an assistant librarian at the Presley Public Library in Middlebury. She rented a small two-room apartment within walking distance of the library. It overlooked Otter Creek Falls and was adjacent to the rusting water-powered generator plant abandoned in the 1920s. Around that time, she developed tinnitus. Fortunately, the rushing water over the falls helped drown out the hum she struggled to ignore. But in the quiet library stacks the relentless drone made her irritable, which led to being argumentative. Coworkers would become upset because she would say whatever popped into her head, as nonsensical or embarrassing as it might be.

Her disconcerting, unabated lack of control became more unmanageable as Tilda's employment at the library dribbled on. Sadly, she was never able to deal with this insidious handicap despite a recommendation from the head librarian to see a therapist. Tilda brushed it all off with, "Everyone has the right to be angry at idiots!"

Within a few years of living in Middlebury and away from the inn, which was only a fifteen-minute drive away, Tilda had finally weaned herself from the constant interference by her mother. Poor Rose had by then slipped into dementia and was spending her final days in a Pittsford care home. The Dewy Drop Inn was being run by a surrogate management firm, part of the Best Western chain, and Tilda was left without responsibilities.

* * * * * *

Unlike most of her school peers who wanted steady jobs, to get married, and breed, Tilda went her own eccentric direction. For a decade, she became a weekend hippy: a love child steeped in pot, whiskey, and loud rock and roll. Unfortunately, her cantankerous nature hardly made her acceptable as a love-and-peace advocate, though she had adapted to the free love aspect of the movement. Having lost her father in World War II, her rabid, beat-the-shit-out-of-them-in-Vietnam attitude didn't sit well with the younger activist antiwar crowd, causing her to be shunned by the unconventional communities she visited that had sprouted up all over Vermont.

Outside of a few public events and the Halloween parade in Middlebury, Tilda didn't socialize or meet men or women for companionship. Once in a while, she'd meet a young tourist or an athletic out-of-town cross-country skier and return to his motel or lodge for anonymous sex. After each encounter, she'd leave him with the memory of a kooky experience and a bogus phone number.

It took Tilda most of her youth to realize that true and enduring love would not be found with mere mortals. Their sloppy, demanding acts were too often downright unpleasant, especially if the occasion came with the peril of wanting a further relationship.

The few contacts she had in town would speculate why she shaved her shapely legs but never her armpits. Other than that eccentricity (but not so strange for Vermont), which some men found enticingly erotic, her few pals from school and more recent library associates were kept in the dark about her nonexistent social life.

CHAPTER 5

The reason she had such beautiful
white porcelain skin

On Tilda's birthday, Mama Rose Wilcox Duclos passed at seventy-five years old, wheezing in her emphysema sleep. For Tilda, it was not unexpected; Rose had smoked Lucky Strike cigarettes since age fourteen, fuming nonstop like the nearby copper smelting furnace that Salisbury was known for.

Tilda was willed the entire estate of Rose Duclos and family—except for five hundred dollars that went to the Rosicrucian Order, a membership Mama Rose had cherished. The Dewy Drop Inn was sold to the Best Western motel chain and, as there were no other heirs, the probate court awarded Tilda a substantial inheritance; most of which she put in an annuity and savings bonds. Any furniture Tilda wanted from the inn was already in her Otter Creek apartment.

* * * * * *

Having kept a portion of her inheritance in liquid funds, she had more than enough cash to buy a rundown farm on Grover Hill Road in the Village of Lincoln. She was happy to leave the Otter Creek apartment.

The history of Tilda Duclos' quaint farmhouse and hay barn was a mystery. When she bought it, there were few disclosure laws about the previous owners' wrongdoings or any God-awful happenings in the house. It wasn't like the place was cursed, it was just that inhabitants never flourished or made any sort of name for themselves. The previous owners, an aging couple, had let the farm and property decay. Tilda didn't care. She fell in love with the place and knew it would be her home for a long, long time. She bought it a week later with cash.

"If the shoe fits, wear it!" Is what Mama Rose would have said about anything— even if there were doubts, and Tilda had none.

The farm had none of the traditional shanty outbuildings for agricultural storage or, as in Vermont tradition, old cars. The single wood barn was larger than the farmhouse and in better condition. It had the typical low-ceiling basement with animal pens and pigsties. Above that was the main ground-level space for farm equipment, twin-side hay lofts, and two mammoth doors that hung on rusted sliding runners that opened to the outside facing the farmhouse.

The farm's water originated from a small hutch built over a hand-dug cistern. The cistern created a shallow pool that was fed by a slow-running spring. A buried underground iron pipe from the pool gravity-fed the farmhouse and a branch line split off to the barn. Because the spring was fed from a glacial moraine lying only a few feet below the rocky topsoil, there were questions as to the potability of the water from ground contamination.

It was rumored the success of Tilda's later neighbor, Williams Dairy, came from dosing their fledgling herd with antibiotics at a time when overdose and substance longevity results were unclear. For certain, the antibiotic residue in the multitude of cow piles from the Williams dairy herds was leaching under the ancient stone wall dividing their property and right into Tilda Duclos' spring-fed cistern. Perhaps it was the reason she had such beautiful white porcelain skin.

The rocky moraine under the farm site drew potato-size or larger rocks through the thin topsoil. After decades of being unattended, the fields had become too dangerous for cow grazing. Previously cleared swathes of land used for corn and hay crops had long gone fallow. Out of simple neglect, the farm was now useful only as a homestead—or as an attraction for wandering tourists to gawk, "Look at the quaint old farmhouse and barn—the stories it could tell!"

Gilmore Brook bound the farm's west side, across from which was a mature pine forest planted in the early fifties. The trees had gone decades without trimming and had grown too misshapen to be harvested for telephone poles or even 2x4s for Lowes or Home Depot. From what was Tilda's second-story bedroom window, she could gaze across the unproductive hay fields to that distant, majestic pine forest on the other side of the brook. When she first visited the farm with the chatty real estate agent—who refused to enter the decrepit farmhouse, the tall, unharvested forest must have reminded her of her tree-feller father, Pierre Duclos, who was said to be tall and handsome.

Because of that, Tilda named her new home The Lost Pine Farm.

Irregularly drawn, the south quadrant ran alongside an odd-shaped tongue of virgin land belonging to the Green Mountain National Forest. That property, covered with forest, would never be disturbed. The north boundary of Tilda's land was delineated by an eighteenth-century colonial stone wall that had protection under Vermont's preservation laws and regulations. Tilda's hay barn sat parallel to that wall, and when Tilda first bought the farm, there was a small vacation home on the opposite side of the wall used only in the summer months by an out-of-state family.

Decades or so later, a suspicious fire destroyed the neighbor's small vacation home; Williams Dairy pounced and bought the property from the Jersey owners before it was on the market. They cleared the charred remains of the vacation home with backhoes, dug up any cow-tripping stones, and returned the acreage to grazing land. Still, the bulk of Tilda's

124 acres existed as an isolated 82-acre patch on the other side of the main state road where her gravel drive originated. That parcel was better suited for cows because it had fewer cow-tripping stones and was targeted by Williams Dairy as a future purchase and expansion possibility.

* * * * * *

As soon as Tilda closed on the property, she had a Shoreham carpenter create a robust two-legged pine sign: The Lost Pine Farm. The lettering was curved, or horseshoed, as if it were a sunset or sunrise, having the two words "Lost Pine" at the peak and "The" and "Farm" in slightly smaller lettering. It ended up looking similar to the logo for a local creamery. Tilda dug the two holes for the two support legs at the top of her gravel drive where it intersected with the tarmac of the main road. The sign, of which she was very proud, was large enough to announce her presence but small enough to make it a tough target for bottle-throwing hooligans.

Before moving in, Tilda wisely hired several village boys to clean the farmhouse, do minor repairs on the roof, and re-nail the warping siding. They helped her turn the gas stove and electricity back on, and reglazed several cracked windows. In the low-ceiling basement, they set a used clothes washer she bought from Bing's Antique & Collectable Bazaar on bricks to keep it off the dirt floor.

Perhaps, because of that economic investment with the Village of Lincoln youth, whom Tilda generously paid, she was measured as a worthwhile citizen by the Lincoln community. They likely did not have library-using children.

No one, except Sam Piper, the easy-going local Subaru mechanic, got to know Tilda Duclos beyond a friendly nod at the Grand Union grocery.

CHAPTER 6

Opened for a life clouded
by mental illness

Holding on to the library job became more and more demanding for Tilda. She had a twenty-minute commute to the library, meaning she had to get up much earlier than she liked and deal with winter weather. Worse, she was tasked with helping children learn the rituals of Boolean searches and dealing with the library's out-of-sequence check-ins and returns on tired, dog-eared 5x7-inch file cards. It was a no-brainer for a while—as long as she didn't have to talk to anyone over twelve.

Eventually, handling the rambunctious children at the library was beyond her patience level, causing Tilda's abnormal behavior to surface too frequently. After several children whined and complained to over-concerned, caring parents, Head Librarian Jane Franken asked Tilda Duclos to resign. Tilda did, and was happy to leave the Presley Public Library and the no-neck monsters she no longer had dealt with.

* * * * * *

Tilda welcomed the quiet life. She stopped drinking Jack Daniels and cut down smoking weed to only evenings after chores. She tended a proper garden, one large enough for a single person to maintain, and at the most, called for squatting three days a week. She grew most of her food, only buying eggs, meats, and canned items at the Bristol Grand Union. For a while, her life became simple, settled, and void of conflict.

Tilda's days and evenings were spent reading home shelter magazines or watching television while nibbling on radishes and carrots from her garden. On TV, she was especially fond of heart-wrenching, homey series like *Little House on the Prairie* or shows that featured imaginary characters like *Bewitched* or *I Dream of Jeannie*. They often made her cry.

Two fateful events years apart followed Rose's passing and Tilda's acquiring the farm. Tilda was driven to find out what had happened to her out-of-wedlock child, which led nowhere. Then, out of the blue, she witnessed a disastrous accident that left her grieving and despondent. Not having emotional support from family or friends, her ability to cope was stretched. Repeatedly, she'd stay up until dawn smoking her homegrown pot to revisit her tough times. This depression, a distinct, separate illness, was piled onto her already fragile state.

In some forms of mental illness, as errant thoughts arise and are not tempered by the psyche's normal balancing mechanism, a separate reality may be created. Over many lonely years, Tilda became dependent upon her imagination to create companionship. She nurtured imaginary characters that were borne out of her whims, desires, and, unfortunately, paranoia. Her creations were, by all standards, relative to her overall unhinged life, as real to her as day. Mumbling while hanging laundry or talking to garden plants would seem harmless to any normal person. Unfortunately, such innocuous behavior led Tilda to sit on the porch in her rocker, knitting surreal scarves, while explaining the ins and outs of the Dewy Decimal System to an audience of rapt students seated symposium-style on the overgrown grass. She would allow some good students to sit on the hood of her cherished Subaru.

* * * * * *

Her profane brother, Timothy, didn't materialize overnight. One afternoon after having furiously smoked her powerful homegrown weed all day, Tilda slipped off the proverbial lily pad into the proverbial pool of despair. Tormented, she contemplated suicide and prayed for someone to help her. Shortly thereafter, in a perplexing phenomenon, a young man in red cowboy boots appeared ambling down her driveway. His name was Timothy, and he had come from the village for a chat with his older sister.

In the beginning, Timothy would linger for only a few minutes to engage her rootless mind and give her a short shot of comfort. Tilda would usually have a headache after one of his visits, which may have come from having to imagine all his particulars. But over the years, she had worked-out who he was so clearly, he became an effortless process and could come and go on his own. He also became successful in telling her what to do.

Unfortunately, Timothy grew into a vile creation: a primal, pleasure-seeking wacko. Her superego, which Timothy's animal-instinctual-based id was supposed to answer to, and whose behavior would normally be tempered by, was nullified by the progressive mental illness that he stimulated in her. As he settled in, she finally had someone else to focus on, and real people hardly mattered.

This was evident in Tilda's wardrobe she had simplified to gray sweatpants or short plaid skirts, faded message or event T-shirts, weird blouses knotted at the waist, bizarre scarves she knitted herself, and her mainstay—yellow rubber galoshes. No doubt her strange appearance further isolated her from the quiet community.

Whether Tilda's disconnect was caused by nature or nurture was immaterial. Had Tilda gotten timely medical help, any attending psychiatrist would have recognized the door was permanently opened for a life clouded by mental illness.

CHAPTER 7

The sacred wall had been breached

Tilda arrived home in her faded red 1992 Subaru Legacy Wagon as the sun was creeping behind the misty ridges of the western face of the Green Mountains. The tired Subaru dieseled, it continued to run after the key was turned off, and backfired several times before dying. It would only be brought to Sam Piper's Garage when it wouldn't start or an irritating red light remained on for more than a month. Often as not, even after a short run, it wouldn't restart until it rested awhile.

Tilda and Timothy christened it Slobberu because it continually leaked unrecognizable fluid, a fluid that killed the grass and forced her to park in rotating spots about the front yard. They enjoyed giving inanimate and unfamiliar things engaging names. The woodchuck living under the barn was named Fartsy because Tilda stumbled upon him one afternoon and scared out a loud fart from him as he dove into the home he had dug under the stone foundation. The Canadian geese that transited twice a year were named, unremarkably, Shitters.

Tilda loaded both arms with brown bags of groceries from the backseat, having just returned from the Grand Union. She cursed out loud, "Damn, my foolish mind!" Forced to squander ten cents each for bags when she had a handful of canvas shopping bags hanging from a dowel on the kitchen door. The irritating oversight made her so cross she raised a galoshed foot and kicked Slobberu's door shut.

Glancing downward to rebalance the bags, an ominous shadow came into view between her short, pleated skirt and yellow galoshes. Startled, she swung about to face two enormous brown eyes beset with flies. Streams of goo slid from the pinkish nostrils of the inquisitive, yet harmless, Holstein. Tilda warily backed away, then sprinted to the front door, raining a trail of groceries as she went. Short of breath, but relieved to be out of the gaze of the errant black-and-white, she double-locked the door behind her.

Who knew what powers were harnessed onto that diabolical beast?

Unloading the bags and finding spots on the open kitchen shelves for gelatin packets, Joy dish soap, Campbell's soups, and two six-packs of Dr Pepper, Tilda hummed her favorite ditty, the advertising tune from the seventies' Dr Pepper commercials. A glance out the sink window and its tattered, frilly curtains caused her heart to skip a beat. The beast had ventured nose-close to the window and was intently staring inside.

When it pressed a gooey nose against the glass, depositing a big wet mush, Tilda boldly racked open the window and flung out a can of corn chowder that bounced off the white blotch between its bulging brown eyes. The startled cow let out a big moo, turned, and lazily trotted off, wagging the plastic yellow ID strip punched in its ear.

Unsettled, Tilda couldn't escape the conflict the delinquent beast had drawn to the surface.

The sacred wall had been breached, and that was an omen!

She sat at the kitchen table and put her hands to her head, feeling sullen and glum. Fortunately, Timothy appeared, framed against the classic rounded door to the living room.

Tilda's younger brother was tall and slim with a mullet of blondish hair. He was of an indeterminate age, adolescent in appearance, but eerily mature. Most often, she'd have him in a James Dean outfit: extra-long blue jeans for him to grow into with extended turned-up cuffs riding atop red cowboy boots. As so often seen in films of the fifties, his pristine white T-shirt held a compressed pack of Marlboros rolled under the sleeve. He never appeared without a red paisley bandana knotted around his neck, just like Gene Autry.

But today was different. He wore a brown khaki shirt with twin flap pockets and epaulets that gave him an official, manly appearance like a game warden, forester, or surveyor. Timothy had forced himself off the couch, his favorite haunt, and had stopped to scratch his back against the door jamb while dramatically exercising his arms.

"What's got you so bummed, Sis?"

"There's a vicious heifer loose. Damn beast chased me into the house, then came to the window." She pointed as if there was a question about which window.

"Really? That's new. What'd you do?"

"I beaned it with chowder and it ran off. Haha, I hate those smelly cows. I think when it crossed over, it must have absorbed some pernicious spirit."

"What the hell are you talking about, 'pernicious spirit'! Yes, the wall's monstrous, but it won't do shit to a cow." Timothy relished chastising Tilda when she said something really stupid.

"Don't you get it? It's come over. Nothing should come over our wall!"

"Jesus, Tilly, some rocks discovered gravity and Moo Moo climbed over. Big deal, it's happened before. They'll fix it."

"That may be," she said listlessly.

"See how you're becoming more and more a drama queen? Don't know how I put up with you."

Timothy returned to the living room couch.

"Timothy, you're supposed to help me! Don't you see you're not helping?"

Irritated, she jumped up and stormed outside to rescue the dropped groceries and the tossed chowder can. On a second trip, she grabbed the two plastic containers of purified water resting on the bare metal frame where Slobberu's back seat had long ago been—but had disappeared.

CHAPTER 8

Never ever dress better than MJ!

Meanwhile, obtusely linked to Vermont Association Maple Products and the aberrant life of Tilda Wilcox Duclos, three hundred miles south on the Upper West Side of Manhattan, the Romance Agents & Writers Guild, or RAWG, had been struggling with membership since its inception in 2010. Or the lack of it. The upcoming Book Expo XII at the Jacob Javits Convention Center on the Hudson was where over two hundred book trade companies, publishers, agents, literary associations, and guilds would set up booths and try to make a year's business in three days.

This year's book expo was crucial for the guild's survival. The owner, founder, and head is Martha Jane Sidel, better known as MJ. A thin, silver-haired dynamo whose fame rocketed in the late nineties with a series of turn-of-the-century romance novels that flew off the shelves. MJ was very crafty. In her short biography, she used every heart-pulling string to dramatize her rise from an orphanage in upstate New York to her resounding success as an indefatigable loner in the dog-eat-dog literary world.

Of course, she marginalized the impact of her adopted school teacher mother who taught her to read when she was four and her engineer stepfather who read her fairy tales every night before bed.

Finding none smarter or more capable than herself in arm-twisting, back-stabbing, and self-promotion, she became her own literary agent. When a detached retina (likely caused by excessive black coffee, vodka overindulgence, and screaming at assistant Pamela) made writing difficult, and she couldn't find anyone to sit long enough to transcribe for her, she took advantage of her contacts and business acumen and put everything she had squirreled away into setting up the guild.

The guild's world headquarters was in MJ's Third Avenue two-bedroom East Side apartment. On workday mornings, Pamela Jean Gadfrey, her shrinking violet of an assistant, came in at nine after collecting the mail from the lobby mailroom. Pamela was MJ's life raft. Her common-sense Pennsylvania Dutch approach had to slave relentlessly to resolve the numerous and usually mindlessly created problems that MJ's abusive nature generated.

Among other particulars, one of the first things she learned about working for MJ was to *never ever dress better than MJ!*

MJ's official bio portrayed her as a passionate student of literature who rose from obscure, humble beginnings in upstate New York. Though she rarely talked about her youth, one drunken afternoon MJ confessed to Pamela she regretted never having had a real family. In contrast, desiring both a career and a family with Jeffery, her lover, Pamela was determined to work as long as she could at the guild and to learn everything about the business. This came down to yet another fundamental principle: *Don't be anything like MJ!*

* * * * * *

This morning, MJ was up and about in her black power suit with a ruffled white blouse and glossy red flats with little gold chains. Typically, MJ would spend the next hour on the phone at her desk with a small mirror finishing her makeup while Pamela would dutifully bring her successive cups of black coffee.

Pamela had already wasted two minutes looking at twenty-four new query submissions and finding nothing worth a response. MJ put her palm over the phone, "Pamela, be a dear and bring me the rouge compact from my bathroom. Oh, and Cecil Rhodes is going to call any second."

Her office landline phone rang just seconds after hanging up from her previous call. As advertised, it was Cecil Rhodes, CEO of the fastest-growing self-publishing empire, C. Rhodes & Associates, based in Canberra, Australia.

"Yes, Cecil, how are you? . . . Oh, it's been a long, long year for me, too! Cecil, listen, darling, I rang you to discuss getting on board with us! . . . Not kidding, we're going gangbusters with a tented symposium at the expo . . . Cecil . . . Let me finish. You know we're the must-go-to for wanna-be romance authors seeking representation. Our members, you bet they're indulgent! . . . I understand you've got to go . . . I'll have Pamela email our website rates. Hang on just another minute . . ."

Pamela stood nearby with butt cheeks balanced against the back of a Parsons chair, one of two that faced her desk. MJ didn't like her sitting around when she was going to rattle off important instructions. Pamela dutifully keyed into her iPad: Send $ info Cecil R@ C & B Pub.

"Cecil, there's an ad space available in our quarterly packet that'll be mailed to every member . . . Oh? I didn't know you'd do such a small print run or I would have called you immediately . . . Of course! Love you. Bye-bye, sweetie!"

MJ slammed down the phone.

"That man's a fucking alligator. The bastard trapped me, angling for our pitiful press work. I'd like to wring him by the gonads, that unctuous Australian hippo."

Pamela frowned, quizzically.

"What Pamela? What now? You're going to tell me Australia doesn't have hippos?"

"No, not at all. I was wondering how this will sit with our membership. Advertising self-publishing on the guild's site when we're all about getting an agent?"

"Good point. We're not going to say anything unless Cecil wants to join us or until the expo is nearly over. Can you be really clear about that and not flub up in your little chit-chats with board members, Pamela?"

"Yes ma'am."

"We need to nail down the speaker's roster with the gang. Take care of the bills while I make a few calls. Pay anything under two hundred. Anything over, do a part pay."

MJ had the roster of speakers on her laptop from the guild's hierarchy of agents. They were the reliable few who could be available to respond to blog questions, put a human face on the guild at events, and contribute one article a year to the guild's website. Being in the hierarchy had one requirement: to have written a best seller on any subject or to have represented an author having a best-selling book in the past five years. That was, alas, a flexible requirement since, even though MJ led the speaker's list, she hadn't been on a best-seller's list in two decades.

MJ would begin with her close friend, Phylis Cartland, of Cartland & Associates Literary Agents. She picked up the phone.

"Phylis, it's MJ. Am I calling too early? . . . Great! I saw your *How to Get and Keep the Agent of Your Dreams* is still selling—hurray, hurray! I know you'll love talking about it at the expo. You're our opening act in the best slot, mornings at nine! How cool is that! . . . What about the money? It's a generous 10 percent of our net, the same as last year . . . Phylis, let's not delve again into the past! We'll work it out, I promise . . . I've got another call coming in. We'll talk soon, ta-ta."

Anticipating her next request, more coffee, Pamela came in from the kitchen with a refilled cup. MJ was shaking her head, irritated.

"Phylis can be such a pain in the colon. She should be paying me to be a speaker! Let's look at the Javits figures again."

Pamela scrolled through her laptop.

"We paid the one-half deposit for the 30x40 floor space. A tent and a hundred chairs are set for the three days and paid for. Javits' union crew will meet everything at the loading dock and move it to our space. We do all the tents, display set-up, et cetera, and we have to arrange the chairs. We're obligated to restack afterward, and they'll move everything to the loading dock."

"Our commitment to that booth, that's not in concrete, is it? We can change to a less expensive booth until when exactly?"

"After today, the whole fee is due or we're canceled without a deposit refund. And they're sold out," said Pamela nonplussed.

MJ inhaled like she was headed underwater. She figured the guild should be able to sign up two hundred new members over the three days. With the yearly membership a reasonable sixty dollars, success at the expo should allow the guild to survive another year.

"Let me check in with Jennifer." MJ punched in a number.

"Another fuckin' machine . . . Oh, morning Jennifer! It's me, sweetie. Calling to make sure we're on board with the expo timetable. I've got you in the very best slot and when the crowd should be the largest. Hugs, hugs!"

Jennifer Rousch. MJ knew Jennifer as an unpleasant, overconfident braggart. Of course, she would talk endlessly about her frequent publishing coups until she ran out of time at the dais. Especially grating was how her cheesy book on self-editing netted her $75,000 in the first six months. Now, as an agent, she crows about private editing and writing lessons for the rich and talentless!

Next on MJ's must-call list was Betty Sampson at Ready to Print Literary Agency. Betty Sampson was a real crowd pleaser as she'd spend her hour telling an audience how to use descriptive sex in their romance novel without becoming pornographic or library-banning offensive. She delighted in reading aloud from her work, which disgusted MJ. But she'd never tell her that since Betty drew big crowds.

"Machine again, thank God . . . Hi, Betty, sweetie, it's me. Just checking in with you about the symposium at the expo. I have you in the very best slot, right after lunch for each of the three days! I'm sure you'll have a packed audience! Bye-bye, my love!" she disconnected.

"Pamela, darling, what do you think about inviting that new Latino agent, Silvia Martinez, as a special guest? She's been getting new writers out of Brazil. I wouldn't mind showing we're a 'with it' organization, ready to lend a hand in discovering new talent in South America. You know, a synergy thing, north meets south."

"I hear most of her clients are in jail or going to jail, so I'd think twice, MJ."

"I could let her do my opening slot one morning instead of my standard spiel. I'll ring her later. Get me her number: Silvia Martinez Literary Agent. I think she's upper, upper, and beyond Upper East Side."

"Yes ma'am."

So, the four of them: Martha Jane Sidel, Phylis Cartland, Jennifer Rousch, and Betty Sampson, would be touted along with the legions of other Jacob Javits Book Expo XII participants in the flood of press releases that fed the media. Web announcements, trade advertisements, and television video clips—everything was falling in line for the media onslaught to begin in two weeks.

CHAPTER 9

What's for dinner, and will I ever get laid again?

Just a cab jaunt south from Martha Jane's RWAG office apartment, and barely missing the Williamsburg Bridge afternoon shadow, sits the Lower Manhattan Seventh Police Precinct, Special Investigations Division. As of yet, uninvolved with Tilda Duclos and Timothy's ongoing saga, Detective Charles White is plopped at his desk reading a notice from his condo board announcing its intention to raise everyone's maintenance fee for repointing the building's historic facade.

Fittingly, Detective White's hair had begun turning a mature white in his thirties, which many women found appealing. Overall, he was considered to be attractive, but not movie-star handsome.

A meticulous and steady officer with less than a year until retirement, White had been recently assigned to manage the squad investigating suspicious deaths and unsolved crimes involving any sort of weirdness. The squad consisted of two other detectives who had been assigned regular homicide duties until some mishap occurred that White couldn't handle alone. On the force for twenty-six years, among other anxieties, he was unprepared for the drastic life realignment brought on by both the passing of his wife and approaching retirement.

Detective White had been serving under unit Commander "Crime Never Takes a Holiday" Mahoney. Usually a nice guy with the old timers, Mahoney was generously allowing Detective White to comfortably glide into retirement, which meant keeping him away from bullets or having to be on his feet most of the day. As if to make up for having the same name as a police cadet caricature in a goofy motion picture, the best result came from taking Mahoney very seriously. If you wandered the other way, he could be a real dick.

Unfortunately, Mahoney couldn't do anything about Detective White's condo maintenance hike.

A fly-fishing aficionado, White spent most of the morning contemplating the snap of his new Scott bamboo rod and Tibor Signature reel being put to the test in the rippling waters of upstate New York, or maybe Vermont. The custom-made rod and reel combo with the top grade #3 line had set him back nearly a half month's pay. But to those knowledgeable about fishing, the combo would signify that this man knew his stuff and that there was no limit to his devotion to the art of fly fishing. Indulging in the fantasy, White was hoping to sneak out of town for a three-day weekend, using one of his sick days. That is, if nothing lands on his desk.

Having spent a month tying his fly designs patterned after the famous "Dog Puke Golden Stone," Charles was sure his alterations to the classic would draw even the cagiest, largest trout out of the deep, dark recesses of the nation's waterways. For this season, in addition to the new rod and reel combo, he'd be properly decked out in a new Simms vest (festooned with his self-tied flies), a green wader combo, and a new Tilley hat.

Yes, Charles was a man of action, and he liked casting the rippling and chaotic river waters, not lake fishing for "gulpers."

Somebody, please take my picture for the Cabela catalog cover!

Sadly, his portly wife Mary, who adored chocolate, hated exercise, and had struggled with diabetes consequently, would not be joining him.

A massive stroke while at her paperless desk at the West Street Verizon phone company headquarters was a surprise to everyone except her indifferent HMO cardiologist. While his police duties kept him fit, he tried to get Mary to eat right and exercise. Her passing before attaining a ripe old age was a foregone conclusion to the prissy gym-committed colleagues in her office. Charles was assured by the emergency room physicians that her stroke was only momentarily painful.

Ironically, *had* Mary pounded the pavement the short distance to her downtown office or pedaled Charles' exercise bike on the terrace overlooking the Hudson, and *if* she had gotten an iota of exercise or stuck to a low-carb diet, he would have never been able to splurge on the expensive fishing tackle or his other adolescent-driven indulgence: a slightly used, shadow-grey 2020 Corvette with Adrenaline Red leather interior.

Charles and Mary's two daughters grew up in the family nest in New Jersey. One had recently resettled in Colorado with a boyfriend and the other, married to an insurance claims adjuster, was sticking it out in Teaneck, New Jersey. Selling the home in Teaneck at the peak of the market, Charles and Mary easily afforded an expensive two-bedroom condo near Battery Park with Statue of Liberty views.

As for vacations, to get an afternoon of trout fishing, Charles found it necessary to glamorize Vermont antiquing to Mary, an avid *Antiques Roadshow* watcher. She'd drop him off in her Volvo wagon near the chosen stream, commit to reappear in five hours, then drive off in search of an undiscovered eighteenth-century pie crust table like the one auctioned at Sotheby's for a cool quarter million.

After thirty years of marriage, few things interfered with how deeply he loved Mary. Sex was roly-poly good, but not experimental enough. Worst vexation: Mary was incapable of watching television alone. Charles, tough on the beat but a pussycat at home, would be roped onto the sofa for programming she'd select. Within minutes, she and their mischief-making short-haired terrier, Mister Fritz, would be snoring while Charles would be sinking into the overstuffed s ofa w atching *Midsomer Murders*, a show he loathed. Sloppy police work and three inane murders being solved by the phony-baloney DCI was engaging, but professionally irritating.

Another pet peeve absorbed by Charles, there was no such thing as "free time" when at home. The grinding refrain he heard over and over again for thirty years was, "*Charles, please fix this!*"

And then there was the walking of Mister Fritz. That was not so much of a chore, it was just that Mary wouldn't ask until it was a matter of necessity for Mister Fritz and had to be done right away. With so many duties, Charles scarcely had a moment to tie his flies or fantasize about sneaking off for a day to cast the rapids. The basic gripes, so simple to amend, were ignored by Mary. But Mary was gone, and there was now no need to argue about who would feed and walk Mister Fritz.

Life with the NYPD had been good for him. Outside of paper cuts at his desk and having his right hand crunched in a cruiser's back door by his reckless partner (instead of the perp's head), he had been seriously hurt only one other time in the line of duty. A bullet from a hopped-up pimp's gun got him.

As the Channel 4 reporter gravely opined, "In an armed robbery gone bad . . ." Unfortunately for Charles, the small 22-calibre bullet missed his Kevlar vest. Fortunately, it passed only through a side roll of baby fat that he had acquired from too often eating eggs and double bacon on a Kaiser at the all-night Sunrise Diner, the precinct's greasy spoon hangout. The round left a tiny puncture wound where it entered, but an ugly scar where it tumbled as it exited. A week in the hospital, several nice police commendations, and a coveted bump up to Detective First Grade followed. As far as he was concerned, the bad guys got enough years in Attica and he made out like a bandito.

So, with two years of grieving behind him, Detective Lieutenant Charles White had solid reasons for anticipating happiness as a civilian bachelor. Except for the feisty Mister Fritz, the dog he had once planned to gift to their New Jersey daughter, he was free of most adult responsibilities. Months away from retirement, he was nonetheless grappling with a widowed retiree's most existential dilemma: *What's for dinner, and will I ever get laid again?*

CHAPTER 10

There was something amiss
with her ethereal brother

As an only child, Tilda Duclos had always wanted a little brother. The incestuousness of rural Vermont, marrying cousins and such, tickled her childish imagination. Tilda, as an unbounded adult, had no limits for imaginary family bonding. So, when Timothy Duclos showed up, this impulse took on a bawdy new direction.

Satisfying sexual play came guiltlessly with Timothy, plus the added blessing she was in control and couldn't get pregnant. Satiating her raging sexuality by fondling herself in front of Mama Rose's antique mirror, pivoted in front of the bed on a mound of pillows, and accompanied by stark-naked Timothy doing a dervish dance urging her on—their play solved most of her physical needs.

During those times when Tilda was not entwined with her second state and she had bouts of behaving normally, she recognized there was something amiss with her entertaining brother. He would show up unannounced and then disappear with hardly a word, which she didn't like. Unable to proclaim his existence or reveal him to others, she nonetheless was determined to maintain his companionship. She fantasized he might be a sexual predator and unsuitable to engage with the few people who might have reason to be in touch with her. In reality, none of the people she interacted with would be surprised to learn her intimacy needs were met by a phantom brother. After years of interactions with townspeople, she had become sort of an oddity in the community; the yellow galoshes she wore all the time gave her freakishness away.

During those times when Timothy's existence collided with reality, reality would step in and her dear brother would vanish in a puff. Like the time a skinny character came to her door in a wrinkled white shirt under a wrinkled brown suit, a wrinkled wide tie, and a crinkled plastic county tax assessor's office ID around his neck.

"Ms. Duclos, how many adults reside in your residence?" he asked, looking up from an electronic clipboard, preparing to check off boxes with a candy-cane stencil. Tilda answered one, but her exclusion of Timothy left her anxious for days.

* * * * * *

Decades after her dismissal from the Presley Public Library, Tilda read in the *Addison Independent* a benefactor had gifted the library a mountain of refurbished Acer laptops from a settlement in a big box store liquidation. She had to have one. But since she hadn't worked at the library for decades, the new head librarian saw no justification for Tilda Duclos to receive one gratis.

Since Tilda's forced retirement from the library came without fanfare or a gold watch, Ms. Tilda Wilcox Duclos had sent the library a scathing letter stating her dismissal had been mishandled and was a flagrant breach of Vermont State employment laws. The library's board of directors felt they had better defuse the situation as there was no statute of limitations on bad publicity, especially for an institution with programs relying on the largess of donors.

Tilda was sent an Acer laptop, along with a thick folder of documents for her signature. The documents stated the laptop was a temporary loan or she could purchase it outright by paying a monthly stipend.

Tilda spent six months learning the basics of computing on the laptop through long and mind-numbing telephone conversations on the Acer information hotline, which undoubtedly stressed the lives of many Indian and Pakistani tech operators—and surely did not help America's overseas reputation.

Now, having the means to express herself in a manner that lent to universal dissemination, Tilda was determined to write a story that would make her painful life experience a savior to others. Her romantic narrative was one young people would innately understand and would help them through the despairing and hopeless years of adolescence. For Tilda, this in itself was life-reenforcing bliss.

Soon, she was spending hours on her Acer laptop, creating the most important romance novel since, as she unabashedly proclaimed, *Gone with the Wind*. She was not unlike The Blues Brothers' "on a mission from God."

Her novel, *Final Love,* is a turn-of-the-century tale of a gifted, misunderstood waif-like girl. She seeks love with a shy lad whose hand had been mangled in a devastating accident. Also an only child, he lived on the other side of a colonial stone wall with uncaring, cruel parents. Over the interlocking stones of the fortress wall, they are magnetically drawn, by the power of love, to bravely reach across—and touch.

As alluded to in *Final Love,* Tilda knew for a fact the colonial stone wall dividing her property had been a nefarious participant in an horrific act that had years before permanently scarred her. Sinister emanations from the stone wall were also set on bewitching the young lovers Tilda had created.

She revisited the epic line that came to her in an inspirational bolt from the Acer: "It was only a simple wall of keenly placed stone three feet high, but it became a barrier to unwavering love that stretched to the heavens…"

Now, the unscalable wall had been breached by an ordinary, snot-dripping, milk-leaking bovine, something her child characters were never able to do!

"Perhaps, I need to rewrite that crucial twist to my saga," announced Tilda.

"Nah, it's perfect!" bellowed Timothy, coming into the room at just the right moment as was his habit. "Don't change a fucking word! The flaw lies not in our words but with Moo Moo!"

"Timothy, Timothy, it's not that easy," voiced Tilda.

"Ever since those buggers at the Burlington Historical Museum christened our wall, 'a notable example of eighteenth-century colonial homesteader construction' . . . it's been rocky for us," Timothy said, enjoying his pun.

"It's infuriating!" Tilda proclaimed. "A green car, one of those with the sliding side door, was stopped at the top of our driveway. Tourists in disgusting shorts, wearing ugly T-shirts—who's John Mayer anyway? Wearing Jesus-freak sandals, snapping shots of our wall with their iPhones! For God's sake, taking pictures of our wall!"

"Is nothing sacred?" noted Timothy smoothly.

"If they knew it was destined to become a shrine when *Final Love* is released, they wouldn't be so fucking cavalier," said Tilda. She remembered the few historically accurate lines she had plagiarized and inserted into *Final Love*.

The magnificent wall in Addison County was created by feverish settlers who felled trees, dragged rocks out of the sod, and meticulously laid the stones to follow land contours, all meant to contain their growing cow or goat stocks. Stone was also the best material to define one's land. As much of unoccupied Vermont had been eagerly granted, in fact, surreptitiously sold to settlers by the unscrupulous Crown's Governor Wentworth in the mid-1700s, some parcel boundaries remained in question. For all to see and touch, a stone wall made a faded surveyor's line on a map clearer and, to many settlers, dearer.

Tilda left the kitchen, crossed into the living room to her desk, and sat at the revered Acer. Oh, yes, the library asked for it back when she ignored the required monthly payment—even sent her an invoice for $880. They were going to have to come out to the farm and pry it from her tenacious fingers. They owed her that Acer, those bastards!

"It's time, Timothy. Stand beside me? You're such a comfort when I read responses from publishers."

He returned to the couch and draped one foot over an armrest. "I'm not getting up. This is just going to make us both feel bad."

It did, too. Checking her email account, there was only one form rejection from CEO Janice Westland of Westland Publishing LLC, an obscure New Jersey publishing company.

Exasperated, Tilda shut down the Acer and sniffled, "I'm crushed."

Timothy was obligated to say something since she was terribly hurt. "I want to lash out, slap that wretch Janice across her skanky face!" he howled.

They had a moment of reverent silence.

"There's nothing we can do," said Tilda with her wrinkled brow signaling helplessness more than her few words could convey.

"I'll make us a plan," said Timothy, stroking his chin as if he were a contemplative, wise man.

Tilda hid her concern by turning away. Timothy had a way of devising plans that often guided them into unwise outcomes. Like the time he used a Havahart trap to snatch Fartsy, the woodchuck residing under the barn. The plan was to resettle him in their screened-in garden to keep out burrowing rabbits. That disaster came about because Timothy insisted Fartsy was a carnivore.

Big mistake. Fartsy loved everything they grew in the garden and had no trouble sharing with his pals, the rabbits.

CHAPTER 11

There once was a lady from East Cabot . . .

The feuding families, characters, and locations brought to life in Tilda's *Final Love* were pure fiction. When she began writing, she could have done research on the net or in the library to give *Final Love* an authentic, historical context. There was a rich tapestry of local history to be uncovered and already written about where she lived in Addison County. But research—that was too time-consuming. If she found something she wanted for *Final Love*, she'd simply plagiarize and hope she'd not get caught.

Ultimately, Tilda's notions of turn-of-the-century rural life sprung from bingeing on television oaters and serial reruns discovered on YouTube. Productions like *Little House on the Prairie* became the authoritative sources for her knowledge of late nineteenth-century rural life.

Much of *Final Love* dealt with the consequences of the feud between the two families and their entwined, in love, adolescent children. Their principal conflict had been sparked by a competition for the coveted blue ribbon for the best black-and-white Holstein at the spring fair.

However, Timothy had other ideas about the blue-ribbon competition as a conflict creator between the two families. "Sis, seriously. Having characters compete over a silly blue ribbon based on udder and teat size is hardly dramatic. Where's the excitement, the sizzle? It's so boringly unsexy!"

Unfortunately, Tilda had allowed Timothy to contribute what resulted in obscene limericks opening each chapter. But she hated it when he whined, especially about her writing, "Well, what do you suggest to make it more exciting?"

With his encouragement, Tilda rewrote the family feud aspect by altering the confrontation from teat size and beauty of the udder (principal calculations for the blue ribbon) to an accidentally toppled milk can. With Timothy's direction, her meticulous description of the spilled milk face-off was tediously framed by competing narratives as witnessed by different bystanders. It was sort of a takeoff on Rashomon's *Kurosawa*, a film she had once helped project in the library's monthly film series. Timothy loved the revision, especially how the milk was sprayed on both families and onlookers.

Notwithstanding other major plot and character difficulties, Timothy's deviant input made him the principal creator of chaos throughout the narrative. There were only two responses from publishers and a slew of emails offering ways to self-publish. The two concerned publishers who did write back advised that 866 pages were far too many, and the inane limericks opening each chapter were distastefully pornographic. Thusly, making *Final Love* unsuitable for public libraries or any sane page-turner. Both closed their letters by stressing the author should seek psychiatric help.

Now that Timothy's limericks were identified as a problem, Tilda was in a tough spot. Timothy had begrudgingly agreed to limit his contributions to the short, spicy rhymes opening each chapter. He described his contributions as sort of like having musical overtures before the feature film. Going back on their agreement was going to be difficult for Tilda.

The limericks for the first two chapters had been tame and sort of harmlessly cute, but by the third chapter things had gotten out of hand:

In Addison lives one hell of a whore

who lies like a dog on the floor.

She wiggles her ass in the air,

plays with her long pussy hair,

and prays for a stud at the door.

By the sixth chapter, Timothy's limericks had crawled to a yet higher level of depravity. Where this perverse obsession came from is anyone's guess.

There once was a lady from East Cabot

who stretched her anus with cuke and carrot.

When her husband complained the salad was lame,

she said it should taste just the same

but next time I'll add a shallot.

In her introductory letter to publishers, Tilda had always included, *Final Love* is an important novel that will outsell the Bible!" After so many rejections, perhaps that was a little too bullish? Maybe insensitive to Christians? Timothy responded she was being ridiculously picky. He was going to use his law practice mainframe computer to apply a super-duper comparative analysis to *Final Love* and the Bible just to prove how wrong she was. That closed further debate.

Frustrated with writing to publishers, Tilda mounted an Internet search on how to break into the book-selling universe. Her search led her to conclude that if *Final Love* were to ever gain a spot on the shelves of the Middlebury Book Exchange, the cozy Zackers; or her previous employer, the Presley Public Library, she'd need a feisty literary agent to hammer out a deal with a publisher. Preferably an agent with a prestigious New York City address.

Acquiring an agent demanded sending a query, a descriptive hype to get the agent excited enough about a book for them to peddle it to a publishing house. Unfortunately, some literary agents demanded special treatment and had different requirements for queries, making each query a massive, creative endeavor in itself! She did all that. After three months of sending queries out for *Final Love*, only two agents out of 312 queries bothered to respond. And they were nasty, dismissive notes.

Tilda fumed at the hundred or so autogenerated responses, and the multitude of others who didn't even bother to acknowledge her submission. To Tilda, a retired librarian, being forced into the query merry-go-round was a sin comparable to judging a book by its cover.

* * * * * *

As requests for more pages did not fill her inbox from queried agents as anticipated, Tilda painfully accepted she should return to the keyboard for a rewrite. Timothy, unusually supportive, disabused her of any pretense of the honesty and fairness of literary agents. He framed those who did not respond at all as callous, heartless buggers. He had a very convincing spiel that captured Tilda's shaky sense of justice.

"Two pedestrians pass on the sidewalk and one says, 'Good day' and the other ignores him? No fucking way! This rudeness is tearing at the moral fabric of our civilized society! It's not right! It's not Christian, not Muslim, not Jew-like either!"

He slammed a fist on the kitchen counter, making her jump. "Sadly, I'm unable to represent your powerful and moving story due to an overwhelming, tragic death in my dear family. Please accept my heartfelt apology and deepest regrets. Is that too much to ask from those fucking agent whores?"

Timothy, not unreasonably dismayed at indisputable evidence of crumbling opportunities when it came to breakout literature, created a new classification for the multitude of foul literati and selfish literary agents who never respond to queries:

"Disregards!" he screamed. "That's what they are! Fucking Disregards!" He ranted and stomped around the room in his red cowboy boots, stressing out Tilda. "From now on, they're Disregards! And Sis, we're gonna make them snotty snobs pay!" He used his fist again, this time against the kitchen table, upsetting the salt shaker and pepper grinder.

"Seriously, Timothy, maybe your contributions should be less controversial. Here it is in black and white," referring to the sole agent's response. "He writes: 'Your limericks are a vile desecration to paper.' Read it yourself, Timothy!"

"Tilly, that's cowpie! My contributions to *Final Love* are electric! They light up, they excite, they give spice to your tepid romance! 'He kissed her on the lips.' That's what you think is sexy! 'He fucked her like a dog in heat!' That's what today's reader demands!"

Unable to contain his brutish disdain for her love scenes that made him nauseous, Timothy had greatly wounded Tilda. She became painfully silent. A trickle of tears found the back of her hand. Timothy knew silence from Tilda was not good, tears even worse.

She struck back. "Young people won't get to be saved because of your demented limericks! Is that fair, Timothy, is it?"

Initially, Tilda considered Timothy's limericks and the odious query task she had innocently undertaken to be minor nuisances on the path to literary fame. Now, they were poised to smite her life's work. No one would get to read *Final Love*.

"I apologize, Sis. Your peerless point of view from the omniscient eye of a vindictive but loving God will be a tragedy if not shared with humanity. But seriously, Sis, why should we take advice from those agent clowns? I mean, them soulless Disregards!" As if to punctuate, he spat on the floor.

He made little sense, but what he said soothed the waters and served to reshape Tilda's brooding. She put the kettle on for tea and warned, "Don't spit in the house."

Timothy went to his perch on the couch to ruminate. "You decided all on your own, *Final Love* is all about finding love. And love may be clean and innocent to a few nitwits, but more realistically, it is also very, very dirty! Stinky, too. Tilly, everyone wants love because it's about sex. My limericks are a vital counterpoint to your sappy writing!"

"But love is about love—it's not always about sex! I think you've let that evil wall get into your heart. Do you want tea or instant coffee while we discuss editing your limericks?"

Timothy slid off the couch. "I'm flabbergasted at having to revisit this boring conversation again and again. Instead of arguing, why don't we go upstairs and yen-yang?"

Yen-yang? What an idea! I'll calm down with some reefer and have a diddle in front of Grandma's antebellum mirror.

This sexual escapade had been ignited years before from a voyeuristic episode that Tilda had witnessed one evening walking home after leaving Slobberu to be retreaded at Sam's Garage. Passing the only home on the three-mile trek from town, the one that always had a baby blue antique Ford F150 truck parked proudly in the yard, she had glanced to an open window to espy a frenzied dance by her scrawny, butt-naked neighbor.

Little did Tilda know, the erotic dancer, Slim Littlejohn, was practicing for the Zumba-style class he taught two days a week at the Middlebury YMCA to adults sixty-five and over. This senior life-enhancing activity was only one element of his profitable retirement home scams.

The image of the naked scarecrow-like reprobate gyrating at the window was forever available to excite Tilda's not-so-virgin privates and refresh her memory of bygone sex with real men. When the mood of a yen-yang struck, it was as if lightning hit the railroad tracks. She would aim Grandmother's credenza mirror at her soft overstuffed bed and finger walk into her baggy underwear. If Timothy was in the mood, which he always was, he'd join her by gleefully prancing around the oak-framed bed buck naked with his member swaying left and right.

That singular occurrence, the unsettling dance at the window, had persuaded Tilda to allow Timothy to write a titillating limerick opening each chapter of *Final Love*, thereby adding more pizazz to her tame love story and reaching a wider readership. But, as so often, generosity towards Timothy had come back to bite her in the butt.

In any case, Tilda was always up for some yen-yang.

CHAPTER 12

We're not going to do anything really bad, are we?

Though Timothy made it clear Tilda would never understand the mathematics of diminishing returns, efficient space management, or how important things worked, she needed to have a clear understanding of the power Disregards had over writers. To wit, Timothy used the metaphor of bobbing for apples at the Vermont State Fair. His explanation was based on a complicated mathematical formula using standard mouth width, average apple diameter, and emerging chaos theory. By applying nihilism and removing the larger agent apples, i.e., the Disregards, only sensitive agents would remain! It was axiomatic; when the snubbing, snotty literati were removed from the barrel, the kinder, gentler agents—the smaller apples, could flourish!

When Tilda heard the apple-bobbling analogy and how it crystalized the agent query problem, she jumped right in, "Timothy, you brilliant cad! We'll be celebrities! Every struggling writer will reap the reward of our Herculean efforts!"

"Thank you, thank you," he said returning to the couch.

After several minutes of silence, Tilda wondered, "How can we do this? Get the Disregards together to bob for apples, and then push them into barrels?"

"Too complicated, Sis," he said. "We'd have to then kidnap 'em and feed 'em."

She was undeterred, "I think we should confront Disregards by going to their offices or whatever they call the evil place where they hang out to ruin writer's lives. Then, I'd give them a face-to-face tongue-lashing. Take them out to the woodshed, so to speak."

"Sis, we ought to do something, something on a grand, epic scale! Nothing would be better than going to New York City where I'd pinch every Disregard's nipples and slap them hard on the ass. Ooooh, make it rosy red."

"Timothy, I don't like that talk! Pinched nipples. Ugh! Do any decent ideas ever tumble out of that creative, overactive brain of yours?"

"Tilly, darling, most Disregards spawn in Manhattan, way out of Slobberu's range. We'd have to make an exhausting bus trip to and from New York City. Besides, they'd know us, and that would limit our punishing possibilities."

"So what? We're not going to do anything really bad, are we?" snapped Tilda.

"Sis, it's a shady undertaking to become a heroine for the world's oppressed writers. Them agents can't know it's us," he asserted.

That took a while to sink in. It ran counter to her sense of personal esteem after years of fawning student accolades at her lawn symposia. But yes, her ego could be stifled for the well-being of all struggling authors.

"That's okay, then. I'll feel good doing something for the betterment of our unpublished comrades."

"You'll come to what I've known a long time: literary agents must die!" With that, he smashed his fist on the table for emphasis. "Carpe diem, carpe diem. Now is the time to act, Sis!"

"God dammit, stop it, Timothy! You're going to break my table!" scolded Tilda.

For sure, Tilda wouldn't buy into Timothy's suggestion, the one where they'd go to New York City, pull on the agents' nipples, and do all that ass-smacking. But after so many futile queries and no requests for more pages, she began to warm to a more Machiavellian way to handle the Disregards.

Correction, those fucking literary agents.

Sweet revenge. When there's a will, there's a way, and patience does not reward the impatient. So, go with the flow and something will turn up. Such was Timothy's sage advice to Tilda, her brother-in-arms.

* * * * * *

It had become night too quickly, and since Tilda didn't like driving Slobberu in the dark, she was on edge. Plus, she was alone because Timothy hated their old hometown, Salisbury. Wouldn't be seen there. These factors made her overly cautious, and she drove slowly despite the line of cars that piled up behind her. After a while, they'd honk and speed by with the passengers shouting nasty things out the windows.

She had come to Salisbury to pick up sets of sprouting lettuce and tomato seedlings at the Green Seed Garden Store. She had wanted to work part-time ages ago at GSGS, before the library stint, to make "real cash" instead of paycheck-less slavery at the inn. She just knew something exceptionally bad could happen any minute—like running out of gas, which a red light on the dash seemed to indicate.

Fortunately, a newly opened Swift & Quik gas station appeared like a florescent island in the growing darkness. Tilda was relieved her card was accepted without issue by the shiny, stainless-steel pump.

Standing beside the pump and fueling, Tilda glanced into the large plate glass window of the mart to observe the turban-swathed foreigner at the cash register playing some idiot game on his cell phone. She couldn't help but notice in the other window, resting under a mesmerizing big "V" formed by angled flickering neon lights, a towering basket of dark mini bottles were balanced on a pyramid of cardboard cases.

A hand-scribbled sign, large enough to be read from the pumping station, declared: "Maple syrup samplers $1 apiece / $84.00 case of 100! Secure mailing boxes included!"

Aha, a veritable maple syrup steal was available to alert motorists and sugar junkies!

Tilda's happenstance observation occurred precisely as Barry McGuire's *Eve of Destruction* came blasting out of Slobberu's radio. His catchy refrain and embracing orchestration were mysteriously synchronized with a whispering voice that emanated from the gushing gas as it pulsed into Slobberu's tank: "The spirit compels you, the spirit compels you . . . "

While Barry McGuire crooned:

And you tell me

over and over again, my friend

Ah, you don't believe

We're on the eve of destruction . . .

Slamming the gas nozzle into the cradle, Tilda ran inside and bought two crates of maple syrup samples on her Visa.

* * * * * *

She arrived safely home in the dark with Slobberu hiccupping and dieseling from the cut-rate gas. Carefully checking all 360 degrees for the manic Holstein, Tilda hustled the two crates into the kitchen. The garden flats, stacked where the back seat used to be, would have to wait until daylight to be unloaded.

"My, my, my, little sister, what have you got here," said Timothy, sitting at the kitchen table. She plopped the cases down in front of him. He carefully inspected the contents.

"Where were you two minutes ago? How come you're not around when stuff has to be carried in from the car? You know these are heavy. A little help would be appreciated."

"I was engaged in the other room."

Tilda needed a cup of something warm, but not a Dr Pepper; it might keep her up.

"I snatched up these little bottles of syrup at Swift & Quik as a treat for our coffees. I had a cosmic revelation, a sign that couldn't be ignored, so I don't want to hear any back talk."

She started boiling water and prepared a cup with two scoops of Nestle's instant hot chocolate. Timothy rose from his chair, ready to present a fresh, yet more draconian idea for handling the Disregards.

"A sign? You can't fool me, Sis! You're thinking these little soldiers could go to our Disregards."

Timothy had hoped Tilda would catch his drift without having to spell it out. She poured the boiling water into a cup.

"No. Why would I want to give them something nice?"

"Maybe we mix in something naughty? Maybe something to upset their precious little tummies? Eh?"

"Jesus, Timothy, God doesn't want us to do evil things like that!"

"Sis, this is God-sent! He wouldn't give you the idea if he didn't want you to act on it!"

"Timothy, that's ridiculous, and you don't even know if he's a he," she snapped back.

"It's a sign for us! We're to become saints for the unpublished! Carpe diem! These syrup samplers are our righteous warriors! They're our vehicles of vengeance!"

"What about the labels on the bottles? There's a return address printed on the boxes, too. We'll get into deep trouble if we do something illegal. Look:"

Enjoy this sample of authentic Vermont maple syrup courtesy of Vermont Association of Maple Syrup Products LLC. 49 Green Mountain Sap Road, Burlington, Vermont.

"Sis! That doesn't matter! Who'd suspect anything's wrong with Vermont's finest? Them agents are all in New York City! They sit around eating Chinese takeout with those little sticks. They'll get a tummy ache. They'll think it came from the dog meat in their chow mein!"

"They don't eat dogs in New York City, Timothy!"

"Yes, they do. That's why it's chow mein, named after their ugly rat eating Chow Chow dogs!"

"You have such fantasies." She took a careful sip of the hot chocolate. "Timothy, this sounds very naughty. What if they found us out?"

"For Christ on the pole, Tilly! The bottle's emptied on one pancake and gets tossed! I bet millions are sold all over the state! Pretty hard to track two little cases, wouldn't you say?"

"I don't like being mean to people we don't know, even if they deserve it. Sometimes, Timothy, I think you've got a malicious streak that wants to lead me astray."

He reminded Tilda how the Disregards, them literati types, were hardly people in the sense of real people.

"It will be *sweet revenge,* Sis. And proportionately just compared to the lives they've destroyed and the loose bowels their meanness created."

He had a point. Writing all those pointless queries had run amok in Tilda's sensitive digestive tract. Thank God for Dr Pepper! Isn't that reason enough for God to want to wreak vengeance on the Disregards?"

Timothy began pacing about the room. "We begin with the agents we sent queries to in that romance writer's guild. *Final Love* is a love story, it seems the right place to start. Also, the agents' mailing addresses are posted on the website."

"They've had months to accept my book. Not a peep for all my days and days of hard work and toil." Tilly became more agitated just thinking about the cruelty she'd endured.

"Well, la-dee-dah, since we haven't gotten one friggin' word back from them. Them Disregards in that snotty guild—they go first!" shouted Timothy, and he stamped down hard in his cowboy boots, causing the kitchen overhead light to blink.

"Damnit, stop it, Timothy! You'll burn us down!"

For the appropriate spiking ingredient, Tilda and Timothy didn't have to look far.

CHAPTER 13

Come on over here, you big beautiful monster

The next day, they stood at the end of the wall where the earth and grass t-boned at a small pool of crystal-clear water. Tilda had named the pool *the pit*. The pit was fed by a tiny offshoot from Gilmore Brook, a hidden waterway that snaked between the pine forest and Tilda's and Williams' Dairy property. The ground was too rocky for heavy Holsteins, so to isolate the area, more low rock barriers had been built over the years, blocking off swaths of land. Although many of the top stones had slid from the walls, they stood proudly as they had a century before.

Tilda had her hands in oversized yellow rubber dishwashing gloves and held a contractor's black plastic garbage bag.

"What do you think, Timothy?"

"I think these are the most beautiful flora I've ever experienced in my long years."

Timothy was referring to the healthy clumps of aconite, or wolfsbane, the pretty but deadly leafy blue flowering vine growing abundantly in cavities at the end of *Final Love's* inspirational wall.

"No, not that. What do you think about my yellow gloves matching my yellow galoshes?"

"You are very fashionable at times."

"I'm only going along with this because if we use wolfsbane from the evil wall to straighten our Disregards, we are in a way messing up its evilness. We're turning the wall's evilness into a positive outcome. Oh boy, it's not going to like that!"

"Whatever, I don't give a shit about the details," said Timothy.

"Here goes," she said squatting down and grabbing one of the snaking vines, ripping it from between the rocks and shoving it into the bag. "How much do you think we need?"

"More than that," adding, "Sis, if you squat a little lower, your love nest is going to be sitting on wolfsbane."

"Oh, shut the fuck up!" Tilda began stuffing handfuls of leaves, flowers, and stems into the bag until it bulged like Santa's tote. "I'm tired, that's enough. You going to help carry this to the barn?"

"No, I'm going to the pit to watch my trout take mayflies."

* * * * * *

It would be too dangerous to bring all that wolfsbane into the tiny farmhouse, so, the dilapidated but still usable barn would hold it. It had everything they needed: ancient electric wiring, a dripping water faucet, and a large vegetable sorting table. They were ready to go. Tilda quickly set up shop on the table and collected all the necessary tools to begin processing.

They had only to wait a day for the wolfsbane, tightly packed in the black plastic bag, to shrivel, condense, and sweat into a foul, mucky mass.

* * * * * *

The next afternoon, they began in the barn. Wearing the yellow dishwashing gloves, now grossly stained a vivid magenta, Tilda crammed handfuls of softened and putrid wolfsbane into an antique wooden apple press. Replacing the circular wooden cap of the press, she twisted the handle until the screw plate compressed the wolfsbane mess. A yellowish liquid and pungent oil oozed steadily into the catch pan.

"How much of this do you think we need for each Disregard?" asked Tilda, glancing at Timothy who was posed dramatically on a hay bale. He was in his natty James Dean scheme: blue jeans with long cuffs over the red cowboy boots, a red paisley bandana knotted at his neck, and a white T-shirt with a pack of Marlboros in a rolled-up sleeve. A hay stalk played in his mouth.

"I don't know fer sure, Sis. We need an efficacy test, don't we?"

"Well, professor, think of something. We don't want to go off half-cocked," said Tilda.

"Don't use that word or you'll give me a boner."

"Oh, really, Brother. And don't you dare light up one of them fags in this barn!"

Over time, Tilda concluded her brother was a sex fiend, but it was necessary for her to tolerate his crude outbursts. Almost like he was part of her, and by rejecting or chastising his sexuality or messing with his lewd nature, it might have some untold negative effect on her carnal desires and masturbatory fantasies. All in all, she was fine with his oddness—as long as she remained the rational and sane one to protect him. He could go hogwild in the bushes for all she cared.

Timothy wondered aloud, "Say, what happened to our Moo Moo girlfriend?"

The errant Holstein, with the unique white nose marking and yellow ear tag, still posed a threat to Tilda's fitful psyche. After confronting Tilda, the malevolent cow had returned through the breach and, upon hearing the milking bell, dutifully trotted back with the herd for the evening milking. The efficient operations manager in charge of the Williams Dairy

Products facility discovered the breach in the wall during his morning ATV rounds. He dispatched a crew of muscular locals who had returned the wall to its original height in an hour. Of course, the stones were only stacked, not resolutely laid and interlocked as the pioneers originally had artistically done.

* * * * * *

One crisp dawn later, having been released from her pen with scores of other cows, the inquisitive wall-busting Holstein, aka Moo Moo, returned to the wall and was tempted to the edge by a handful of hay laced with wolfsbane oil. Tilda and Timothy had added a drizzle of maple syrup to make it more attractive and to overwhelm the wolfsbane's oily scent.

"Come on over here, you big beautiful monster," mouthed Timothy luringly.

"I've got a little treat for you," continued Tilda. "Might give you a tummy ache—wait, that's incorrect. Cows do have a tummy but they call it a 'rumen.' That's where the grass becomes cud and gets regurgitated for a second chew." Tilda was proud for remembering what every Vermont child gets drilled into their brains in fourth grade.

"Sis, forget the lesson. Just feed Moo Moo her damn breakfast," said Timothy impatiently.

Enticed to stretch across *Final Love*'s rocky wall by Tilda's trembling hand, the snorting and snot-dripping Holstein chomped down on the offering, blissfully unaware she was laying waste to eons of atavistic evolution.

"I bet Moo Moo is going to barf and have a bad, bad day," said Timothy triumphantly.

"It won't do anything bad to the milk, will it? I mean milk is sacrosanct, Timothy. We don't want to hurt any children." The gravity of their largess was catching up to Tilda.

"Sis, for screaming Jesus, stop it! You're babbling! They're not going to milk Moo Moo when she's spraying shite all over her stall!"

"Timothy, why must you be so disgusting and crude!"

By evening's call, the pasture was empty except for Moo Moo. She was flat on her back in the middle of the field, her hooves drooped on legs aimed at the darkening sky. Her engorged udder was flopped to the side and oozed soured milk.

* * * * * *

The sounds of grinding and heavy machinery awakened Tilda. Cautiously peering through rumpled blinds and an unwashed window, she was dismayed to see fly-infested Moo Moo being dragged by a steel cable looped around its neck onto a flatbed truck. Within minutes, Moo Moo was whisked to the far side of the plant's property and buried by a pristine, yellow backhoe. This was not Tilda's intention, naively believing the stricken cow would be ill only for a few days and recover after a nice rest.

As reported two weeks later in the *Ripton Crier* interview with the local vet, Dr. Nasir Faarhab: "The poor ruminant must have been mad to have eaten leaves of the wolfsbane, a poisonous plant that eons of bovine evolution had taught to seriously avoid!"

Moo Moo's death, an act Timothy proclaimed the wall-breaching beast deserved, meant testing was over. The wicked consequences of their deed began to seep into Tilda's splintered psyche. She wasn't a hateful person, except when it came to their new enemy, the Disregards. The death of Moo Moo seemed to impress upon her the fleeting aspect of life and the perverse role she would play by making strangers, although contemptible literary agents, very sick.

After more exhausting work on the apple press, Tilda had only about a cup of wolfsbane extract.

"Making them sick is our objective, right? Timothy, if they're dead, they won't realize they're being punished."

Timothy howled, "No, we want fucking deathbeds for Disregards! You turncoat! Literary agents must die or nothing will change!"

"I'm not sure, Timothy. We're not an evil family. We fight evil, don't we?"

"Apples, apples, apples! Don't you remember the friggin' apple bobbing analogy? Jesus, Sis! What you're proposing is only taking little bites out of the big apples. Them big evil apples are going to still float up and crowd out the good little helpless apples."

"You must help me be strong, Timothy. I know you're right."

"Of course, I'm right," boomed Timothy, retreating to the living room and his couch.

Tilda was clumsy in the ill-fitting yellow dishwashing gloves, and it was sweltering hot in the barn during the day, even with the fan she had set up. She lined up ten bottles like a squad of soldiers. It was easy to open the sample's screw top and eyedropper in two drips of extract. Why waste more than two drops? That should "fry 'em like Raid on a roach," opined Timothy. The cap threads were smeared with a small touch of melted wax to give the impression of a tight seal. Tested, the bottle would reopen with a reassuring snap.

"Stop messing around, Sis!" Tilda had dripped extract on the rim, causing it to run down the outside of the bottle. "We don't want anyone to question the maple syrup as a reason for their demise. Too much extract and someone might suspect foul play and call CSI."

Tilda marked each doctored bottle top with a small black point from a magic marker. God forbid, they mix up the laced and unlaced! Tilda addressed a sample box while it was an unfolded flat surface, then got screamed at by Timothy.

"For God's sake, don't use your real handwriting!"

"What?"

"You know how to do that stylish block lettering architects and engineers use? That'll throw them off good."

"That's very clever. Should I do some little hearts and stars around their names like we used to with birthday cards at the Inn?"

"Fuck no! It's from a cutthroat business. Keep it businesslike."

"Okey dokey. I'll start with Disregard Martha Jane Sidel at the Romance Agents & Writers Guild. She's never responded to any of my queries," said Tilda, snapping her gloves for dramatic effect.

"The witch must die!" screamed Timothy, throwing an arm into the air.

After addressing the carton to Martha Jane Sidel, Tilda unfolded the sides and snapped the tongues into the precut slots. The sample bottle slid inside with plenty of cardboard protection. The lid and bottoms got tucked tightly into the sides. No need for tape.

"Ready to be shipped out," said Tilda, proudly rolling off the gloves. "Only a few hundred more to do."

"You'll go to an out-of-town post office and find out how much these little puppies are going to cost us to get to New York City."

"Me? Aren't you coming with me?" Tilda was astounded, she'd be all alone!

"You're a big girl, Sis. You have to learn how to do some things on your own."

"Go to hell, Timothy! You're always leaving me to do the real work, and I don't appreciate it!"

CHAPTER 14

Step up, young lady. Counter service way up here

Friday morning, Tilda drove Slobberu to the Shoreham Post Office. The tiny little white box building, set in a residential neighborhood, had one door and two windows facing Main Street. The door was wedged open for the line of patrons that led around to the far side of the building. Tilda parked Slobberu in the back lot that had a single space available.

Timothy had cautioned her to remain unmemorable, so she dodged conversation with a matronly woman in a vile flowery dress by looking away. When a woman tried to start a conversation about Tilda's yellow galoshes, Tilda pretended to be deaf by tapping her ears. A busybody behind her announced she knew sign language and offered to translate. Tilda ignored her.

She eventually reached the counter to face the harried bearded clerk with thick, black-rimmed glasses. She kept a step back, counting on his poor vision to not remember her.

"Step up, young lady. Counter service way up here," he said, drumming an index finger on the counter.

She slid the sample box over to him and endeavored a smile. "Would you be so kind as to tell me how much postage I need on this little box? I'd like to send a bunch off before Christmas."

"Does it contain any flammable liquids, like gasoline or ethanol?" he asked, shaking the box.

"No."

"Does it contain ammunition, explosives, hazardous, liquid waste, or airbags?"

He was already suspicious.

"No, no. Why airbags?"

"Might explode if roughed up. Something about the aircraft's pressurization system."

"Oh."

"Does it contain maple syrup?"

Tilda looked at him blankly, speechless.

"Miss, it says so on the carton right here."

"Well, it might. I haven't looked yet."

"If it's in a glass, tin, or durable plastic container and well-secured, it's okay. Is it in one of those?"

"It must be if it's maple syrup."

"Good. Maple syrup can be mailed. Wasn't that easy?"

Tilda thought of what Timothy would have in mind: *You prick. I should claw your eyes out.*

"They're all going to the same zip codes?"

"Yes, for now."

"Do you want picturesque issue stamps or do you want machine stamps that I can conveniently crank out in two minutes?"

Tilda—think fast.

"I want pretty colorful stamps. Most of our missionaries are in Manhattan helping the disadvantaged."

She flashed on a TV trailer for *Men in Black*. "Flushing, Queens, too!"

"You said Christmas presents. I've got stamps with Santa by the tree with cookies. Santa on his sled, wintery snow scene—you pick."

"Forget any of the winter or Christmas scenes."

"Manhattan or Queens, that's pretty much the same rate. Let's see, to Midtown 10038 from 05770." His fingers tapped on the keyboard, "Regular postage comes to four dollars and eighty cents. Be there in two, three days tops."

Tilda was nearly floored. "What? Five damn bucks!" she exclaimed. The line of patient Shoreham natives behind her shuffled nervously.

"Washington sets the rate. Take it up with Bernie and Peter."

"Yeah, what else is new," Tilda huffed.

"It's going to be an odd collection of stamps to make that exact amount. Four different stamps for each box."

"That'll be fine. Stamps to send sixty boxes, please."

"Good Lord! For sixty boxes?" He rolled his eyes.

Tilda just stared at him.

Flapping open the large binder of stamp pages, "Let's see, scenic Vermont views sound right?"

"Oh yes, they'll like that."

"We got your typical rural views: ah . . . a wooden bridge or I Love VT with the big red heart? Personally, I don't like that one. Reminds me of my heart attack."

Tilda bobbed her head sympathetically while the crowd behind groaned impatiently.

"Here's a sugaring scene or how about trout fishing?"

"No."

"There's the seasonal yellow-to-red maple leaf. Leaf peepers' favorite. Frankly, looks a little too Canadian for my likes. Here's a new issue: wolfsbane growing on a rock wall. A beautiful stamp, colorful vine, isn't it? These are going to go fast."

"No, no, not that one! Use the others! The sugaring, the trout! That type of thing."

It took him excruciatingly long minutes to tear out four different sheet styles from four different binders to make the odd postage needed. All to the disquiet of the customer line piled behind her, now reaching well into the parking lot.

"That'll be $288 even. Cash, debit, or credit card?"

"Visa."

Boy, what an ordeal, thought Tilda as she scampered to Slobberu.

Driving home, Tilda was getting cold feet. Just to smack down sixty agents was already way more money than she thought they'd spend in total. Sending two hundred plus literary agents, though despicable Disregards, to the great unknown? They'd be broke!

* * * * * *

Logically, they should begin with the earliest unresponsive agents queried. Then, those Disregards sending form letters should be next for the syrup treat.

Tilda's sense of fair play was especially enraged when reading a form response that contained misspellings. Timothy agreed. Sending a form rejection was barely a step up from being a total Disregard. But the two agents who took the effort to write a note, indicating they had read at least one page, although a painful rejection, should get unlaced maple syrup.

Tilda had a saucer with a soaked paper towel ready to moisten the stamps. Timothy was quite certain if suspicion arose, CSI types would take over with their DNA analysis machines. Ergo, no stamp licking. This made Tilda wonder if Timothy was sneaking off nights and involved in some aberrant behavior? What if he was leaving DNA samples on a neighbor's laundry clothesline? With the help of the NSA, if the CSI types matched her saliva and some kind of sticky deposit from his weirdness, the genetic trail could lead right back to her!

In any case, Tilda felt good about taking to task the earlier Disregards like Martha Jane Sidel of the Romance Agents & Writers Guild. Her sample mailer and three more agents from the same guild were ready to go: Jennifer Rousch of Rousch Literary Associates, NYC; Betty Sampson at Ready to Print Literary Agency, NYC; and Phylis Cartland of Cartland & Associate Literary Agents, NYC. All would get the first batch of samples.

"You know, Timothy, looking at our agent list, I bet over 80 percent went to women! I mean, this is shameful! You'd think it would be them ogre men with wrinkly peckers that would be the worst Disregards!"

"That's a veritable damning statement on the lack of feminine-stick-togetherness between agents and authors if I've ever heard one!" responded Timothy, leaving Tilda pleased about agreeing to several things in one day.

Working down the mailing list from the guild site, only six more boxes had to be addressed and stamped:

Recognizing the necessity to cover their tracks just in case someone wondered about the illness or demise of so many literary agents in such a short time, Timothy demanded they mail only one box at a time at any given post office. Each had to be a healthy distance from Lincoln. That element, distance from home base, would confuse any gumshoe.

Tilda's hand was cramping. "This is exhausting, transposing all these addresses. My fingers are numb and my eyes are aching. Why does the Internet thing have to use such tiny print on the screen?"

"It's a conspiracy to keep the elderly misinformed, that's what it is. Shit like that doesn't happen by chance," said Timothy wisely.

"Brother, it would help if you would read addresses off the computer as I address the boxes."

"I have things to do outside. Maybe later," said Timothy, beating it out the door. "And don't forget to rub them with your hankie before mailing. We don't want any latent fingerprints leading them to our door."

CHAPTER 15

Jesus God, what have we done, Timothy?

In the early morning, surrounded by a ghostly mist, Williams Dairy's cows began their unhurried ramble from the evening pens. On the other side of the colonial stone wall, Slobberu awoke with a hiccup and then settled to a loping idle. Tilda had the stack of addressed maple syrup boxes in the front seat next to her. Timothy was behind her, where the back seat had once been, on a cushion and blanket so he could lay down and snooze.

They set off for the first stop, the main post office for Burlington. Number 11 Elmwood was a semi-modern six-story, concrete government structure, a typical budget-driven and universally bland building. It could have been built in the 1970s on the wrong side of the Iron Curtain. Two blue freestanding mailboxes were set on the sidewalk just outside the twin glass door entrance.

"Turn left, go into the parking area next to Papa John's," directed Timothy.

She did and parked. Tilda hurriedly arranged her clothes.

"Sis, pull down the beret! Further! Yes, it makes for cool and passes you off as a U.V.M. art student."

"I shall wear it more often."

"I think we're out of sight line of their cameras at the entrance. Shut off the motor; you're wasting gas," rattled Timothy, like they were on some big heist.

"I'm scared."

"Don't be. You're totally unrecognizable. Keep your head down and your raincoat tight around you."

"No, I'm scared Slobberu won't restart."

"Oh. Let her run. And don't forget to mail Martha Jane's maple syrup," he said, teasing her.

Tilda got out of the car and briskly crossed Pearl Street to the blue boxes. As she tugged open the metal slide to send Martha Jane's syrup on its way, she was startled by a bony man with a Brit-style handlebar mustache bumping through the glass doors with a canvas postal cart. Decked out in an official postal cap, a light blue pinstripe short-sleeved uniform shirt, gray shorts, and his skinny calves covered with amusingly tall black socks. With florescent green sneakers, this postman took individuality over official dress guidelines.

Big engaging smile, he rolled to a stop next to Tilda.

"Morning, Madam! Don't drop that in, I'll take care of you! First, let me empty last night's catch," he said disarmingly. From a ring of keys, he unlocked the access door to the second postbox. "Always surprised at the amount of post that comes in overnight." He began transferring handfuls of mail from the box to his canvas cart.

Giving him polite attention was Tilda's downfall. Sample box in hand, she reached again for the box's flap handle.

"Whoa, Miss, hold on! Gimme that," he said, causing her heart to flutter. "Gotta warn you—you go in this way head first, this baby's gonna get jammed, for sure. If you put it in long ways crosswise," he showed her, "no problem. I see you have postage on it. You weighed it properly, did ya?"

Tongue-tied, Tilda could only bounce her head, affirmative.

He shook the box. Seems okay. No rattling. I'll take it right now. It'll get to Ms. Martha Jane Sidel a day early," he cavalierly tossed it into the canvas cart.

"Thank you, officer."

"Sorry, not an officer. Just doin' my job."

Fighting panic, Tilda weaved down the sidewalk, looking both ways for traffic, then bolted across the street and leaped into Slobberu. She managed to squeal four tires backing onto Pearl Street and, with another screech of tires, left the postman scratching the bald spot under his official cap.

"Jesus God, what have we done, Timothy?"

It took only a half hour to reach the Bolton Post Office, a one-story tin-roof shack-like building that shared half the space with the Janesville Antique & Collectables shop. Oddly enough, both were without a customer. Entering through an atypical residential glass-paned front door, Tilda found the mail drop box set into the wall between rows of antique rental P.O. boxes.

She carefully slid the carton for Jennifer Rousch of Rousch Literary Associates sideways into the box. Turning away, her eye caught a movement across the lobby. A lone postal clerk with frizzy hair, white beard, and granny glasses had suddenly appeared behind the counter. Tilda darted out the door but glancing back, the postal clerk was now excitedly waving for her to return.

Nofuckingway, Santa! She hightailed it back to the idling Slobberu and took off.

Tilda didn't realize the postal clerk was waving because she had dropped her crumpled hankie. He had to crawl beneath the counter as the hinge on the lift-up section was bent and inoperative, and pick up a used handkerchief from some rude out-of-towner! Didn't that just make his day? Those people!

Equally irritating, it would have to remain tacked to the lobby bulletin board for four weeks before he could trash the eyesore.

* * * * * *

Rolling into Middlesex, Tilda and Timothy were seeking a post office that didn't exist. It should have had one, but in actuality, Middlesex residents shared postal responsibilities with Worcester and other small nearby towns. Tilda warned Timothy she wasn't up for any goofy jokes about having "sex in the middle."

"I wasn't going to say anything, but since you've brought it up, Sis . . ."

They traveled to Montpelier where the main post office was another mammoth government building. It had a row of circular concrete flowering planters and two drop boxes by the front doors. Tilda and Timothy were fed-up with being secretive; there were two handicapped parking spaces in front near the bright, freshly painted blue boxes. Tilda leaped out, tossed in Betty Sampson's just desserts, and was back in Slobberu before anyone could accost her.

Back on the road, Timothy had moved to the front seat and kept himself entertained by making an airfoil with his arm and palm held out the open window. Tilda drove carefully and slowly, striving to keep the broken yellow lines rolling under the left front tire.

By the time they passed Sharon, Tilda was exhausted. They decided to visit <u>any</u> post office on the way home. Continuing to Hanover on I-91, they backtracked to Lebanon where they found a contemporary one-story post office with a drive-up blue box on the corner. Tilda was elated she didn't have to get out of Slobberu to send Phylis Cartland of Cartland & Associates Literary Agent's sample on the way.

"Shit, we didn't get to mail Ima Foch's syrup—Inkspot Foch Associates, what a fucking name. Anyone who'll keep a name like that should be put out of their misery. We'd be doing her a favor."

Then, disaster struck. Slobberu began to misfire and smoke. Slobberu's radio was always tuned to WCKO, the golden oldies station, with the volume set deafeningly loud, so loud that Tilda was unaware of any mechanical malfunction until the damage became catastrophic. Catastrophic this had become, and the rising and falling roadway became a trial for the ailing car.

"We're not going to make it," announced Tilda, somberly.

"I don't want to sleep out on the highway. Do we still have triple A?"

"No."

"Sis, we got to get home."

"If Slobberu will make it to Sam's, he'll fix it right away or give us a ride from the shop."

"Call him," ordered Timothy.

"You know I don't have the cell phone anymore."

But Slobberu wouldn't die. It kept chugging along, covering one mile after another toward home.

They were relieved as they came to Bristol and crawled through the blinking yellow light that usually had a nazi, female state trooper hiding in the bushes. That green cruiser would come charging out with lights and siren blaring for the simplest of infractions: like having no license plates or driving without lights! Once, she even stopped Tilda just because a big tree limb had gotten jammed under Slobberu and was being dragged along. Big deal. The nazi cop said it was gouging the macadam. What an idiot!

"We're gonna make it, Timothy!" said Tilda, all aflutter.

"Don't get your undies in a knot, Sis."

Slobberu was leaving a trail of smoke like a diesel semi when they arrived at Sam's Garage. The trusted auto repair shop was closed. Tilda balanced the keys on the front tire inside the wheel well and left a note on the windshield: "Fix Me Please, key on left front tire."

* * * * * *

Tilda stashed the remaining samples in a shopping bag and began the long walk in the twilight to the farm. A faster walker, Timothy forged ahead and disappeared. She had hardly gotten out of town when a baby-blue antique Ford 150 truck pulled to a stop next to her.

"Hey, you're Tilly Duclos! I'm your neighbor, Slim. I saw your car parked back at Sam's. I'll be more than pleased to give you a lift home before it gets too dark."

It was Tilda's erotic dancer, a man she had never met in the flesh. She just stared at him, transfixed as she remembered him and his swaying penis.

"It's darn near two miles to your driveway from here. Long way on foot, and it's getting dark fast."

"That'll be real nice; my bunions are killing me." Tilda climbed inside.

They drove silently to where the blacktop met her gravel driveway. She motioned for him to stop before he could turn in.

"This will be fine. I'll walk the rest," she said, remembering to take the bag of unmailed samples.

"You sure?"

"I'm sure. Thank you for the lift." Nothing more to be said, he drove off.

Their first mailbox expedition was over, and they had only gotten four samples mailed. But Tilda slept more relaxed than she had in months. Not for sending off the samples, but for making it to Sam's Garage. She was indifferent to the fact that they had just booked four innocent women for a visit with the Grim Reaper. Six more Disregards had received a stay of execution only by Slobberu's misbehavior.

CHAPTER 16

Sometimes you're so simple, I think you're stupid

It was the weekend but it could have been any other day of the week for Tilda and Timothy who generally didn't have much to do. They lazed on the porch. Tilda continued knitting on a new scarf while serenely planted in her wooden rocker. The wooden rocker was one dug out of the allergy-inducing basement of Bing's Antique & Collectable Bazaar (the same place where she had found the used clothes washer) with a red tag marked twenty dollars or less. The rocker was the first piece of furniture she had bought after closing on the farm; it held a special meaning to her.

Timothy admiringly studied Tilda, something she made him do. She liked being watched, even if it was by herself. Timothy had a foot cocked on the first step, and today he was deep into projecting the modified James Dean look, which was a combination of clothing elements found in *East of Eden* and *Rebel Without a Cause*. Well, actually, she assumed the bandana she gave him was red as it came from the oaters she watched as a teen on the little black-and-white TV at the inn's front desk.

As he so often did, he kept a strand of straw twiddling in his mouth.

"I've been thinking, strategizing our next move. We don't have enough money to send samples to every Disregard." Timothy worked the hat brim, perfectly projecting the rugged cowboy mannerism Tilda so admired. "Can't afford it."

"You're telling me something I don't know? I'm dreading next month's Visa. Maybe you'll help me out with some funding from your law firm." As usual, Timothy ignored any conversation about using his money.

"How will we know the success of our crusade? Since all the syrup went to the guild members, we'll have to rely on their website to see the results of our undertaking. *Undertaking*, get my pun?"

"Sometimes you're so simple, I think you're stupid."

"Well, anyway, we ought to start watching their websites in about a week, I reckon," he said.

"Because you got syrup in the mail doesn't mean you're going to have pancakes the next morning. A week's hardly enough time," said Tilda.

"I think not. In a week, we're gonna see on their website the tragic demise of four precious members. I can already hear their whimpers, 'Why me?'"

"That's just outright mean, Brother."

"Wait 'til the rest of our little soldiers arrive! New York City Disregards will be dropping like flies!"

"I pray to God the others get our message and change their evil ways before we have to send more," said Tilda.

"We should send a postcard to those who didn't get a sample! *You're next!*"

"That's a precious idea, Timothy!"

CHAPTER 17

Maybe I'll put it on ice cream

Days came and went with so little change, except for the steady compression of so many things to be done in a shortening amount of time. This was creating high anxiety at the Romance Agents & Writers Guild, especially for overworked assistant Pamela.

MJ looked up from her DayTimer. "I hope there're checks in today's mail," she snapped at Pamela who was bringing her coffee and a handful of mail. MJ had been anguishing over the many things she had to do in the two days left before Book Expo XII opened at Javits Center. And there was her dwindling checkbook balance.

"Usual bills. Two new membership checks and this looks like a sample. Open it?" asked Pamela, shaking the small carton from Vermont.

"Please do. You're brewing me more coffee, hon?"

Pamela un-flapped the box and displayed the syrup sample bottle to MJ.

"Oh, isn't that interesting, maple syrup! So good for my diabetes. You can take it home, darling."

"You sure?" *Maybe I'll put it on ice cream*, thought Pamela, then wondered: *how many calories?*

* * * * * *

Noted literary agent Jennifer Rousch picked up the pile of mail that had cascaded through the door slot in her East Village flat. Stuck halfway inside and jamming the exterior flap open was a cardboard carton. She had to crunch its sides before she could wrestle it through the slot.

The free sample of maple syrup was secretly troubling. Jennifer had an unusual obsession with maple syrup, one not even confessed to her misanthropic therapist. The obsession began when she was fourteen. She had dabbed Aunt Jemima syrup on her nipples and let Putties, their household cat, clean it off. The cat's sandpaper-like tongue not only made her nipples gloriously sensitive and cherry red, but Jennifer believed they gained extra length from Putties' delicate grooming.

Fearful she would descend into that adolescent indulgence if given the opportunity, Jennifer strictly forbade ever having a cat. Alas, Jennifer had been tested a second time when her sister dumped Pussyboots on her for a weekend while "slumming" overnight in the Hamptons. Her visit kept Jennifer inside with Pussyboots, and a half tin of Top of the Notch Vermont maple syrup from Balducci's disappeared. The cardboard box went in the garbage, and as soon as the coffee was perked, all the syrup would go into her morning coffee, vowing she wouldn't save a drop!

Yes, Jennifer was looking forward to the Book Expo XII and addressing a large idolizing audience. She was confident that in the Q&A given at the end of her casual off-the-cuff talk, someone always would ask about her how-to book, *Self-editing: The Road to Successful Publishing*, and how she made a bundle six months after release. Before leaving the dais, everyone would know Jennifer Rousch was brilliant, available as an agent, and could be talked into providing writing lessons, editing documents, and overseeing all publishing aspects for the rich and talentless!

* * * * * *

Betty Sampson was at the office of Ready to Print Literary Agency when the postman arrived with the morning mail. Betty had an empire; she kept seven other agents under her wing, taking in projects and authors of their own, but always reporting on their progress or lack of in a weekly assembly over coffee and Danishes.

After office manager Susie distributed the morning mail to all the agents' desks, she stood Tilda's sample box on end and asked Betty, "I'm not sure what this is, but if you want to share, count me in."

The box, standing end up on her desk, reminded Betty of her Ralf's erect penis. Which wasn't happening, but her husband was working on that with some erectile pump he had found on eBay. At least twice a week, they would enclose his penis in the hard plastic sheath, connected by an air evacuator that worked by squeezing a rubber bulb. After some titillation, she'd squeeze the bulb like crazy, removing the air around his penis, engorging it with more blood. It stretched the cells and grew unnaturally larger. The only trouble was the flesh became more sponge-like, making erections less satisfying to her.

Opening the box, Betty was pleased to find the maple syrup sample. She envisioned exactly where she and hubby Ralf would use it that evening. No, she would not share it with the rest of the office at their weekly meeting.

* * * * * *

Phylis Cartland, also recognized as the "Agent of the Stars," specialized in helping develop bios of Hollywood biggies. *My Agent: Maker of My Dreams* was written not to help newbie writers, but rather to broadcast about the celebrities she had coached when writing their sordid tales. Oh my, the stories she would hint at! Needless to say, she'd get the audience at the symposium listening to every name-dropped utterance. It was still way down on the best-selling list of how-to books, but it wouldn't slide into oblivion until after Expo XII.

The small cardboard surprise that arrived bundled with her mail was left at the door of her Tribeca loft that she used as an office. She loved maple syrup as it revived memories of Dad's pancakes, crisp bacon, and weekends at the lake. The sample wasn't large enough for a stack or even double waffles, so she'd use it in the morning when she got her usual Egg McMuffin at McDonald's on Tenth Avenue and 34th Street. She'd order the hotcakes instead of the Egg McMuffin and ditch their synthetic corn syrup tinted to look like maple syrup!

CHAPTER 18

The syrup had an underlying tinge of tartness

Pamela returned to her Brooklyn apartment late; Martha Jane had kept her past six printing out the speaker schedule. She was exhausted, but the syrup carton rattling around in her knapsack reminded her to buy a pint of Ben & Jerry's Straight Vanilla at Mama Boy's Bodega on the corner.

She climbed the three flights of stairs to the apartment she shared with her boyfriend, Jeffery, a classical musician and oboe player studying at Juilliard. She came through the door, hung her satchel on the hook, put the bag of ice cream on the kitchen counter, kicked off her shoes, and threw herself atop Jeffery who was half asleep on the couch. He groaned.

"I am so tired. MJ drives me nuts."

"It won't be long. Another year I'll have the degree. We'll move to New Hampshire and I'll teach and you'll write that fairy tale."

"I can't wait," she said, rocking onto his hips.

"Move over a little bit, you're crunching my package. What's in your hand?"

"I brought some B&J ice cream! And look what else!" Raising her eyebrow seductively, she drew the maple syrup sample out of its carton.

"I'll have something for you, too," he said, rolling her over, sliding his hand up her dress, and smoothly working a finger under her panty's elastic.

"Stop it! Not now, silly boy! I have maple syrup for the ice cream. We could start dinner with dessert. Okay, my prince?"

"Capital idea, my Cinderella temptress."

After polishing off the ice cream, drenched with the maple syrup, they began watching NPR's *All Things Considered*. Soon, both began having stomach gurgles and odd, tingling sensations in their arms. Disentangling themselves and trying to stand, they became dizzy. Intense spasms began in their abdomens. Jeffery, who had pigged-out and finished the pint, was struck first with nausea, making him retch on the couch before he could reach the bathroom.

Pamela barely made it to the hallway and to Tina Barnes' door, a neighbor and an E.R. nurse who was enjoying her night off at home and was in the midst of vacuuming the living room. She took one look at Pamela and caught her as she melted to the hallway floor. She called 911 for an ambulance and, from experience, recommended Brooklyn Hospital Center, which was geared for overdoses and suicides. Finding Pamela's door open, she discovered Jeffery had made it to the bathroom, was draped over the bathtub holding his groin, moaning, and evacuating in his shorts. She called for a second ambulance.

* * * * * *

At about the same time, Betty Sampson in her black bra with holes cut out for her nipples and sheer crotch-split panties, lay beside her chunky hubby, Ralf, in their California king bed with red satin sheets. They were watching a *Columbo* rerun on Tubi.

"I love this man. Especially his cross-eyes. I bet Columbo is a hero to those with disabilities," said Ralf, nonchalantly fondling his penis through his gray jockey shorts.

"Why's that?"

"No matter how messed up you are, there's a place in Hollywood for you."

Betty took the maple syrup bottle off her night table.

"You ready, honey bunny?"

"What have you got there?" Ralf eyed the sample.

You'll see, my lollypop."

With one hand, Betty opened the split in his shorts and took out his flaccid penis. Opening the syrup, she carefully dribbled some on his growing member. It didn't take long for Ralf to have a raging hard on. In between the oral sex and their deep, slobbering kisses, most of the syrup disappeared.

Unfortunately, pretty soon Betty began to feel nauseous, and it wasn't from taking him too deeply.

"Something's wrong, honey bunny. I've got to go to the potty." She wobbled out of bed.

"I'm dizzy, too. Something's going on with my heart." Ralf was turning green.

Betty never made it to the bathroom, upchucking along the way. Ralf reached for his cell phone and weakly punched in 911 before rolling off the bed, sparing their expensive red satin sheets. He puked in the wastepaper basket, then passed out.

* * * * * *

Hours later across town, literary agent Jennifer Rousch dumped three measures of robust Brazilian coffee into her French coffee press followed by boiling water. She had time to do her eyes, brush her teeth, and fuss with her hair before the coffee had steeped. The maple syrup, how divine, went into her first cup followed by low-fat milk. Avoiding the temptation of running into a stray cat by saving some for later, she emptied the rest of the coffee and syrup sample into her 24-ounce plastic carry-away mug of coffee.

Jennifer quickly got dressed and left her apartment. While trying to hail a cab, an uncomfortable gurgling began in her stomach. An odd tingling in her arms was followed by more pronounced grumbling in her bowels. Having more sips of coffee from the carry-away cup didn't help.

An early-model Chevrolet yellow cab stopped. She managed to get in, and as they pulled from the curb, she began retching. This was followed by an uncontrollable, obscene gastrointestinal explosion.

She slumped across the rear seat, begging: "Take me to a hospital! Quickly, please."

"No shit, lady, you're real bad sick!" said the dismayed cabbie, Ansel Baptiste, or AB. AB was a gifted Haitian folk artist who became a New York City hack after Haiti's recent hurricane hurled his Labadee studio into the sea. No, he didn't care much for vomit in his pristine palace. "You pay, have mess properly cleaned up, too, lady!" Another repulsive odor reached the front seat, "What you doing, lady? You crapping now in my cab, too?"

"Hurry, hurry, I'm dying." Jennifer groaned louder.

* * * * * *

Phylis Cartland left her Hell's Kitchen studio apartment on 34th Street and Ninth Avenue and walked briskly to her McDonald's. She liked that particular McDonald's because it wasn't far from B&H Photo where several times she had met attractive young photographers in the ordering line. Sadly, they seem to lose interest in her upon learning she was a literary agent and not a photographer's agent.

Phylis was a diehard romantic, energetically representing several talented romance authors. But she could write, too—and not just how-to books like *How to Get and Keep the Agent of Your Dreams* that made her reputation. Phylis had a fantasy of meeting a talented young photographer, preferably African American, whom she would take under her wing. It would create a stir and whispers in the industry as she would be thirty-five years his senior.

In her fantasy, when they first met, they would struggle to keep their lust under control but would eventually resign themselves to furious nights of guiltless banging. She would bashfully brag to her closest girlfriends how she loved that he was uncut, something she was unfamiliar with having spent most of her sex life sweating under Ivy Leaguers. To get away from the growing scandal amongst their clique, they would move to the south of France. Along the Mediterranean coast, they would find a cottage amongst the olive trees or, just as well, grape vines, and would produce two beautiful light-brown children—a boy, Cicero, and a girl, Ariella.

Phylis ordered her double order of hotcakes and coffee after waiting in the line that backed out onto Tenth Avenue. She was fortunate to find a two-seat window table that had just been cleared and wiped clean. She used the complete sample of maple syrup on the hotcakes and shook out the last, precious drops into her coffee. The hotcakes were marvelous, although the syrup had an underlying tinge of tartness.

Minutes later, she was squirming on the terrazzo floor, retching violently and losing control of her bowels. Nearby seated customers, observing Phylis' frightening spectacle (several to be sprayed with her vomit), were assaulted with the overbearing stench and began barfing. In a chain reaction to the stomach-churning spectacle, children who had been occupied with Happy Meal toys, smelt doom and began wailing. Customers pulled their shirts up over their noses and raced to the double doors, jamming the entrance, giving time for those stuck behind to initiate fresh rounds of retching.

One elderly man panicked and with his trembling cane raised into the air began screaming, "It's a gas attack, it's a gas attack!"

Never had a McDonald's been more quickly evacuated. In the confusion about the magnitude of the event, emergency dispatch sent a slew of ambulances screaming down Tenth Avenue. They found sick customers and McDonald's workers lying on the sidewalk or sitting up on the curb gasping for breath. Fortunately, Phylis got thrown into the first ambulance.

* * * * * *

MJ was freaking out; she had had to make her own coffee! It was ten a.m. She had called Pamela six times in the last half hour.

Where was that girl?

Finally, Pamela and Jeffery's neighbor, RN Tina Barnes, their savior, became so irritated by the constant ringing from Pamela's satchel hanging on their door that she answered the cell.

"Hello?"

"Pamela, where the hell are you? Do you know what fucking time it is? We have to be at Javits, God dammit! Get your ass in gear!"

"This isn't Pamela. Pamela and Jeffery have been taken to the emergency room at Brooklyn Hospital Center. I'm a neighbor waiting for the police."

"Oh, my Lord! What happened? Is she going to be alright?"

"It's very serious. I can't tell you anything. Call the hospital, Brooklyn Hospital Center."

"This is very important: when she's able to get up, tell her to meet me at Javits."

"Are you out of your mind?"

"No, I really need her there. This is our big day!"

Tina Barnes shook her head, confounded, and disconnected from the crazy woman. She put Pamela's cell phone back in the satchel as two uniformed police arrived at the top of the staircase.

The concerned female officer nodded toward the open apartment door, "Crime scene?"

"I'm thinking—it's got to be more like a suicide," said Tina dryly.

CHAPTER 19

The aforementioned earnest and likable Detective Charles White

The reprehensible results of Tilda and Timothy's battle with literary agents, the Disregards, were to land in the capable hands of the aforementioned earnest and likable Detective Charles White.

Detective White was at his desk mulling over the pros and cons of asking Inspector Mahoney if he could spend the rest of his active year looking into a few cold cases that he would be leaving behind when his desk phone buzzed, "He wants you. Glass Palace. ASAP." That was Sergeant Bookus, Mahoney's insufferable gopher.

White strolled to the other side of the detective's area, continued down the hall, and entered the realm of the most powerful man in the division. They called Inspector Mahoney's office the Glass Palace because it sat in the center of the floor, had three walls of oak paneling that came up to knee height, and then regular glass up to the ceiling. It was filled with all sorts of computers and radios that continually blinked tiny red and green lights while making scratchy radio noises.

Without comment, Detective White went past the desk of Sergeant Bookus. Bookus ignored White as he was engaged in an animated conversation on his cell phone. Bookus was not fat but had a bulging beer belly, which, along with his puffy, ruddy face, made him look a little like he was pregnant. He wasn't keen on White because of the preferential treatment Mahoney afforded him.

White entered the Glass Palace through the open twin glass doors and stopped a respectful distance from Inspector Mahoney who was seated at his desk at a new Mac and typing with two fingers. After a minute of looking at Mahoney's law enforcement citations and pictures of him and buddies in khaki Marine fatigues that were scattered about the room on little round glass tables, Charles finally asked, "What's going on, Captain?" Which made Mahoney look up. No salutes, no handshakes.

Detective White could address Inspector Mahoney as Captain because White had known him for a decade plus, and Mahoney liked being called Captain among his old-timers. To him, the higher rank of Inspector had an intrusive aura to it. Mahoney was five years younger than White, a towering man six feet, five inches, and a fit, if not robust, 260 pounds of muscle. His short Marine recruit haircut revealed where his balding spot was expanding.

"As of 0600, we have four incidents. Six victims, all life-threatening"

Charles also liked Mahoney for the simple reason he called him Charles rather than Whitey—the way some irritants down the hall in homicide used to knock him.

"First reports by patrol officers on the scene indicate poisons came in maple syrup samples from Burlington. I'd like you to get to each scene ASAP. Blues are holding at all locations."

"Terrorist? asked White, hoping he'd be able to pass it elsewhere— like to some fool in one of those other departments. White wasn't looking for long, drawn-out cases to fill his last months.

"Don't know. Let me know what you find out; the sooner the better."

"I'll be on my way."

"Detective, I'm counting on you to be circumspect. If we have to liaison with Vermont's law enforcement and judiciary, maybe it should stay up there. Know what I mean?"

"I'll tread lightly and ensure it's a Vermont problem. Am I reading you correctly?"

"Yep, exactly," said Mahoney; then, "How long?"

"One hundred and twenty-four days, eight hours," said Charles, all smiles.

"You got time to solve these. Go, Charles. It sounds like some real evil doings."

Charles passed Sergeant Bookus' empty desk but caught a glimpse of him briskly walking down the hall. The phone was still in his ear, and he was gesturing wildly.

Yep, he's on that divorce track again, thought Charles. *Come on, Bookus, try to be happy with what you have; it doesn't last forever.*

As Detective Charles White would later uncover, there were only two nutty people (both in one shell), to blame for the debacle set in motion to right the depressing world of unpublished authors. The details of the daunting cases would be simple to unwind, but like a ten-pound monster trout spinning out yards of #3, it could take a light touch to reel in.

CHAPTER 20

She was thinking about suicide, right then and there

The worst wasn't over for MJ. That afternoon and evening were designated for display and booth area setups; the morning would bring the opening and the public.

Phylis Cartland's part-time secretary called and tearfully said Phylis was near death at New York Presbyterian Hospital. She was being pumped full of activated charcoal and was connected to a hemodialysis machine that would filter out some unnamed poison. MJ asked if Phylis would be able to make at least one of her scheduled talks. The secretary slammed down the phone.

Jennifer Rousch's cab driver, Ansel Baptiste, called, having found the Romance Agents & Writers Guild phone number on a business card in her satchel. He had taken her to Mount Sinai Beth Israel Hospital, and the fare was twenty-six dollars. He wanted to know who was going to pay for cleaning and sanitizing his cab and whether there was going to be a reward offered for the return of Rousch's pocketbook and cell phone. He wasn't sure where the pocketbook and phone were located exactly, but he thought he might be able to find them.

If the cabbie didn't cough up the Jennifer's items gratis, MJ was tempted to fix his ass. Recalling she had once forgotten a precious

Saint Laurent bag with all her IDs and personal crap in a cab—and had gone that nasty direction and filed a complaint with the Taxi & Limousine Commission. Alas, it was returned, insides soaked with what smelled like urine.

She made a speedy, all-inclusive offer of two hundred dollars to Ansel Baptiste, which included the outstanding fare, vomit cleanup and the return of all items. This was grudgingly accepted by AB. The whole exchange would be handled by her doorman who would have to be tipped at least a ten. Well, better make it a twenty. Miss Jennifer was going to owe her big!

MJ had hardly had a chance to catch her breath when Ralf Sampson called from Lenox Hill Hospital. Fortunately, MJ didn't pick up but she had to listen as he left a ridiculously long message which she erased immediately. He was in better shape than Betty, having had only a small amount of wolfsbane absorbed through the skin of his erect penis rather than what Betty ingested. She lay senseless in a white hospital gown connected to a hemodialysis machine getting the charcoal treatment. Betty's racy outfit was unceremoniously hung in a clear plastic bag at the foot of her bed in open sight to the ward's hallway, gaining the attention and chuckles of the staff and visitors.

Ralf was hoping MJ would send someone to their flat for a clean nightgown and robe. He knew it was an imposition, but he knew how close MJ and Betty were.

Good luck on that one, Ralfie, dear!

MJ's head began to spin even before she could handle the chilling fact that she had no one to set up the display and had lost all her eminent speakers! Before she could collapse, the phone rang again. It was the loading dock at Javits Center. The guild's truck had arrived, but there was no one there to move everything to the booth space. Martha Jane wanted to shriek. Instead, she calmly told the Teamster's chief her crew was stuck in New Jersey and to please get everything off the truck and move it to the guild's space. She would pay for their extra time.

She was thinking about suicide, right then and there. *Pills*. She had enough stockpiled from multiple plastic surgeries and touchups to put down half the population of Manhattan.

CHAPTER 21

She was okay, I guess kinda hot. He was a jerk

Detective Charles White parked his duty car, a beat black, 10-year-old Chevy Trailblazer with dents on every panel, just past a green fire hydrant. He leaned the official police sign against the windshield. It took him a few pushes on the buzzer before being buzzed in by one of the officers waiting at the third-floor walk-up of Pamela Gadfrey and Jeffery . . . some unpronounceable last name.

"Hi, all," he said to the two officers and a neighbor who had brought over coffee for them.

"I'm Detective White." Looking at the involved neighbor, "And you are?"

"I called the ambulances last night. Tina Barnes, I'm an RN. It's been a long night, but they are great kids. It's so sad."

"Good work, Ms. Barnes. You may have saved their lives."

Charles shifted his focus to the female officer. "Tell me what you know."

She nodded for him to follow into the kitchenette where she pointed, with a straightened index finger, sequentially to the empty Ben & Jerry's vanilla ice cream pint, two dirty ice cream bowls, spoons, and lastly, the empty maple syrup bottle.

"Detective, do you think it could be Ben & Jerry's ice cream? Maple syrup doesn't go bad; it'll last forever."

"You think?" he said, cocking his head to the side as if to better hear her.

The other officer, a buff weight-lifter type stepped in, "From what Ms. Barnes told us, it's a no-brainer. Poison."

"Something else." The female officer showed White the open garbage container next to the dirty dishes and sink. Using his ballpoint pen, Charles lifted out the cardboard box and put it on the counter. He took iPhone photos of all sides, making sure the Vermont Association Maple Products address came out clearly. He pulled a plastic evidence bag from his coat pocket and slid the empty bottle into it.

"Can you help us out, anything at all about your neighbors, Ms. Barnes?" She had remained silently at the door.

"She's with some publisher or agency, something like that. He's a student at Juilliard. I hear him practicing the oboe all day and night. It's classical, so I don't mind. Detective White, I'm sorry, but I did a rough rinse of the tub in the bathroom. It was making our whole floor stink unbearably. I didn't think it could be evidence."

"Don't worry, it's not," he lied. He would have liked to have at least a picture of the dirty tub.

"Thank God."

White handed both evidence bags to the female officer. "Should go to the midtown lab ASAP. I've got to be elsewhere."

He acknowledged with a nod all around and hurried down the staircase to the street and his Chevy.

Fuck me! In the fifteen minutes I was gone, someone, a street person or dog, had pissed on my front tire. I'm starting to hate this fucking place!

White drove to the next crime scene, the McDonald's on Tenth Avenue. On the way, he speculated if it was really dog piss or if someone had simply tossed a cold coffee in the gutter and hit the tire by mistake.

At McDonald's, the enormous mess Jennifer Rousch had instigated was cleaned up, but the fast-food titan had closed its doors until the Department of Health checked out things. The shell-shocked manager, John Augueri, was exhausted. He was certain, beyond any doubt, the maple syrup sample "that fucking woman" had brought in herself was responsible. Not his hotcakes and corn syrup, no way! Their syrup had a minuscule amount of maple flavoring extract and came in sealed plastic packets. *That woman* had gotten two packages of syrup with her order and they were found unopened on her table. Despite the overwhelming, nauseating cleanup, Augueri's clear-thinking staff had the presence to save her empty syrup bottle. Detective White bagged the bottle and handed it to a patrol officer to give to forensics.

On to the next crime scene.

* * * * * *

Driving across town, Charles conjectured how curious it was when happenstance became elevated to a coincidence. Coincidences, on the scale of happenings, rank pretty high in his mind as being equal to planned events. He remembered the British television series *Midsomer Murders* on *Masterpiece Theater* and recalled an episode where the evil-doer used wolfsbane to dispatch an innocent character. Detective White wasn't going to stick his neck out by broadcasting the toxin used was wolfsbane, but it sure acted like it.

* * * * * *

When he got off the elevator, a patrol officer standing in front of the apartment door exhaled a thankful sigh. Charles had been there, too, the first lawman on a crime scene and locked out, only to twiddle thumbs. He gave the officer a recognition nod and alerted him that more officers were on their way.

Access to Betty Sampson and Ralf's apartment was provided by a sweaty superintendent pulled from the bowels of a basement cubicle. He was reeking of beer. His hanging belly hid his belt and strained every button of his soiled uniform shirt. Following the super and his ring of pass keys, they entered the apartment, which was pretty stinky, too.

Of interest to Charles, in the living room were wall-to-wall bookshelves lined with multiple copies of books. He pulled one from the shelf: a how-to book on living off the grid. First edition, signed by the author. *Boring.*

The bedroom had them holding handkerchiefs to their noses. On the bedside table next to the enormous bed with flamboyant red satin sheets stood an empty maple syrup bottle. Charles took iPhone shots of the bottle and mailing cardboard found in the trash, bagged them, and gave them to the patrol officer to hold for the lab.

"Good tenants?" he asked the super. The super was busy casing the joint, eyes going to the jewelry on top of the dresser, to the watch and rings on the night tables, to the pocketbook on the plush sofa seat that had a beach towel with coconut trees printed on it.

"She was okay, I guess kinda hot. He was a jerk." The super eyed the penis enhancer on the floor, "Always fucking complaining."

"About what?"

"Heat, water pressure, slippery floor in the lobby. You name it, he bitched."

"What type of work did they do?"

"He's retired, sales or something. She went out mornings with a laptop. That's all I know, Detective."

Charles glanced to the super then to the patrol office, "Don't let anyone touch anything." The officer got the message and nodded.

CHAPTER 22

You going to eat that other half?

Back in the Chevy Trailblazer, Charles tried calling each of the victims at their hospitals. They were mostly still incoherent, except for Ralf Sampson. But he was indisposed, evidently able to sit down on a toilet.

Charles did a quick Google search on every victim, updated what he knew into the department's information service, the Real Time Crime Center, or RTCC, then drove back to the precinct and went directly to Mahoney's office. Bookus was nowhere to be found, probably out to lunch with his phone. There had to be a juicy backstory of how Mahoney got saddled with Sergeant Bookus.

Mahoney was at his desk, working on the first half of a Pastrami sandwich with a Dr. Browns Cel-Ray soda and a sour pickle standing by. Someone had ordered out to Katz's.

"You going to eat that other half?" asked Charles.

"I'm sorry, it's so big you won't have time to eat it."

"Be that as it may . . . Cap, bad news."

"Explain," *chomp, chomp, wiping mustard off chin, chomp, chomp . . .*

"I Googled our victims. Didn't do a deep dive, but they're involved in publishing, authors' representation. As far as I can tell at this stage, they are personally unrelated but all belong to the same writer's guild. I'd have more, but their IDs went to the hospitals with them. All have been poisoned by samples of maple syrup sent from a trade association, a collective in Vermont."

"I knew it, worst-case scenario! Why couldn't it have come from a New York business? Law enforcement upstate could taken care of it without our involvement!"

"Does New York make a lot of maple syrup?"

"You'd think so! Fucking Vermont, they're like Massachusetts. Think they have something profound to say about everything."

"Maybe, I should take a drive north?" mused Charles.

"Yes, do, before the press gets wind and we have a big brouhaha between Montpelier and Albany. I need not tell you; this could be a massive cluster fuck for everyone."

"And then there's the FBI and the U.S. Postal Inspection Service question," said Charles.

"I didn't hear that." Dead silence while he took another massive chomp out of the massive sandwich, followed by a quick snip out of the sour pickle.

Of course, the FBI and the U.S. Postal Inspection Service should be involved; it's an interstate crime! So, Charles knew—but wouldn't utter a word about that.

"Understood, Captain. Postal cancellations indicate they were all sent from Vermont, so it's impossible they were tampered with here."

"That's a plus. What's your plan?"

"I'll head for Vermont as soon as I get something to eat. I haven't eaten a thing all this morning. I can call, make sure someone's there to meet me—if I don't expire from hunger first."

"As I suggested, it might be unwise to alert Vermont law enforcement as to what you're up to. You're on an unofficial fact-finding trip. But not a vacation. Got it?"

"I think that's prudent," Charles agreed, eyeing the other half of Mahoney's sandwich.

"Want more people on it?" *Chomp, chomp.*

"I'm sorry, Cap—you asked me if I want mustard on the other half?'"

"No, you misheard me."

"Nah, don't need any help. Nobody's dead. We need to know what was in the syrup."

"Forensics will be done by tomorrow. I want to know if are there more coming?" grumbled Mahoney, wiping his chin again and taking a slug of Cel-Ray.

"Vermont might have all the answers. So, let me get going." Charles headed for the door.

"Ah, Detective, I am a little reticent about sending you to the Green Mountain State. I'm trusting you'll not be screwing the pooch on our taxpayer's dime."

"Really, Captain! If I didn't know you so well, I'd think you were questioning my integrity."

"Not your integrity, your ability to fight off irrepressible urges to kill little fish and burn more time than necessary in vacation land."

"Cap, for Christ's sake, I'm fresh water. We take snaps and release. Rest assured, no wet lines 'til the wrongdoers are cuffed."

"Well, glad that's settled. Detectives get antsy or is the word ballsy, as they near retirement," said Mahoney cocking his head, attempting to signal a threat that White will ignore.

"Won't happen. I'll go up and come back like a good little puppy."

"You want something decent from the motor pool?"

"If you don't mind, I'll take my wheels."

"I'll get a notice on the air. You're going to be busting limits up there and back in that new toy. I don't want anyone wasting your time."

"Thanks, Cap." Charles paused at the door, "Are you really going to eat the other half of that greasy Pastrami sandwich? Thought you were watching your weight."

"Yeah, I'm going to eat the other half as soon as you get the fuck out of my office. I'll expect a phone briefing later today, Detective White."

"You bet, Cap."

Unsharing asshole, thought Charles. He couldn't take the time to wait in line at Katz's for a sandwich.

* * * * * *

Back at his desk, Charles grabbed his sports coat off the swivel chair and closed the laptop he used to tie into the RTCC. Across the aisle and a desk away, a spirited officer, Jeannie Jones, or JJ, stopped working on her computer. She swirled a cold coffee and took a sip. Detective White was sort of her unofficial mentor in the division so she kept an eye on him.

"What's going on, Charles? Need a hand?"

JJ was his favorite out of the team. She was a top-notch Officer II, a detective trainee, and still in uniform, whereas everyone else could wear street clothes. She'd often charm Charles by spontaneously coming up with a humorous twist to murder, suicide, decapitation, missing limbs, and the like. Most comments would be aimed at the woman, the hairdo, the type of shoes, or maybe the gross activity that had put her in their orbit. Nothing was sacred, which delighted the hell out of Charles.

In some sad happenstance, it turned out JJ was an avid saltwater fisherman—ah, a fisher*person*. Unfortunately, this put her on the wrong side of the aisle. But she had a valid reason for her offending preference, a reason stemming from her hometown of Cleveland, Ohio, which she called, "Mistake on the Lake," referring to the time when Lake Erie had become so polluted by the Cuyahoga River that it caught fire from floating industrial debris and petrochemical dumping. JJ wouldn't touch or eat anything that spawned in fresh water.

She was too young, way too smart, and too pretty to want to mess with an old widower. The only lewd thought Charles had about JJ was what type of belly button she had: an innie or an outie?

"Nah, I got it, JJ. Poisonings in our patch. But it's not out yet, so mum's the word. I'm off to Vermont to open it up. I'll be putting everything on RTCC."

"That's a sneaky way to beat town, go for them little freshwater fishes, Charles," snickered JJ.

"Hey, we freshwater guys, we're all about control and finesse," he responded while activating his desk telephone answering system. "Not like you saltwater putt-putters, chumming and then praying for a nibble from a bottom sludge eater."

Charles left JJ with a big grim. Both were used to ribbing and dishing it back. The precinct was filled with saltwater guys and gals that he derisively called "putt-putters," a term he knew they loathed.

What Detective White hadn't told Captain Mahoney was that he'd make two pit stops before getting on the road to Vermont. He'd stop at the Sunrise Diner for a sausage and egg on a bun with mayo because he was, actually, really hungry. Then, drop the duty Chevy at the motor pool and grab a cab to the condo.

* * * * * *

Instead of Mary's Volvo wagon parked in her old spot, Charles' newer Corvette was parked there now. With the purchase of the 'Vette,

Charles decided to pay extra to the condo association for two spaces one story above the flood level reached in 2012. The Volvo carried too many memories, so he passed it on to his daughter in New Jersey. When giving her the keys, he took the opportunity to suggest the Volvo was exceptionally safe and a great family car for kids, hoping she'd get the hint. Nope.

Charles transferred his "war bag" from the SUV to the Corvette. A war bag is a canvas tote officers carry that contains an extra flashlight, gaffer tape, Tylenol, pens, paper pad, zip ties, a tool kit, toilet paper, and several flash drives—even out-dated computer discs. Anything that might be needed in the field before the backup trucks or vans arrive. Charles' war bag also had fishing flies and lures.

After Mary died, the barely used but immaculate shadow-gray 2020 Corvette Z51 Stingray with Adrenaline Red leather interior and the performance package came up for auction on eBay. It was the only big thing he bought, which was not meant to be a distraction from his misery for losing Mary or some intangible reward, but as a stimulus to think ahead and begin life anew while looking good and going fast.

CHAPTER 23

Don't bother getting up, Mister Fritz

Unlocking the double lock to the condo, Charles was rarely greeted at the door by Mister Fritz who had remained mostly indifferent to him since Mary passed. Going into the living room, Mister Fritz eyed Charles, but remained flat on his back stretched out on the sofa, clearly waiting until called.

Mister Fritz was assumed to be a terrier: short white-brown coat, cute little flopped-over ears, and long whiskers. Having a big personality, he acted like he was ready for his close-up. Anytime, just whistle.

"Don't bother getting up, Mister Fritz."

Which made him leap off the sofa and dash over, wagging his little white tail and wedging himself between Charles' feet. "That's better, buddy. I was thinking you forgot me." A little vigorous head-scratching always warmed up Mister Fritz to him.

"I see your leash at the door, so Mrs. Wilson took you out for the afternoon poop-a-thon. I'm going to say hello to Mrs. Wilson. Sit tight."

Charles left the apartment, walked down two doorways to unit 32, and hit the door buzzer. As soon as Mrs. Wilson opened the door, the hallway was flooded with the mouthwatering aroma of a long-simmering pot roast. A retiree from the IRS, she wore a Pottery Barn apron over her colorful smock. It was in the same outlandish vein as her reckless, hennaed red-brown hair.

"Come in, darling. I got some pot roast that's going to knock your socks off."

"Boy, wish I could! But I've got to hit the road to Vermont. Official business."

"That's a shame, I made so much of it!"

"It won't go to waste," Charles said.

"That's the trouble, I'll eat it all! We had such a lovely walk this afternoon. Mister Fritz, he's such a sweetie, but I tell you, he doesn't care for chipmunks or squirrels!"

"Mary used to tell me he'd pretend not to see them and then jump at 'em like a tiger." Charles opened his wallet, finding two Andrew Jacksons, "I want to give you something for taking care of him."

"You can't keep trying to make me take money! Walking Mister Fritz is the only exercise I get, and he's a joy for company!"

"That's too generous of you. It's been a tough year, and you've been a lifesaver. Unfortunately, I have to go away for a few days, so your walking companion is going to be gone for a while."

"If I wasn't so allergic to dogs, I'd snatch him away and have him all for myself. Putting on his leash and an hour's walk doesn't affect my breathing in the least bit, but Charles, it makes my day."

"We'll be back soon, just don't know exactly when," he said, sadly realizing there was no chance of enlisting Mrs. Wilson to take Mister Fritz. He went back to the condo and found him posed at the door.

"Hope you're looking forward to a nice visit with Caroline? You know how she loves you and takes you for long walks around the common yard. And there's all the other little dog friends you have there."

Mister Fritz looked up for a moment, then scurried to the kitchen. He reappeared with his plastic dinner bowl in his mouth. More endearing quizzical looks with cute head rotations.

"You rascal. It's too early for din-din and then I'd have to walk you. Can't do that, papa gotta run to Vermont. I heard they don't allow little dogs in Vermont, only ones big enough to fight bears."

Charles flopped down on the sofa, opened his cell, and punched in his daughter's number. Mister Fritz climbed up beside him and rested his head on his thigh.

"Hey, Sweetie! I'm in a hurry so I'll be brief . . . you, too? You're on the way to Newark airport? . . . Well, you and Steve have fun in the Bahamas. I'll let you go but call me when you get back. I'll be worried if I don't hear from you. Love ya!" Charles looked at Mister Fritz, "Looks like you're coming. Don't you dare leave any little hairs in my 'Vette. Got it?"

Charles went into the bedroom, paused to enjoy the spectacular view of the busy water traffic on the Hudson, then began packing his YETI overnight bag (that he had gotten for Christmas from Santa), for a two-day-away change. He remembered to take from the bedside table his nightly read, *Landon Mayer's Guide to Flies*. Always tucked into his wallet, his expensive Vermont fishing license was current but expiring in three months.

With Mister Fritz trailing, they went into the parking garage, loaded the overnight bag next to his war bag, then secured his brand-new, never-seen-water fishing gear into the safe compartment of the 'Vette's hidden wayback. One never knew when an opportunity to wet a line might open up, despite his no-fishing pledge to Mahoney.

Mister Fritz would sleep on the motel bed with him but would eat and drink off plastic from fast-food joints, ensuring the 'Vette was kept nice and clean from doggie-bowl smells and the like.

CHAPTER 24

CEO Thomas is out in the bush killing things

They were good to go. Mister Fritz was perched in the passenger seat with his leash off, but snaked around the dash of the Corvette. Detective Charles White and his frisky traveling companion, were soon crawling up the Westside Highway in bumper-to-bumper traffic. They crossed the George Washington Bridge, made a quick jag onto Route 4, then blasted onto I-87N, which would take them all the way to Glens Falls. They'd cross into Vermont onto Route 7 and would reach Burlington from New York City in five-and-a-half hours if he adhered to the legal speed limit. That, he was not going to do.

With his cell phone clipped onto the dash and with the speaker on, he called the number on the maple syrup mailer for VAMP.

"Vermont Association Maple Products, Kirby Clark speaking. How may I help you?"

"Hello, Ms. Clark. This is Detective Charles White with the New York Police Department."

"You're calling about a parking ticket for the Elton John concert? Jeez, that was two decades ago!"

"No, not about a parking ticket. I'm with NYPD's suspicious death squad."

"Oooh, that sounds real creepy."

"It is creepy. We have a situation involving maple syrup samples from your organization."

"That sounds even worse."

"I'm afraid it is, Ms. Clark."

"I'm on my way up to you, crossed the G. W. Bridge a few minutes ago. Ms. Clark, are you the person I should be speaking to?"

"Call me KC. Would you hold for a minute?"

Kirby Clark was at a crossroads. She had to decide whether to be a powerless pawn, passing along messages to Bill or an employee of substance, a person empowered with judgment and responsibility.

"I'm back, Detective. I'm the Director of Promotions and the one who can help you. CEO Thomas is out in the bush killing things."

Wrong description, thought White.

"So, how may I help you?"

"GPS says I'm 260 miles from you. I'll be at your door in two or so hours."

In two hours? That made her chuckle. She needed to hear something ridiculous in her tedious day.

Kirby Clark, aka KC, sat in a microscopic cubby between two glass partitions and a floor area mostly occupied by metal file cabinets. Adjoining her cubby was a small six-seat conference room that doubled as a kitchenette with a microwave and coffeemaker. Wall art consisted of a smattering of member-supplied maple sugaring images mounted on unframed posterboard. Every picture was sleep-inducing to Kirby, a jaded country girl when it came to hackneyed, sugarbush images.

The only sunlight came from the one-bay loading dock, and that was only if the sliding corrugated metal door was raised. This lack of sunlight could be emotionally trying for Kirby in the winter months if she had to keep office hours. She'd have to talk to Bill when deer season was over.

Kirby worshipped the sun's warming rays and had been thinking of getting a small sun tattoo with radiating rays on her ankle. That was before her son, Davey, related to her that his former, almost-became-wife, had a tramp stamp—a tattoo of a soaring eagle across her ass cheeks. He once bragged that his lovemaking skill could make the wings flap, pissing off Kirby to no end. But Kirby was blessed with Davey's infant son, leading her to reconsider: *What sort of self-respecting grandmother would have a tramp stamp?* She'd wait for the sun tattoo until he was old enough to understand. Maybe she'd add a little trout tattoo on her other ankle?

"Sure, I'll see you in maybe four hours, Detective Lead Foot. We close at four-thirty, so I'll be waiting outside on the loading platform. Try not to be too late since I'm not paid overtime."

"That'll be appreciated. See you then." Charles disconnected.

* * * * * *

Before the detective arrived at VAMP, Kirby had to make essential decisions based on their short telephone conversation. First, no matter who he turned out to be, she made a promise not to hop right into bed with him. If by chance, he had to overnight in a Burlington hotel, she would need extra hormonal control—sleeping in a hotel was like a brief vacation with a bed she didn't have to makeup and a minibar she wouldn't have to pay.

Experience reminded her it is better to go into a relationship showing restraint and that she be super selective. Of course, the consideration of involvement would hinge on whether he was cool and the intangible can't-put-a-finger-on chemistry.

Waiting, and having nothing else to do but fantasize and sip water, Kirby confirmed to herself that all consideration of sex mostly had to rest on his charm, intelligence, and the particulars of him in the flesh. No-go things were if he were a total ogre, ridiculously old, alarmingly overweight, had offensive body odors and bad dandruff, was effeminate, wore Bermuda shorts, and married. Actually, the married aspect was adjustable if he had a convincing explanation for his sad and lonely marital circumstances.

It had been a long, long time since she had slept with a man. She had been relying on a satisfying vibrator she bought on a trip to Connecticut and kept in a hideaway niche under her bathroom sink. It was well hidden so she could say, "Must have been forgotten by the condo's previous owner."

Never knew when Davey might be rummaging around looking for a Band-Aid or something for Simon. Best to have a cover story ready.

* * * * * *

Charles had the office laptop on the red leather seat beside Mister Fritz and the E-ZPass on the dash. As the Corvette effortlessly sucked up the miles, it was gobbling gasoline. They had to tank twice because averaging between 100 and 140 mph (all he could do between clusters of traffic), the Z51 would average under ten miles to a gallon. It was the first time he had the speedometer in deep triple digits, and he was screamingly happy. Sensing the potential for doom, Mister Fritz remained trustingly calm while snuggling deeper into the leather seat and closing his eyes.

Several times, the shadow-gray 'Vette ripped past speed traps. The state troopers in their blue-and-gold striped cruisers would flash their lights, letting him know he was recognized and that his mission had been blessed from their headquarters in Albany.

His cell toned with Beethoven's Fifth, his selected ring. *Unknown caller.*

"Who's this?"

"An officer in your office gave me your number. My name is Martha Jane Sidel, and I want to know what the hell you're doing to get my people back."

"You need to be a little clearer. What's this about?" Charles started to cringe. *What asshole in the chain would give out his cell number?*

"I'm at the Javits Center getting ready to slice my fucking wrists."

"I'd hold off on that."

"I have to set up a massive display, and there's no one to help me! My assistant and three irreplaceable speakers are in hospitals dying! If that isn't a terrorist attack, what the fuck is it?"

"Ma'am, you break up when you scream. Your speakers are the ones in the hospital, correct?"

"My God, are you policemen all morons? Yes, by tomorrow I'll have no business and you don't get it!"

"What type of event is this? Where are they speaking? About what?"

"This is unfathomable. Everything is collapsing, and I've got Barney Fife on the phone. It's the book expo at Javits Center! My agents are the greatest audience pull in the literary world!"

"Literary agents?"

"Yes, yes! Jesus, don't you know anything?"

"What's your name? Your organization is what?"

"I'm Martha Jane Sidel, founder of the Romance Agents & Writer's Guild. We provide writing courses and help writers get published."

"Who would want to hurt your people? Who would gain from disrupting the book expo?" Charles didn't have time to mess with a distraught civilian, but he was learning more of what he needed to know.

"Good Lord, where did you go to school? On the friggin' moon? Everyone here at the book expo wants me to fail. They've always hated me, my success, the business I've built from nothing."

"Ok, got it. There's another call coming in I've got to take. Don't call me again. Someone from my office will get back to you. He's going to want your speaker list."

"It's on our damn website!" He heard her screech as he disconnected.

He immediately slowed and banged off an update into the RTCC, letting Captain Mahoney know all the victims were literary agents belonging to the Romance Agents & Writer's Guild, and were to attend an event at Javits Center. Further information to follow. And tell the dickhead who gave out his cell number to the guild's distressed owner, to go fuck himself!

Definitely wasn't JJ or one of my guys. Maybe stressed-out Sergeant Bookus couldn't handle Martha Jane Sidel?

The 'Vette had a quick top-off at Mobil, then Charles blasted through the gears onto I-87N. A few minutes later, he slowed to text JJ to prepare an email blast to every Romance Agents & Writer's Guild member alerting them of the maple syrup tampering. Charles thought a few minutes, then revised his recommendation. The email should stress the announcement was a precautionary measure. The more he thought about it, it wasn't the right time to start that either. Maybe the samples had targeted only the guild speakers? He'd hold the text to JJ a while longer.

He gave Mister Fritz a reassuring tummy scratch, then got back to pressing on the gas pedal. He had his Motown collection and *The Iceman's Make it Easy on Yourself* to carry him to Vermont. Jerry Butler: smooth, smooth as ice.

CHAPTER 25

Mister Fritz. He pretends to be a person but he's all dog

Detective White and Mister Fritz made the drive to VAMP's office in Burlington in two hours and fifteen minutes. They arrived at the single-story building with two small loading docks. One belonged to an outfit making cast iron heating kits that burned reconstituted wood pellets from tree bark and the other was for the Vermont Association of Maple Producers or, as the sign abbreviated, VAMP.

Kirby Clark was reclined in a blue plastic pool lounge chair on the concrete loading dock face up with her aviator Ray-Bans throwing off a cinematic glint from the afternoon sun. Ideally, she'd like the detective's first impression of her to be one of a laid-back, sophisticated woman belonging on the French Riviera. The lack of sand and water and wearing blue jeans and her red-and-black-checked flannel shirt would kind of ruin that fanciful scene. Unless he was a real creative.

As soon as she saw the late model Corvette enter the parking lot, emptied the water bottle into the planter of daises, and signaled him to pull into the space next to her red Jeep Cherokee. Her Jeep, as she was advised by the architect seller, was not a simple red, but a special Frank Lloyd Wright Cherokee Red. Which made a lot of sense.

Detective White climbed out and stretched his arms, giving her a glimpse of a holster and badge under his brownish tweed sports coat, all of which was quite acceptable. She knew her bang 'em or not on the first date might be a trial, especially when he came with a frisky little mutt of a dog bouncing around inside the Corvette desperately trying to get out to greet her.

"NYPD's got new patrol cars?"

"Not quite. It's all mine."

"Too bad I didn't know you in high school. You might have gotten lucky."

"There's still time," said Charles, baiting her back.

"What's that riding shotgun? NYPD's latest attack canine."

"Mister Fritz. He pretends to be a person but he's all dog."

"Just goofing, I love dogs. I just happen to have a baby myself. I named her Teddi after my grandmother."

"Quite a name for a grandmother."

"Yeah. Neither Granny nor my puppy were keen on being called Theodore."

"Sorry, got to do this." He took a small pad and pen out of his sports coat, "What's your full name?"

"Ms. Kirby F. Clark."

"Middle initial stands for . . .?"

"Fried." Kirby burst out laughing, which was infectious and had Detective White cracking up.

"It was hell in school. I was called KFC by everyone until I knocked a few heads. It's actually Frank. As in frankfurter." More uncontrolled laughter, "Name came from my dad's father—seriously."

Kirby Clark had Detective White pleasantly surprised. She was enticingly attractive, especially to a desperate old single dog like himself. She had sort of a demurring look framed by longish blond hair with strands of grey tucked behind her ears. All was neatly ponytailed with a tortoiseshell barrette. She was uncorrupted by makeup and her lips seemed to be set for a smile. But, as he was to soon learn, those pretty lips were just preparing to say something.

She was definitely smart, and that came with the right amount of silly fun and non-confrontational sassy talk, too. She liked his wheels. Well, that may have been one reason why he brought it. She also took to Mister Fritz, which was a real plus.

Maybe she'll take care of Mister Fritz so I'll be free to quickly wrap up this phony-baloney investigation and afford me some time to do a little fishing?

Kirby dragged out a second plastic lounge chair from the office, and they ended up relaxing on the loading dock drinking old coffee. Mister Fritz was very obedient; after he watered the daisies, he stayed put between their chairs licking his paws.

"You carry a gun?"

"Oh yeah," he said, unsurprised by the question.

"Where is it?"

"Hidden."

"So you think. Well, I have a carry permit. Got it to dissuade my former from stealing the furniture when we split. Told him I'd be waiting for him."

"That's nice . . . nice to know."

Through the rollup door and stacked against the back wall Charles could see a slew of cardboard cartons with stenciling identifying them as containing maple syrup. "That how the samples come?" he asked. She nodded.

"How many?"

"Five thousand were filled by our bottler in Vergennes. Take out the hundred I have at home and I think board members grabbed a case or two. And there are still eight cases here. That's maybe 3,800 distributed so far."

"Where'd they go?"

"Originally, in the dumbest of dumb marketing schemes, we had them going to wholesale channel buyers, candy makers, ice cream producers, and the like. A massive flub-up has us now saving our asses by dumping them on the retail market: small grocery stores, local restaurants, diners, minimarts, gas stations with marts, touristy haunts. That type of thing."

"One could buy a case or single samples at any of those places?"

"Yep, you got it. So, tell me, what's the problem?"

"Samples sent to New York City have been tampered with, making people very sick. Life-threatening, but no one's died yet."

"Really?"

She made a big show of pouring a sample bottle of syrup into her coffee. Stirred, took a big slug, then another. "How much time do I have?"

"Not long," Charles answered. "Before you leave us, would you guess who would want to do this type of thing?"

"That won't be a guess, I know for sure."

"Refreshing. Tell me so I can start for home before dark."

"It's the Canadians, no doubt. They'd love Vermont syrup producers to go under and our products pushed off the market. They already undercut us whenever they can."

"I'll keep that gem of a motive in mind."

"Well, it's just a thought, backed up by my years of professional experience in the business."

Charles' cell phone toned Beethoven. After a few minutes, he disconnected.

Just as I thought. I ought to send Midsomer Murders *a Christmas card.*

"The toxin in the syrup is aconitum, also known as wolfsbane or monkshood. Ever hear of it?"

"No kiddin'. It grows all over. Anyone with half a brain knows not to touch it, much less try it on their pancakes."

"Someone's targeting people in our literary community."

"Well, we didn't have anything to do with it."

"I believe you. But they were all mailed from different post offices in Vermont, which raises questions."

"That will keep you busy."

"Let's see if a malcontent has been using wolfsbane elsewhere to sow chaos and disorder," he said, winking at her.

He worked on the laptop with Kirby hanging over his shoulder, catching and correcting his spelling. Finding no wolfsbane deaths in over twenty years, it seemed Vermonters were pretty savvy when it came to recognizing the plant.

"Here's something. Recently in the *Ripton Crier* about a cow dying in Lincoln from eating wolfsbane."

"That's very, very rare. Cows know better. They have an atavistic awareness to pass on the wolfsbane entrée."

"Come again?"

"They've learned to avoid the plant and its flowers over centuries of evolution."

"Oh, that's interesting. May I take a few of your samples and mailers? Ours are locked up as evidence."

"No problem. We still might have just a few," nodding toward the cases stacked against the back wall.

"If you've finished your days' work here, a sample was mailed from the Elmwood Post Office in Burlington. Want to go for a ride?"

"Sure. Twenty minutes away, five minutes if you let me drive," said Kirby.

"I think not," said Charles, standing.

Kirby put away the chairs, dropped the roll-down garage-style galvanized door, and snapped on a tough-looking padlock. "This is so cool! I'm assisting in an official investigation and will be chauffeured in a new Corvette with incredible red leather. Can't wait to put my fanny on it. I'm just like going to be—all excited!"

She did an exaggerated but cute little excitement shiver.

"Excite away!" said Charles, wondering what he had gotten himself into.

"You don't know, I'm a gearhead! Always wanted a Porsche 356. Sunroof, German racing silver. Red leather, just like that," referring to the 'Vette, "But this American iron will do for now."

"It's mostly aluminum and carbon fiber," he corrected her, and added, "You're going to have Mister Fritz on your lap."

"I'd be delighted. Is he lap-broken?"

Charles didn't respond. She hesitated at the open door and said, before dropping into the beckoning seat:

"I mean, really Charlie, you look like something out of Central Casting. In cop flics, white hair usually comes with a pot belly."

"Well, I don't eat all those donuts anymore with the boys."

"No complaints, really. Frankly, I'm charmed by your lean, good looks without looking like you work out twice a day in some stinky gym.

"I ride a bike on the terrace," and added as an afterthought, "and eat White Castle cheeseburgers or Oreos before turning in every night. Is that okay?"

"You such an honest liar. My ex has a growing bald spot. He's not nuts about it, well, neither am I. So, I'm real partial to your head of white hair that coincidentally, matches your name!"

"Will wonders ever cease."

"So Detective White, is your Harry Callahan appearance something you've worked at, or inherited?"

CHAPTER 26

Get up! Get up! MJ, you lazy whore!

Meanwhile, back at the Javits Center, Martha Jane had lost all hope of having a successful expo, much less any future. All around her exhibitors were working like mad to get their displays erected. She was immobilized, boxed in by cartons of the guild's display materials and a mountain of folding chairs. Defeated, she had plopped onto the carpet, sitting with legs splayed apart. She reasoned it was the proper position to be in to have a coronary, sitting up. A stroke would do just as well. She was not going to survive Book Expo XII. It was over for her and the guild.

That is until she was surprised by a rap on the shoulder from Cecil Rhodes of C & B Publishing. Cecil was the family scion, destined to be an industry titan. And, as rumored in the industry, he had unlimited resources to reshape the emerging self-publishing market. Although short in height, he was giant in bulk. He was marching his setup crew out of the Javits Center after they had finished putting up the C & B Publishing display. When Cecil saw MJ on the carpet, he raised his arm like a Boy Scout leader and stopped his parade.

MJ looked up with pitiful, bloodshot eyes to see Cecil towering over her. Rivulets of black mascara continued to roll down her cheeks.

"Cecil, darling, I'm screwed. Pamela's almost dead. My speakers are in the hospital dying. I swear, I'm joining them soon."

Cecil, all rotund three hundred Australian pounds, took a deep breath, grabbed her arm, and gave it an impolite jerk.

"Get up! Get up! MJ, you lazy whore!"

"Huh?"

"Get up! Stop this nonsense, you pathetic wretch. Your tent's up, your display's off the loading dock, and you're sitting on your skinny little ass babbling like a fool!"

"I want to die."

Cecil, not completely heartless, decided to respond a mite more humanely to her rarely experienced, vulnerable state. He wrapped an understanding arm around her shoulder.

"Now, now, MJ. You may be the biggest bitch in the industry but you're not going down like this. No friend of mine is going to be reduced to childish sniveling because of a little bad luck. Come on, stand up."

Martha Jane was speechless, mouth agape. Cecil motioned to his crew to gather around them.

"Guys, this is MJ, an old friend having a little difficulty. Let's get her stuff set up and made ready for tomorrow's opening. Don't leave until it's done. Right, guys?"

Martha Jane choked back bawling, but more mascara tears began streaking down her cheeks.

"For Christ's sake, MJ, get to work! Tell them what you want done! I've got a cocktail party to attend. See you tomorrow." Cecil turned and was gone.

CHAPTER 27

I was a wee little thing and didn't know better

Kirby and Detective White got to the Burlington Post Office minutes after closing. Inside, Manager Donald Picard was hustling about, ensuring staff was properly shutting down the teller windows as he shuffled cash trays. When he heard Charles pounding on the revolving door and saw his badge pressed against the glass, he let them in. Picard appeared to be an outdoorsy type: unshaven, in a wrinkly shirt and cargo pants with multiple sets of keys attached to several belt loops.

He was not keen on being interrupted at the most crucial part of the day, closing time, which made him even more sweaty. He perked up when he saw Kirby.

"Hey, KC! What'd you do now?"

"Not a thing, Donnie. Just trying to make our hometown industry bigger, better, and safer."

Charles knew Vermont was small, but what a coincidence!

"I used to go to the lake with Donnie when I was a wee little thing and didn't know better."

"Yeah, back when you were nice," snapped Donnie.

"Okay, you two. Cool it."

Charles flashed Donnie his wallet I.D. and gave him a brief spiel without mentioning maple syrup. It was dramatic, lives were at stake. Slightly perturbed, Donald led them to the surveillance cubby, a distasteful room with colored printouts on the walls of him holding a crossbow and standing beside dead deer. The room was made worse by Donald's pervasive body odor.

He found the disc for the exterior camera recording at the date and time when the sample was postmarked. He loaded it into an ancient and grimy white Dell. Within a few seconds of scrolling through grainy and choppy images, they were surprised to see a woman in a beret and raincoat, walk up to the blue mailboxes carrying a small carton. Charles took a video of the scene off the computer screen with his cell phone.

"She's probably local; look familiar to either of you?"

"Not me, boss," said Kirby.

"I'm drawing a blank, too. Can't see much of her anyway," said Donnie.

In the video, they could see a postman coming out the front doors of the post office pushing a canvas mail transfer cart. He stopped the beret-wearing woman from dropping a box into the mailbox. They chatted for a moment, and he then dropped the carton into his cart.

"Damn, *he* just mailed our package," moaned Charles, and added, "*She* didn't mail it." Kirby and Donnie exchange quizzical glances. "It's a legal thing, a minor hiccup for a prosecutor."

"That's postman Nathan Alberts. He's off today at home watching the PGA. I'll get you his address and phone," said Donnie.

"Would you dupe that disc and send it to my attention?" He gave Donnie his card and added, "Can you get it off by tomorrow?"

"Think you can manage without calling Fed Ex?" Kirby said wryly.

"Give Alberts a heads up that we're on the way, okay?"

"No problem. There's not going to be a situation, you being from New York State, is there?" Donnie seemed to be awakening to the fact he had done everything he shouldn't have done without a sign-off from bosses in Rutland or, worse, Washington D.C.

"Nope, none whatsoever. Interstate collaboration and criminal pursuit agreements rule our day every day," he answered somberly. Then, he gave Donnie a reassuring shoulder pat.

"Just had to ask," said Donnie, relieved and happy to get back to his regular work, shuffling stamps, toting teller trays, and assigning vacation schedules.

"Hey, Donnie, I do miss you. Once in a while, I think of some of the good times we had," said Kirby, winking at Charles.

"Well, shoot, let's get together sometime. Get back on the lake or something. I got a new boat. You can swim, waterski, smoke pot, go topless. Whatever you want."

"No thanks, better not," answered Kirby, rolling her eyes for Charles to see.

When they got into the car, Kirby scooted Mister Fritz to her lap, and asked, "Were you fibbing? There's no problem you being a New York detective and this being Vermont?"

Charles gave her a withering glance.

"Never mind. Just asking.

* * * * * *

Kirby and Charles didn't have time to get out of the car before Nathan Alberts charged from the Craftsman-style cottage, slopping a tallboy Budweiser can in one hand and a filter-less Lucky Strike cigarette in the other.

Nathan Alberts was certainly the postman with the odd handlebar mustache seen in the surveillance disc. Even on his day off he wore the same shorts and green sneakers, confirming his identification—as if there were any doubt. He set his Bud on the roof and threw himself against the car door before Charles could open it. *Postmaster Donnie must have phoned ahead.*

"Nathan, please take the beer can off my roof." He did.

Charles held his cell phone out the open window so Nathan could watch the clip of the woman and him.

"You're sure you've never seen her before?" Charles asked politely.

"Nope. Only that once." Nathan picked a wet tobacco fleck off his lip from his cigarette, and wiped it onto his shorts.

"You're positive?"

"Only that once. Put her in a lineup. I'll pick her out though," snapping his fingers, "just like that!"

Nathan had no trouble remembering her details: elderly disorganized woman, black beret, pearly white complexion, too. Maybe a bit nervous. He offered to sit with an artist to do a facial rendering. No thanks, wasn't necessary, the surveillance disc, that'll be enough.

"You didn't see her transportation, did you?"

"Yep, red Subaru, early 1990s wagon. Parked across the street at Papa John's Pizza."

"You didn't happen to see if she was alone, did you?" asked Kirby.

"Nope, didn't see if she was alone."

They had gotten all they needed out of Alberts. They shook hands and drove away, leaving an enlivened Alberts waving goodbye as if they were off to some war.

"Let me do future questioning. Okay, KC?"

"Sorry about that—this is too much fun," she said sheepishly.

"I understand."

"My lips are sealed, except for needing a cocktail. Like a disgusting Mai Tai since it's well after five," she suggested, flirting eyebrows at him. He was receptive.

"Where do we find that?"

"Burlington's worst, the Tiki Bar."

"Okay. What's it called?"

"Tiki Bar."

"Right. Tell me where to drive." He had completely forgotten about calling Captain Mahoney.

CHAPTER 28

Not totally naked. You know, figure of speech

They found a parking spot just across the street from Tiki Bar where Charles could watch the car and Mister Fritz, who kept his nose glued to the slot left open on the passenger window. They sat at a varnished ship's hatch table next to the street-facing window that was framed by hanging baskets of philodendrons.

Tiki Bar was a hangout, not only for the student population but also for those locals who had a yen for enamel-rotting sugary drinks. Also, a great place for those on a first date to loosen up and be able to profess they didn't know what they were doing the next morning.

Kirby had to order from the bar, no table service. She rose from the table, went to the bar, ordered, and came back. Charles had noticed her eyes, when seen slightly off-angle, appeared to waver between blue and green. They would drift about the room, find something to momentarily hold an interest, and then settle back as if to remind you she was actually listening to you.

"You wear contacts?" he asked.

"No. Why?"

"Your eyes . . . they're beautiful. You know, they change color from different angles."

"So I've been told. Hold tight, be right back, our Tiki Bar Specials are almost ready."

The Tiki Bar Island Specials came with umbrellas and speared red dye #9 cherries. They loaded ice in a shaker, added splashes of vitamin C from exotic canned juices such as orange, banana, pear, and maybe lime, filled the rest with cheap rum, and shook it all up.

While Kirby waited at the bar, Charles logged into the RTCC on his laptop. He added the information about the mature female mailer and that she drove an early model red Subaru wagon. A follow-up from forensics had just been entered, confirming wolfsbane in all poisonings. Mahoney must have lit a fire—all out of the lab in one day!

Pity, thought Charles, *the syrup ended up in Sidel's assistant and roommate's ice cream, not with hers. Which would have been just dessert.*

Kirby returned with the Tiki Bar Island Specials.

"I'm just fascinated with your job! Do you, like, every night go over what you've done? Think about clues you may have missed?"

"No," but he lied.

"Do real life-and-death situations get lost in bureaucratic red tape? And evidence gets stolen?"

"No," but he lied again. "You watch too, too much TV, KC. Seriously, you do," he said, smiling and not wanting to open up a tedious subject that could run on all night.

"I guess, I do watch a lot of TV. Mostly movies. It's easy to get cabin fever up here around January. As for me, by March, I don't care how cold it is, I'm a bare-assed lady on the terrace if the sun is shining."

"Interesting . . ."

She followed with, "Not totally naked. You know, figure of speech."

"No problem on my end, either way."

"It's so cool you're linked to an information system you can access anytime, anywhere. Do you have to have that laptop with you all the time?"

"Real Time Crime Center. We say, RTCC. It's a valuable tool. And yes, I keep it with me all the time. I'm sworn to protect it with my life and destroy if I'm captured," said Charles, maintaining a straight face.

"You are a good guy, Charlie. You ever let the bad guy go? You know, weird circumstances?"

"No, I'm pretty clear on the law-and-order thing. Courts decide, I just catch them." Charlie lied once again.

Once badged, police officers were obligated to be ever vigilant for evil-doers, 24/7. Detective White took that very seriously, although he generally ignored petty infractions.

When living in Jersey there was a dim-witted, stoner neighbor kid and his tatted girlfriend who stole his dad's treasured '67 Camaro for a joy ride. Hardly down the block, he skidded off the road, across a lawn, and smacked into a telephone pole. Fortunately, both came out of the wreck unscathed. The toppled pole sparked and flared wildly on the collapsed hood, knocking out electricity for two blocks.

Charles had seen the son take the car and confronted him as he sat dazed on the grass.

The delinquent son, assuming the classic car would not be covered by insurance because of the circumstances, begged him not to report him. From neighborhood gatherings, Charles knew his dad, a town employee of modest means, and his mom, a bank teller. He felt confident the incident would destroy the family, so he let the youth and inked girlfriend sneak back home like they had nothing to do with it.

* * * * * *

Loaded with the Tiki Bar Island Special and beaming with red cheeks, Kirby was waiting for Charles to continue. He didn't know how to keep up the entertaining chatter—it was exhausting.

"These tables are actually faux ship hatches that are cranked out by the thousands in the Philippines," then his stomach growled.

"You're hungry!" Kirby exclaimed. "Me, too!"

"I haven't eaten since this morning's takeout breakfast from a greasy spoon diner in New York."

"We've got a greasy spoon here, too! I worked there one summer. Learned how to make authentic New England crab cakes without crabmeat. What do you get at your greasy spoon?"

"Nothing like your crab cakes. Mostly grease with donuts, egg sandwich with double bacon."

"Greasy spoons, God I love 'em! You know, Charlie, you're like living in a TV series. That's so cool!"

"If you think so, but it ain't so glamorous." They were quiet for a minute. "Today has been special. Working with the entertaining and beautiful Kirby Clark, Promotions Director at VAMP."

"I like that, what you just said."

"It's all true."

She then hesitantly asked, "You're not married, are you?"

"No, widowed. Not big into dating yet."

"Sorry, that must hurt. But I'm glad you're not hung up with someone. Or a cheater."

"Honestly, never into the cheating part. Mister Fritz and I have a new life now. And you?"

"Divorced, one grown boy, Davey. He's with Fed Ex. He wants to fly their planes but is stuck as a loader. I've got a baby grandson, from Davey's foolish lust, and a puppy maybe you'll get to meet. I'm bored, but not looking for a good man."

"Very good. I should be naughty?"

She ignored his remark. "You have kids?"

"Daughters. All grown. One married in Jersey, one single in Colorado. No grandkids. I have to be patient. I've found there's no pushing with them."

"That generation is holding off. God knows what for," stated Kirby.

"There's a lot to be uneasy about. New York City struggles with overwhelming social issues. It's because they elect scumbags. At least, we're out of the mask-wearing and vaccination farce."

Charles, finishing his Island Special, said, "You must love Vermont?"

"It's home. It's changed since the sixties. We've been inundated with out-of-state transplants who keep voting for Bernie. Sure, he's well-meaning—bless his drooling liberal heart—but he can't get shit done. Thank God, Leahy's taken a hike."

That made him laugh, but Kirby kept on without missing a beat, ". . . and our winters, once you give up winter sports, old age is miserable. That's why my folks dwell in the perpetual sunshine of Tampa."

"Mine are in The Villages, Florida, too. They love it, but their lifestyle would kill me overnight," responded Charles.

"Ditto. Besides, I need room to shoot my guns," she replied.

He smiled and glanced out the window at the car across the street. Mister Fritz's nose was mucking up the windows something terrible.

"Charlie, tell me about your family. Brothers, sisters?"

"One brother, Reid, an account exec with Levi Strauss, married with two kids. A sister, Julie, lives in Kentucky. She's married and has two kids."

"What'd your folks do for work?"

"You'd never guess. Mom was a couples' therapist. She liked helping people stabilize their lives. Dad was a full-blown head shrink, a psychiatrist in our local hospital system."

"Wow! Ever feel like you were walking around in a test tube?"

"Not at all. We all came out good. I'm very proud of my family. Especially my daughters. Okay, KC, your turn. Out with the family tree."

"Well, nothing very spectacular. I have a brother who lives in Connecticut and works for a medical instrument company. Before retiring, Mom was a high school teacher and Dad was Athletics Director for Burlington County Schools."

"Jeez, that's pretty cool. Were you an athlete in school?"

"Little bit. I wanted to be seen as an intellectual . . . damn, Charlie, you're looking a little glossy-eyed. We better order so you can eat something before you go weak and pass out on me." She pushed a menu at him.

"What do you suggest?"

"Tiki Bar Lover's Leap. It's French-style grilled steak with thin fries and served with mayonnaise. It's the French Canadian influence, which has its merits."

"Leap, I will. And you?"

"The same." She got up and went to the bar to order while he took a cup of water out to Mister Fritz, gave him a quick walk up the block and back, and promised him a good din-din later.

Dinner was memorable, but the food wasn't. Charles had a momentary pang of guilt. Having such a good time while six victims, deadly sick but recovering, were relying on him to atone for their pain. Instead of working, he was getting a buzz, having a good time with an alluringly attractive, shiny-eyed woman. Maybe, probably, ten years younger? They were on the way to knocking down a second mai tai while she was polishing off the last of his fries.

He couldn't take his eyes off her.

Charles paid the bill, and Kirby remarked, "I like the skinny *pommes frites* way more than the burger. Mister Fritz must be ravenous," she said, thoughtfully bagging the rest of her burger for him.

If Mary was watching . . . ah, fuck it, what will be will be. Unfortunately, this was going to end soon. I'll drop her at some house, condo, or apartment, and probably never see her again. Maybe we'll have a wrap-up chat on the phone. Hope not, I'm digging her—but man, does she talk!

* * * * * *

Mister Fritz wolfed down the rest of Kirby's burger and had another go at filling the gutter while they stood by chatting about Burlington and its quiet streets. They slipped into the 'Vette and settled into the soft red leather. Charles needed to give her a hand getting buckled in. Kirby accommodated by lifting Mister Fritz into the air above her chest as he reached across her torso and snapped her in. It was awkward, and half intrusive, but she didn't seem to mind.

He was maybe a little too loose to be driving—but did anyway.

"Where can I drop you off?"

"Drop me off? Drop me off?" She repeated it like it was the most absurd thing said all day!

"I'm going to take you home, and GPS will navigate me to a motel."

"Like hell you will. I've got an extra bedroom upstairs with private bath. You and Mister Fritz are staying with me. You're overnighting in my palatial townhouse so you can't sneak off tomorrow morning without me."

"Really?"

"Shit, Detective. You'll be calling me partner by the time we close this case."

Wouldn't that be a gas! Do I have any Cialis in my war bag?

This and other fanciful notions ran through his well-juiced brain as his head hit the clean sheets and cold pillow. He noticed Kirby's guest bedroom had a few pieces of long-ago, but familiar, furniture like the crib and baby carousel hanging from the ceiling. As Mister Fritz snuggled up at his feet . . . *didn't she say she had a dog?*

CHAPTER 29

Please, MJ, it would be very good for everyone!

The booming PA system announced: "The Jacob Javits Center is closing in twenty minutes. Please be prepared to leave your booth and exit through 4B or 5B. See you at the opening of Book Expo XII at eight a.m. tomorrow! Thank you for your cooperation!"

MJ was dazed. Cecil's crew had put together the guild's display in an hour. The tent had the folding chairs organized in rows ten deep, just as Pamela planned. The dais, microphone, and amps were tested and ready. The blue skirting was clipped around the tables that displayed books, and 30x40 color enlargements of reviews of books by members were set on easels. All just as poor Pamela had designed but wouldn't get to enjoy.

So busy, MJ had forgotten about the speakers' roster until Silvia Martinez, the portly Latino literary agent, came out of nowhere, announced herself, and pressed her enormous breasts against MJ in a long hug. In any other circumstance, it would have been strange; today, it was reassuring. She released the slender MJ before crunching her bones and stepped back to admire the guild's finished booth.

"This is all wonderful! *Maravillosa!* I heard you are going through a terrible time. I am so, so sorry I did not reach you after your helper called. I was engaged with my writers."

"Not to worry. It's come together, despite my dreadful problems. Cecil Rhodes' crew did all this, they set up everything. I'm overcome with his generosity."

"How are your friends in the hospital?"

"You are so sweet to be concerned. I called each hospital and they're all recovering. It's going to be a long time before they'll be up and about, but thank God, alive!"

Making the calls was a fib . . . but she did mean to call them when she had time.

"It looks like you're all ready for tomorrow. Yes?"

"Yes, I'll be here but won't have the symposium. I've got no speakers."

"No speakers?"

"I'm thinking, make this a rest area: Romance Agents & Writers Guild invites you to come under our tent, rest your feet, and chat with friends. Maybe an open discussion? A forum?"

"That is such a wonderful idea! But MJ, I can help you with speakers! I have writers from Brazil, Venezuela, Mexico, and three countries in Africa. They would love to speak about their country's literature. Even if your audience is resting their feet!"

MJ's jaw could have bounced off the floor.

"Please, MJ, it would be very good for everyone!"

Without batting a drooping eyelash, MJ responded, "How does 9:30 to 10:30 and 10:45 to 11:45 sound? I'll buy everyone lunch right here. After lunch, they can rotate through and speak as long as anyone wants!"

"*Maravillosa!* MJ, you are so generous. I love you!" She gave her a big kiss and then darted off as fast as allowed by her fleshy frame, calling out over her shoulder, "I set it all up tonight. No worries."

No matter what tomorrow may bring, thought MJ, as she rode home in a cab . . . *swear to God, I will forever after be a gentler, more understanding woman like Silvia Martinez.*

* * * * * *

It was late, well after ten, and past her bedtime. Tilda Duclos was sitting at the Acer in a fretful state. The first samplers to the Romance Agents & Writers Guild should have been flattening recipients like unlimited free shots at an alcoholic's buffet. But there was nothing on their website except babble about some big deal book expo in New York City and how the guild was going to make a splash.

Timothy appeared from outside, startling her.

"Timothy, don't do that. You scare the hell out of me wandering around outside!"

"I was on the porch having a smoke. So, what's going on that's got you so wired?"

"There's not one damn word on the guild's site about our gifts. You'd think out of the four we sent off, a few would be telling the world about tummy aches, like our Moo Moo."

"Moo Moo. Ah, I miss her already."

"That's because Moo Moo never scared the hell out of you. We've got stamps for fifty-six more. Are we going to start sending again?"

"Let's wait a few more days and see what happens," Timothy said, going to his couch.

CHAPTER 30

I'll let you in on one of my hot spots

Charles awoke to a familiar, but distant scent. What was that? It came to him slowly, eventually taking him back to their first child, Caroline. Baby powder and the ever-recognizable—no matter how long one airs the room—fragrance of poopy diapers. Mister Fritz was AWOL but had left a compacted, empty impression in the comforter where he had created an overnight nest between Charles' feet.

First thing he needed to do was to check his overnight bag where he had stashed the SIG Sauer and the belt holster. It was there along with the extra magazine. He brushed his teeth, gargled, put on clean underwear, pants, and shirt, and drawn by the aroma of hot coffee, danced down the flight of stairs.

"Good morning, Detective Charlie! Sleep well?" Kirby asked, sliding over a steaming mug. She was dressed in jeans, a lumberjack's checkered long-sleeved woolen shirt, and white sneakers. Charles dropped onto a stool at the counter across from her.

"I went out like a light. Slept like a baby! Jesus, KC, you look great. Very outdoorsy, too."

Mister Fritz had already staked out a spot on the sofa but leaped up to greet him.

"Don't worry about Mister Fritz. He came down as soon as I did. Did his business in the backyard and mooched the food I had for Teddi. Acts like he wants to move in, at least on my sofa."

"That can be arranged."

"What do you need for your coffee?"

"Little milk, that's all. Still got Tiki Bar cobwebs," said Charles, massaging his temples.

Kirby passed him a ceramic cow with the nose open to pour milk and the sugar bowl decorated with a farm scene of grazing black and whites.

"It was the two mai tais we each had. Don't think the beer chasers were a good idea."

"Should have taken three aspirin," he said, getting his first sip of coffee.

"You were tired. Don't forget the long drive at rocket speed, recruiting a ravishing blond as a partner, and big, exciting breaks in our case. Yes, yesterday you were very busy," she said nonchalantly.

"Yes, indeed, all wonderful things. Hope I was a gentleman last night? It's a little fuzzy."

"We walked in the door and I pointed upstairs and said, 'You and Mister Fritz are on the right.' You said something like, 'Goodnight.' I said, 'I'll see you two in the morning over coffee.'"

"And here we are." Charles opened his laptop and logged into the RTCC while Mister Fritz returned to his indent on the sofa, keeping one eye open on them.

After a few minutes of hitting the keys, "Good news. There are no more cases of wolfsbane poisoning in New York City in the last twenty-four hours. And let's see . . . not surprisingly, there are 68,324 Subarus registered in Vermont."

"If finding a Subaru in Vermont is the key to our case, we're going to have to work out some rent arrangement."

"I'll narrow it down to wagons that are red and fit the years Alberts saw."

Charles paused to sip the coffee. He took a few minutes to take in the many photos on the walls and several small end tables. Most were photos of a happy child with Kirby and her with a young man. There was also a smattering of frames with the typical family mix, weddings, and parties. There was a picture of a bearded man, a hunter on his knees holding a scoped rifle, with his arm resting on a black Lab pup. The bearded man had a red grease penciled X over his face.

Kirby unloaded the dishwasher.

"That's some grandchild."

"My best work, he and Davey."

"Does he have a name?" asked Charles, repressing a grin.

"Hardy har har. It's Simon. Davey's my son."

"What's the story with the X on the guy and the dog?

"Judge temporarily gave Teddi to my former. He emotionally needed my best friend riding around in the front seat of his damn pickup because he was sooooo depressed from our breakup. He had a skank living with him and a big backyard. I'm single in this townhouse with only an itty-bitty backyard and now work nine to five. He has her weekdays, and I get her weekends unless he has a field trip and needs her for work. They're off together in Canada for the next three weeks." She finished unloading the dishwasher, snapped the door shut, and sighed, "Yes, I feel abandoned."

Charles had a sip of coffee and nodded, understanding.

"As soon as I get a house with a real yard, I get Teddi full time," she declared. She finished tidying up, sat down on the stool across the counter.

"Mary bought Mister Fritz from some unscrupulous puppy farm in Pennsylvania. I don't think he's purebred anything, except mutt. As much as I enjoy his company, he is a cute little guy. Caroline, our youngest, is probably going to have him most of the time. It's tough for both of us, my job's 24/7."

"Aw, no, don't say that, Charlie. You'll have to find a way to keep him with you. Just look at that lovable little mug!" She nodded toward Mister Fritz on his adopted sofa. At least one eye was aware they were speaking about him.

"Well, not to change the subject, but little Simon must love cows! You've pictures of him everywhere. Sitting on a cow, feeding a cow; here he's got his little hands on a teat. Pretty lucky four-year-old!"

"You're not a perv, Charlie, are you? Simon's useless mother was more concerned about her perky breasts than his health and well-being, so she cut him off as soon as they left the hospital."

"Selfish."

"You said it! Thank God, my son never married that greedy, unpleasant, pole-dancing bitch."

"Now I know how you really feel about her."

"If you're lucky, someday you'll meet Davey and Simon and get to pet my Teddi."

"Sounds good," he said, quietly dealing with the double entendre.

Behind him was a niche with a rarely used formal dining table. Charles could tell because the chair legs were embedded in the thick carpet. The staircase ran up one wall to the master bedroom and guest bedroom, each having a bath, already explored. To his right, through sliding double-glassed doors, was a rectangular fenced-in yard with a stone patio, a gas grill, and a haphazard arrangement of potted plants.

From his stool to the left, he looked into a double-height living room with a traditional arrangement of a comfortable sofa, deep-sided chairs, and a brick-surrounded fireplace. Lo and behold, to Charles' delight, over the mantle and next to the wall-installed TV set was a monstrous mounted rainbow trout.

"Where did you get that incredible rainbow?"

"Get? What do you mean, get? I caught that sucker in my secret brook, deep in our lovely Green Mountains."

"No way. Really? Tell me about it." Charles rose from the stool and moved in to inspect.

"Eleven pounds, eight ounces," she said.

"That's got to be a record," he said, studying the fish from several angles.

"Not quite. Record's thirteen pounds, twelve ounces, but close enough to get me in all the papers. I took him with a green-and-yellow jig on a #3 line. Took forever to reel in. It was a one-fish jig; he tore the hell out of it."

"The coloration, mounting, is really first class. The eye follows me wherever I go. Shoot, you could lose a thousand jigs to catch one fish like that. Still be worth it."

"Maybe when you're not working, I'll let you in on one of my hot spots."

"I would be ever so thankful to try out one of your hot spots."

Both paused, had to think twice. They were going to either burst out laughing or be awkwardly embarrassed. Charles quickly picked up the slack; "My gear's squirreled away in the 'Vette, so maybe we'll find time to fish," he said, projecting optimism.

"You are a clear-thinking man, Charlie. By the way, I called my boss this morning. He says to stick to you like glue. VAMP wants to keep the maple syrup details of this fiasco off the radar."

"Good idea. FYI, we call it a tragedy, not a fiasco."

"I will be more aware of that." She watched Charles scroll through more RTCC pages. "So, where's today going to take us?"

"Forensics found one of our victim's mailers postmarked from the Bolton P.O. We've got a pretty good image of our culprit, now it's just a question of finding her and building a case for the D.A."

"Do you think you're lucky enough for me to drive you to Bolton and uncover new leads?" Kirby had placed her hands on her hips for some earnest emphasis.

"You really have a flair for the dramatics, don't you?"

"I'm really just lovin' it. Truly, I am. It's so thrilling."

Charles couldn't help laughing. "I'm glad. Yesterday was such a winner with your pal, Donnie. Let's go see what Bolton has to offer."

"I know the way. I'll drive."

"We'd need to pick up your car back at VAMP, wouldn't we?"

"I'll drive us in yours. Save time."

"Nice offer. No thanks," said Charlie, heading for the door.

"Hmmm, Charlie. What about Mister Fritz?"

"He's happy, let him be. He's attached to your sofa and he's been walked."

CHAPTER 31

New Yorkers do really stupid things

The town of Bolton and the East Main Street post office, where the sampler was postmarked, were only a short scoot from Burlington. They cruised with the windows down on I-89 on a stretch renamed the Vietnam Veterans Highway, thoroughly enjoying the sunny day. Their route ran parallel to the exciting rapids of the Winooski River. It was very tempting to stop and throw a line, but Kirby didn't have her gear and he couldn't face letting her use his new never-seen-water gear. Besides, they were chasing a dangerous criminal. Better not.

They arrived at the tiny one-story, tin-covered shack-like post office that shared a facade with the Janesville Antique & Collectables shop. There were several parked cars in front, but they found an empty spot to one side of the entrance. They instantly garnered the interest of two teenage boys across the street who were chemically stripping the bottom of an antique mahogany Chris Craft Runabout. It was set atop a jury-rigged wooden frame in the yard. Both wore tattered T-shirts from a Kiss concert and very stringy cutoff jeans.

They came over as Kirby and Charles got out. Charles activated the door locks. The boys eyeballed the New York plate, FST - ASU2, then circled the car, making an inspection.

"Hey, Mister, can I sit in your car?" asked the taller. Charles noted their clothes.

"Can you sit in my car? No." Charles looked at Kirby. "Some Vermont affliction, wanting to get into other people's cars?"

"Depends on the car."

The second, likely a younger brother, said, "We gotta try. Sometimes New Yorkers do really stupid things."

"That's an understatement," responded Charles. "Look, don't touch, guys."

The post office door had a little bell attached that twinkled when Kirby and Charles entered. They waited in line behind two other patrons; one, a lean grey-haired man with a ponytail wearing an orange hunter's jacket and the other, a young brunette woman in a jogging suit that had the word "Fly" scrolled on the back and up a leg. Both held familiar boxes with return labels—shoes being returned to L. L. Bean.

"That was mean to those two boys," whispered Kirby.

Charles whispered back, "They're already delinquents."

The line moved quickly due to the snappy work of the elderly postman, a man cursed with forever looking like a counter-culture granddaddy: wispy white hair, sagging cheeks, and granny glasses sitting on a ruddy nose. A nameplate on the counter read: T. S. Frasier. His image drew Charles to remember a Norman Rockwell painting— or was it the Santa Coca-Cola ad? An Eliot literary moment? A Jerry Garcia fan?

Charles placed a syrup sample box on the counter and in the other hand exhibited his NYPD badge. "Mr. Frasier, I'm Detective White. Do you remember a woman mailing one of these? It would have been in the past week."

"Yep." The postman began wiping his granny glasses, ignoring Charles. Kirby gave Charles a little nudge to his ankle with a white canvas shoe.

"Could you elaborate? Perhaps a little more about her physical characteristics. It's important."

"I'd imagine so since they've sent a New York City detective all the way up here."

"That's right. What can you tell me about her?"

"Never saw her close, she kept outside. Elderly, black beret, heavy tan raincoat—too heavy for this weather. Saw her mail a carton, just like that one, in the box outside. Then, she took off."

"Anything else?"

"When I emptied our box at closing, I saw it was on its way to New York City."

"You've been a great help, Mr. Frasier."

"If you'll take that hankie tacked to the Community Board over there, I'd consider it a real favor. She dropped it running to her car."

"Consider it gone. You saw her running to what car? What color, year?"

"Let me think a bit."

He concentrated with eyes closed and finally hit on it. "Just like my neighbor used to have. An early 1990s, red Subaru wagon. I did not see the license plate.

"That's a great help. Thank you very much," said Charles, turning to go.

Kirby stepped in, "Would she have been alone in that red wagon?"

"Couldn't say." Pointing across the lobby, "Please don't forget that filthy hankie. Every time I see it, it makes me want to blow my nose. Besides, it looks like hell on my board. Crowds out important community notices."

Charles dropped the hankie into an evidence bag. They nodded goodbye to T. S. Frasier.

The adolescents working on the boat had disappeared. Charles did his inspection, a quick walk around verifying he still had four wheels. They slid inside.

"KC, I do the interviewing, okay? You gotta stop jumping in!"

"Sorrrryyyyy. I thought you forgot to ask about another person in the car."

"It's a technique. I ask a series of questions and pretend like I'm all finished. Then, after a timely pause, I flip back with another question as I head for the door." That sort of disarms the person.

"Gotcha! Just like Columbo!"

"Well, yes."

Perhaps there was nose discharge, like snot or a bugger, on the hankie, which would be filled with DNA and could seal the miscreant's fate.

CHAPTER 32

How long have you wanted
to be an author?

The turnstiles were open and attendees flooded into the Jacob Javits Book Expo XII. There was a rush to the Romance Agents & Writers Guild booth where a line formed to hug and sympathize with Martha Jane Sidel over the dastardly event that had befallen the guild. How brave MJ was to press on. Damn the torpedoes!

At nine-thirty, Silvia Martinez led a parade of her foreign guests to the booth. First, a soft-spoken author from Ethiopia stepped to the dais, adjusted the microphone, and began to speak of the new literature coming from the Christian fighters who had beaten back the Islamic extremists in their capital city, Addis Ababa. He was followed by a petite Iranian woman who was writing a report to the United Nations about forced abortions in the Islamic State of Iran.

Around eleven, right before lunch, at a time when many attendees were wondering where they could get off their tired feet for a few minutes, they would remember Silvia Martinez's rather primitive poster in multiple languages, "Come here and rest your tired soles." It was clear when someone asked, "Where should we meet?" it would be in the guild's tent.

Throughout the day, there was a steady procession of speakers—even a few in comprehensible English! The important thing for the

Romance Agents & Writers Guild was that it had picked up a rhythm, and that rhythm had an international pulse. By the end of that first day, the three major networks had come to the guild's booth and videoed the symposium for the ten o'clock local news. The stream of passionate foreign speakers would carry on nonstop all three days of Book Expo XII.

* * * * * *

In New York City's 7th Precinct, Inspector Mahoney had tasked a Serial Crime Evaluator to massage out, from her experience and thousands of digitized essays, what would motivate an individual or group to poison six individuals in the literary field. First, she determined that none of the stricken agents had publicly expressed radical views or belonged to any out-of-favor political groups, nor did they have any odd leanings, besides all being registered democrats. She thought that was too broad a reason to trigger the poisoning. Although the four women victims were in the literature hustle, none of them had written on subjects or had published anything that would have stimulated that level of disdain. Even to the most whacked-out, spiteful literary villain.

Might it have been a senseless attack by a madman, simply to experience the high of committing murder? Murdering at random happens, but the victim is usually a homeless person. Was this heinous crime conceived by a competitor, as mentioned in Detective White's report—say, a Canadian syrup producer aimed to cripple the Vermont maple syrup industry? That would be unusual and unlikely, but not to be dismissed. Canadians were generally believed to be docile people, but they had their share of rednecks and outdoor nutcases capable of understanding market share and supply and demand.

What Mahoney desperately needed to know was whether the offender was a one-timer or had serial motivations. That, the evaluator couldn't say—until he or she struck again. Which seemed somewhat circular to Mahoney, and not very useful. He decided he'd have to rely on White to ferret out the big picture of the miscreant's motivation and plans—and dump it into Vermont's legal system.

* * * * * *

Meanwhile, in Kirby's comfy Burlington townhouse, Charles decided the best way to get a handle on the wrongdoers' motivation required research on literary agents. Regretfully, it was pretty clear to whom he had to turn: Martha Jane Sidel and the guild. Charles wasn't keen on phoning her.

Normally, he would have to do a face-to-face, but that would require him leaving Vermont. A nice arrangement was developing with Kirby, and so, when Captain Mahoney suggested he should stay until he got what was needed, Charles was elated. He knew from experience, however, Mahoney's largess toward time away from the precinct was fickle. He wasn't going to go back to New York City early unless everything went south, and Charles wasn't going to let that happen. He had begun doing his laundry in Kirby's new machines, and she had spontaneously begun doing his folding.

Charles and Kirby settled on the sofa in her living room. His laptop was open on the guild's site. He put his cell phone on speaker so she could follow.

"Good day, Ms. Sidel. This is Detective White, NYPD. We briefly spoke several days ago. We were opening our investigation, and things were a little hectic for both of us."

"I'm in the middle of Book Expo XII. Can we speak later in the week?"

"This should only take a minute."

"Officer, seriously, I'm afraid there's no time for me to talk."

"I'll be brief. The guild's main function is to aid aspiring writers in finding an agent. You, yourself, represent writers. Correct?"

"Yes. We have a submissions page and we look at anyone who sends us a query."

"I'd like to understand the process of how a novice would get an agent."

"Officer White, go to the guild's website and follow the instructions under "Submissions." It's all there, plain as day."

"It's Detective White. Who exactly reads the query submissions?"

"Normally, Pamela does. Since she's dying in the hospital, I'll be reading queries that comes in."

"How often do you look at submissions?"

"We try to every other day, first thing in the morning before phones start ringing. Our business model is helping new authors find an agent. In a few select instances, we may choose to represent an emerging author. I can't afford to pass up on the next Irene Hannon."

"Who?"

"Officer, you're wasting my very valuable and limited time."

"That's Detective White. So, the expo is going to be successful?"

"Except for the chaos and disruption of my speakers getting poisoned!" she ranted. "Jesus, where the hell have you been for the last week? Asshole!" She abruptly disconnected.

Charles scratched his stubble, trying not to telegraph his discomfort from Sidel's rant. No need to shave this morning, the case was becoming a vacation. He studied Kirby. She returned his gaze with an open-mouth gawk.

What's with the telephone call???

"Nothing. Just that Romance Guild woman causing trouble. Let's get to work. When did you decide to become an author?"

"Always had literary aspirations. Got an A in Creative Writing. Why?"

He slid the laptop around so they both could see the screen. He worked the keys and found the submissions page on the guild's site. It didn't take long for them to get the gist of what a submission to the guild required. A brief biography, a limited two-page scenario covering what the novel's about, and the query. Charles read out loud what the query should contain:

"The query is a succinct teaser designed to interest the targeted agent in the novel. It could be envisioned as the blurb found on the front flap of the novel's cover. It should excite, be pithy, and draw the agent into a page-turning plot. The query should also indicate to the agent they can work together, and importantly, that the author has potential."

"You up for this, KC? Think we can write a query?"

"Are you kidding? Piece of cake."

"What's our story?"

Kirby stood and aped a Moses pose with arms apart, "It was a dark and stormy night. Ten Boy Scouts sat around a blazing campfire. One scout asked, Scoutmaster, tell us a story . . ."

"You belong on stage," said Charles grinning.

They had a titter, having no idea what they had bitten off.

* * * * * *

Meanwhile, only a short distance south, Tilda was on the phone to Sam's Garage, getting the scoop on her hurt Slobberu from mechanic Sam Piper.

"Tilly, I'm not pulling your leg. It's a blown head gasket. I can replace it, but it'll take a day or so for my supplier to deliver a new gasket. And I'm backed up with other cars. It's going to take more time."

"Sam Piper, you may be the only black man within five hundred miles, and I like to use minority businesses, but that doesn't mean you can rake me like those rich New Yorkers who run out of gas on our highways. So, what's it gonna cost, and when can I have her back?"

"Tilly, don't you honestly think it's about time you stop driving? The car is ready to permanently expire, and whenever I see you driving, you're swerving all over the road. Really, you know you're dangerous and shouldn't be behind the wheel!"

"Cow pies, Sam! I drive just fine, maybe not as fast as I used to, but I drive fine. So, tell me what you have to do and how much you're going to rip me off for!"

"It's a hell of a job! Got to pull everything off the top to replace the gasket and put it all back. Who knows what else I'll find? It's an $800 job that I'm going to do for $500."

"That's way too much, Sam. You can do better than that."

"Tilly, it's a lot of work."

"Why get it fixed at all? At $500, I won't be able to go out and buy groceries! My starvation will be on your hands!"

"It's been two years since you've had a filter and oil change. I'll throw that in free."

"Go ahead, do it. I can't live without a car. Thank you, Sam. I know you mean well even though you often act like a purse-snatcher."

Sam Piper had been a tough one for Tilda to keep her mind straight around. He was so kind, it was easy for her to slip up. One day, early in their relationship, she called the garage after he had replaced the battery and made the profoundly stupid mistake of saying she'd send Timothy to pick up Slobberu. Goodness, Sam didn't know Tilda had a brother! Well, send him around. Love to meet him!

In subsequent conversations, she'd make elaborate excuses for Timothy's disappearance. She'd settled on the ruse that he had moved to California for tax reasons, which was even more baffling and unbelievable to Sam.

CHAPTER 33

Crime and violent conflict, war, are inescapable conditions

They went for an early dinner in downtown Burlington. Kirby wore a black sleeveless cocktail dress that shimmered in the candlelight of the Farmhouse Tap & Grill. The black high heels exhibited another side of an athletic country girl that made Charles feel like she was out of his league. Dinner was very enjoyable.

Back at the condo, Charles put away his tie and jacket and took Mister Fritz out for a short walk through the complex. When they returned, Kirby had changed into gray sweatpants, a white loose-fitting V-neck pullover blouse, and no-show red sports socks. They settled on the sofa and drank a merlot someone had left at Kirby's Christmas party.

Charles learned about Kirby's gig at VAMP, also bringing up Davey and fishing as a life-restoring activity. She had a few words about realignment as a single mom after tossing out her husband. Charles spoke of a few trips to southern Vermont to work his homemade flies in whitewater rapids and swirling eddies. He omitted Mary's passion for antiquing.

He ended with, "I've talked enough about me."

Prompting her to ask, for the umpteenth time, "I'm trying to get why you do it. I mean, you're a smart cookie, Charlie. You could be doing anything, why the police force?"

It took him a pause to think where to begin.

"When I was a teen living at home, there was an unsolved murder in my neighborhood—Mr. and Mrs. Smith. I cut their grass. They were a quiet couple whose lives seemed to just go off the rails."

"Really? What happened?"

"I think, now that I understand it better, they were clinically schizophrenic. Mr. Smith was an insurance salesman and evidently, his business had merged with another and he was left behind. His depression may have triggered an underlying mental illness. Unfortunately, within several years, she began to slip, possibly with Alzheimer's. Couldn't take care of him, much less herself."

"That's so sad."

"I was doing their grass one afternoon, thinking only of the three-dollar check I was getting when they both came outside. They gathered around me and just looked up to the sky, gazing about their property like they were prisoners on yard release. I asked if there was anything wrong. They said no, nothing was wrong. They just liked being outside once in a while. I got a chilling sense they felt I was providing some sort of protection, like nothing would happen to them with me beside them.

"That's paranoia, Charlie."

"Yeah, it is. I finally spoke up and said they seemed to be uncomfortable about something. I suggested my mom would help if they wanted to speak with a professional. You have to know, that was a scary thing for me to say."

"I'm sure it was."

"You'd not believe how nice they were, thanking me for my concern, and how much they appreciated I was willing to be frank with them. They were so normal, our conversation so refreshing and disarming."

"That took some guts, Charlie."

"Walking home, I felt foolish and embarrassed I had brought it up. Anyway, by the time of their murders, months later, they had lost it."

"What do you mean, 'lost it'?"

"Washing their car when it was freezing and snowing outside. Discussions about poisoned vegetables in the grocery store. Locks were being changed on their doors every week. No more grass cutting, the property was neglected and looked abandoned. But they never made threats or were violent toward anyone. It was schizophrenic behavior that people live and die with when they could be fine, if they were on meds."

"How do you feel about that now, Charlie?"

"I was fourteen. I should have been more convincing, more committed to getting them help. I might have followed up. I didn't. I still have regrets."

"Shoulda, woulda, coulda! Fuck, Charlie White! You were fourteen; you couldn't have done anything more! How'd they get murdered?"

"Someone entered their house and shot them. Investigators never found a reason why. Nothing was stolen, things weren't tossed. Police concluded they were victims of random, senseless violence. Possible scenarios were a confrontation with a real bad egg, a simple misunderstanding gotten out of hand, or maybe a road rage thing. He or she followed them home and offed them."

"And you wanted to solve it?"

"Yes and no. I wanted to learn why, as a general supposition, a person would murder without justification."

"Oh, Jesus, it's a real horror story."

"Their murders led me to John Jay College of Criminal Justice and the force."

"Your interest wasn't solving the crime; it was more why does one have the capacity to murder without reason?"

"Exactly. I'm lucky, what interests me and what I do professionally are closely related. A detective's assignment is collecting facts for the district attorney's office. I uncover the basics: who, what, when, and why. And on the side, I get to pursue the mysterious and unrevealed, *why* of a certain type of violence."

"How's the 'underlying *why* different from the mundane why?"

"Murder is one of the most unsocial acts a human being can do, and it's usually about drugs, money, envy, violence from insanity, and so on. They are the 'whys' of crime: He murdered her out of jealousy. He killed the guard for the payroll. These well-defined behaviors may result in murder. But some murders have no connection to any circumstances. I wondered how a person could have so little disregard for the life of another and kill for no reason at all."

"Wrong place at the wrong time?" suggested Kirby.

"That doesn't explain killing without reason. We're all wired from indecipherable events driving our emotions and actions. The 'why' may never be understood because an individual is far too complex. For a while, scientists thought there was a 'murder gene.' Today, most agree, that criminal behavior is a combination of genetics and environment. They've determined that empathy has a genetic basis. It appears some people, a very small number in the population, have little or no conscience controlling their violent behavior. 'Survival of the fittest' offers no answer; there's no explanation for the evolutionary necessity for that behavior to exist. So why does that gene, or collection of genes, exist at all?"

"So, a defective gene or genes makes all the trouble?" Kirby wondered aloud.

"Think on this: What if we were able to zap that gene or genes out of a convicted murderer? Should he or she be set free? Should we test everyone and allow law enforcement to give those with the criminal defect, special attention? Put them in camps?"

"Dissecting crime and consequences on that level, freaks me out," said Kirby, giving an emphatic exhale. "In your family of all those shrinks, you're definitely a case of 'the apple doesn't fall far from the tree.'"

"Maybe, KC, you shouldn't be doing this with me."

"Freaks me out, but I want to learn more. Seriously, you ought to do guest lecturing."

"That's been suggested before," said Charles, enjoying the praise.

"So, keep talking."

"Crime and violent conflict, war, are inescapable conditions of our world. The only difference between war and individual violence is one of extent and the degree of monetary investment. . ."

* * * * * *

By late evening, Charles had recounted several cases he'd worked on, keeping Kirby spellbound. She left the sofa to go pee, giving him a moment to ponder a more personal issue: why was he hesitant to make an overt sexual advance? On first meeting Kirby, her attractiveness and sassy mind had charmed him . . . and those ever-changing green-blue eyes. Now, on their second day, he realized she had seriously gotten into his head. But he didn't want to read more into their relationship without resolving the one primitive, human bond agent: were they sexually compatible?

Sitting together on the sofa, they had minor, unspecific contact. Her bare feet resting against his outer thigh or a jostling hand on his shoulder when laughing. When she came back from the bathroom, adjusting her blouse and sweatpants, he decided to test the unclear waters.

"Miss Clark, gracious hostess, I'm beat. Regrettably, I must turn in."

"Me, too. I try to read every night, and I'm on the last chapter of *Breakfast with Buddha*. Ten minutes to finish, but I'll be out in two."

"Is it good?" asked Charles. Then, before she could reply, followed with, "Do you do yoga, meditate, wellness, that type of thing?"

"Book is good, yoga is good, meditation is good, going to bed is also good."

Charles gave Mister Fritz, occupying most of the sofa's end, a wake-up nudge. He then leaned over and, before Kirby knew what was happening, gave her a simple peck on her cheek. He remained close to her, taking in the scent of her shampoo—or was it perfume? Would she draw him into a long, wet kiss?

Instead, his move led to an unusual turndown.

She placed both arms on his shoulders. "Not tonight, Charlie. Now's not the time to try to bugger your partner. When the time is right, it'll be good, real good. You'll like it," she said and broadly smiling, gave him a gentle pushback.

Sensitive to the awkward situation he had put her in, he rose and emoted, "Alas, hope springs eternal in the breast of Man."

Kirby, momentarily at a loss for words, hid her smile with a palm. Finally, straight-faced, she responded, "Coffee, eggs, toast, and juice in the a.m.?"

"You bet!" He said, hitting the first steps to his upstairs bedroom with Mister Fritz trailing. At the top of the staircase, on impulse, he sang out, "Tomorrow, tomorrow is only a day away!"

"Sorry, Charlie, those aren't the correct lyrics to *Annie*," then yelled, "Goodnight, sweet Prince."

By the time he had showered and fallen into bed, Mister Fritz was already asleep at his feet. Charles, too, was snoring within minutes.

Kirby rinsed their wine glasses, checked the exterior door locks, turned off the lights, except for the small one over the stove, and went upstairs. She quickly showered, put on a long ACDC T-shirt Davey had given her, and slipped into her bed. Comfortable between the soft cotton duvet, she moistened two fingers with saliva and noiselessly masturbated. She came in less than a minute, which was rare.

More than ever, she was proud of herself for resisting someone she passionately wanted, and she would for certain live the next day with greater anticipation. Also, good was honest Charlie used humor to wash over his letdown. A big difference between him and her former.

CHAPTER 34

An alluring innie belly button was revealed under her rising shirt

At eight-thirty a.m., they were working on refilled cups of coffee after the promised breakfast. Kirby had an old dog bed that was three times larger than Mister Fritz and had placed it on the kitchen floor. He took to it without hesitation. For napping, the sofa was still his preferred perch, the best place to stay in the center of things.

Their laptops were online, ready to be tickled. Since Kirby hadn't gotten far with the query writing, it was time for a distraction by working on something else.

"We could check off the biography item?" politely asked Charles.

"Hey, I'm ready!"

"We have to use your real name but cook-up a believable resume."

"Why?"

"With a fictitious name, I'd be asking you to go undercover. I'd have to present it to Mahoney and our legal department for approval. Waste of time 'cause they won't do it, and we don't want to do it anyway."

"No, I mean why cook-up my resume?"

"Well, I was thinking, we can jazz you up a bit. Maybe give you a degree in English, make you a contributor to a local paper, that type of thing."

"Aren't you an assuming douchebag! My B.A. in Education from Middlebury College isn't enough? Associate Editor of the Middlebury campus newspaper doesn't count? Sports Editor-at-Large for my high school newspaper doesn't make me capable of writing some dumb-ass query?"

"Fuck me!" he exclaimed.

"Yeah, don't get your hopes high! Just because I apply a veneer of being a little ditzy, don't get suckered by my innocent charm. My idol, Dolly, said it nicely: 'I don't mind being called a "dumb blond" because I'm not dumb and I'm not blond.' Well, in my case, I am blond, all the way blond. And this blond's got plenty upstairs to go with this bitchin' bod."

"I apologize, and I'm at a loss to explain my stupid assumption."

After a minute of frowning, "You are forgiven."

"Jesus, KC, what are you doing working at VAMP? It's so unconnected to your abilities?"

"I got pregnant and married a bush-hopping loser. So, I got sidetracked for a few years. Besides, I kinda got tapped out of over-achieving. Today, I just want to love my kids and be loved."

She looked downward, giggling at some old silliness and brushing back strands of blondish hair that had fallen across her never-know-what-color eyes.

Charles was amused—well, entranced, really. "Stop me from laughing 'cause I'm honestly very happy about your divorce."

"That's greedy. Marriage was the best thing I ever did. Our divorce was the second best. Correction. Having Davey, and now little Simon, would be first, but has to be second because I needed a husband to have that first. But third for sure, right there would be the divorce."

They went back to their laptops.

"Interesting," said Charles having a rethink. "We need the scenario roughed out before we can create a query. Nothing comes to me right off. You?"

Kirby left her laptop and walked about the room, thinking out loud, "Creative writing's all about conflict and resolution."

"Boy meets girl romance?" he added, "We'll give it a twist—parents approve?"

"That makes sense because we're sending it to a romance guild." They had a quiet think.

"Charlie, we're in the middle of a big case that's nearly killed people and we don't have a story!" said Kirby, after gently slapping her forehead for emphasis.

"I cannot stress this enough, we must tread lightly. This is an ongoing case. I have professional responsibilities, obligations to the public, and so on."

"How about this: the deadly instruments are watermelons? Someone's injecting poison into watermelons in a steamy small Southern town. Watermelons are being shipped all over the county, dropping people left and right. Our protagonists are young, adventurous characters. Sort of Huck Finn meets Lisbeth Salander."

"Who's that?"

"The girl with the tattoos."

"Got it, Swedish serial killer."

"They're in an intense love triangle with the actual killer. The killer isn't just doing her, he's having a homosexual liaison with her guy who swings both ways. They set out to solve the case in between their prelaw classes at the state university, and enlist the help of an old, discredited chemist."

"I'm in. Put it on paper. Meanwhile. I'd better enter something into the RTCC so Mahoney thinks I'm working."

She plopped down next to him at her laptop and took the first step in creating her first novel—the title. After a half hour of struggling, the title became *TBD*, or to be determined. She'd type furiously for a while, rise from the sofa, walk about the room talking to herself, and then return to the keyboard with a long sigh. An hour later, she announced, "I've got writer's block."

Charles concurred, "I'm stuck, too. We need to get outside. Fresh air brings new ideas."

"Change of venue wouldn't hurt," said Kirby rising.

She took a long stretch, exhibiting her pleasing torso and an alluring innie belly button was revealed under her rising shirt. Charles thought of offering a back massage but got lost in a fantasy of burying his tongue into her enticing belly button, a deed successfully exploited while in high school with his first real girlfriend, leading to both losing their virginity.

Decades later, an innie belly button still punched his buttons. He wondered if he was drawn to belly button tonguing because it was a more acceptable first step with a reticent partner as it had the appearance of innocent cavity exploration and also tended to lead to a successful glide downward.

Unfortunately, with Mary, she'd begin hysterically laughing, which kinda ruined it for him.

For the origination of that pubescent urge, he was once tempted to ask the force's psychologist during his annual review . . . *ah, maybe not!*

Charles had been thinking romantically of Kirby, all soft-core and quite innocent. Now, their dynamics were changing and it was time for a road trip—excitement! He might as well fantasize about having her legs around his neck and furiously having sex on the hood of the 'Vette. That was make-believe awesome, but physically impractical and would likely dent the lightweight hood. It was a good image though.

Back to work.

"Remember the blurb about the cow dying from eating wolfsbane? Let's visit Williams Dairy Products in Lincoln. It's a long shot, but there might be something for us."

"Good idea. I know where it is. Maybe leave Mister Fritz to guard? He seems happy here, and we're not going to be late."

"It's your sofa," replied Charles, gathering his firearm and sports coat.

CHAPTER 35

We call it Bristol Falling Bra Falls

The drive to Lincoln took them past Bristol Falls. Through the breaks in the roadside trees and bursts of warm sunlight, Charles caught glimpses of a plummeting waterfall that sprayed a rain-like mist as it dropped into a circular gorge and emptied into a large pool of swirling waters. Scattered about the surrounding rock outcroppings were sunbathers on colorful towels, swimmers of all ages, and kids gleefully battling with squirt guns. Charles pulled to the side of the road to have a clearer view.

"This is amazing," he exclaimed.

A boy and girl, high school age, leaped off the twenty-foot ledge and disappeared into the foamy, swirling water. When they sprung back up from the depths, the girl's top had slipped off and was twisted around her neck. This caused clapping and wolf whistles from onlookers.

"There's always something going on at Bristol Falls," said Kirby cracking up. "We call it Bristol Falling Bra Falls."

"Happened to you?"

"Nah, I did this." She cupped her hands to her breast. "No free shows when I jump. I used to be very straight."

"That's hard to believe."

"Bristol Falls is the best swimming hole for miles around. This is sad because right under the falls, turbulence has scooped out a big cavern where monster fish hang out. Upstream, people toss food—you know, sandwich scraps, potato chips, anything. It goes over the falls, whirls around in the eddy. The trout jet out of the cave, grab the snack, and then shoot back to safety! With all the people carrying on above, they get enough food for the winter, and won't take a lure, jig, or worm."

"You'll have to make itsy-bitsy sandwiches on #12 hooks," responded Charles, demonstrating with two clasped fingers as if they were holding a tiny sandwich.

"You may be on to something, city boy. Let's go, investigation awaits. 'Crime never sleeps.'"

They got back on the road. Charles was grinning at her fluke connection to Captain Mahoney and his office moniker.

"What? What's so funny?" asked Kirby.

"Well, actually criminals do sleep. I've caught them sleeping, for a fact."

* * * * * *

The Village of Lincoln was pretty low-key. The downtown had one small ma and pa grocery and nothing else.

A few yards past the grocery, directional signs immediately appeared for Williams Dairy Products, Inc. But they didn't need to follow the signs. Kirby directed them through the gates to the enormous dairy facility. On both sides of the dairy's gravel road were humongous corrugated-metal buildings, a collection of smaller outbuildings, and several silos. Boxed in with split-rail wood fencing were several connected areas containing herds of fifty or so grazing black-and-white Holsteins.

Approaching the administration office, a massive stainless-steel milk tanker forced them to pull off onto the grassy side. It roared past, leaving a plume of dust and creating a shower of small pieces of gravel, making Charles cringe.

"You're going awful slow, Mr. Lead Foot," said Kirby.

"My car is getting destroyed!" said Charles despairingly.

* * * * * *

On a well-trimmed, residential-style lawn peppered with kitschy red and green gremlin figures lining the concrete walkway, was the administration office.

They parked in front and walked inside to face an elderly woman wearing pink pajamas sitting behind a large wood-appearing but Formica covered, reception desk. Next to her mug of coffee was a laptop, a landline phone, a cell phone, a portable color television set, and an open makeup kit holding all sorts of small vials, combs and brushes. She was working her nails with an oversized emery board. An open vial of brown nail polish was in use.

Directly behind her desk were open double doors to the CEO's office. "Be right with you," a woman's voice boomed from inside.

The woman at the desk stopped on her nails, glanced up at them, and pointed with a brown thumb, "Might as well go in."

"Good color for gardening," reflected Kirby.

They entered a large office. Across and behind a massive oak desk was a panoramic window with a sweeping view of the rear of the facility. Another milk tanker roared by on the gravel road, this time throwing crazy reflections off the shiny stainless-steel tank and strobing the office with eye-blinking flashes.

The boss, an attractive middle-aged woman in a business suit and reading glasses hanging from her neck, rose from her desk. She pushed back her shoulder-length brown hair that must have been getting in the way of her reading from a large pile of uncut light-green computer printouts.

"My MIRG report's due next week, and I've been to Montpelier with the bankers. I'm dressed to project fiscal stability. Normally, I'm in jeans but just as financially stable."

"I'm Detective Charles White and this is Kirby Clark. Thank you for seeing us."

"Hey, KC! Fess up, still chasing that puck?"

"Nah, got rid of him long ago. I'm a single mom with a grandson. Lovin' it."

"Alright! Go girl! Since I saw you last . . . let's see, I've dropped three more: boy, girl, girl. Got six altogether. Same pain in the ass husband, too."

"Way to go, Susan! Charles, this is Susan Williams, my very dear friend."

Detective White thought for the umpteenth time: *Jeez, Kirby Clark really gets around.*

"So, to business: how can I help you two today?" Williams asked, motioning them to take seats facing her desk.

"Recently, you had a cow die from wolfsbane," stated Charles, all copper-like.

"Oh yeah, one of our old ladies. Terrible waste, even though she was getting up in years. Frankly, yields were dropping and her future wasn't very bright anyway. We were planning on moving her next year to the great pasture above. Timing dependent on the chuck market. Hey, KC, ain't we all gettin' older faster than we'd like?"

"That's for sure," noted Kirby.

"You've had trouble with wolfsbane before?" asked Charles.

"Nope, never. When my folks bought the place, there was some growth on that old wall, so we cleared it when we ran the lines for the water troughs. During construction, Phase II on the back nineteen, a flatlander jackass picked a flower for his wife and then his nose. Pretty soon, he was in the hospital getting the charcoal treatment. Jerk tried to sue us. Well, that ended our free tours. But to answer your question, never before with our ladies."

"That's interesting," noted Charles glancing out the window, expecting another truck to come ripping past any second. "I'm struck by how big this place is."

"We're big for the neighborhood, middle-sized for the state. Give you an idea of what's here: we've eighty milking parlors with stanchions, meaning we have to rotate the herds at different times to be milked. Let's see . . . we have two separate feed and manure storage buildings and four different-sized barns for hay storage. Three outbuildings for tractors, hay balers, numerous water pumpers and three trucks to move stuff around. I've got twelve employees with eighty-six extended members of families that I take responsibility for. At least that's the number that shows up for the Christmas party."

"That would turn me into an old lady," opined Kirby, making Susan burst out laughing.

"Would I be wrong thinking the basics of your business haven't changed too much in a century?" Charles was just making conversation; he knew it was a dumb question as soon as it came out.

"Don't I wish. We're having all our ladies wear telemetry collars. These days, I'm hiring geeks, not cowboys. Down the hall is our tech room with two of them keeping track of everything. And they don't know a cow pie from a mud pie. It's a sad world we're entering. Pains my heart, too."

"What was here before you bought it?" asked Kirby.

"Nothing. We're all new construction over forty years. Over yonder, there was a vacation cottage owned by a family from New Jersey with a healthy amount of acreage on both sides of the road. Cottage burned down after a fireworks accident in '76. We acquired it since that swath had enough acreage for my folks to expand the dairy. Jim and I took over twenty or so years ago when my folks retired to Arizona. Jim's family hangs around in Middlebury to give us regular, unwelcome advice. That's Jim's mom, my delightful mother-in-law, managing the front desk."

"So, this has all been built in the last four decades?" asked Charles, expressing a degree of awe.

"Just about. Whenever property values dropped, we added more acreage and cows. If you're wondering, we're having lots of kids so they can fight over who's running the show when we're gone. Survival of the fittest will determine future management."

"What a plan," said Charles.

"My Davey's studying to be a pilot. He's worried he'll be just another passenger in the nose but on a salary," offered Kirby.

"I hear ya. This AI stuff freaks me out," said Susan, nodding her head dolefully.

"About that dead cow. How'd it get to eating the wolfsbane?" Charles asked.

"Well, Detective White, we'd certainly be most happy for *you* to tell us! Cows never eat wolfsbane, that's a fact. But this old Holstein may have forgotten. Come here."

She got up from the desk and herded them over to one of the large side windows.

"Right over there, that's the south boundary. We have a lot of cows out there that'll mosey back when they hear the bell. There's an old stone wall that T-bones from the blacktop, the road you came in on. My ops manager tells me there's a nasty stretch of wolfsbane right where the stone wall ends. I'll let him get to it sometime, but it's a hell of a job 'cause you have to be suited, and it's got to be pulled out by the roots."

"Can't spray BeGone and get rid of it?" ventured Kirby.

She must have hit a nerve because Susan Williams went off like a shotgun.

"Good Lord, no! We won't use anything that might affect our ladies. And that damn wall's a historical structure! Can't touch it even to get rid of wolfsbane! Fact is, if it falls down, I have to rebuild it! I don't even own it! The damn wall belongs to the nutcase next door."

"Bummer," said Kirby.

"I don't want to sound sexist, but Tilda Duclos is an unwell, crazy-sick bitch. Sick is being generous—bitch is being accurate!

"You mean sick as in bedridden?" Charles inquired.

"No, that would be understandable. This old coot is plum out of her mind. Decades ago, we tried to buy her property. Made it so she could stay in the farmhouse with a few acres. We only wanted the land on the other side of the blacktop. She said she wanted to sell. Christ Almighty, we didn't even dicker about her price! It was all above board."

"It became complicated?" guessed Charles.

"She kept saying we had to deal with her brother, but he'd never show up to our meetings. We spent more on legal fees with all her messing around than the damn place was worth. It got so frustrating, we finally threw in the towel. We'll end up buying the property when it's on the courthouse steps for half what we offered when she's six feet under. God forgive me."

"She's having financial problems, too?" asked Kirby.

"Let's not even go there, KC. I don't know anything except she's crazy as a loon."

"You mind if we go take a look?" Charles asked.

"Not at all. Go back to the blacktop, make a right, and follow our white fencing about a quarter of a mile until it butts into that old stone wall by her gravel drive. That's Tilda Duclos' property. Park on our side of that wall unless you want a nasty lipstick note on your windshield. Hop our white fencing, stay on our side, and follow the rock wall over the crest. You'll find all sorts of wolfsbane. There's a stream down there, so don't fall in."

As they walked out of Susan Williams' office, she followed them to the front desk nail filer, "Hey, Mom, you remember Killer Kirby?"

She looked up from her nails, "No, can't say I do."

"Think back, say, twenty-five-plus years. She was skinnier back then."

"Weren't we all?" She got back to her nails.

"Mom's living weekdays in our office conference room so she doesn't have to commute from Middlebury for our God-awful crack-of-dawn eight a.m. office hours."

With that, Susan Williams dramatically rolled her eyes.

CHAPTER 36

I'mmm guessing it's the crazy lady

That's what they did; they parked in the grass on the side of the road, hopped Williams Dairy's bright-white rail fence, and followed the old stone wall. After a short walk on the Williams' side of the wall, they came to Duclos' red farmhouse and barn. The two neglected structures conjured up an image of ancient wooden ships, afloat on a sea of long grasses swaying in an undulating breeze.

On the house, white timeworn paint was peeling in sheets to expose the dangerous pre-1978 lead-based sealer. Sections of siding were twisted and separated from the backing board, and rotting eaves were peppered with holes drilled by pileated woodpeckers that Kirby said were common in the area. Tilting hazardously, a rusted hundred-pound propane gas tank was sinking into the soft earth, stretching the green copper tubing that snaked into the house. It looked very dangerous.

A clothesline ran off one corner of the house and was hung with an assortment of women's undergarments that fluttered in the breeze. To one side was a small garden surrounded by a chicken wire fence.

Across the yard was a large barn that was once painted red. It had developed an unacceptable sag in the roof ridge. The board and batten siding in various places had warped so badly the nails had worked themselves out, allowing the ends to pop and twist like pretzels.

"Teddi and Simon could play here forever," Kirby said wistfully, encompassing the scene with open arms. Puffy white clouds like cotton balls crawled across the bright blue sky. "That's the opening to *The Simpsons*. You know, when they roll the credits."

"From what your dairy pal said, getting involved with this place . . . like buying it, sounds like big trouble."

"Charlie, don't be so negative. The house only needs a little paint and cleaning up."

"Dreaming is healthy. Let's follow the wall to the wolfsbane."

They continued on the gentle upward slope. Their biggest threat to their well-being came from the minefield of cow pies. A smattering of nearby grazing cows saw them coming and ambled away disinterested. When they topped the rise and had the farm and barn behind, they lingered again to take in the pastoral view broken by distant patches of tended fields and scattered farms. The view might have been the same at the turn of the century.

"That old gal's got some great view out her top back window," said Kirby.

Charles started to comment, then held back his thought.

"I'm pretty jaded," Kirby panned one arm across the horizon, "but that's a classic Vermont postcard."

They continued on the downward-sloping terrain until it leveled out. Just as Susan Williams said, they found the stone wall covered with wolfsbane's bright magenta flowers. Further along, and still out of sight, should be the water.

"Let's go all the way," Kirby said.

They followed the wall until it ended. Only a dozen feet further, they stood at a precipice where the terrain plummeted about a man's height to expose a small, irregular pool. It was obscured on all sides by heavy brush and thorny thickets. At one end, it narrowed, and a lazy current flowed out of sight under a floating clump of reeds.

They couldn't see the bottom in the crystal-clear water from where they stood above.

"There are sheer faces on each side. Who knows what's collected at the bottom?"

"Shopping carts," guessed Charles.

"You're in Vermont, not New York City."

"Cut back the thickets, it'd make an awesome swimming hole," said Charles. Simultaneous glances, then in unison, "Or a fishing hole."

They climbed along the edge upstream, found the pool was being fed by an offshoot from a larger fast-running stream that ran parallel. The rapids were barely a foot deep, but fifty or so feet wide with large boulders and jutting rocks splitting the surface and kicking up white caps of foam and bubbles. On the other side were rows of tall mature firs that had been planted but never shaped for harvest.

"This must be an offshoot of Gilmore Brook. Gilmore's got good, good fishing, Charlie."

"If you're on the brook, you'd never look here. Bet no one's fished it for years," Kirby said.

"So far from the road, no one knows about it," said Charles, wondering about what their next step might be: *fishing or solving a crime?*

They headed back to the stone wall. Approaching from a lower angle, Charles noticed something glossy crammed between the first course at the wall's end. They squatted to inspect.

"It's a wad of cellophane jammed between the stones." He cautiously tried reaching between the rocks and purple wolfsbane flowers, hoping to dislodge the cellophane.

"Charlie, for Christ's sake leave it! It's got wolfsbane all over it."

Their exploration was interrupted by a shrieking voice. They turned to see an elderly, white-haired woman a distance up the rise, on the other side of the stone wall, on a trajectory directly at them. She was stomping down the slope, frantically swinging a gardening hoe and screaming like a banshee.

"Stop! Stop right there! What the hell are you doing at my pit?"

"I'm guessing it's the crazy lady," warned Kirby.

Tilda Duclos was in baggy gray sweatpants, her knees marked by caked dirt from kneeling in the garden. She wore a stained and muddy Walk for Cancer sweatshirt and, wrapped loosely around her neck, was a homemade scarf with a yellow, psychedelic flower pattern. The scarf was so long the tails hung past her knees and were swiping the ground. Fittingly color coordinated, she wore bright yellow galoshes that squeaked loudly as she approached.

Incised, she flung down the hoe and then almost tripped over it.

Charles glanced at Kirby, "I do the talking, okay, KC?"

"Right. I'll listen while you muck up access to our fishing hole," she grumbled.

Tilda Duclos stopped before the wall, several yards from them. All the hollering had left her gasping for breath. She squatted, braced herself by placing both palms on her knees, and began taking deep gulps of air.

From across the wall, Charles attempted to calm her. "Take a few breaths. We're out taking a walk, that's all we're doing."

"You two, what the hell do you want?" She stood, having regained strength.

Finding a place where some stones had slid off and the wolfsbane growth was thinner, Charles moved closer and extended his hand, intending to shake. "I'm Charles. This is Kirby."

Tilda ignored his extended arm, "Stand back! Get away from that wall!"

"Be careful. Those flowers . . ." Kirby was saying before Tilda cut her off.

"Stop telling me stuff I already know. Cross the evil wall, you're looking for trouble. Touch the pretty little flowers, you'll get sick and die."

"Is this some sort of poison ivy?" Charles retracted his arm.

"You don't look too stupid, but that's sure a stupid question. Everyone knows wolfsbane."

"Wolfsbane? I'm a city boy. This is new to me."

"Where you from? You talk funny."

"New York."

"I visited New York City once a long time ago. Swore I'd never go back," she muttered as if it were a sad admission.

Kirby pointed up the slope. "You're in the cute little farmhouse?"

"This is private land and posted. What do you want?"

Charles hemmed and hawed.

Kirby jumped in, "We're just out walking. This is a cool pond. There any fish in it?"

"You'll have to ask Timothy about the pit. He's around here somewhere."

Tilda exaggeratedly looked about as if he was going to pop up and join the conversation.

"I didn't catch your name," asked Charles.

"Didn't tell you my name. It's Tilda Wilcox Duclos. It's French and has an 's' on the end, but it's silent. You say it, 'Du-clo' with two clear syllables. My friends call me Tilly."

Tilda sniffled and wiped her nose on her scarf. "You two married?"

"No, we're buddies," he said exhaling. "I'm a widower. Lost my dear wife."

Kirby managed to keep a straight face. *Charlie you sly, manipulative fox!*

"How about you? There a Mr. Duclos?"

"No, Lord no. I live with my kid brother. He's all I got."

"I'd love to meet him," said Kirby warmly.

"I think he's out for a hike. Timothy's an active outdoorsman when not practicing law."

"I haven't seen anyone. What does your brother look like?" asked Charles.

"Oh, you'd remember Timothy if you saw him—spitting image of James Dean. Has kind of a cowboy look to him; that's not by chance. I make him look and behave right."

"Tilly, you know what I'd love to do?" continued Kirby.

"Can't imagine."

"I'd love to get down to where I can hang my little toes over the edge and put a fishing line into your cool little pool. You ever do that?"

"No, I don't fish and I don't want you fishing my pit. Timothy might do that thing with his toes. He does a lot of goofy things."

"Maybe Timothy will fish with me?" She glanced at Charles, "This lonely old man can't catch anything. Fish see him and they jump out of the water to get away from him."

Charlie grimaced.

"That side of the wall belongs to them dairy people. You stay there, there's nothing I can do. But I don't want you taking any fish. And that pit's my property. Now go. That's final and that's all she wrote. At least for now."

Charles and Kirby were momentarily at a loss for words.

"Wait a minute, KC! Did you call me a lonely old man? I'm standing here talking to this beautiful lady, and you're bad-mouthing me."

There was an awkward silence.

"If anything bites, I'll drop it right back. What do you say?" Kirby decided to refocus on fishing the pit.

"Well, I'm not saying either way, but Timothy might consider it," said Tilda, fussing with her scarf, then pretending to hear something, "Hear that, that's his law firm calling from Boston. I've got to go."

"This is such an awesome place. You must keep very busy, especially in wintertime with the snow," Charles remarked, trying to slow everything down.

"House needs a paint job. Timothy isn't doing his part, and I'm busy all the time."

"You're busy? Active in the community, maybe help out in the church, do you?" probed Kirby with a disarming smile. Wrong.

"Church, fuck no! I don't do any goddamn church! Can't stand them, two-faced hypocrites. When I went to church, thought I knew the people. But when I started to have some troubles, they dropped me like a hot potato. Got me fired!"

"I'm saddened to hear that, Tilly," said Charles.

"How'd you know my name?" she blurted.

"You just told us," answered Kirby.

"Oh. Sometimes I forget things."

"Often, when things get rocky, good people just don't know how to react. They may not realize what they're doing isn't right," calmly stated Charles.

"I was a librarian, helping their no-neck children through years of poor schooling, and it meant nothing!" She paused to catch her breath,

"Now I'm an author. They'll see what I say when they come asking me to sign my novels at their stinking library."

"You're an author! How exciting!" exclaimed Kirby. "Tell me what you're writing!"

"Well, you'll just have to buy *Final Love.* But I can tell you this much: it's a true story about love between two sweet adolescents old enough to know love but who are misunderstood by their mean parents who keep them apart."

"That's so sweet," gushed Kirby. "Go on, tell me more."

"Well, my message is to the young: they will have to face life, and life can be difficult. There's no escaping tragedy and sadness, but they should always be proud of themselves and work to find love and happiness."

"That's very moving," said Charles.

"That's all I want to do, bring people together and let them know love is worth pursuing—and they shouldn't let evil forces conspire against their enthusiasm and desire to be together."

Charles took notice of how upliftingly and sincerely she spoke. What she said was a refrain that sounded like it had come from suffering, unfortunately.

"I don't want you to have sympathy for me because I have dark forces collected against me. I can be a cranky old fool and at times not have all my wits about me. But I'm heartbroken for those children who have to struggle without proper guidance and love from a decent family. My book may make their lonely times bearable."

Before Charles and KC could respond, some regretful thought seemed to have swept into her mind, disrupting the intense atmosphere she had created with her impassioned words. She wiped her nose with her long scarf to disguise another sniffle. After a reflective pause, she readjusted the scarf to cover up some of the dirt caked on her sweatshirt and pushed her gray hair off her forehead.

"What was I saying?"

"Tell me more, Tilly," said Kirby with a note of enthusiasm.

"You'll be hearing about *Final Love*. Just wait 'til I get an agent and publisher. By chance, do you know someone in publishing; maybe they could help me?"

"We'd better be off," said Kirby.

Avoiding answering, Charles reached across the wall, "How about a friendly parting handshake?"

"Put that hand back, nothing goes or comes across the wall," snapped Tilda, having recovered in a blink from her emotional moment.

"Tilly, this wall needn't be 'tween us. Come on, we ought to be friends," ventured Charles.

Tilda rolled her eyes. It was all too much.

The spontaneous appearance of strangers at the wall: a handsome hunk having an interest in her and his sweet-talking hussy asking about fishing. What was that all about? His steady hand was there, palm and fingers aimed at her. To touch across the dark chasm of the wall? Has a powerful force, more powerful than the wall, arrived?

Taking a path to avoid the wolfsbane, Tilda hesitantly extended her wrinkly arm and pinkish palm to Charles.

"You have a nice handshake," he said, buttering.

Dumbfounded, Tilda looked at him. She then abruptly pulled back her hand, turned, and began trudging up the rise toward the farmhouse and barn. Kirby called out, "Can I come back and meet Timmy?"

"Too late to meet my Timmy. You might meet my brother, Timothy," Tilda shouted back.

"How about me? Can I come see you?" implored Charlie.

"Hell, no. You stink of trouble."

"Oh, come on, Tilly. We just shook over the wall, didn't we?"

Tilda hesitated and turned to face them. "That's the trouble. You're too friendly. Touching me and everything, before I'm ready."

"Come on! We ought to have tea or coffee or something together one afternoon." That caught her attention.

"You bring me tea and some fancy chocolates, we'll see then. Maybe."

"Deal," said Charles.

Tilda flushed with a smile, continued up the slope.

CHAPTER 37

Charlie, you're a complicated copper

They stood and watched her until she reached the top of the hill and had become a diminishing speck moving down the other side. They started back to the road.

"Duclos is a riot! Jesus Christ Charlie, she reminds me of a Lilly Tomlin character! Of course, I don't know if Tomlin's on a crusade to ease adolescent suffering." Kirby said uncharacteristically cynical.

"KC, that could be taken as petty and heartless"

"Well, I've never met anyone as nutty as Tilda. I did have a crazy aunt, she ate sand," said Kirby. She paused and took a deep breath. Then, gave Charlie a wide-eyed stare and confirmed, "It's her, isn't it?"

"Afraid so. She's the one dropping off samples at the post offices," said Charles, his voice relaying frustration.

Passing Tilda's farmhouse and barn, they noted there was no car to be seen and the undergarments had been taken in from the clothesline.

"Well, Charlie, her fucking brother, Timothy, I bet he's the warped mind behind all this," said Kirby.

"Most likely. But did you see the way her eyes lit up when I said we'd bring her tea and chocolates? It was like we were bringing her a birthday cake."

"And she is so caring about kids, that's really endearing."

"But something's not kosher with this situation. It doesn't add up."

"Easy to forget she's out of her mind and trying to kill people. So, where's this brother Timothy fit in?"

"Hold on. Let's think critically about what we've learned. Tilda Duclos is disturbed. Senile, Alzheimer's, schizophrenia—take a pick. She has Wolfsbane in her backyard and recognizes what it can do. Professionally, we say she has the *means*. Using syrup VAMP blithely provided and pal Donnie delivered, that gives her *opportunity*. Now what's the *motive*, KC?"

"Pain and suffering?"

"Yes. But why?"

"Motive? With a frog name like Duclos? Duh, Charlie, collusion with Canadian maple producers! Who else? Someone's got to pay for all them 'Nam draft dodgers and Trump escapees!" exclaimed Kirby, but not too seriously because she was smiling ear to ear.

"Tilly told us, 'I'm a writer.' Our victims are literary agents. What do we do next, KC?"

"We beat out a confession! Kill her cat! Jesus, Charlie, you're the detective. You tell me!"

"Ask the obvious: does she belong to the Romance Agents & Writers Guild? Has she been published? Does she have an agent? It's all stuff we need to know to uncover her motive."

"I 'd have said all of that if you had given me another second or two."

Charles remained quiet. They walked a little further and then, Kirby had an epiphany.

"Wait just a minute! Why didn't you take her picture just now with your phone? Run it by postman Alberts or the Santa-clone postmaster in Bolton?"

They took a few more contemplative steps. "If they recognize her, it'd be all over, wouldn't it, Charlie? *Finito*! He kept his head down as if watching for cow pies.

"Charlieeee, fess up!"

"Yes, and I'd be obligated to enter everything into the RTCC."

"You don't want to do that, do you, Charlie?"

He looked blankly at her. "Mahoney would call me back to New York. With a positive I.D., Vermont law enforcement would arrest her."

"There's got to be a better way, Charlie."

"I know what's ahead for her, and I don't like doing this to anyone her age," he said. "It's not how I see myself. Know what I mean?"

"Gotcha. Never simple, is it? Real life isn't like on TV. Your job doesn't unfold between snippy commercials and isn't wrapped up with sweeping orchestration, is it?"

"That's stunningly insightful and very aptly put, Miss Clark!"

"Charlie, you don't think it's clear? She's trying to kill literary agents because they don't like her writing. Duh, I don't get it?" said Kirby sarcastically.

"Yes, that appears to be the case. But remember, the court decides if guilty or not. I'd like to know 'why' on a subconscious, internalized level. Remember our conversation last night, the reason I became a detective? The elusive 'why' of Tilly Duclos is a case made for study."

"Charlie, you're a complicated copper."

"No, I'm not."

"Jesus, just be happy we've solved the case. Anyway, changing gears. Don't think I'm being too forward, but I don't want to lose you before I got ya. Frankly, I'm getting some real good vibes from you."

"Hmmm. Me, too. So, all in all, why'd you come up with the unkind idea that I'm old and lonely?"

"Because you've been a real gentleman. Means you might be in for the long haul."

Hoisting his arms toward the sky as if calling to the Almighty: "Thank you! She's beautiful, experienced, and wise, too!" He took a second to reconsider, "But at this early stage, I'll qualify that outburst with *so far.*"

"Play your cards right, might find out before you're too rickety and weak to enjoy my finer hidden qualities," she replied, then had to leap over a cow pie before tripping into it.

They came to the blacktop road and found the 'Vette parked where they had left it, and the windshield, fortunately, unmolested. Once aboard, Charles sat behind the wheel for a long moment. He glanced up Tilda Duclos' gravel drive, then messed with his itching nose.

KC twisted about on her seat to face him, "What's up Charles?"

"She asked us to help her."

CHAPTER 38

We may be cutthroats, but we're not blue meanies!

It was time to shut the doors on Jacob Javitz' Book Expo XII. After three intense days, attendees were numb from inputting on their iPads and laptops, yakking up deals, and being upbeat with new contacts that might make the upcoming season profitable.

Sometimes, publishers, writers, and agents at book expos collect around an exhibitor's space near closing hour to get a final look at a new product or perhaps a celebrity might drop in. At today's closing hour, many wandered over to the Romance Agents & Writers Guild tent to say goodbye. The tent and booth were festooned with garlands and flowers from well-wishers, including an enormous vase of roses from the expo's organizers.

When Cecil Rhodes walked up to the dais, exhibitors and workers paused from breaking down their booths and tables and came over to listen to him.

"I'm here to honor the sweetheart of Book Expo XII, Martha Jane Sidel. I'm not going to use this time to bash my competitors. At C & B Publishing we've already had three days of doing that! We may be cutthroats, but we're not blue meanies!"

Big laughter from the gathering audience.

"But seriously, MJ had the rug pulled out from her. Hell, you know the story. Our poor friends are in the hospital, and our hearts and love go out to them for a quick recovery—a senseless tragedy beyond comprehension." Cecil drooped his head as if in a little prayer. "But with all this crap thrown at her, look what happened, she got her ass off the floor! So, isn't what we have here today amazing? MJ, come on up here before my crew has to rip this place apart and you don't get a chance to say a few words."

MJ worked her way forward amongst pats on the back and variations of "way to go, MJ!"

"I'm touched, so very touched. I'm tongue-tied with emotion, so excuse me if I roll over and die. I don't have . . . I've never created a character who has more to be thankful for than me. I'm struggling— struggling to find the words to express to Cecil, you big Australian bully, that I love you to death! And to Silvia for so much help and understanding. Without question, I am so indebted to you two for these past three days."

Tears with sooty black mascara began streaming, making her look like a witch from hell and beyond.

"And to all you who came, who spoke with passion in a free-for-all of ideas of how our industry is most important to our ever closing-in world, and for those who just came to rest your feet, I'm so happy I could provide a chair. Thank you all from the very bottom of my heart."

Among the writers Silvia Martinez had enlisted was a cadre of musicians, and for a sendoff to end that tiring week, out came their instruments.

* * * * * *

Meanwhile, Kirby and Charles were settled on the sofa having glasses of wine. Mister Fritz was perched on his end, keeping an eye on them.

Once in a while, Charles' fingers danced on the laptop investigating Vermont DMV.

"Tilly's 1992 red Subaru wasn't at the farm, but it's registered to her," thought Charles out loud.

"Timothy's driving it," offered Kirby.

"Okay. So, we assume the brother is making her post the samples. Why is he trying to kill literary agents? A frustrated writer, too? I don't think so."

"Charlie, we can't let the old bat go to the slammer while her brother skips town. If she has anything to do with the poisoning, they are going to—what's the thing they say on TV, the 'aid and abetting' thing?"

"Aiding and abetting. But the word you're looking for is, 'accessory.'"

"Exactly. So, what happens?"

"She'll be locked up until a trial. She may sit there a year as the states fight over jurisdiction and details, which they will do. Six hospitalized in New York City, that's bad. Vermont's overriding interest will be softening the hit on the maple industry and all the bad press. There's a lot at stake— justice versus money. Guess who wins?"

"She's God-awful sick. But it's not hatefulness toward one person. She and bro have their own class action suit against literary agents. Maybe they're justified on some level?" she said, as if it was not such a bad thing.

"Don't go there, KC. In any case, it's the end of the road for someone her age and mental condition if she goes into the system."

"Charlie, you're such a good, understanding heart." She gave him a pat on the shoulder and ran several fingers through his white hair.

"I'll get onto RTCC, see what Mahoney's been doing. I recommended to him we get one of my guys to interview the guild head, Sidel."

"Where's that going to lead?"

"Nowhere. It's a red herring but it'll keep the office busy. The upshot is, I'm not entering anything definitive on Tilly Duclos until we're clear about her role."

"It sounds like you may be crossing some symbolic blue line?"

"What's entered into the RTCC limits our wiggle room if we want to give her some cover until we get the brother."

"I got it," Kirby nodded in agreement.

"How's our scenario and query coming?"

"Done the query. It was easy. The query is all about hype. The scenario is the concept—plot with characters doing what they're going to do. I'm pushing it off for now."

"Let's not knock ourselves out. I simply want to get a feel for the process of becoming a professional writer."

"Gotcha," said Kirby, "Think the guild will answer my query right away?"

"How long can it take to read two paragraphs?"

"What am I going to do when they want the manuscript and I have to go on book signing tours?"

"Cross that bridge when you come to it. Let's go out and find some dinner before you send it. Give your words time to mature," teased Charles.

"Aren't you tired of eating out? How about a steak on the patio? I've got a porterhouse in the freezer, lettuce, broccoli, and plenty of wine. Put the steaks in warm water, be ready in no time for the grill."

"You're a single woman and you keep porterhouse steaks in the fridge?"

"Davey rides into town often enough. I know how to rope men in."

"If you have a grocery receipt, I'll expense it and give you the cash."

"I like that! What about lodging expenses? I'll type up a receipt?"

"I'll have to think about that."

* * * * * *

Just a few mountain ridges away, Tilda was preparing dinner. After telling Timothy about the strangers at the fish pit, she heated a can of clam chowder. Rinsing the can, she dropped it into a crude hole cut in the floor under the sink that emptied into the basement coal box that had gone unfilled with coal for the last sixty years.

She slurped down the heated soup, not needing a spoon until she faced a few clams and potato cubes at the bottom of the bowl.

Timothy was miffed. "Now you tell me the babe wanted to meet me! All you had to do was yell! Sis, you know I need stimulation."

"You have to get off your fanny if you want to meet my visitors."

"Think maybe she got a little hot thinking about me?"

"You know, Timothy, one of these days you'll find you've gone too far. I spent all these years bringing you up right, and now you're going to make me kick you out?"

"If you'll be so kind as to describe her physical characteristics."

"She was blond and had a full chest. That's all I'm going to say."

"Big knockers, my favorite. Tell me more."

"Well, if you insist, they were nice like mine." Tilda's thoughts had turned to the stranger, how she might be able to lure him to her nest.

It wasn't too late to sit at the Acer and put down a few fiery words from their arousing encounter. The stranger, Charles, and his harlot, Kirby, who were they really? He could be a time traveler, a Roman centurion transported by the powers confronting the wall to swoon her! He had thrown himself at her, unconcerned about breaching the wall and unafraid of its underling, the deadly vine! A handsome devil, a bold and demanding lover he would be. He had commanded, "Take my hand."

He was no keyboard creation borne from her keen imagination. This fearsome warrior appeared and was captivated by her. The harlot with him, they weren't having satisfying sex. No, she had to be a block of ice. Maybe that's why she wanted young, fiery Timothy slipping between her thighs. A fishing partner, duh!

Tilda worked at the keyboard until she collapsed onto Timothy's couch. As she drifted off, she realized what had occurred: she had been delivered a man who would shower her with love and tempestuous sex! She understood he would have needs—all men sought carnal release—and she felt the same. So often, she recognized her lusty cravings were a little strange for a woman of her age and stature. Would she get to see him again, feel his strong grip? If she did, she'd go all out to keep him.

CHAPTER 39

You're very good with women, aren't you?

It was a late dinner. They had vodka tonics while Kirby made a side of broccoli smothered with cheese sauce and a mixed greens salad with a balsamic dressing. Charles grilled the steaks perfectly on the patio gas grill. They ate at the counter on the stools and after the 1.5-liter bottle of Beaujolais was emptied, they collapsed at opposite ends of the sofa. Greasing up the tiled kitchen floor, Mister Fritz was having a field day demolishing two porterhouse bones.

On the cocktail table were two open laptops, each running screen savers. On Kirby's were images of her folks and friends at parties, but most were of Simon: Simon sprawled on the sofa, Simon in the crib, Simon bundled in a Road Runner car seat, Simon touching a cow's nose, and so on. Charles' shots? They were of him in rubber waders stream fishing, another of him holding a large caught trout, Mary and the girls on ATVs in Colorado, and promo shots of many, many different year Corvettes.

"I'm not up for working," Charles expressed definitively.

"That's because we're both shit-faced drunk. Want to read my query for *Desperate Measures* before we shut down?

"I can't imagine having anything to contribute. Besides, any corrections I'd suggest, you'd likely end up getting pissed at me."

"You're very good with women, aren't you?" she asked, a wee sarcastically.

He didn't respond because he could have droned on all night about what he did not understand about women. Why were so many women dissatisfied with their lives? Why murder a husband and run off with a bigger loser? And very sad women, taking pills or using a razor in the bathtub to swim into Freud's oceanic eternity. But one thing was certain, the 'whys' of misbehavior were genderless.

Charles was familiar with all this sadness and rage but fortunately, not with women he held precious. While in their teens, his daughters had emotionally separated from Charles after he had gotten shot. Not angrily distant in the traditional estranged manner of teenagers, but out of necessity. Perhaps to have a protective veil were he to depart, "unannounced."

And then Mary died before him. *What the fuck*!

Kirby cleared her throat to get Charles' attention. "I think we're good to go."

"Got 'Query' in the subject line?" He was just checking.

"Yes, it's done," she answered with a touch of irritation.

"Hold on. *Desperate Measures*? There's something familiar about the title," mumbled Charles. His mind was clouded by too much wine and food.

Kirby hit the Enter key. In a swish, it was on its way.

"What'd you just do? Thought we were going to go over it!" Charles groaned.

"Too late. We must visit Tilly Duclos," said Kirby. "The pursuit of criminals can never stop, even if we're hungover."

"You want us to bribe her to let you drop a line in her pit." It was easy to see Kirby's end game.

"Exactly. We bring her some tea and chocolates and she'll open the door. That's what she said."

"Well, I'm conflicted about seeing her. We've enough grounds for me to turn this over to Vermont. That, Mahoney will be glad to hear, and he'll have me driving back that very day.

Both wanted to get away from that thought. His eyes wandered to the mounted rainbow trout over the fireplace.

"I'd rig a split shot about five feet from a brown worm jig. Keep it off the bottom, but in enough light to see from below," Charles said, matter of fact.

"You're going to need more split shot to keep it from walking downstream in that current," offered Kirby.

"You're right. Might have to use a bobber, too," said Charles.

"White side down so fish won't see it," cautioned Kirby with a pointed finger.

For a second, they looked hungrily at each other and glanced at their laptops. *Fuck work!* Kirby leaped onto Charles and mashed her lips onto his, causing them to fall back onto the sofa. She hurriedly stripped off her sweatshirt and unhooked her bra as he wiggled out of his slacks. He jammed his shorts down to the floor and with a free heel kicked them off. He started to drop his head between her legs.

"No, no, don't go there. I'm not clean enough for foreplay and I'm plenty wet. We'll take showers later," she said.

"Good idea." He went atop, settled between her legs. At first slowly, then gradually all the way, making her grunt. His mouth found her breasts and nipples.

"Too hard?" he asked.

"No! God, no, just right. Give it to me how you like it. I'm easy to please."

"Pounding okay?"

"Yes! Fucking pounding's great!" she said, tossing her legs around his waist.

They went at it. Kirby shook and got there twice. Charles held it together like he had something to prove. He was really, really out of breath but hadn't lost a functioning brain. "Stupid question, you safe?"

She hesitated. "Maybe," she said perplexed. *Hadn't thought of that in a long time!*

Not wanting to miss the moment by too much thinking, she used one hand on him and one on herself, making him spray on her honey-brown curls while climaxing once again. They didn't budge for minutes, savoring their new relationship.

"God, about time. I was wondering if you were ever going to make a move!" said Kirby, catching her breath while smearing his stuff around her belly button. He feigned surprise—*after last night's rejection?*

"Can I assume any sexually incompatible issues have been resolved?" Charles entertained himself by twisting a finger into her moistened pubes. *I am one lucky dog.*

"I'd say so," and responded by giving him a long kiss. "About getting pregnant, no worry, I'm on the pill. Every day I take pills, frankly, I've lost track of what they are all for."

After another minute, "Charlie, I felt a scar on your back. What's that from? Let me look."

"Hero stuff. Scratch it a bit as you look. It can itch like crazyeeeeee!"

* * * * * *

MJ was in her apartment stretched across her leather Chesterfield sofa wearing sexy red silk pajamas. She was making mini whirlpools in a half-consumed martini using two speared olives on a sculpted plastic toothpick snatched at a book release party at the Plaza Hotel's Champagne Bar. It was red and had the clichéd devil head with twin fork horns for olive stabbing. For some vague reason, she favored it and managed to leave the event with a pocketful.

"I've no one to play with," she thought out loud.

Inside her tossed brain, MJ was out to sea with doubts and anxieties. Right-hand assistant Pamela would come back to work at the guild in a few days—but only with conditions. First, a raise and elevation of status to no longer "being your slave." Pamela's very words. And she would only return as a bona fide literary agent in the guild. Moreover, if she were to continue reading queries, she wanted to sign her own writers. Of course, only from queries MJ wasn't interested in representing.

MJ sensed Pamela was carrying a bit of resentment toward her. How unfortunate that Pamela had snatched the maple syrup right out of MJ's hands! Why did fate select doll-like Pamela to get the deadly juice? Just chance? Well, that's not the way MJ would have felt if the roles had been reversed. Maybe there was someone up there looking after her? Nah, that's fairytale crapola!

After Book Expo XII closed, MJ implored Silvia Martinez to join the guild as an Associate Partner. Having her name on the masthead, an international agent focused on South American, Latin, and African writers would help the guild enormously. Not yet committed, but Silvia was thinking about it.

As for Cecil Rhodes, MJ didn't know how to thank the man who truly saved her guild. She'd be willing to bang him if required, but no way could she survive him on top of her. Her limbs weren't limber enough or long enough to straddle him. It might come down to oral sex or an enormous fruit basket with French champagne, an assortment of exotic cheeses, crackers, and little jars of jellies. She'd have to think about it. One was distastefully expensive; one was simply distasteful.

MJ was obligated to call Phylis Cartland.

Phylis had used the complete sample of syrup on her pancakes, so she was still struggling in the hospital. Her debacle at McDonald's had garnered all the press attention; oddly, the other poisonings went unnoticed. Luckily for McDonald's, vomit wasn't as newsworthy as the two mutilated bodies found in a Chinatown dumpster. Later, Phylis would receive a certain amount of derision from her office cohorts for taking morning breakfast at McDonald's rather than the egg sandwich and coffee from the friendly Olympik Greek Deli on their building's ground floor.

Poor Phylis was going to be a tough call for MJ. Better put that call aside for a day . . . or longer.

Jennifer Rousch was going to be a tough call, too. Her coffee-to-poison ratio was so high, the concentration would keep Jennifer on the detoxing hemodialysis longer than anyone else. Because of Jennifer's sad progress and fearing an emotional outburst, MJ did not want to discuss anything over the phone. She decided to write her a reassuring note about how she rescued her bag with all her IDs, cell phone, credit cards, combs, nail polish, breath freshener, and more assorted crap Jennifer toted about. It had cost MJ $200 to get it from the hack and twenty to the doorman. Would it be unseemly to ask for reimbursement? Better get Pamela to make that call, too.

The easier call would be to Betty Sampson. Neither she nor Ralf had absorbed as much of the toxin, and Ralf went home after three days in the hospital. Somehow, in all the chaos of the day, MJ had managed to get them bathrobes. No, she didn't go to their home and rifle through their closets. She picked up the phone, called Macy's, and had two of their best terrycloth robes sent to the Sampson's rooms at Lenox Hill Hospital. MJ went into arrhythmia when she opened Macy's email with the itemized charges. Expensive robes, that was expected. But a hundred bucks each for two door-to-door rush deliveries to the same hospital?

That was obscene! Bastards! They could have gone in one box! Macy's lame explanation: Men's and Women's were two different departments.

After topping off her martini from the stainless silver shaker and reassessing the blowjob or fruit and cheese basket quandary for Cecil Rhodes, it dawned on MJ that she didn't have to squeeze Betty to pay for the robes or Phylis for the expensive cab fiasco! There was another way to even out her largesse on the balance sheet. She wasn't obligated to pay them a percentage of the take because they didn't speak! Why the hell should they expect payment? With that common-sense rationale, she could manufacture an explosive scene to stifle any grumbling. All those situations were "people" problems, which MJ knew how to deal with, but she'd get Pamela to do the dirty work just the same.

MJ was still troubled why in her interview with the obnoxious police officer Mahoney had sent (not that hapless NYPD officer in Vermont) he'd hinted there must have been something she did to bring this on! What an asshole thing to suggest!

As she worked on the martini and lit another Kent, she couldn't help catching a glimpse of her messy kitchen. It was strewn with three days of Chinese food cartons, pizza boxes, unwashed plates, and dirty cocktail glasses, which made her wonder:

Who's a neatnik I can call to come for a visit who will sympathetically offer to clean what Pamela would have done reflexively?

Dishwashing always ruined MJ's nails.

CHAPTER 40

Come on, White, get on the stick!
We haven't all fucking day!

Detective Charles was luxuriating in Kirby's California king bed: comfy mattress, silky gray sheets, pillowy duvet. Kirby was tucked against him, curled in a fetal position, sexually spent from a night of melding bliss. They had showered together; warm water flowed between their soapy bodies, making him hard again. Charles wouldn't disagree when, looking up from her knees, she told him, "My former told me I gave the best head he had ever gotten from a girl." Charles was overall very pleased but wasn't keen to dwell on Kirby's past sexual exploits or her ex's description of her blowjob skills.

A morning light was filtering through the sheer chiffon window treatments. It was time to rise. He knew Kirby was awake even though she was motionless. After just a few days of cohabitation, he already knew that as soon as it was light she would to get up and pee and turn down the air conditioner.

"I'm faced with a dilemma, KC. Help me out."

She rotated to face him, pulled herself up, and arranged the pillows so she could rest against the headboard.

"About us or the case?"

"The case."

"Good. It's too early to talk more about us."

"I need to call Mahoney."

"Okay. How soon?"

"This morning. He'll ask for clarification on the lame stuff I filed in the RTCC report yesterday.

"Hold that thought. I've got to pee. It's too cold in here, isn't it? I'm turning down the air conditioner."

Charles put on fresh boxers and pullover while Kirby slipped into a loose-fitting man's white terry cloth robe. As they headed downstairs, Mister Fritz was waiting at the bottom step, eager to visit the lawn.

"Okay, my friend, I'll let you outside." Charles opened the sliding glass door, let Mister Fritz scoot onto the patio, and closed the door behind him.

"I'll make him a little snack," said Kirby from the kitchen.

Charles opened his laptop but was distracted by Kirby strutting about in the kitchen. Well aware she was being eyeballed, she'd purposely let her robe split apart variously exposing a white breast, a peachy thigh, or a flash of pubic hair. Then, she'd do a fussy little act of covering up. He couldn't *not* watch her. Her plan all along.

His cell did the Beethoven.

"Good morning, Captain." Charles immediately stood. It was too weird talking to Mahoney, lounging on the sofa in his boxers while voyeur-ing his undercover girlfriend. Attempting to avoid further distraction, he cupped his hand over his eyes, listened closely, and said nothing for a while.

"I'm glad to hear our victims are recovering, Captain … Understood. You'd like me to wrap this up … "

Kirby came over with a steaming cup of coffee. Charles indicated thanks, bobbing his head like a dashboard Jesus. Mahoney was doing police blah, blah, blah. Unfortunately, Mister Fritz had completed his business in the backyard and began barking and pawing the glass door to come inside.

"What's all that barking, Charles?" groused Mahoney from 350 miles away.

Kirby rocketed outside, snatched up Mister Fritz, and quieted him with nose-to-nose snuggling. Meanwhile, her bathrobe was flapping open, exposing more for her neighbors. Charles rolled his eyes and spluttered his conversation to Mahoney.

"Yeah, Captain, damn motel's lousy with dogs. Ignore 'em. I visited a dairy where a cow recently died eating wolfsbane . . . That elderly woman lives next to the dairy . . . Tilda Duclos. It's French Canadian, D-u-c-l-o-s. You don't pronounce the 's' at the end . . . Well, she's not all there. I'd say unbalanced, mentally scrambled. Her license says she's seventy-eight . . . That's correct . . . yes, sir."

He walked into the kitchen, allowing Kirby and Mister Fritz to sneak inside. Mister Fritz quietly went to his spot on the sofa. Kirby tiptoed over to Charles to overhear Mahoney shouting:

"Come on, White, get on the stick! We haven't all fucking day!"

"Cap, I'm on it! Duclos owns a red Subaru wagon, the type identified by two postmen where the samples were mailed . . . No, sir, they can't identify her. She has a flaky brother, Timothy. I can't find anything on him in New York, Vermont, or Canada . . . That's right, I think she's doing her brother's bidding. We could never get charges to stick on her. I mean, what's the point? . . . I will get something actionable on the brother for the Vermont D.A."

Charles was quiet for a while, listening.

"Kirby Clark? Who? . . . Oh, her, the gal at VAMP. She wasn't helpful . . . No, Captain, didn't tell her any more than she needed to know. I may need to backtrack to her at some time"

Kirby frowned; her feelings had gotten stung: *Oh, Charlie, my dear, you shouldn't have said it THAT WAY!*

"That makes sense . . . I can assure you, Captain, I'll get him one way or another . . . I need more time . . . Yes, well, it's nice to be missed."

He wrapped his free hand around his throat signaling Mahoney was choking him. Kirby unobtrusively slipped her hand into his boxers and began a pleasurable fondling. He became hard instantly.

"Captain, I have a pile of sick time, so if I need a few days, I can take that time, okay? . . . No, sir, certainly no disrespect. Yes, sir, I'll update RTCC. You'll let me know what to pass on to Vermont's D.A.'s office, if that's your call . . . Yes, sir." Charles disconnected.

With her index finger, Kirby gently wiped a smear of clear fluid that had collected at the tip of his penis and theatrically touched it to her extended tongue.

"That's quite nice. Don't stop," encouraged Charles.

She stopped. "Well, since I don't know anything, what now?"

"He's thinking it's time for Vermont law enforcement to step in so NYPD can step out. If I stay past the weekend, he'll take it out of my accumulated vacation and sick days."

"Is that a deal breaker?"

He groaned, "No. I'll have to talk to Bookus and have him block me out of the office schedule—but Mahoney's on to us, KC."

"First, I have some observations. You avoided telling your NYPD big cheese that two postmen could identify Tilda Duclos. And did you forget about Donnie's surveillance tape? Also, Duclos knows all about wolfsbane, and has it growing all over!"

"To hell with it, KC, only results matter. Besides, we have bigger fish to fry," stated Charles. He was not thinking of the case—he was pondering how to get her on to her next move. And that move wasn't about frying fish.

"Come again?"

"Where's your fishing gear?"

"Behind you in the locked closet next to the rifle rack."

"Is there a Balduccci's in Burlington? Somewhere where can we buy quality tea and chocolates?"

"For quality and selection we'll go to Trader Joe's. I'll drive."

"We'll have to stop at VAMP and get your car."

"Charlie, I know the way!" she said, projecting a little more testiness than he was used to.

"KC, for you to drive my car, I'd have to recalibrate the presets on the driver's seat and realign all the mirrors. I'd have to show you how to use the stalk shifter. Sweetie, honestly, it's a real electronic pain in the ass to set up! I spent a whole day . . .

She stopped playing with him, pulled herself up, and retightened her robe. "I'll get dressed."

"Are you seriously going to leave me like this?" Charles referred to his erection.

Smiling, she leaned over close, eye to eye, "Oh, since I've not been helpful, help yourself." She gave his penis a bye-bye pat, then tucked it back into his shorts. "Sorry, Charlie, no time for play. Maybe you'll figure it out before I'm too ditzy to drive your precious car."

Mister Fritz got up from his bed and did a shake, expecting to go for a ride.

"Fritz, stay and protect the fort. We'll be back in a while."

Unrelieved, Charles was now looking for his pants and gun.

* * * * *

Back in New York City's 7th Precinct, Mahoney was in a stew. He loathed being taken advantage of, especially by someone he'd given a long leash to and was now screwing the pooch in scenic Vermont.

Probably boning that maple syrup girl or fishing. Likely both.

He'd better look into the situation before it got out of hand. Because the office's twin glass doors were closed, he had to shout. "Hey, Bookus! Get off your personal business. I'd like printouts of White's RTCC reports. Just his reports, no one else's."

Sergeant Bookus disconnected and rotated about to his new desk computer, a Dell that he despised. His main peeve was its bright-white plastic cover. Not like the classy Mac Mahoney had gotten, which had a subtle, soft ivory tone—his Mac wouldn't show messy fingerprints from pastry dribbles or coffee spills.

"Right away, Inspector."

He waved a thumbs-up to Mahoney in the Glass Palace and began searching for White's RTCC reports.

He didn't ask for it, but I might as well look at everything White is up to. Let's see, when he accesses RTCC, I think I can piggyback into his laptop's hard drive without him knowing . . .

CHAPTER 41

I'm a trollop you picked up
as a sex toy on vacation?

Charles stashed Kirby's fishing gear, a two-section rod and reel, a wicker creel packed with lures, and a Kryptek S2 hand net. All nicely fit into the 'Vette's rear hatch. They were taking only items necessary to get a line in the water, foregoing waders and nonessential stuff. She noticed the large black zippered bag jammed into the right recess of the wayback.

"That your fishing gear?"

"That's my war bag. It's everything I might need in an emergency before backup arrives."

"Cool. I know what I most often need in emergencies: toilet paper!"

"Got that and hand wipes, too. I've got a hidden compartment for my treasures."

He unsnapped a carpet flap, lifted a cover plate, and drew out a long graphite tube. Inside, in two sections, were his new fishing rod and reel.

"Charlie, wow! Nice stuff! Awesomely expensive, too. You're not on the take, are you?"

"No! For God's sake, KC! Don't even think that! Jeez, fucking TV crime writers are ruining the world.

"Sorry! Just joking."

* * * * * *

An hour or so later, they left Trader Joe's with a box of Japanese matcha green tea packets, spiced chai tea, a box of organic mint green tea, and a bright red package of Trader Joe's Pound Plus dark chocolate bar. Kirby suggested Tilda may not have the teeth to crunch the harder chocolate, so she added a box of the softer Trader Joe's S'mores bars to the large brown paper bag.

"It's noon, not going to catch anything, even if she lets you fish. But I figured we'll drop in hoping Timothy's there," said Charles, as they turned onto Route 7.

"You going to cuff him, call for backup?"

"KC, you've got to get with the program. If we see Timothy, I can't arrest or detain him unless I have a substantial reason—like he's going to commit a felony in front of me. If it goes south with him, the best I can do is hold him until Vermont police arrive."

"For real?" she said, adjusting on her lap the Trader Joe's bag stuffed with Tilda's treats.

"If we prejudice the investigation, anything we'd uncovered would be inadmissible. A homicidal maniac could be set free because we botched it."

"That's why I brought this," she reached behind into the antique creel fishing basket and removed a .32 caliber pistol in a canvas holster. It had a Mallard duck stenciled on its snap flap.

"Oh, Jesus Christ, KC! Why'd you do that?"

"Why? You just said 'homicidal maniac'! No sweat, I've got my permit with me."

"Okay, okay, just leave it in the car."

Kirby grunted back disapprovingly, "Go back to what you were saying."

"Had I come to Vermont officially and I didn't have the courtesy to contact the local district attorney, guess how are they going to react?"

"Charlie, if you leave town without getting Timothy, you'll be sending that poor lady to jail, not to a treatment facility."

"I'm aware of that. If this becomes a cluster fuck, Mahoney will say I'm on vacation so NYPD has deniability. Mahoney will save his skin and haul me into a disciplinary hearing. When it comes out you're involved, that would cost me everything."

"Oh shit, it's that bad?"

"Yes, it's that bad. I'm here to collect information, not confront suspects or look for fishing holes."

"Well, asshole Mahoney's got none of that esprit de corps I hear about."

They drove silently with Charles pretending to be distracted. Finally, he had to confess.

"If we solve the crime and bring justice to the felon, then we're stars. And all the shit we're wading in will disappear."

"And when your semiofficial status is terminated, I'm a trollop you picked up as a sex toy on vacation? Not your civilian liaison-turned partner?" She said, annoyed.

"Works for me." He chuckled, then leaned to the far-left side of his seat, expecting a wallop.

Set on changing her mood, Charles was already tapping the 8-inch touchscreen, bringing up his Motown collection on Apple CarPlay. "Want to listen to some great Motown?"

"Yes, I do remember Motown. I was just getting out of my diapers then," passing him a droll look.

Snaking through fourteen speakers, the 'Vette was immediately filled with the intoxicating sounds of Blue Magic's hit, *Just Don't Want to Be Lonely.*

"That drummer's on fire!" Charles said, feeling twenty years younger. Glancing at Kirby, she looked twenty years younger. That morning, he had removed the overhead roof panel, making the 'Vette like a convertible. As they sped along the sun was kicking off Kirby's Ray-Bans, her hair was swirling about her most awesome smile; all a glamorous scene right out of a Detroit advertisement.

Just beautiful.

The smooth and twisting road reminded him why he had sunk an un-Godly amount of savings into the shadow-gray Corvette. The smooth paddle-shifter with rev-matching had them blasting along Route 116 at speeds causing Kirby to beam with excitement while her right hand white-knuckled the door grip.

So exhilarated, they roared through a blinking yellow light at an intersection with a hidden gravel road. Unsportingly well-camouflaged, lurking behind a towering mass of brush was a green Vermont State Police Dodge. With all lights ablaze and an irritating tickling siren, it took but a few seconds for the green cruiser to fill the Vette's side mirrors.

"Shit," said Charles. They pulled off the road onto a dirt patch created by others flying through the same blinking yellow. He reached into his rear pocket for his wallet, found the registration in the door's side compartment, and put both hands high on the wheel.

"KC, don't say anything, *please.*"

* * * * * *

The siren was killed and State Trooper Francine Forget, wearing wraparound sunglasses, tan shirt with darker brown twin pockets with snap closures, a long tie of the same dark brown, leisurely got out of the cruiser and sauntered to the Corvette with palm readied on her holster. To round out the traditional trooper uniform, she wore the hideous greenish slacks with bold yellow stripes, designed to make a trooper visible on the highway in the dead of night or in a snowstorm.

Trooper Francine Forget came from a long line of hugely successful statewide businesspeople. She was initially headed for law school but decided a mean-ass bully in uniform with state powers fit better. She aced all the trooper exams, physical and written. For multiple reasons, the department was pleased to have Fran Forget.

Glancing past Charles as soon as she got to his window, Trooper Forget recognized Kirby in the passenger's seat.

"License and registration, please. Know how fast you were going through my intersection? The one clearly identified with the impossible-to-miss bright flashing yellow lights?"

He passed everything out the window to her. "Sorry, Officer. My new car just loves these roads; thrill of the moment got the best of me."

"Well, that's nice you've come all the way to Vermont to test your toy. Over sixty in a thirty, Detective White. What do you have to say for yourself?"

"No excuse. I hear you loud and clear. Won't happen again."

"You carrying?"

Using both arms to stretch out his jacket, he exposed his badge and the SIG Sauer.

"Why are you in Vermont, Detective Charles White?'

"Fishing."

"I see your gear in the back. You have a license?"

"Of course."

"Let's see it."

Charles gave her his fishing license.

"She going to fish, too?"

"Probably."

"Kirby, you have a current fishing license?" Trooper Forget asked impatiently.

"*Here it goes again,*" thought Charles.

"Right here," Kirby responded by digging in her wallet, finding her license, and passing it over.

"What are you up to today with that brown thing between your legs, Miss Clark?" Trooper Fran asked, biting her lip so as not to burst out laughing.

"It's a bag of assorted teas and chocolates from Trader Joe's," snapped Kirby, adding a scowl.

"Huh. I'm sure you don't remember me. I was in Champlain Elementary School when you were puckin' with the guys in high school."

"How could I forget you, Francine," Kirby said, her face flushing.

"Detective, I'm giving you two tickets, not warnings. One for speeding, and I require touching the brakes before going through a blinking yellow. Which you did not do. That'll cost you $380 if mailed in on time and uncontested. You're not going to contest it, show up in court for a hearing, are you?"

"Highly unlikely I will contest. But, really $380? Ouch!"

"Yeah, we're very protective of our people up here. Don't forget to put on a stamp. If I made it out for what you were really doing, we'd have to go in front of a judge, who happens to be my sister-in-law. She'd probably be extra mean."

"Thank you, Officer . . . Francine Forget? Or is it pronounced For-jay?" Charles asked, tongue in cheek, hoping she might think he was being friendly in a cute manner.

"That's Trooper Forget, pronounced 'Forget.' It's not like the retailer Target, which is often said as 'Tar-jay.' I'm not French-like, nor is my name Frenchie. Both which I do not like at all."

"Thanks for the clarification."

Trooper Forget used her handheld PocketJet mobile printer to print out Charles' two tickets, one for speeding and one for busting the intersection. Charles took a minute to look them over and noted two blaring mistakes.

"Where're you staying?"

"I'll be in an inn or motel along the way. Miss Clark has her own place."

She glanced at Kirby, "Sure you are. Well, as of yet, there's no law against Flatlanders breeding with Chucks. I suggest you slow down, Detective White."

"Gotcha," answered Charles, somewhat bemused.

They gingerly pulled off the dirt strip and got back onto Route 116. Trooper Forget in the Dodge cruiser turned off the car's flashers, made a u-ie, and sped back to her haunt.

Charles looked over to Kirby, "What's this about you and every person we run into?"

Kirby shrugged innocently, "I was popular. Even with the girls."

* * * * * *

Tilda sat serenely in the antique rocker on the front porch reminiscing. This morning, she had decided to dress up a bit, wearing her favorite frilly white blouse and a skirt that looked like a Scotsman's kilt. All the colors nicely clashed with her insanely multicolored knitted scarf and her indoor yellow galoshes.

Timothy was nearby on the porch top step, mirroring James Dean in his blue jeans, check-patterned shirt, and paisley bandana. For some unfathomable reason, today was a good day for a short black leather vest. Of course, the red cowboy boots were there. In the beginning, Timothy's details were limited by the extent to which Tilda was willing to imagine.

Years before, when she was addicted to television, Tilda loved the Dr Pepper commercials with the flashy dancing and catchy music. And didn't the young dancer wear a short black vest? She did love seeing Timothy in the black leather vest. Who could forget the zippy, unforgettable lyrics: "I'm a Pepper, you're a Pepper?" She remembered move for move the dance routine and the marvelous granny character she planned to emulate when she got old.

Tilda had spent most of this morning revising what she had written the night before. That masculine hulk, Charles, who forced his way into her steamy thoughts, had been urgently entered into the hallowed pages of *Final Love*. Occupying fewer words, but also inserted, was his harlot, the one determined to yen-yang Timothy.

"Timothy, you want the rest of my refreshment before it gets warm?"

"No thanks, Sis. I want reefer."

Tilda opened a small tin, previously used for Altoids mints, now stuffed with her homegrown marijuana. Inside the tin were two fat joints already rolled and set to be fired up. On the table beside her was a box of wood matches and several packs of Bambú rolling papers.

She had hardly taken a few unladylike tokes when a cloud of dust appeared up her driveway where it met the tarmac. A vehicle was coming to the house.

"Timothy, someone's coming on our road!" Salivating her finger, she extinguished the joint and put it back in the Altoids tin.

"I'm not at home." In a puff, he disappeared.

The car-like thing pulled up to the house and stopped a few yards from the porch. On closer inspection, it was either a spaceship or some big mechanical roach. When she saw who got out, she was dazed.

Was her passionate plea heard over the evil forces of the wall? Had he been compelled to return? Damn! Why'd he bring the harlot?

"You two again! What do you want?" Tilda said, coming off the porch and flaying her arms as if she was being bothered by insects. She wanted to start off with an aggressive show rather than simply caving to his awesome powers.

"We come bearing gifts," said Charles, offering her the Trader Joe's bag. "We brought you three different teas and a sweet selection of fine chocolates."

Tilda pretty much ripped the bag out of his hands and dove into it. Kirby stepped forward.

"Hi, remember me? I'm Kirby, friends call me KC. I was hoping your brother was around so we could talk fish down by the pit."

"Nope, he's gone. Won't be back until late tonight."

Tilda was satisfied with the gift.

"Handsome, we gonna sip this tea you brought?"

"I'd love to."

"Well, come on in."

Kirby was only a foot behind and ready to hit the first step of the porch when Tilda shrieked: "Not you, girlie! You can go to my pit and talk to the fish all you like, but no fishing!"

"Okay, thank you, Tilly. I'll mosey down and have a look-see. Maybe come back in . . .?"

Charles put his hand by the pocket where he kept his cell. She acknowledged by patting her pocket where she had hers.

"One-half hour," he said, precisely.

Following a few steps behind Tilda, Charles noted the porch floorboards were soft underfoot, a sign of a rotten support structure. The outer screen door was loose and flimsy on the hinges. When Tilda had to give it a muscular tug to open, it went out of kilter, leaving doubt as to how tightly it would close. The traditional main inner door, with four small glass panes at eye height, was held open by a circular antique umbrella stand that had dancing deer painted around it. That door had been recently replaced and new rubber insulation was added around the frame.

By whom? wondered Charles.

Stepping directly into the living room and near darkness, Charles was hit by the offending odors of mouse droppings and decaying wood. The few pieces of furniture were obscured by stacks of boxes loosely bound with string, piles of junk mail, collections of magazines, and old newspapers. The boxes were so high and overloaded, they had collapsed and fallen against the window blinds. The slats had crumpled so that the only light in the room came from a few errant rays of sunlight peeking through.

Completely wrapping the four walls of the room and directly at head level ran a clothesline strung with empty plastic water jugs, the type of gallon jugs people bought for homes with bad wells.

"I see you're saving water jugs," mentioned Charles, watching Tilda spend a moment considering where they were to sit.

"I try to recycle everything. Maybe I'll donate them to the high school. I'm thinking art classes can make candle holders out of them."

In the middle of the room on a Victorian roll-top desk sat Tilda's Acer laptop and a single antique ladder-style seat. Catty-corner to the desk were two smaller antique chairs whose fabric seats were well worn, exposing the base threads. Across the room near the kitchen was a tattered couch partially covered by an antique broken-star quilt. It fleetingly reminded Charles of his grandmother who had two heirloom quilts saved from her immigrant family who had settled in Detroit. Centered overhead was a ceiling light fixture whose multiple bulbs were black.

"Tilly, why don't you fix that light? It'd make getting around all your boxes and things a lot easier."

"I keep forgetting to buy bulbs. I'm too busy to remember everything, so you needn't point out my shortcomings if you want to be friends."

"I understand." Charles was immediately struck with another unexpected oddity—no framed snapshots of family or any hanging art.

Of course, one could consider the string of empty jugs some sort of art statement.

"Follow me, we'll visit in the kitchen. Timothy agrees to clean the living room. He promises a lot and then disappears. I can't get that boy to do nothin.'"

The kitchen was slightly cleaner than the rest of the house. Long ago, it had been a quaint country kitchen. Frilly curtains hung over a deep white ceramic sink. A scrubbed worn, yellow Formica counter rested on Sears catalog 1940's wood cabinets. Above, on two walls, were open shelves wrapped in red-and-white check-patterned shelf paper, exposed layers of dust and grease.

Tilda indicated he should sit at the table in the middle of the room on one of the four ancient cane chairs. Unceremoniously, she dumped the Trader Joe's bag of goodies on the table.

"Oh my, don't these look good. You remembered! Remembered what I like!"

Instead of water from the sink tap, she poured water from a new plastic jug into a kettle and fired it on the 1960's four-burner gas range.

"I only use tap water if I boil it. Get the trots if I don't. See, I'm going to the use the expensive water so we don't take any chances. I keep the store-bought water upstairs to brush my teeth and down here for tea or coffee. I keep my hydration by drinking Dr Pepper. It's approved by a doctor, Dr. Pepper. You knew that, didn't you? It provides me with all the vital nutrients I need and gives me a burst of energy when I get sluggish."

Tilda drew two cups and saucers from a shelf and placed them on the table. "I've extra empty water containers in the living room if you like 'em. Just untie the line and slip them off. Take all you want."

After a quiet moment, Charles remarked, "I don't see a television. That surprises me."

"It's upstairs, and I'm having antenna trouble. I spend more time now on the Acer anyway."

While she fussed with the boxes of tea and chocolates, Charles studied the splitting lathed walls, sloping plank floor, and cracking ceiling. Rehabilitation was an expensive fantasy. A buyer would be best served by shutting off the electricity, capping the water and gas lines, and using a bulldozer to take it all down.

Who in their right mind would be foolish enough to keep it—Kirby.

"We're all set! Let's go with the matcha green tea, shall we?"

"Sure."

"We'll follow up with the S'mores. Sound good?"

"Definitely."

The water was steaming. Tilda arranged the cups, filled them with boiling water, and gave Charles a tea bag.

"Forty-seven seconds will do exactly right," she said, dipping her tea bag. He could see by her little mouth quivers she was silently counting. Forty-seven seconds would be an eternity, he couldn't wait.

"I'd like to know more about you, Tilly. You're an authentic Vermont original?"

"None of your beeswax," she said and stopped counting.

"Okay, just wanted to know where you got the name Tilly. Is it an old family name?"

"I wasn't around then to have an opinion, but from where I'm living, it might well have been from a cow," she said, followed by an unladylike raspberry. "Timothy came later. He was named after a neighbor."

"Well, it's a big job keeping a farm together. That's a lot of work." Charles was fishing to keep the conversation going.

"Timothy, he pitches in when around. Sam comes by and helps, too."

"Sam?"

"Sam's Garage. Sam Piper is a sweet but over-priced mechanic in Bristol. Do your own tea bag. I can't do everything for you."

"Sure." Nonplussed, he worked his bag around the chipped tea cup. The tea had a nice aroma.

"You were telling me about Timothy and his work."

"Oh, he's all over the place. Very, very successful lawyer. Advises companies from Montpelier to Chicago. Spends way too much time in the Boston headquarters."

"You miss him, do you?"

"That's hard to answer."

"I'd like to meet him."

"You'd like to meet him? Thought that girlie friend of yours wanted to meet him. For fishing, huh? She wants to do something else; I wasn't born yesterday. I'm opening these S'mores," she clawed into the box with her nails.

"I'm guessing you might be like all the others, thinking I'm crazy or something because I . . . well, you know how old folks get."

"Why should I think that?"

"I may get a little confused once in a while, but all I want to do is spread my message of love and happiness. You couldn't have known this, but I ran the library in town. They gave me the Acer for my decades of outstanding of service."

"What an honor," said Charles.

"At first, I thought she was just a tool to write poetry and do shopping. Well, wasn't I surprised to find I had been chosen to combat an evil presence!"

"Really? That's interesting. Tell me about it?"

"Sure! It comes down to the wall's devilish aims. You know, the wall where we met at my pit. If you must know, *Final Love*, my latest novel, infuriated the malevolent forces radiating from the wall. She came to the rescue; *she* being my dear Acer. Well, anyway, Timothy and I devised a plan using the wolfsbane against it. You see, the wall's not covered with wolfsbane by chance—they're in cahoots."

"In cahoots?" Charles hesitated. *Hold on, Detective, do you seriously want to go further into Tilda's psychosis?*

"Yes, the wall and wolfsbane. Ah, but here's our trick! Timothy and I have turned the wolfsbane into an instrument of good. So, the baddie force in the wall is pretty pissed off. If you get my drift."

"I'm not sure I follow," he said.

"Oh really, come now. You've seen those spooky movies. You know all about evil forces in inanimate things. You can't kid me."

"I wouldn't try to kid you, Tilly. Anyway, what can I say? That's all very exciting."

"Yeah, that *exciting* part has been a problem. Timothy says I have to have more sex in it, spice it up. You know, do what the market demands and everything."

Charles' mind was racing. *She was mentally ill and clearly took no medication but still carried on a semi-normal existence. Was it because she could slough off her abnormal behavior to Timothy? Or because she was driven by an engrossing goal, a message of love to help others? Her alliance with a laptop to fight evil emanations of a rock wall, that's pretty hard to reconcile with sanity.*

Tilda crammed a whole S'more in her mouth, crumbs tumbling down and off her blouse.

"Excuse me! Please help yourself. Lordy, where are my manners!" She flicked a few crumbs off her blouse, took another s'more, then slid the box over to him.

"No, thank you. Tell me more about your book."

"All I can say is, literary agents are dying in New York City to present it to publishers."

"Outstanding, Tilly. Bravo!" Charles stroked down the small hairs rising on his neck. *Nope, wasn't the brother doing the crime. It was Tilly. All her show.*

"I haven't signed with a big agent. Timothy wants us to deal with the smaller, nicer apples."

"What do you mean?"

"There's a group of big bad apples that control who gets published. Those big bad apples ignore all the fine work done by starting-out writers. *Final Love* is being blacklisted but, as we all know, 'what's good for the goose is good for the gander.' So, them big apples are getting their comeuppance by the wolfsbane."

"How are you doing that?"

"What's your name? Sorry, I forgot."

"Charles."

"What do you do anyway, Charles?"

"I'm a public employee, retiring. Thinking of Vermont as a place to live permanently."

"Oh. So, Charles, as I was saying, literary agents, they're a pretty rough bunch. We call 'em Disregards. They're the big apples that crowd out the little good apples who, in a just world, would be representing writers like me. The Disregards are in cahoots with that evil wall."

"Disregards are in cahoots with the big bad apples and the wolfsbane?"

"Jesus, Charles, you've got to get this straight. You're confusing the whole point! Disregards are literary agents who don't write back and send insulting form rejection letters about my lovely queries," Tilda was exasperated.

She took another sip of tea. "I know for a fact that cursed wall is colluding with them big apples to keep my message from getting out."

"And what are you doing about that?"

"You are slow, did anyone ever tell you? I'll explain it again. We've cross-circuited the wall's power by using its underling, the wolfsbane, to do good. We're teaching the Disregards a lesson by using the wolfsbane against them! Are you getting what I'm saying or do I have to repeat it ad infinitum!"

She latched onto another s'more.

"Yes, now I get it." Charles stood up. "I have to be on my way. Thank you, Tilly." He pushed back from the table and rose to leave. "How do you get around? I don't see a car."

"Slobberu. She's getting a new head gasket at Sam Piper's Garage in Bristol. He's a dear brown man and swears he'll be finished soon. I've known Sam for years but he's a car mechanic so I'm not holding my breath."

"Slobberu must be a Subaru! I see you in a red wagon."

"That's pretty good. Before you leave, would you help me adjust my TV antenna? It's a two-person job, one to turn the rabbit ears, the other to watch the screen," she said, wiping her lips with her palm.

"Sure."

"Come this way, it's just upstairs."

They left the kitchen, weaving through the living room's chaos to the staircase.

He followed Tilda up the well-worn stairs onto a second floor and a short hallway. There was an open door on each side and a center door at the very end. The bathroom? He peeked into a room on the left, an empty room without a stick of furniture. The floor had a layer of dust and small white pieces of plaster that had fallen from a cracking popcorn ceiling. Two small windows with the frames sealed with gaffer's tape, unwashed in decades, let a yellowish glow invade from the outside. No curtains, no shades. Only a dangling wire from the center of the ceiling.

She led him through a door on the right, her bedroom, which was surprisingly spotless and tidy. Her two windows, similarly placed as in the first room, were clean and had frilly transparent curtains. A small four-lighted chandelier hung from the ceiling. The plank-board floor had a large faded oriental rug covering most of the room. Against one wall was a five-drawer credenza and an open closet niche, which revealed a clutch of haphazardly hanging women's clothing.

A neatly made duvet-covered queen bed, sheet tightly tucked in as done in a hotel, rested between two circular marble-topped side tables. Both had newer lamps and shades. The left table had a half glass of water that was likely filled by the plastic jug on the floor. Beside the glass was a small faded framed photo of a young Tilda and a child with a straw hat and some sort of costume. Who was that? Resting on the credenza between a mess of combs and hair brushes was an early color TV. The TV was unplugged.

A full-sized antique mirror on pivots was in front of the bed. The unusual placement of the mirror should have alerted Charles because a millisecond later, Tilda reached out, grabbed his wrist, and tugged him toward the bed.

"Don't say a thing," she whispered.

"Hold on, Tilly. That's not going to happen," and forcibly undid her grip.

"Why not? Because you have that tramp? I don't care! It will work out fine for us."

Tilda flopped onto the soft, engulfing bed and rolled onto her back. Seductively hiking up her Scotsman-like kilt, she created a jaw-dropping scene reminiscent of vintage black-and-white pornographic films.

"Would you like to watch me first?" she coyly asked.

"Tilly, this is not acceptable behavior, is it?"

"Who cares? Free yourself from the harlot. We can be together."

Charles turned away and swiftly charged downstairs while speed-dialing Kirby.

"KC, where the hell are you?"

"On the porch, right out the front door. Be careful, the steps are rotten."

"Let's go. Double-time into the car."

CHAPTER 42

Imagine Mrs. Robinson thirty years older, on crack, and very, very horny

As soon as they hit the blacktop, Kirby blurted, "Alright, Charlie, spit it out—what the hell happened?"

"Imagine Mrs. Robinson thirty years older, on crack, and very, very horny."

"Who is Mrs. Robinson? Never mind, I'll google later."

"Right now, GPS us to Sam Piper's Garage. She said Bristol."

Kirby worked the touchscreen panel. "Bristol. Four miles, turn left before the speed trap."

"Great."

"Charlie, we want to buy this farm. We want it for us, Charlie."

"Figures," he said with an exhausted exhale. "I'm guessing there's fish there."

"Correction. There's big, big fish there. Monsters."

They stopped at a yield sign to make the left turn as directed by the GPS. Charles had a thoughtful moment with his fingers playing on the steering wheel, obviously not onboard with her enthusiasm.

"I sounded greedy and selfish, didn't I?"

"Our suspect is mentally ill. I can't scheme against her best interests. Understood?"

"Completely understood. I got it and agree!"

He took a big breath, recapturing her attention, "But if things were to fall our way, and taking care of her needs in an honest, fair and legal process, well, we'll see."

"I got it. Don't think bad of me, Charlie."

"We're cool." They drove on.

"Charlie, I got excited and felt you were going that way, too. I just got carried away by our whole adventure."

"I agree." *Carried away?* Charles twisted uncomfortably in his seat. *Did KC just toss Tilly a lifeline?*

"If we can save Tilly Duclos from jail and want a crack at her farm, we're going to have to exterminate Timothy," he said quietly, but she heard him.

"Charlieee! What the hell are you talking about? Exterminate Timothy! Jesus Christ! After the Saint Charles lecture? I'm with Jeffrey Dahmer!"

He reached into a side pocket and fished out a pair of fancy and expensive Roka Phantom Ti Aviators sunglasses. This elicited a deadpan gaze from Kirby.

"Your way of changing the subject, putting on sunglasses?"

"It's my Miami Vice look. Gift from the department after getting shot."

"They do nothing for me. Turns you and your car into a pimpmobile. They'd look better on me."

"I'll know what to get you for Christmas."

"So, the way I see it, Charlie, doesn't sound like Timothy would be a great loss to mankind or the performing arts."

He laughed. "You're something else. Timothy exists in some twilight space with Tilly. We'll have to get rid of him to save her."

"Sam's Garage is here," she blurted. "Stop, stop, it's on the corner!"

They pulled off the road at Sam's Garage and parked behind the open bay with Tilda's red Subaru on the lift. Noting all the parts strewed about, it was getting to be an expensive repair.

The corner lot had been a gas station in the fifties and sixties until the new self-service pump became a necessity. The little Bristol gas station didn't have the volume to be supported by the smallest independent distributor. Despite an exterior patina of neglected paint and a striking collection of vampire graffiti on the concrete block walls, Sam's garage was not rundown. Inside was a single bay with a hydraulic lift that was kept in new condition. The rest of the shop was meticulously equipped with the metric tools needed to keep every model of Subaru alive. Over the years, Sam Piper had become the local go-to guy for ailing Subarus, especially the early models. Behind the garage and crawling up the slope to a defining tree border was a huge graveyard of early-model Subarus. Dozens of cars and parts of cars were slowly being overcome by a rising forest of shrubs and high weeds.

* * * * * *

Sam Piper was a muscular tall black man somewhere in his late fifties to early sixties with short, curly black hair going grey on both sides. A poorly trimmed patch of white whiskers on his chin was an attempt to disguise an odd-shaped scar. There were so many grease stains on his military surplus flight coveralls, the underlying khaki hue was blotted out. They watched him wet the sealing ring on a new oil filter with an oily finger and twist it in. When the screwing ended, he stepped out from under the car.

"You must be Sam Piper," said Charles.

"Before you say anything, I can't touch that Corvette."

"It runs fine, but breeds tickets." Charles looked at the lift. "Tilda Duclos' Subaru?"

"It is. Let me clean up." Taking a red rag to his oily fingers, "What's she done now?"

"Hard to say."

"You the law?"

"Detective Charles White, NYPD. No big worries, I'm on sort of a vacation. This is Kirby Clark."

"Yeah, I know about Kirby Clark. Didn't remember she was so pretty."

There's some backstory about KC I'm definitely not in on, thought Charles.

"You better come inside. It's air conditioned."

Kirby and Charles sat down in two old oak wood secretary chairs, the scary type that would let you lean back a few inches then jerk a notch or two, alerting you that you were destined to topple. They faced Sam's desk which was piled with receipts and work orders. His chair was one of those massive green leather things, the type normally found in a 1930s bank president's office. Period-correct with the furniture, he had a manual adding machine—the one with large buttons and the big yank-it handle. Old steel file cabinets lined the walls between the two doors. Atop one cabinet was a small color TV. One door led to the shop and the other to the outside.

Sam relit a nasty-looking cigar stub. The engulfing puff of smoke made him cough and rub his tearing eyes.

"Smoking's permitted," after a final, nasty cough. "How much trouble is Tilly in today?"

"Couldn't get worse," said Charles.

"Ah, shit. Anything I can say or do to keep her from being arrested?"

"That's why we're here, hoping for a better outcome."

"I love Miss Tilly despite all the craziness she puts me through— things you'd not believe. But there's something sweet, maybe not sweet, but kinda like a lost puppy you want to look after. Something's sad in those bright eyes. Beats me."

"She does get your attention, I give you that," said Charles.

"Can you tell us where to find her brother," asked Kirby.

Sam howled and fell back into his chair. "What brother?"

"Yeah, I figured that out as soon as I stepped inside her house," said Charles, catching Kirby's surprised look. "There hasn't been a man there in decades. Bro Timothy is only in her mind."

"Did she try to get you to do anything . . . uh, like yen-yang?" asked Sam, apprehensively rubbing his forearm.

"I was able to resist her in the bedroom, if that's what you mean." They burst out laughing, ignoring a glower from Kirby.

"Come on, guys." She looked at Charles like he was expected to say something. "Jesus, Charlie, stop fucking around and tell Sam everything!"

"Tilly and her nonexistent brother gave six New York City residents near-death experiences. I'm here trying to get a jump on how it happened."

"No shit." Sam Piper was at a loss, unsure what to say. He took a moment to calmly pick cigar crap off his lips. Finally, "New Yorkers? Does she get a medal?"

Charles leaned forward, nonverbally messaging that this was no time for games.

"Sam, tell us everything you can about her," responded Kirby.

"Guys, I've never said nothin' about Dizzy Tilly to anyone. Frankly, telling you two will be a sort of confession for me. Get comfortable. It's complicated."

They resettled their feet and cautiously leaned back in the sprung chairs.

"I grew up in Salisbury, graduated high school at least two decades after her. By the way, I was the highest grade-point average black student in our school. Truth be told, I was the only black student."

"Yeah, this part of the state is racially challenged," said Kirby.

"Anyway, I went into the army and did a tour. Mostly in the Philippines repairing rotorcraft."

It was time for Sam to pick more bits of tobacco crap from the slimy end of the cigar.

"Mama Rose was real old or dead when I saw Tilly again. Her dad had died in WWII; that's an interesting story in itself. The Wilcox family owned this rustic old inn run by her mom."

Sam stopped, played with the stogie, and seemed to be debating whether to carry on.

"I remember she was called Dizzy Tilly because she drank like a fish and she'd laugh at anything. She wasn't all that attractive. I mean, she was nice-looking, but any attention a boy gave her was appreciated. You know what type of reputation you can get for that." Sam thought he was finished.

"There's more, Sam," probed Charles.

"Oh, yeah. From what I heard, she went to the Winter Ball alone, followed by a midnight party in the woods with some of her pals. I'd assume a large amount of hard liquor was consumed. Beside a blazing campfire, being drunk, and smoking, along with all the other carryings-on, she lost clothes. I heard, to use the crude phrase, 'took on the football squad,' or at least her male friends who were up for it. She crashed hard and ended up in Rutland Hospital for a few nights."

"Police report filed?" Charles asked.

"Nah, no one ever brought it to the police. The hospital's got an overdose record, you'd think."

"I can check on that."

"She was an item for years around Salisbury, then she just dropped off the chit chat."

"Yeah, things have a life, and then everyone gets tired of it. Sorry, go on, Sam," said Kirby.

"Decades later, she's an assistant librarian in town. I'd get a call to fix what she's done to the Subaru so she can get to work. There are times when she's totally normal—I mean, grounded in reality. Other times, she's a space cadet and her mind's all over the place. Over the years, I'd see she was struggling. And then, all of a sudden, this brother 'appears.' That's where the real insanity comes in. She makes like he's real. It's crazy. That's all I can say, without sounding more stupid than I am."

"No father, no family, a victim of sexual predation, being mentally ill. It's a nightmare," said Kirby, voice cracking, turning away from the men, not wanting to show how affected she felt.

"Anyway, we won't know what goes on in her head 'til she writes a book about it," said Sam.

"She's doing that," said Charles standing up. "All our targeted victims are literary agents and women. But two male partners were mistakenly poisoned."

Kirby looked up from her phone. Held her hand up, stopping the conversation. "I googled 'Name for poisoning literary agents'. There's no official name for killing literary agents."

"That's good to know, I guess," said Sam bemused.

"There's not one connection to another human being in the whole house except for an old framed picture in her bedroom of her and a child in a straw hat. The shot was so small, I couldn't tell if it was a boy or girl. But no pictures of a mom or dad. Not even a blinking Jesus on a wall."

"She's been a loner since I've known her. Believe me, she's got no one," said Sam.

"I hesitate to tell you, but Tilly believes the old stone wall behind the barn has taken on an evil presence. It's what's kept her novel, *Final Love*, from getting a literary agent and published. She's combating this evil presence with the help of her Acer laptop that does some sort of automatic writing when she touches the keyboard."

Charles indicated with tossed-up hands that it was all unfathomable.

"This is too effing freaky. You sure we want to get further involved?" Sam asked, after searching and then finding a longer cigar butt in the large porcelain Michelin ashtray. "Sorry folks, I'm out of smokes." He fired up the butt, then went through the whole coughing, teary-eyed thing again.

"That's only part of it. Let me finish. Tilly and Timothy are using wolfsbane, an underling to the wall, to get back at agents who don't respond to their queries. These agents are called Disregards or bad apples. Tilly is convinced using the wall's precious wolfsbane to get rid of the Disregards will essentially be an act of goodness and will diminish the evil powers of the wall."

Kirby and Sam simultaneously burst out laughing. Sam's stogie flew out of his mouth and bounced across his desk. "Man oh man, this is fucked up."

"It's so sad," said Kirby, burying her face in her palms.

"I've known people who believe a stop light is sending them messages. If this suspicion becomes embedded and isn't treated, it's full-blown paranoia. I had encounters with a young man who acted normal but was certain the CIA had planted a chip in his brain. Didn't know why, couldn't explain it. There's little doubt in my mind Tilly Duclos has a schizoaffective disorder with heightened, aggressive sexual urges. That we can't do much about; it's the criminal route she's taken to get her love message out that must be stopped."

Sam found and revived the wayward cigar. "Timothy, the freakin' wall, the wolfsbane—this is crazy shit! If you think we can do something for her, *you* might be delusional."

"That's counterproductive, Sam," cautioned Kirby.

"Timothy, her odd creation, must've had the idea to take revenge on literary agents. If we can isolate him, keep him from controlling her, there's a chance for us to sidetrack the investigation."

"If we can do that, I'm all in," said Sam.

"Now, I know what you meant when you said, 'we're going to have to exterminate Timothy,'" said Kirby, pointing a finger at Charles.

It was time to leave. Charles and Kirby carefully rose from the hair-raising chairs.

"Let's think about solutions before I have to put the law on her," said Charles.

"I'll do whatever I can," said Sam Piper, extending his hand for a shake. Kirby hugged him.

Charles took one of Sam's business cards from the stack on the desk. They walked through the garage under the steel rollup door to Charles' car.

"Sam, don't fix her car. You can't get the right parts or whatever she'll believe."

"No problem, Charlie. We're a small community; we try to look after each other. Dizzy Tilly kinda slipped through the cracks, she being so confrontational."

"Happens all the time," Charles dug out his wallet and gave him his card. Tried to hand Sam two fifties. "Can you make sure she has some food?"

"Nah, keep the money. I help Tilly 'cause I like the old fruitcake and maybe it'll make up for all the shitty things I've done in my past. I drop in on her every few days with staples: soups, veggies, that kind of stuff. Man oh man! She eats a lot of hamburgers, and I can't get her enough Dr Pepper! Anyway, I stay five minutes. Gives her a chance to bitch about how long I'm taking on her car."

Kirby turned to Sam as they got into the 'Vette, "If Tilly has no heirs, would you be up for buying her farm?"

"Fuck no! Living next to herds of crazy shit cattle! When the wind blows the wrong way, hell, I grew up with that. *No mas.*"

"You're sure?" asked Charles.

"I've got a cabin by Sugarbush, my boys are in Pennsylvania, and I've got secret plans with a young thing when I retire. God's been good to me: got all I need and want."

"If we bought her farm fair and square and were able to get proper care for her, which is going to cost a bundle, would you feel bad about us?" probed Kirby.

"KC, you're getting carried away. It's premature to . . . "

"Fuck no!" interrupted Sam. "Please, please, buy the damn farm while it's still worth something! Get her into a facility and therapy. One that will keep her off the road, too. That'll be a winner for everyone."

"We'll be on our way. See ya," said Charles, starting the 'Vette, which idled to a low rumble.

As they backed out, Sam cautioned, "I highly recommend cooling it, under thirty, well past the blinking yellow. You don't want to meet hell-on-wheels with a badge, Trooper Francine Forget."

"Been there, done that," bemoaned Charles. They drove off.

* * * * * *

Later that night, Charles did an investigation of Trooper Francine Forget's family. First a look into the RTCC database, then into the National Crime

Information Center, and finally a dive into the crime database shared by the U.S. and Canada known as the Automated Canada-U.S. Police Information Exchange. After hours of digging, what Charles found led to an uneasy conclusion: the Forgets were sort of a rural-based mafia but without guns and bloodshed. Eek! He wasn't going to complain to Trooper Fran or say a word to anyone.

CHAPTER 43

Is it too early to start drinking?

Charles was on the sofa scratching Mister Fritz, who was nestled between his legs. He was blankly staring at the laptop wishing it would begin writing on its own, like Tilda Duclos' Acer. Kirby sat on the floor in white shorts directly in front of him, her feet crossed and tucked, looking much like a fifties bobby-soxer. She was waiting for the right moment to launch into Charles; she had a lot on her mind. After a string of sighs from Charles, there was no better moment.

"Are we going to do something, Charlie? Before something happens to mess this up for us."

"What?" he said, not looking up.

"Is it too early to start drinking?" she answered.

"I've got to catch up with RTCC," evading her question.

He leaned toward his laptop, fingers getting ready.

"You want some lunch? Tuna fish on toast?"

"No, thanks. KC, let me get this taken care of, then I can relax."

"Fish! Damn! Charlie, I forgot to tell you! Remember down at the pit, the cellophane stuffed in Tilly's wall?"

"Vaguely."

"So, I'm watching the water glide by, there's a small current in the pit, and I'm wondering how deep it is. And guess what happens?"

"What happens?"

"No, guess."

"Please, don't do that. What happened?"

"What comes up to the surface but an enormous rainbow! Followed by another and another. Maybe not a state record yet, but each is a monster. Eight, nine pounds at least. I'm stunned! It so odd they just came up, did little gulps of air, then went back down."

"Fish do that sometimes naturally. Gulpers."

"That's true, but back to the cellophane stuck in the wall. I got a stick and dug it out. It had a grocery store label. Guess."

"Please don't do that, just tell me."

"Ground beef 80/20 from Grand Union in Bristol!"

He was taken aback. "Campers?"

"Jesus, Charlie, you *are* a city boy! Tilly's feeding her fish hamburger! That's why they came up when they saw me at the water's edge. Feeding time!"

"What a hoot! Don't tell Sam Piper. He's buying chuck and she's feeding it to her fucking fish!"

"That explains why she doesn't want anyone fishing. They're her pets."

Charles closed the laptop, no longer interested in punching keys. "I now have a craving for a burger. You?"

"Great diner not far from VAMP. When they're baking pies, I can smell 'em."

"What about Mister Fritz?"

"He'll stay and protect. I'll bring him scraps." Kirby looked at Mister Fritz, "I promise."

On the way to the diner, they went past the VAMP office. Kirby's red Jeep Cherokee was still parked in front but now covered with a coat of yellow pollen.

"Shouldn't we bring your car back to the townhouse?"

"Nah, not now. I'd have to go to Quickie Wash. The interior is filthy from Teddi, I'd have to vacuum. Getting her hair out is a pain. It's real work, skip it."

* * * * * *

Wood's Sunset Diner's exterior was like every boxcar diner Charles had ever visited, except inside it had stuffed deer heads at each end of the counter and multiple displays of antique fishing gear tacked to the walls. It was also oddly empty of customers. Passing by the register they could not miss the basket of maple syrup samples. Dollar apiece.

"Your good work?" asked Charles.

"You got it," she answered.

Both tempted to reward themselves with dessert first, they lingered over the display cooler filled with pastries and cream-style cakes. Undecided, they walked to the far end where the circular stools that spun around and Formica counter curved to a stop. They chose the last booth where the red Naugahyde was glossy and slick from decades of sliding butts.

"Fair warning: don't feel under the table," advised Kirby.

Betty, the waitress with her name stenciled on her blouse, came over carrying menus. "KC, why do you two want to sit way back here in the boonies?"

"I need to make a call or two, don't want to be rude to your customers," Charles answered, testing different pockets for his phone.

"Don't worry, you won't be. We'll be stone dead until the tree crew arrives, and they're deaf from their chainsaws. Coffee? Tea, water?"

"Water will be fine with a little slice of lemon, if you will."

"Ditto," nodded Charlie.

Betty sighed and lingered by their table, desirous for more conversation.

"This used to be a place to have a nice smoke and a quiet coffee. People didn't yell or get excited unless they were going to beat on each other. Kirby, you remember how it was. Chef would come out and beat on both of them, then toss 'em out. Now, with these cell phones, people blab away. Like we want to listen to their dreary day or sorry sex life."

Kirby ordered the special of the day: macaroni and cheese with chunks of lobster. Charles went for a cheeseburger made like a Whopper with onion rings, then asked Kirby for picking rights to any unfinished lobster macaroni.

Outside, a pair of trucks with buckets on folding arms for tree felling and limb trimming, parked on each side of the Corvette. Two crews dismounted, eyeballed Charlie's pride and joy, then came into the diner. Weathered men in grimy jackets and jeans speckled with wood chips, they sat on counter stools rather than soiling the booths. The eldest of the bunch, probably in his early seventies, wiry and surely having arms of steel, walked to the end stool, the one nearest Kirby and Charles.

"Well, I'll be damned, Kirby Clark! What a treat seeing you!"

Kirby was puzzled. Charles peered down into his glass of water, concluding *I'm a fucking idiot; there's some backstory she's not letting me in on.*

"You used to hang with my boy, Wilbur."

Waitress Betty came from the kitchen carrying six cups of steaming coffee. Each cup was sent sliding down to the end of the counter.

"Oh, geez, Mr. Clayton! Of course! How's Willie?"

"Lawyer in Baaaaaston. Two big kids, boys. Tolerable wife. They're all fine."

"That's great. Give him my regards. Sorry 'bout the wife."

"Hey, I remember your boy. How's he doing?"

"Davey's fine. Got me a grandson, Simon!" Kirby said gleefully.

"God bless. So, what have you been up to, sweetie?"

"I'm Director of Promotions at VAMP selling maple syrup."

"That sweetness must have bought you those nice wheels outside."

"Well, no," she pointed across the table, "this is Charles. He acts like an only child and won't share his toys. And I've known him for a whole three days! Can you believe it?"

Mr. Clayton chuckled, "That's a tragic mistake, but at least he's smart."

Charles dug out his cell and started to slide out, "Excuse me, got to go outside, make a call."

Mr. Clayton looked up, "No, no, sit right down. Call where you are, unless it's private. Won't bother me. I just need my coffee."

"Who you calling, Charlie?" asked Kirby.

"Martha Jane Sidel, the guild woman."

* * * * * *

In New York City, MJ was on her third cup of java sorting through receipts from the expo. In the last hour, she had arranged to have a colorful bouquet sent to her fallen speakers still in the hospital: Phylis, Jennifer, and Betty. Sending flowers was more like completing a business tradition from the guild after an expo and less like a personal message of friendship or caring about their illness. Pamela recovered, was wrestled back to work and was presently downstairs collecting the afternoon mail. MJ didn't need to spend sixty-eight dollars on flowers for her.

The office landline phone rang.

"Yes, this is she . . . Oh, Officer White. No, I don't have some time— I'm busy. Unless you're calling to inform me you've made an arrest?"

In the few prior conversations with Martha Jane Sidel, Charles had revisited the saying, "Familiarity breeds contempt." In her case, he hadn't decided where disdain and loathing ranked on the ladder of contempt.

"You'll hear from the office if we have new information or anything changes. I'm here with a very talented writer friend," he said, trying to sound upbeat.

"That's nice," MJ said, firing up a Kent.

"She sent a query to the guild several days ago. *Desperate Measures.* Sound familiar?"

"Yes, it does, but not for a query submission. Your friend should be aware, the title was used for a Hollywood film with megastars. Good luck using it."

"Oh. Title's not important at this stage."

"Normally, a query review takes six weeks. I'm at the computer. I'll take a look right now."

Charles gave Kirby a thumbs up and a reassuring wink. She signaled Betty for more coffee.

"Put her on speaker phone, Charlie. I want to hear, too."

MJ came back on. Kirby signaled crossed fingers for luck.

"Here it is . . . Yes, I've read the first paragraph. It's drivel, crapola. Couldn't read another word."

"What?"

"Officer White, it's tripe. That's 't' as in terrible, 'r' as in revolting, 'i' as inane, 'p' as in pathetic . . . "

"I get it! You'll send her a note. Maybe, 'Thank you very much for your submission'?"

"Hell no! Sometimes we get fifty queries a day! That's 'd' as in dumb, 'a' as in . . ."

"Got it, got it! So, you'll never write back something constructive like your story is not up to our standards?" Charles was squirming.

"Jesus, not for crapola like this. Oh, maybe Pamela would. God bless her pity-patty little heart. She'll write a ditty to anyone just to keep her little conscious clean. Only one query in a hundred or more do I ask to see more pages. To this broad, I'd write—and only if I had a gun to my head, 'Don't quit your Dollar Tree job.'"

"Isn't that a little harsh?"

"Officer White, Kennedy said it best: 'Life is tough.'"

"It's Detective White. Thank you for your time," he disconnected.

* * * * * *

Betty brought their dinners and both dug in, trying to ignore the upsetting conversation with Martha Jane Sidel. They said nothing for a while. When the last bite of macaroni and lobster disappeared and only a few cold onion rings remained, Kirby came back to business with a vengeance.

"It wasn't tripe! She's a fuckin' whore! Bitch!"

"They all are," announced Clayton, who had overheard everything. "Well, most agents are."

"Why is that?" Charles asked, relieved to not have to respond to her.

"I've been writing for close to ten years, mostly fiction and thrillers. My latest is *On the Line: Tales from a Vermont Linesman*. I'm thinking a new direction might work."

"Mr. Clayton, I had no idea!" said Kirby.

"You're old enough now. It's Bob, please."

"Bob, you have an agent?" asked Charles.

"No, I don't have a damn agent! I've sent hundreds of them queries. Might get a little form letter back. 'I appreciate your sending the story, but I do not believe I can properly represent you . . .' Do they care if you've put your soul into something? I get pissed being so easily disregarded."

Charles' ears perked up on "disregarded", recollecting Tilly used the same term. "Does that make you feel like striking back, Bob?"

"Me? Hell, I'm an old toughie. I can take it." He took a sip of coffee. "But when my query goes unanswered or I get a form rejection letter, I do want to rooster 'em, wring their goddamn necks! I guess most wannabes suffer the humiliation and just let it slide."

"I think a lot of people feel that way," said Kirby.

Bob returned to his coffee while Charles and Kirby went for dessert, sharing a slice of banana cream pie and a cup of cinnamon rice pudding. When it was time to say goodbye, Kirby went to hug lineman Bob, but he unexpectedly shied away from her.

"I've been climbing all day and I'm covered with poison ivy. Hug me double-deep next time."

"You *are* a charming, thoughtful man, Mr. Clayton—I mean, Bob!"

Waitress Betty worked out their bill and rang it up on the classic door popping register.

"Hey, Betty, anyone not finish a burger? I've got a pup at home not too proud eating after others, if you know what I mean," stated Kirby.

"I just dumped half a sirloin. Hold tight, I'll doggie bag it."

"That's going to make someone real happy," said Charles.

He over-tipped Betty if there's ever such a thing.

Back in the 'Vette, Charles rotated his head a few times attempting to dislodge some building tension. Kirby reached over and began massaging his neck.

"Just thought of something, KC. I wonder if Martha Jane Sidel has an arrest record?" Charles opened his laptop and went into the RTCC.

After a few minutes watching him on the keyboard and tired of being in suspense, Kirby asked: "Well, is the bitch out on parole?" followed by a guffaw.

"Nothing. One nuisance complaint against an unknown person accosting her on Third Avenue decades ago. Never found out who it was, and the complaint was dropped."

"What does it mean?"

"It means nothing to us."

CHAPTER 44

That little tart is getting quite uppity!

Pamela returned from the lobby with a load of mail. It was her first day back at Romance Agents & Writers Guild, and she was having a hard time reconciling being in the house of hell again. Using earphones, she was able to ignore MJ's request for a coffee refill. Undeterred, MJ devised a yet more demeaning manner of beckoning her: crumpling a Kleenex and tossing it across the room to skip across her desk.

"I spoke earlier with that dense Officer White," uttered MJ, shuffling papers around her desk when Pamela finally looked up.

"What did he want?" Pamela dropped the junk mail into her wastebasket.

"He had a writer friend send us a query. Days ago, I directed him to our submissions link. Guess he doesn't know how to read because the query was a piece of crap."

"Any news on the case?"

"Not a word, darling. Be a dear and take a look at the receipts in our in-basket. They need to be scanned and entered into our checking account for payment."

"That's what I was doing before you sent me to get the mail," replied Pamela smartly. "We need to cut speakers' checks."

"Let's hold off until we see how many new members we get in the next few weeks."

"MJ, everyone's out of the hospital. A check would give them a boost."

"Well, you know, they didn't actually speak at the expo. I mean, it wasn't my fault they got sick. Of course, you're getting paid for the time you were out. Call them and say the guild can't pay them for work not done."

"You want me to call them?" Pamela was incredulous.

"You can also say I had to find replacement speakers and cover all their expenses."

"What additional expenses? All I see are receipts for lunch trays of slice meats and cheeses and a few cases of bottled water. They total less than $400 for the three days," Pamela replied brusquely.

MJ thought: *That little tart is getting quite uppity!*

"While you figure out what's the right thing for our loyal guild associates, I'm going to take a look at our new queries." Pamela took out her frustration by arbitrarily rejecting any queries with a misspelling, too many semicolons, or run-on sentences.

Our new queries? Feeling a tinge of anxiety, MJ recognized there was another sheriff in town, and she was going to have to share the spoils.

* * * * * *

Charles had risen early, thrown on a sweatshirt and slacks, and was updating notes on his laptop. Kirby slept late, came downstairs, and made coffee. Afterward, she settled next to him on the sofa and, as she often did, tucked her feet under like she was thirty years younger. Mister Fritz ignored Charles and snuggled up to Kirby, looking for a tummy rub or more chow.

"Traitor. Just because she's feeding you sirloin," said Charles.

"Charlie, what's going to happen to Tilly if we don't help her?"

"Mahoney will send me to the Vermont D.A. to turn over what I know. Statements will come from Donnie, Alberts, and T. S. Santasomething in Bolton. They'll get a warrant to toss her farm and collect evidence. She'll be arraigned and put in some holding facility. Eventually, the Vermont Department of Health will step in . . . "

"Charlie, stop! Don't tell me more!"

"In six months, if she's lucky, she'll go into a permanent facility and avoid a trial. If New York wants punishment, it's a whole new ballgame. I'll be a persona non grata in Vermont and you could be in some doo-doo. We have to be careful, very careful."

Kirby moaned and carried on with expressive exhalations.

"And what about her farm?"

"Like your friend said, probably sold at auction. Proceeds might pay for her incarceration, depending on if she's tried in Vermont or New York. That I know next to nothing about. A lot has to happen for this to go our way, KC. You do know that, don't you?"

"Well, I'm optimistic. It's more doable since we don't have to 'exterminate' someone! We'll be doing an exorcism instead."

"I'll always wonder how far you'd be willing to go with that."

"Charlie, move on! I just blurt out stuff. Doesn't mean nothin'!"

"You realize how unethical it is for me to be in a financial transaction with Tilly Duclos. If Mahoney got wind of it, I'd be investigated and dragged in front of the commission. What we're doing for Tilly so innocently, could be misconstrued as a fraudulent, criminal act. Fortunately, they'd have a hell of a time messing with my pension. There are no forfeiture laws in New York for police pensions, but if convicted of fraud, they could confiscate through criminal forfeiture all my other assets. I could go to jail, sweetie."

"You mean your savings, your condo, and the Corvette I don't get to drive? Oh, fuck, Charlie, now you tell me."

He shrugged, "Let's not underestimate public optics and consequences."

"So, why did you ask Sam if he would buy the place?"

"Just kicking around ideas on how best to help her."

"It's hard to believe you're so magnanimous."

"Okay, I had us in mind, too."

"Come on, Charlie. If we figured out a fair way for her to sell to us, she wouldn't be indigent. She'd have cash and Social Security. Our way, she's in a private old folks' home and gets good care!"

"We'd have to ensure she can't launch some other craziness."

"Absolutely," agreed Kirby.

"Between New York and Vermont, millions of taxpayer money would be saved," he said, scratching his unshaven chin.

"And long-term damage to our maple industry would be averted!"

"And the six people she's poisoned, what justice do they get? How's Mahoney going to like having six unresolved attempted murders on his watch?"

"Charlie, your job is to stop crime and catch those who commit it. Right?"

"It's what I signed on for."

"We've caught the perp! We're just not letting the system decide how to punish her!"

"I wish it were so easy, KC. The last thing I want to do is to have her punished for being crazy."

"Charlie, this is all happening kinda quick, even for a loosey-goosey gal like me. I'm a gone-astray Christian, but I want to help Tilly. And it shouldn't be wrong for us to benefit in return. Correct?

Charles started to speak but stayed quiet, making her uncomfortable.

"Charlie, speak to me."

"Seriously I don't think I can, or should, swing all this on my own. If we're partners, it shouldn't be all my money."

"Hey, Charlie, for crying out loud. I'm not expecting you to do this alone! I'll have my half!"

"Really? Well, that's cool."

Two of Kirby's fingers did a walk across the space between them, landing on Charles' thigh. Not wanting to leave the subject of finances, he tried to ignore her. After a period of ambiguous exhales, he reached the necessary and significant point that was bothering him.

"KC, do you honestly have the resources to go fifty-fifty? We might be talking about a hundred thousand or more, each. It may have to be available as cash."

"I don't have that much cash on hand, but I have an income from my former, and I can easily get a second mortgage. Mom and Dad have a little package squirreled away for me, too. Yeah, Charlie, if we do this, I'll do my part. No sweat."

"It'll be a hoot putting that farm together."

"Charlie, Tilly would get what she needs. You'd be getting a low-maintenance, hot woman partner, a new place to call home, and the opportunity to raise monster trout. It's a win-win, dummy!"

"Okay, I'm in. But in the next few days if this doesn't come together, the idea is toast," said Charles, vigorously scratching his head, perhaps hoping to unseat some spectacular idea.

"I hear you," said Kirby.

"There's no way to help unless we get into Tilly's laptop. It's in her living room. I saw it."

"Why is that so important?"

"We need to know she's the only one involved. What if it's an Internet-based conspiracy? If Tilly's gone, will there be more poisoned samples of something else sent from co-conspirators?"

"Got ya. Getting to her computer, that's going to be a trick," noted Kirby.

"Another thing: realistically, can Tilly survive without Timothy?"

"You're thinking, if they're permanently separated, and he's done away with, she may self-destruct?" Kirby concluded with the worst-case outcome, "In that case, maybe she's better off being in an institution."

"You're going to make my head explode, but something's been bugging the hell out of me. How come every man or woman we meet seems to be . . . let's just say, very familiar with Kirby Clark?"

"That's not true. Let's see, well, Susan Williams at the dairy knew me. Trooper Fran, too. And there's . . . " He drooped his head.

"Okay, okay, Charlie. hold on to your britches. It's the Vermont High School Statewide Hockey Finals, televised on a Saturday night. Big time. We're behind two goals. It's only minutes before the final buzzer. Forward Kirby Clark, to the astonishment of hockey viewers throughout the Vermont sports universe, does a hat trick—an astounding three goals in seven minutes, forty-two seconds.

"That'll do it," he felt immediately better.

"Sorry for the dramatization."

Kirby sensed Charles needed a distraction. She rolled up his burgundy Colgate University sweatshirt, just a few inches, and began mindlessly picking at a few hairs around his naval. "You know, Charlie, the clothes you have look like Goodwill rejects. Your slacks are for corporate clowns. We need to buy you some clothes."

"I assumed I'd be home by now. What are you doing to my belly button?" Charles asked, raising one eyebrow.

"Nothin.' Just playing." She unhooked and slid his belt from the first loops.

"Just playing?" Charles raised an eyebrow.

"Oh, another thing, when we get Tilly settled, let's not mess up my alimony, okay?"

"This is the twenty-first century. Who needs to be married?" He put his hand on hers, making her pause. "KC, reassure me, there's no one else in your life who's going to want to pitchfork me to death?"

"Just relax. My ex is out of the picture. There's no one else but you." She began stroking like she was swimming across and around his chest in a relaxing massaging motion.

Charles glanced at Mister Fritz stretched out on the floor, one eye watching them. "Get in your bed." Fritz yawned, stretched, and ambled off to his spacious new bed in the kitchen.

In a tug, his tan permanent-press pants went to the floor. Colgate sweatshirt flew off. Taking him at a perfect angle, she had him aroused in seconds.

She unbuttoned her blouse, unsnapped her red bra, and squirmed out of the rest of her clothes. She slid atop him aiming to make slurpy smooches around his ear lobes, but he scooted further under her for a quick visit to her belly button, then charged south to tongue into her soft and wet place.

Everything was perfect and on the way to being blissfully resolved for Kirby—that was, until the sound of a fumbling key came from the front door. Before they could respond, the door banged open.

There stood Kirby's son, Davey, with three-year-old Simon tucked under one arm, a backpack slung over his shoulder, and a tote bag dragged by his other arm.

"Jesus Christ, Mom! What the fuck?"

CHAPTER 45

Mom, what's with the gun on the table?

Kirby leaped off Charles, grabbed her blouse and shorts, and raced into the half bath. He managed to slip into his underwear and slacks. Sweatshirt went on inside out.

Simultaneously, Mister Fritz came charging out of the kitchen, growling mad, and took to doing crazy leaps into the air at Davey and Simon.

"Get this monster away from us, please!"

Charles scooped up Mister Fritz and calmed him.

"Damnit, Davey! You could have at least called! I get to have some privacy, don't I!" screamed Kirby from the bathroom.

"My cell was dead. When I pulled in, some asshole's Corvette is parked in your spot."

"That'll be this asshole," said Charles meekly.

"I had to park way down the street and carry all of Simon's crap. My arms were full, and all I could think about was getting inside with all this stuff."

Since Mister Fritz was behaving, Davey put Simon down on the carpet. Kirby came out of the bathroom, "Really? Those fingers couldn't hit the buzzer or knock the knocker but were capable of digging out my door key," Kirby said incredulously.

"Mom, what's with the gun on the table? For Simon?"

She pulled Simon away before he could explore the coffee table where Charles had left his sidearm and holster. Charles took his gear upstairs and a minute later, cautiously reappeared.

"Cut it, Davey," Kirby snapped, anger eclipsing any embarrassment.

"Yeah, well, now Simon and I have an image we'll never forget. I bring Simon to Granny's and she's boning some hoodlum on the sofa!"

"Watch your nasty fucking mouth! He won't remember a thing unless you keep mouthing off about it for the rest of his life. This is Detective Charles White, hardly a hoodlum! We've become very close over the last ... we've been seeing each other a long time, and we're serious. Okay?"

While the smoke settled, there was a minute of calm reflection. Kirby fluffed up the flattened sofa cushions, and Charles hid in the kitchen. Simon was on the carpet with his new friend, Mister Fritz. Having a new playmate, Simon showed little interest in granny, which made her more testy. When they began scouting the living room carpet, Kirby had to jump to rescue her bra off the floor before they started a tug-a-war.

Charles wandered in from the kitchen with three glasses and a bottle of white wine.

"Wine?" Charles offered a glass to Davey.

"That'll be great. Thought I'd surprise you."

"You've succeeded," said Charles, pouring wine.

Davey unpacked onto the floor Simon's satchel full of diapers, clothes, and a toy collection of soft and fuzzy cows. Simon was still having too great of a time with Mister Fritz, so Kirby took him in her arms and had him flying around the room.

"Mom, where's Teddi?"

"Your father's got her two weeks in a row. Besides, I have VAMP stuff to deal with."

"Yeah, sounds like you're real busy. Teddi's gonna have that little dog for lunch."

"Well, we'll see in two weeks, won't we," answered Kirby.

Davey stuck out his hand to Charles. "I apologize for being such a jerk." "Since you guys are together, Simon and I are in the second bedroom?"

"Terrific," said Kirby, discovering a wet diaper.

Davey was lean and athletically built with tidy short hair. He took off the Fed Ex-labeled windbreaker, showing a gray uniform shirt and the official dark blue slacks.

"What are you up to at Fed Ex?" Charles asked.

"I'm a ramp agent. It sucks. I'm getting overtime now, but that will slack off after Christmas. I hope to get into their flight program and in the right seat. Right now, I build hours when I can."

"How many?"

"Little over a thousand. I'm getting commercial and instrument time in an Aerostar 700 through a sweetheart deal. I copilot when I can get time off but may be able to be full-time if we go into charters."

"Cool. Aerostar is a hot ship. I had a friend, a colonel, who used a twin Beech to get around Nam. He wanted an Aerostar and said it could outrun a SAM. Fortunately, never got the chance."

"I'm ordering pizza and a salad," Kirby announced. Everyone agreed it was a good idea.

* * * * * *

To mild protestations, Charles insisted on picking up the tab for the pizza. He sat on the defiled sofa, eating pepperoni and mushroom pizza as a pleasing realization formed: *This was like having a new family.*

Meanwhile, Kirby doing most of the talking, explaining what Charlie, a decorated New York City detective, was doing in Vermont.

"I assume VAMP has crashed and burned," suggested Davey, after hearing about the maple syrup poisonings in New York City.

"No, not at all. There's no connection to the poisonings with VAMP. I've been bumped up to full-time and was made Director of Promotions," she explained while feeding Simon little bits of pizza. No pepperoni for Simon, Davey warned, because of the bad poopy experience. "It's a moral situation, Davey. It's about doing the right thing."

"I honestly believe the less you know, the better off we'll all be," interjected Charles.

"We're trying to do the right thing for a handicapped senior citizen. No matter what crime she's done, she *can't* go into the legal system," Kirby answered.

"Really? Handicapped, how?"

"She's mentally ill, in an advanced stage," answered Charles, then turned away, realizing how bad their good intentions were going to sound.

"And what are you two going to get out of it?"

"At this junction, that's irrelevant and not why we're doing it," answered Kirby.

"Well, okay. But what are you getting out of it?" Demanding a reply, Davey shifted his gaze from his mom to Charles. Charles avoided his eyes by looking at the trophy trout over the fireplace.

Kirby gave in, "We're hoping to buy her farm. The proceeds will get her in a decent retirement home where she'll get proper care."

"Jesus, Mom. Sounds really, really shady."

Later that evening, Charles was seated on the downstairs toilet, surrounded by fanciful vinyl animal and cartoon characters stuck on the tiles for Simon. While contemplating Tilda's predicament, he wondered: might Davey pass for the fictitious Timothy Duclos?

CHAPTER 46

Sounds more like she wants
to entertain you

Tilda and Timothy were in the kitchen engaged in a family spat.

"Now that you're all grown up, if you're to be part of this family, you're going to have to stop disappearing when folks show up."

Tilda's disquiet was spurred by a sugar high after eating piece upon piece of the Trader Joe's chocolate bar. With a Campbell's soup can, she pounded the impossible-to-break chocolate into eatable-size morsels and had already polished off half of the huge 26-ounce bar in an hour.

"Sis, you know I'm shy."

"We hardly got started on the Disregards and you've petered out. You've made me make a massive investment in syrup and stamps on my Visa, which I'm only supposed to use for Slobberu gas!"

Timothy did his pacing thing around the living room, as he did when thinking deeply.

"Sis, we can be such fools. Sam's a nice guy but tell him you need to get Christmas gifts off to friends."

"Sam says it won't be ready soon. Days more, he says."

"Ask him if he'd drop them off at the post office as a favor."

"Good idea, Timothy. You always have the best ideas, even if they are devil-inspired."

"We've got to finish dosing them samples."

"Tonight?"

"Right now, Sis!"

"It's too hot, Brother. Can't we wait 'til tonight?"

"No. Bring cold Dr Peppers from the fridge. That'll keep you hydrated. And your Acer for the addresses."

* * * * * *

In the barn, Tilda, nourished with a Dr Pepper, cranked up the fan and got to work. To her aggravation, Timothy soon wandered off. After hours of sweating in the blue latex gloves, she finished spiking fifty or so samples. The omniscient Acer found the agents' addresses, and she addressed the boxes using the untraceable, architectural script. The next step was finger torture: separating the four different stamps from four different pages, moistening them individually, and sticking them to the boxes.

She had drunk all the sodas and had to rest her cramping hand. Flopped across several hay bales, she fell into a snoring nap and had a silly dream. Even Timothy thought it was silly when she told him how the Charles man had tenderly awakened her by gently fondling between her thighs and whispering in her ear: *Tilly Darling, I couldn't sleep after you had drained me, so I read Final Love for the third time. I couldn't put it down. It's a masterpiece . . . Will you love me forever?*

By midnight, Tilda had everything ready to be mailed. The fifty-plus samples would go to those Disregards on her query list of those who didn't respond, not just those evil guild agents. The samples were now on the front porch neatly arranged in a plastic Williams Dairy milk crate she had dragged from the barn in exhausting stages. As always, when there was work to be done, Timothy was nowhere to be found. But it hardly mattered as there was no way to mail them without Slobberu.

Tilda kicked off her outdoor yellow galoshes at the porch steps and rambled upstairs to bed. She collapsed into the antique feather duvet from Mama Rose and The Dewy Drop Inn; it sailed her into a Dr Pepper commercial, which lullabied her right to sleep.

* * * * * *

In the morning, Slim Littlejohn, Tilda's bare-assed dancing neighbor with the baby-blue antique Ford 150 truck, drove up to the house. Tilda was on the porch struggling into her outdoor galoshes with one hand and balancing a mug of Trader Joe's spiced chai in the other.

Before he could climb out, she shouted, "Stay right there!" It took her a few heartbeats to recognize the truck. "Are you stalking me?"

"No, no, ma'am. Don't you remember how nice I was when I gave you a ride from town 'cause your car was at Sam's?"

"It still is. I don't know what's taking him so damn long. He's acting like I don't pay him enough. Why are you bothering me?"

"I saw up the road your mailbox was overflowing with mail and magazines. Your valuable correspondence was blowing out all over the road, so I picked it up for you."

He scooped all the mail from the seat beside him into a huge double handful, got out of the truck, and placed it at her feet beside the milk crate of holding the syrup samples. Tilda couldn't look at him without envisioning him naked and his privates flopping around.

"That's very nice of you, neighbor. What's your name again?"

"Friends call me Slim. Slim Littlejohn."

"Sounds Indian."

"Nope, it's Scottish. Came from having two Johns in one neighborhood, way back when."

"Must have been a Bigjohn running around next door."

"I never heard of no Bigjohn as a last name, but I guess we'd be townies."

"You'd think. What should I call you?"

"Friends call me Slim."

"Come inside for some tea and chocolate, Slim?"

"Oh, no, not today. That's very kind, but I need to get to the Bristol Post Office. Got to get my truck insurance check in the mail. Then, I got the exercise group."

"Exercise? What exercise can a skinny rail like you do?"

"Oh, Mrs. Duclos, you're way out here and don't hear about all the goings-on I do for the folk at Smith's Retirement Villa. I load up the van and take them out for long healthy walks. Trip with Slim's the highlight of their weekly activities."

"You make a living at that?"

"Sure. They pay me, and the folks give me real nice tips, too."

* * * * * *

Slim Littlejohn wasn't telling all. He did use the Smith's Retirement Villa's van to pick up the residents, but didn't mention they were desperate to escape the tedium of every room painted okra-green and their carbo-loaded meals. He'd kindly assist them into the van and make sure they were buckled in comfortably with their canes and walkers stashed at arm's length. Before exiting the complex, he'd stop at the gate and call out: "Where do we want to go today, my friends?" As if he didn't know.

In unison, they'd shriek: "Costco! Costco! Costco!"

"All right, pair-up and have your Costco cards ready!"

Manipulator to the impaired, the senile, and desperately bored, he'd shake his head remorsefully. Costco was too far to go with the measly gas allowance allotted to his program. But if they dug into their own pockets and change purses, dropped a few bills and loose coins into his green John Deere cap that was passed around like a Sunday church offering, he might have enough money for the extra gas.

Sufficiently rewarded, he'd scoot them the ten miles to the Colchester Costco. Not a completely unscrupulous, uncaring nitwit, Slim would relentlessly push the shuffling and cane-toting retirees a minimum of six aisles roundtrip, before releasing them to gorge on the free snack sampling that Costco had finally returned to since the phony-baloney Covid crisis had ended. All in all, it was a winner for everyone. The retirees had six long aisles of exercise and a treasured diet diversion. For Slim Littlejohn, the chump change he squeezed from the retirees made the painful dealings with the tight-fisted Taiwanese owners of the retirement home worthwhile.

* * * * * *

Tilda knew that when it came to mysterious interventions, God had to be helping her combat the evil wall and learn the Disregards a lesson. Why else would the stud Slim Littlejohn show up at her door, right at her moment of need?

"May I get you to do an important favor?" she coyly asked, fluttering her eyes.

"Sure, if I can." Slim was in an awkward place. Normally an avid womanizer any chance he got—but this Tilda woman? Maybe too spooky to even contemplate a womb massage. His specialty!

Tilda shoved the milk crate with her galoshes toward Slim.

"Sam's incapacitated my cherished automobile. Do you think you could drop these off at the post office for me? They're ready to go, stamped and everything."

"I'll take them right now. What are they?"

"Small tokens of appreciation to my literary associates."

He slung the crate into the back of the truck, opened the door, and hopped in.

"Slow down, Casanova. I want a receipt showing fifty-six boxes got mailed. Don't pocket one for yourself. I'll treat you properly when you return that milk crate of mine and the receipt."

"Don't you worry about me. I don't take what isn't mine. I'll stop by in the next few days with both, Mrs. Duclos."

He started the truck and began backing out.

"When you come back, we'll have some tea and chocolates."

"That'll be real nice," he answered.

"By the way, Slim, you ever yen-yang?"

"Don't think I know that game, but I've done the Ouija board and I play Oh Hell and Hearts with the cousins on holidays."

* * * * * *

At the Bristol Post Office, Slim Littlejohn slid the milk crate across the worn counter to the stoic postal clerk. He checked the weight and stamps on two sample boxes, then dumped all fifty-six into the outgoing canvas roller basket set behind him. He returned the Williams Dairy crate to Slim and gave him a receipt. Slim was relieved the clerk didn't ask him where he got the Williams Dairy milk crate.

On the way home, Slim passed Sam Piper's Garage and saw Tilda's Slobberu floating in the air on the lift. He could see the shop floor was covered with Subaru engine parts.

Sam was outside in the hot sun working on a green Subaru whose sunroof was left open in a downpour. Although the three inches of water had drained out of the interior, it still wouldn't start and it smelled like raccoon shit. Sam hated telling the owner the repairs would cost more than the car was worth, and the stink would stay until the floor rusted out.

Slim pulled off the road and stopped alongside the green Subaru. Sam's grimy face peaked out from under the hood.

"What's up, Slim? You having truck trouble?"

"No, she's running sweet. That red Subaru on your lift, that's belonging to the old bat that lives up my way?"

"You mean Tilly Duclos."

"Yeah. Ain't she something? I give her a lift the other night after she left it here. She's a good three miles up the road, wandering 'long like some vagrant. Lucky I saw her."

"That's for sure. It's going to be a while before she gets it back."

"Couple weeks' worth of mail fell out of her beat-up old mailbox. Blew out all over the highway. So, I picked it all up and brung it to her."

"That's good of you. You might get some good karma out of that, Slim."

"Yeah well, she twisted my arm and made me go to Bristol and mail a shitload of little boxes."

"What little boxes?" asked Sam. Anything concerning Tilly Duclos was a red flag.

"Those little maple syrup samples they sell everywhere."

"Come again, Slim? You took maple syrup samples for Tilly Duclos to the Bristol Post Office?"

"Yep. Prickly-ass sow. Wants a receipt for all fifty-six samples and her crate back, too. Seeing her car, I was thinking if you're going to be delivering it to her, I might leave the receipt and crate with you? That way I can hightail it before she wants me to do something else."

That brought Sam upright and made him laugh. "Come on, Slim. I'm not going to have this mess together anytime soon."

"Yeah, I see you got the head off."

"I do have a bag of groceries for her, and she's expecting me. So, leave them. I'll see she gets both."

"That's a relief. She wants me over for tea and chocolate. I can't stand either. Makes my teeth itch."

"Sounds like she wants to entertain you," Sam said cautiously.

"She wants to play some yen-yang game. What's that? Cards? Board game? I don't have time to waste with a freaky woman like that. I keep in shape and I like 'em young."

"I'd be extra careful about seeing Tilly Duclos socially," said Sam forebodingly.

"Why's that?" He put down the empty crate with Tilly's receipt next to Sam and climbed back into the idling truck.

"You'd be begging for trouble. Trust me, she ain't all together." Sam spun his greasy finger around his ear.

"Who is these days? I hear ya. Warning registered."

CHAPTER 47

I wouldn't count on Nasty being friendly

Charles was on the laptop logged into the RTCC when his cell began Beethovening. Kirby was in the kitchen cooking brownies and Davey and Simon were wandering outside, oohing at big trees and hunting for squirrels.

"Sam Piper, hold on, I'm putting us on speaker so KC can hear. What's up?"

"Slim Littlejohn. He lives over near Tilly. He dropped by a few minutes ago. Told me she asked him to drop off some boxes at the post office."

"That's interesting."

"Did Tilly's problem with the law have to do with those maple syrup samples?"

"That's what it's all about. Go on," said Charles, as his neck muscles tightened.

Kirby panicked and began pacing around in circles, mumbling to herself.

"He just dropped off a bunch at the Bristol Post Office. I have the receipt; says he posted fifty-six of the little buggers.

"Jesus Christ! Sam, she's spiked them with wolfsbane. They're going to the Disregards!" shrieked Kirby.

"Well, shit! Now you tell me!" sputtered Sam.

"Bristol? Bristol Post Office, you said? KC, fastest route to Bristol!" Charles said, as he sprinted out the door.

* * * * * *

They wheeled into the post office lot narrowly sliding between two parallel-parked blue postal trucks and screeched to a stop in the handicapped zone. Dashing inside, past the line of customers (one who recognized Kirby), Charles went directly to the service side door and pounded on it.

"You'll have to wait in line like everyone else!" A voice bellowed from behind the door.

"Open up! Official police business," Charles said, continuing to bang on the door.

The steel door swung partway open and they faced no-nonsense Postmistress Boucher. Her grey hair was short and neat in a soldier's crew cut. She had an oversized plastic I.D. badge hanging around her neck. Near retirement age, large and bony, her appearance was reminiscent of the iconic Depression-era woman on a public works mural—the one sowing seeds behind a pair of straining oxen.

Charles flashed his badge and, with Kirby trailing, pushed by the astonished postmistress into a short hallway that led to the sorting facility. On its wall were framed recognitions Boucher had earned as a USAF sergeant. They entered the sorting room and the loading dock as a filled canvas cart was rolled by two postal workers toward the open gate of a blue postal truck.

"Stop immediately! Bring that cart over here!" commanded Charles.

Behind him, Boucher angrily inquired, "On whose authority?"

Peaking over Charles' shoulder, Kirby said, "They've been laced with poison. It's a nightmare. He'll explain."

"Really? We've sent quite a few of these little boxes all over the country and no one's complained. Let me see those I.D.s of yours again."

"Postmistress Boucher, I'm Detective Charles White, NYPD. I'm investigating six attempted murders using poisoned maple syrup samples mailed in small cardboard boxes. Slim-something-or-another mailed fifty-six of the samples at this post office in the last hour."

"They're going into that Rutland truck right now," snapped Boucher, crossing her arms. The man and woman pushing the cart figured trouble was coming their way and cautiously eased away from the cart.

"This is all from this afternoon?" Charles pointed to the cart where a mound of sample boxes were visible.

"We haven't done the outside drop-off box," offered Mrs. Hanson, one of the cart pushers.

"KC, give us a count. Should be fifty-six."

Boucher had her cell phone in hand and it was on its way to her ear—all the while, her eyes messaged *I'm going to fuck you over as best I can.*

Charles swallowed and had a quick think-through of the situation:

The gig was up if Vermont police came, saw the samples, and asked questions. If a whiff of Vermont law enforcement involvement were to reach Captain Mahoney before Charles had alerted him, everything would unravel. There would be a bitter clash between New York and Vermont law enforcement and their hungry district attorneys. Outcome? Misery for poor Tilly Duclos, and he'd have troubles galore. Who knew how it'd work out for KC?

Kirby could hardly breathe. For a few seconds, she panicked, thinking her heart had stopped. Before accepting death, she ran through the cascading scenario:

The sale of Vermont maple products would plummet for years and a salary increase would be out of the question. Poor Tilly Duclos would lose everything. The farm would be sold on the courthouse steps, and she and Charles would never be blissfully raising trout at their secret pit. Worse, her grandchild, Simon, would have a felon for a grandmother, which would not be much of a step up over his pole-dancing mom.

Charles desperately needed to convince Boucher of the dire consequences were the samples to leave her post office. He was ready to snatch her phone and plead on his knees when, mercifully, a savior came quietly into the loading dock.

"Charlie, Charlie! Look, look!" shouted Kirby pointing.

Strolling in like it owned the sorting room, a black-as-night tomcat appeared from outside the loading dock.

"That!" Charles said, pointing. "Who does that belong to?"

Mrs. Hanson, the truck loader, warned, "That feral cat comes in here, hisses at us, and squirts his scent around. We named him Nasty. I wouldn't count on Nasty being friendly."

"Here Nasty, Nasty, Nasty," cooed Kirby, leaning down cautiously. The black cat hissed at her.

"Anyone got a bowl or cup of anything?" Charles asked.

"Sometimes putty-tat gets a little half and half we keep for coffee. That calms him down," suggested Hanson.

"I'll get a saucer for you."

"What in God's name are you up to?" asked Boucher, letting the cell phone dip from her ear.

Charles opened the sample going to Ima Foch at Inkspot Foch Associates and set the saucer on the floor. He filled it with half and half and then added a taste of Ima Foch's syrup. Nasty knew it was for him and got right into it.

Sated, Nasty plumped down onto his rump and went to licking off maple syrup and the cream, which was now stubbornly clinging to his whiskers.

"He sure does like Vermont maple syrup," remarked the second cart loader.

"Everyone likes maple syrup," snapped Boucher. "You've racked up multiple federal felonies in the few tiresome minutes you two have been here. ASPCA will have words to say about this, too."

Nasty, his hind legs spread further apart, began burping.

"This little charade is over. Detective White, I don't give a hoot how big a deal you are in that depraved city, but you're in big trouble in little Bristol. I'm calling the law and . . ."

Boucher's harangue was stopped by increasingly loud gurgling sounds emanating from Nasty's bowels.

Alarmed, everyone took a step back. Nasty released a wet, nauseating fart and unleashed an ear-shattering screech. With fur standing on end, he exploded across the room and leaped onto the row of stainless-steel sorting tables. Now spraying poo, he raced the length of the tables, kicking piles of posts and mailers into the air. After thrashing about, chasing his tail, and continuing to spew, he skidded off the table and thumped to the concrete floor. Following a chain of spastic tremors, Nasty was motionless.

The other postal worker who had been helping load cautiously approached and, with a steel-booted toe, gave Nasty a little nudge. Then another. No response.

"Postmistress Boucher, Nasty's dead."

"Oh my," said Boucher with fingers going to her lips.

"Oh my, is fucking right," said wide-eyed Kirby.

Postmistress Boucher, being of a decisive nature, snapped her fingers at the stunned loading crew. "James, transfer all those cartons into Detective White's vehicle. Make sure you get all fifty-six. You, Hanson, bag that animal and clean up this mess. Snap to it!"

* * * * * *

The samples were packed into the Corvette's wayback next to Kirby's fishing gear and Charles' war bag. Leaning against the blue postal truck, the one with the steering wheel on the wrong side, they spilled the beans to Boucher, relating the complete wretched Tilda story. She listened to the machinations Charles and Kirby were undertaking to keep Dizzy Tilda Duclos out of jail and how they were attempting to avert an economic catastrophe for Vermont.

"We're honestly at your mercy, Postmistress Boucher," said Charles sheepishly.

"You gotta help us with this," pleaded Kirby.

"Now that you've explained the situation, God bless you. Let me know if my church can help. Quite a few of us will be willing to step up," Boucher stuck her hand out to shake.

"Be a big help if you could avoid writing a situation report and keep our conversation private," said Charles with a hopeful smile.

"I have top-secret clearance earned at Creech Air Force Base, and I've managed not to blab about all the atomic bombs we've lost. Of course, it stays here."

She glanced at her staff and they both gave thumbs up and affirming nods. Charles and Postmistress Boucher did a stiff shake, one professional to another, while Kirby gave her a soft hug. Appreciative nods went from Charles to the postal crew for loading his car and being tolerant of the chaos they had created.

As they were buckling up and preparing to leave, a familiar green state police cruiser briskly wheeled into the parking area. It jerked to a stop parallel to the Corvette's driver's side but angled enough to block it from leaving. It was State Trooper Francine Forget. Her window came down.

"Well, here's Detective White and his sidekick, Kirby Clark, now causing panic in the post office."

Before Charles could respond, Postmistress Boucher came between the two cars and draped an arm on the cruiser's roof, effectively blocking Trooper Forget's door from opening.

"Hello, Trooper Forget. What brings you to my parking lot?"

"We've had two 911 callers for a 10-31 in your lobby. A big lug and crazy woman pushing themselves into the back room and causing a ruckus."

"That's a bit of an over-statement. Detective White and I are old buddies and, hell, everybody knows Kirby, our famous pucker. Nothing here to see. You'd like to come in and have a coffee and donut?"

After a moment of silence and sidelong glances all around, no one had more to say.

"If you say so," said Trooper Forget, unconvinced there was nothing to see. In any case, she wasn't going to have a fuckin' post office donut.

"I say so," echoed Boucher.

"How about I write him up for hogging two handicapped spaces? Teach him a lesson?" She took ahold of her handheld PocketJet mobile printer to start the process of producing a ticket.

"We ought to let him go this time," said Boucher, "I insist."

Trooper Forget didn't respond until Boucher gave her a long commanding stare.

"Your parking lot, your call. I guess I'll be on my way." Trooper Forget pointed her trigger finger at Charles, "No more trouble, big-town Charlie."

"You bet," he said.

Trooper Forget wheeled out of the post office lot screamingly mad. She dared not take on Postmistress Boucher as the post office was federal property and Boucher was the overlord. But why the hell would Boucher cover for them? It was the second time they had clashed, and she didn't like it. Whatever White and Kirby were up to, something stank like roadkill at the end of a long holiday.

CHAPTER 48

We dodged a bullet with
Boucher, didn't we, Charlie?

Charles and Kirby left the parking lot and turned onto Route 7.

"Can we talk about what just happened?" asked Kirby.

"Later, KC. Do you know the library where Tilly worked and how late they're open?"

"Presley Public Library. Probably 'til eight. Why?"

"We're near Middlebury. Let's go by and do some research."

"We can research at home online with vodka tonics," replied Kirby. He said nothing. "No? Oh, I get it," replied Kirby sarcastically. "We're scouting out a shelf for *Desperate Measures* and *Final Love*?"

"Bear with me. Information is currency, and we're going broke. Booze can wait."

* * * * * *

Head Librarian Mrs. Alexandre Reddy eased back into her spanking new Lagoon Green Steelcase Series One Chair that sat behind a shiny new Steelcase desk. So new, both still had the protective cellophane wrappings on the legs. On the desk was the latest Mac computer with an enormous color monitor.

Charles and Kirby were across from her, butts uncomfortably crammed into tiny plastic chairs sized for elementary school children.

"Sorry about those seats. They're kid's chairs for the new reading room. I won't have the proper ones until next month," Reddy said.

Charles flashed his badge quickly enough that Mrs. Reddy didn't catch he wasn't a Vermont official. He explained they were only seeking background information on Tilda Duclos.

Ms. Reddy related that when Tilda Duclos was Assistant Librarian Presley Public Library was continually short on cash and in debt. That may explain why she was let go by Head Librarian Jane Franken.

"What else can you tell us about her firing?" asked Charles.

"We don't fire people at Presley. We would have used a budget-driven reason for dismissal. Tilda Duclos, I never met her—way before my time. But I know she was called Dizzy Tilly by school chums, which sort of indicates something amiss."

"Ms. Reddy, seriously, you need to be more forthcoming. This is important," said Charles.

"Understood. As far as I know, she was let go for cause by my predecessor, Mrs. Brown."

"What cause would that be?" asked Kirby.

"I was entering junior high around that time. What I heard from a staffer decades later was that we didn't have the resources some of our children required and it rubbed Tilda the wrong way. She may have been over-burdened and impatient with some of the parents."

"About when did this happen?" asked Kirby.

"Can't tell you exactly. I suspect around 1976, year of the Bicentennial."

"Might the Bicentennial have had an impact on her?" asked Kirby.

"Don't know. Everyone from here to Brattleboro was shooting off fireworks and guns into the air. We had a big reenactment at the town hall."

"I don't remember that time at all. I was born just after, so my folks must have been shootin' off something that year!" commented Kirby straight-faced.

Charles and Reddy looked at each other without blinking.

"That may have been a stressful time for someone with underlying emotional issues," surmised Charles.

"Holidays may not be holidays for everyone. In my family, we almost—I stress almost—enjoy getting together on holidays," responded Ms. Reddy.

"I understand. Are your local newspapers accessible online?" asked Charles.

"We've got the *Addison County Independent* back to 1946."

They thanked Reddy for her considerate help and left.

* * * * * *

They got into the 'Vette and began the drive back to the condo.

"We dodged a bullet with Boucher, didn't we, Charlie?"

"Did we ever."

"You think there's anything more about her job at the library we should know?"

"No. But there's more to Tilly's: 'You didn't answer my query, I'm killing you.' Compulsive writing, determination to spread her message, a willingness to punish those in her way, and aggressive sexuality says to me she wants to come to grips with something."

"Let's stop thinking about Tilly and think about us. Like what could we do with the farm if we got it. Okay?" suggested Kirby.

"KC, KC, the farm's not going anywhere. Taking care of Tilly is top of our list. So, relax."

A long drawn-out silence with Kirby meaning to speak several times followed.

"What's our next step?" she finally asked.

"I saw a garden shovel by the grill."

"There is," Kirby said, somewhat perplexed.

"We're going to dig a hole. Break every one of those bottles and bury 'em."

"Cool. Then what?"

"We need to neutralize Tilly's ability to do more mailings and find if others are involved. We're going to need an outsider to help."

"Sam Piper. He'll do it for Tilly," said Kirby confidently.

"She knows Sam. Davey's got to be our man."

"Charlie, what are you smoking? You can't use my son!"

"Okay, do you have a better idea?" A long awkward silence followed.

* * * * * *

"Good morning, NYPD. Inspector Mahoney's office. Who's calling? . . . I'll have to put you on hold for a minute, sir."

Bookus' hand went to hit the intercom button, thought better of it, and swiveled about in his chair. He peered into the Glass Palace at Mahoney who was absorbed in the *New York Post*. By chance, Mahoney happened to look up just then. Bookus closed his palm over the phone and mouthed:

"Waterbury, Vermont. Colonel Samuel Hanover, Director Vermont State Police."

Mahoney hit the loudspeaker button on his desk landline, "Good afternoon. Inspector Mahoney, NYPD. How may I help you?"

"Colonel Samuel Hanover, Director Vermont State Police. Inspector Mahoney, we've got an NYPD Detective White up here causing a butt load of trouble."

Mahoney took the phone immediately off the speaker and picked up the phone.

"I am aware one of our detectives is on vacation in your fine state ... No, I haven't heard about him with some local gal busting into a post office ... Causing a big scene? That's distressing ... Disrespectful to one of your female officers, too? ... I don't know what this is all about, but I'll damn sure find out!"

Mahoney muttered under his breath, "White, you fucking asshole!"

Mahoney went on to assure the colonel his rogue detective would be properly chastised and punished. Naturally, Mahoney did not reveal anything about the maple syrup poisonings or that he had authorized White's trip. They disconnected after cordially inviting one another to come down or come up for a barbecue.

"Bookus, find everything you can about White's trip—including his cell calls. When and to whom. Talk to whomever you need to, but discreetly. You can backdoor his laptop's history when he's on RTCC, right? Also, get a GPS track of where he's been. Got it?" growled Mahoney.

"Already ahead of you, Inspector. There're printouts of White's RTCC entries in your in-basket. Look to your left, beside your family corner. I'll get on the other stuff," said Bookus, gleefully.

CHAPTER 49

Outright scheming and clever hoodwinking

Charles lay in bed wide awake. Kirby was sound asleep next to him. Mister Fritz, also asleep, had snuggled between them and then rolled onto his back. Charles had just figured out what they needed to do to save Tilda Wilcox Duclos from the clutches of a heartless criminal justice system. It was complicated and risky, and the outcome of success was entrusted to the goodness of the people making up the very same system that would crush her.

Unfortunately, Dizzy Tilly Duclos' future was going to ride in the mercurial hands of Trooper Francine Forget and the young Davey Clark, who were the last people Charles wanted to ask for help. He pondered how to defuse his tenuous relationship with Trooper Fran Forget, marred by the clash at the post office and the speeding ticket for blasting through the yellow light speed trap—which he hadn't paid. Davey could be manipulated into action by his mom. He hoped.

That next morning after reviewing his plan with Kirby over coffee, she called it outright scheming and clever hoodwinking, more in line with what coppers did when they didn't have honest ACLU lawyers looking over their shoulders.

Charles reiterated that she watched too much television.

* * * * * *

Charles spent the afternoon cooking Umberto's inspired spaghetti sauce, a recipe he had gotten from Gianni Ippolito's young and handsome son, Dino. Gianni was known as "Socks" because on one of his run-ins with the law, he was detained exiting a massage parlor wearing nothing but white socks. That was long before Dino, his son, was sentenced to four years in Rochester Correctional Facility where he joined his father who was halfway through twelve years for fraud and extortion.

Axiomatic: bad crooks, good cooks.

Simon and Mister Fritz were watching Mel Brooks' *Spaceballs* and then *Willow* without leaving the television for more than a few minutes. Charles needed to get Davey committed to the plan, so he made robust margaritas for him and Kirby. He over-salted the rims to keep them thirsty and coming back for more.

"It's simple, Davey. You're an Acer field representative come to upgrade her browser. We're going to use your Fed Ex outfit with a little alteration."

"Okay," said Davey, glancing up from the television to knock down the margarita in two gulps. "Nice drink, old man."

"I hate sewing," said Kirby defiantly while sipping her cocktail.

"It's only two patches, KC! Come on, help us out here!" whined Charles.

Kirby, on her second margarita, got on board and patched together believable Acer labels and sewed them over the Fed Ex labels on Davey's jacket. She then squeezed him to commit to the cause.

"Honey, all we need is a few minutes in the barn. We'll make it up to you—and Christmas is coming up fast for you and Simon."

"I'll do it, but it sounds like something I could go to jail for," said Davey nonchalantly, not taking his eyes from the TV, and slugging down the next margarita.

Charles scoffed, "No, no, don't be ridiculous. This is a legit, undercover job. As we say in the force, 'I've got your back.'"

"I still don't like it," he said to Charles, tapping his glass indicating he needed a refill. Kirby picked up the torch . . .

"Son, we can't save Tilly from prison unless we know she's working alone. What if she's part of a conspiracy? Davey, are you listening? As a family, we've got a lot riding on her laptop. If we can get Tilly into care and buy her farm, we'll be out of this condo and have a place for all of us to live."

"Mom, you're putting a lot of pressure on me!"

Charles needed to lockdown the mission; "When you've got her laptop, you'll need her user name and password to do the upgrade. To cover our asses, be sure to ask if you can share her data."

"I can do that, no prob. Hey, Charlie, you think she has enough flat land for me to land an ultralight?"

"Plenty of room for an ultralight. There's another thing about Tilly. She believes that stone wall on the other side of the barn is possessed by an evil spirit. This evil spirit has schemed with the wolfsbane growing on it to poison those literary agents we told you about."

"What? Now you tell me! I'm fucking doomed!" howled Davey.

Charles jabbered on, deftly underplaying the severity of her illness and presenting a sympathetic version of how mentally disabled she is. He then waxed on and on about how she is quite harmless, and that Davey would find her entertaining.

No need to totally freak him out!

Charles brought him the canvas tool kit from his war bag and a clean flash drive. He slapped him on the shoulder, "You're the man!"

Little did Davey realize the meeting with Tilly Duclos was a tame rehearsal for another role he would be called on to perform in Charles' theater.

CHAPTER 50

Poopy diapers don't seem
to bother him either

In the morning, in his Honda Civic and suited in the faux Acer uniform, Davey followed the shadow-gray Corvette up Route 116. In the 'Vette, Simon was on Kirby's lap and Mister Fritz was relegated to the wayback, miffed at having lost his favorite place to his little playmate. They unloaded at Sam's Garage and Davey quickly set up Simon's playpen and toys in the office.

When Sam came from the shop wiping his hands on a greasy rag, only then did he realize what he'd been suckered into.

"Are you guys nuts? I said I'd help with a dog! Now you want me to babysit, too? I got work to do. My hands are full of grease all the time!"

Sam continued his grumbling while Charles handed him Mister Fritz's leash and Davey plopped Simon into the playpen, or "the prison." Simon was in a particularly good mood having relieved himself on Granny's lap, leaving a wet circle on her checkered L. L. Bean flannel shirt.

"He's got all his moo cows and two juice boxes. He won't be a problem!" promised Davey.

"You don't have to worry about him. Sam, I swear, the child never makes a fuss," testified Kirby.

"Poopy diapers don't seem to bother him either," contributed Charles, thoughtfully.

"Charlie, you did warn this innocent young man about the yen and yang thing?" Sam relit a slimy cigar butt and suspiciously eyed his new companions taking over his office.

"Davey's been properly alerted," responded Charles.

* * * * * *

Charles and Kirby parked on the roadside a few yards before Tilda's driveway at the end of the Williams Dairy white rail fencing. Several Holsteins anxiously trotted off when they saw them climb over the fence; others were indifferent and continued grazing. Carefully avoiding the infinite number of cow pies, they reached the rise and paused to enjoy the bucolic view that had captured them only a week before: open pastures of grasses and weeds; a horizon of trees; more puffy clouds; and the quaint but dilapidated farmhouse and a barn.

Ah, Kirby sighed, *almost mine—ours—almost ours.*

The notion it might become permanent in their lives was captivating for Kirby but surreal for Charles.

"I hope, I hope this works," said Kirby crossing her fingers and reaching to grasp Charles' hand.

"If we do the right thing for Tilly, it'll work out for us. It's a karma thing; we obey our ethical compass and let Fate decide."

"That's some laid-back philosophy you got there, Charlie," she said dubiously. "I hope you're not saying that to give you an out if this goes belly up."

Davey had lingered in his Honda on the tarmac until Charles and Kirby disappeared over the pasture's rise. After a few minutes, cued by a call from Charles, he turned down the gravel driveway and drove to the red farmhouse. He rolled to a stop in front of the rickety porch, shut off the engine, and waited to let the dust settle. Upon seeing the farmhouse up close for the first time, he phoned Charles and Kirby.

"Mom, Charlie! What is wrong with you two? Why would you buy this dump?"

"Just do what you're supposed to do!" snapped Kirby.

By this point, Tilda had just enough time to march out the front door, thrust both hands to her hips, and bellow at Davey.

"What the hell do you want!"

Mom had forewarned Davey, "With Duclos, you need to be prepared for the unexpected."

Wrinkly, baggy sweat pants with dirt where she had been on her knees in the garden, a *Free Willy* sweatshirt, and the wacky—no, better described as psychedelic—knitted scarf. She wasn't wearing her signature yellow galoshes, causing Davey to witness the weirdest ten toes he had ever seen.

Jeez! She's more frightening than I expected.

Davey cautiously got out of the car carrying the Acer tool kit.

"Good day, Ms. Duclos. Are you ready for your free Acer system upgrade?"

"What are you talking about, young man?"

"I'm Davey Clark, a field representative for Acer computers. Your Acer's running version 2.0. We're bumping you up to 3.4. No charge, upgrade comes automatically with the laptop."

Tilda puffed up her disheveled hair and fussed with the flowered scarf. "Who are you?"

"I'm here to fix your Acer computer."

"It isn't broken."

"Yes, but it will be soon unless I upgrade to our new operating system. You'll notice a big difference in speed and downloads. Doesn't cost you a cent."

"Why didn't you say so?"

Davey took a step forward.

"Hold on, fella. Let me get on my house slippers."

There were several pairs of yellow galoshes lined up by the screen door, and she tugged herself into the cleanest pair. "Come in and get out of the sun."

Davey took a deep breath and followed her across the porch, through the battered screen door, and into the dark living room. Despite being prompted by Charles, he was taken aback by Tilda's interior. Only a glow of daylight filtered through the off-kilter blinds, and to avoid colliding into boxes, bundles of magazines and papers, he had to watch every step. Encircling the living room at his eye level, hung an ominous string of empty plastic gallon containers. Which was unnerving.

"I know all about you shady geeks, so don't let me catch you touching my antiques or trying to steal my magazine collection!" Tilda called out from the kitchen where she was banging things around looking for the Acer.

"No, ma'am, won't touch a thing!"

Meanwhile, Charles and Kirby were waiting behind the stone wall about fifty feet from the barn, still on the Williams Dairy side of the barn. From where they stood, they had a full view of the farmhouse. If they moved a few meters to the side, the barn would block the farmhouse.

Like many early Vermont barns, the lowest floor was half buried into the ground and rested on a mortarless, irregular flat stone foundation. Pigs or cows were kept on this lowest level in small stalls where they could huddle and keep warm during the winter. Before that arrangement, in the earliest colonial days, cherished livestock were kept inside the house in what was considered to be the kitchen area.

* * * * * *

When Davey disappeared inside the house with Tilda, Charles and Kirby scampered over the wall and snuck into the barn's lower level through a sloppily framed opening made for animals. Inside, they had to stoop down as the animal stalls were barely five feet high. They startled a fat woodchuck who scampered into a den under the foundation while leaving a string of squeaky farts. Looking about, they found an open hatch and rustic wooden ladder that went to the main floor.

They climbed up into the cavernous main workspace. The only light came from leaks around the twin sliding doors or where the exterior planking had loosened and left gaps. From inside, the two sliding barn doors faced the farmhouse. Outside the sliding doors, the ground was graded up from the farmhouse level, and when both doors were slid open, it was wide enough for large farm machinery.

Overhead, on each side were hay lofts, and jammed into corners were defunct farm implements and stacks of old hay bales that had turned ashen gray. Centered in the space was a crudely crafted wood table that had been used for cleaning garden produce or as a canning work area. On it rested a large antique cider press, a couple of half-burnt candles, an open box of CVS latex gloves, a collection of post office stamp pages, and a glass Mason Ball jar containing a yellowy liquid. Scattered on the floor were scores of empty Dr Pepper cans and two cartons of VAMP maple syrup samples. One carton was torn open with rows of samples missing.

Also on the table was Tilly's Acer laptop!

"We're fucked, fucked, fucked!" Charles threw his clutched hands into the air.

Kirby muttered, "Oh shit."

In the farmhouse, Davey was petrified. Searching for her laptop, Tilda was flinging magazines and old newspapers about, sending waves of dust and mouse droppings into the air. "Haven't misplaced it, just can't remember."

In the barn, Charles snapped on a pair of latex gloves and carefully poured the jar of wolfsbane through the floorboards. All finished, he set the Ball jar down and tried to replace the yellow liquid with his urine. This was watched with the tickled amusement by Kirby.

"It's no good KC, I'm dry."

"Moooove." Kirby pushed down her jeans, rolled down a pink thong, and squatted over the jar.

"Don't let the rim touch you," warned Charles, as he backed away. Out of view, he took a snapshot with his phone. Unfortunately for Charles, the auto flash came on and captured the scene in blazing color. Kirby was midstream and helpless.

"You son-of-a-bitch. That phone's going to where the sun don't shine when we get out of here."

"Strictly professional documentation; you're not even in it!" he said businesslike, while checking the shot. *Yeah, he got her good.*

She finished and jerked her garments back in place. When he came close enough, she gave him a hard slug to the shoulder that made him screech, "Ouch"!

"Careful, KC, you can't treat me like you do Davey."

"Well, you better fucking behave then."

* * * * * *

Back in the farmhouse, Tilda was shuffling about reenacting her previous steps with the Acer laptop. After a long think, she exclaimed, "Ah, yes, yes, yes, I used it in the barn!"

"The barn?" Davey envisioned a catastrophe: *Mom and Charlie busted by Ms. Duclos!*

Tilda commanded, "Follow me, young man!" and charged out the front door.

Straggling behind her, he began yelling, "Ms. Duclos, Ms. Duclos! Are you sure the laptop's in the barn? You forgot the laptop in the barn?"

When they were but a few feet from the sliding doors of the barn, she spun around, raised trembling hands over her reddened face, and screamed, "For God's sake, young man! Do you have to holler? My hearing is fine, so stop the goddamn shouting!"

Hearing the commotion outside, Kirby quickly closed the Ball jar and put it where it had been on the table. They hastened to a dark corner and hid behind an assortment of ancient tractor attachments.

Tilda slid open one side of the mammoth doors, blasting the room with daylight. On the table was her laptop.

"Here it is!" She stashed it under her arm.

"What's all this? What are you making?" Davey asked, inspecting the table.

"That's Timothy's doings. Just ignore it. We have more important things to do."

Still, a little out of breath from all the rushing and shouting, Tilda paused and rested a hip against the table. "I bet you didn't know I have a book ready for publication. All I need is an agent and you'll find my books in libraries."

"That's great. We should go back to the house; your router and modem won't connect this far."

"I don't have a router or modem. I'm hard-wired to the dial-up system. That's why I have a stupid landline. You need refresher training, young man."

Davey's blunder got him thinking, *Granny is more with it than we'd thought.*

"What's your name again?"

"Davey."

"Davey, soon as I got your Acer laptop, I was on a mission. How'd I know? My Acer, she'd grabbed stories right out of my mind! I'd set my fingers on the keys," Tilly mimicked placing her fingers on the top of the closed Acer, "and she did everything else."

"That's like the automatic writing thingy in seances. I don't know what app you have installed to do that," Davey concluded.

"Of course, I have to use the spell checker because sometimes I write so fast she gets lost behind my quick mind. Does that ability come with all Acer computers?"

"I don't think so. Can we get back to the house?" Davey's overtaxed mind was getting a little frazzled. *Automatic writing, where's this going?*

She placed a hand on his shoulder.

"Davey, I have an important message. *Final Love* will rally the young and the timid to seek true, and lasting love. Even if at times they have to reach across evil stone walls. You hear what I'm saying?"

"Sounds pretty solid to me. I think people are generally always seeking love—or sex. But that's a great message," said Davey, slowly backing away.

"Tragically now, *Final Love* is being thwarted by them Disregards. They don't want my vital message to spread, but Timothy and I, we're getting things taken care of."

Davey stopped edging toward the sliding door, now more attentive.

"That murderous stack of rock behind this barn is a metaphor for what happens when true hearts are kept from crossing over walls. You do know what a metaphor is, don't you?"

"Sure. But Ms. Duclos, what's happened that's kept *you* from a final love?"

"That's a heavy question, young man. I became absorbed in my mistakes. One day smelling the roses, the next day knocked up. My life had slipped by."

"Wish I knew how to help."

Davey was feeling something like sincere affection for the doddering white-haired senior. She reached over, gripped his arm, and moved in close. Close enough for him to study her bloodshot eyes and disturbing odd hair growths around her chin.

"My little friend was lost forever, and it's pained me ever since. Maybe I didn't scream loud enough, maybe I was too slow to respond? I swear to God, I didn't mean to let it happen."

"I don't know what you're trying to tell me. Why don't you get help for you and Timothy?"

"Hell, that misfit would shun me if he knew I was talking about him."

"Really?"

"He likes to control. He's ruined my book with his fiendish poetry." She whispered, "Frankly, he has a perverse bent that comes out once in a while. I may be a little paranoid, but I'm concerned the evil wall and its underling, the wolfsbane vine, may have an influence on Timothy."

"Explain again to me. That thing about the evil wall and the wolfsbane underling."

"Boy, this country's dumbing down. I'm having to explain things over and over again . . . that colonial wall has an evil spirit in it. It's trying to wreak havoc with my mission by supporting the Disregards, the big-shot literary agents, the big apples, that rejected my love story, *Final Love*. My Acer has taken to battle the evil wall and its wolfsbane cronies."

"Oh, now I understand," said Davey. "Ms. Duclos, why don't you sell this place, get away from that evil wall?"

"If I could get Timothy settled elsewhere, I'd buy a nice townhouse in town. Write all the time."

"You could do that, Ms. Duclos. I will help you. My friends would help, too."

"I never was wanting of anything more than to help lost little ones," Tilda began to fade midsentence like she was going to drift off into a slumber.

"I think we should get back to the house and install the upgrade." He took the Acer from her hands and encouraged her toward the open sliding doors.

"Follow me!" Snapping out of her slumping position, she sprinted outside shouting at him:

"Come on, Davey! Slide that door closed behind you or Fartsy will get in!"

On their streak to the farmhouse, Davey began formulating a plan to handle the evil wall.

Meanwhile, on the rough plank floor with backs against hay bales, Charles and Kirby had taken in every word.

"Davey does that to people. We've got to help her, best we can, Charlie."

"Here we go again. What do you want? To help her or take her farm?"

"I want to help her by buying her farm because she can't handle what's going on in her life and she's trying to kill people. Does that sound better, less greedy?"

"You do just blurt out things, don't you?"

"I'm spontaneous! That's a positive thing, don't you think?"

At her desk in the farmhouse living room, Davey plugged the flash drive into the Acer.

"I need your user I.D. and password for your account," Davey said matter-of-factly.

"It's just my email, Tillysoldfarm@gmail and password," she called from the kitchen.

"Just password, written out?"

"Easy to remember."

As far as Davey could observe, every email she had ever sent went to a book publisher or literary agency. Every subject line contained "*Final Love.*" She received no emails from friends or any other contacts. No spam? How'd she manage that? He opened several files of different versions of *Final Love* and dumped everything onto Charles' flash drive.

Tilda came in from the kitchen with two cups of tea and remnants of the chocolates Charles and Kirby had brought.

"Ms. Duclos, sorry. I can't eat or drink anything. Corporate rules."

"Sugar? My milk's gone sour. Icebox's on the blink."

"Smells nice, the tea. I really shouldn't, but I'll have a sip of tea."

"Yes, some nice friends brought it for me. Slobberu is at Sam's, and he's been coming by with groceries! He can be a dear man, except when he has a wrench in hand and needs money. Then, oh boy, look out!"

They sat resting for a while, sipping tea. He wouldn't touch the chocolates after seeing the packaging. It looked like it had been opened by a famished wolverine.

Davey worked on her laptop another minute, then cleared his throat and sighed. "Ms. Duclos, I've detected malware."

"What's that?"

"That's an unauthorized piece of software maliciously inserted into your Acer. This software is bad news. I've seen it before. It has a . . . I'd say, an alarming identity: Satanic/wall/possession666."

"Satanic wall! Oh, my! You don't know the atrocities done by that evil thing!"

"Don't worry. We're going to neutralize it, rid it forever in your system."

"How? How . . . can you do that?"

"Easy. I'll trash its coding and install a firewall so it can't reinfect your Acer. This cleaning will also zap the power the wall has over some organic thing . . . I see it has its own identity: Satanic/wall/possession/wolfsbane. This will remove the power the wall has over an innocent family, the wolfsbaners, that live nearby."

"Good Lord, that's the greatest news! Thing you're doing won't hurt my garden, will it?"

"Course not! The wolfsbane will still be there, poisonous as ever. But not under the wall's control. Are you ready? Because you have to do it with me. The Acer server requires that only you can do this type of electronic surgery."

"It won't hurt my writing, will it? Or disconnect me from the good Acer spirit, will it?" Tilda was rubbing her hands together, nervously fussing with her hair.

"No, not at all. It will stop a wall from sending out evil thoughts that interfere with your life. It's been controlling your mouse, too. We want our Acer and just you to control that. Are you ready?"

"Yes, yes, I think so!"

"Give me your fingers. Here, place three fingers on these keys: o, u, t, . . . good. I'm going to hold these keys: e, v, i, l, just like this. Now you hit the Esc key."

"What?"

"Push Esc, the escape key, upper left on the keyboard.

"How?"

"With a finger from your other hand."

While she followed Davey's instructions to enliven the event, he whistled a plummeting sound like a passing train.

"We're done! Success! An old stone wall no longer has any power over your computer! It's had all the evil stuff driven out of it! And the Wolfsbane family is no longer involved!"

Davey slapped her on the shoulder, knocking her forward and upsetting her tea cup and saucer. "You did it, Ms. Duclos!"

Tilda was dumbstruck.

"My work here is done!" Davey solemnly closed his Acer tool bag.

"Well, Davey, I'm speechless. You drove the evil from my computer just like that! I have to write about your talent in my book."

"Good idea!" said Davey, rising from the table.

"Can I give you some money? Would five dollars help you out?"

"No, but thank you. It's a free service for loyal Acer users just like you."

"Oh, Davey, that's so sweet."

"If you don't mind, can I share your information with my associates? It might get me a raise."

"Sure! As a reward, I'd like to share with you a little bit of wholesome yen-yang. A virile young man like you has a lot of energy, and tension gets built up."

Wasn't he warned about that?

"Sorry, I'm behind schedule. Gotta run."

He couldn't abandon Simon any longer and by now he'd be into all kinds of mischief at Sam's!

"I insist," she reached out to take hold of his arm.

"I've got to go, Ms. Duclos. Thanks for the tea."

Before she could get a grip on his jacket, Davey flew out of the kitchen and was gone.

* * * * * *

Kirby and Charles were plopped in the grass on the Williams Dairy side of the barn, their backs resting against the now-impotent wall. Charles' cell did the Beethoven. It was Davey calling as he ran to his Honda.

"I've got everything done. Had to do kinda hocus-pocus thing to drive out the malware! You'd have loved it! Damn, should have made a video! I'd get a million hits on YouTube!"

"I've been worried sick!" gulped Kirby.

Charles was confused: *Drove out malware?*

"I've got to get to Simon before we lose Sam as a friend!"

Charles and Kirby hurried to the main road and caught a glimpse of Davey's Honda as it sped away. They vaulted over the Williams Dairy fence and dove into the 'Vette. Charles spun the 'Vette around in the grass, burnt black tracks when they hit the tarmac, and chased after him.

CHAPTER 51

Will he ever learn to keep
his big mouth shut?"

Surprisingly, the scorned Vermont State Trooper's green Dodge was parked in front of Sam's garage. In the bay, Slobberu was still up on the lift and Sam was under the front quarter panel cursing up a storm. In his hand was a heavy wrench that he used to attack the inside wheel well.

"Damn aftermarket morons! How can something so fuckin' simple be made impossible to install without putting a goddamn torch to it!" As an afterthought, "Forgive my cursing, Lord Jesus."

He flung the wrench and it helicoptered across the garage to miraculously clunk perfectly into the open tool chest. *Jesus Christ, nice response!*

Davey piled into the office to find baby Simon on Trooper Francine Forget's knee. They were watching *The Simpsons* on Sam's surprised-that-it-could-work antique black-and-white TV. Trooper Fran had safely stashed her holster cross belt and firearm on the top of the adjoining cabinet. Mister Fritz was still in prison.

Seconds later, Kirby and Charles arrived.

Trooper Forget was pissed, "Add child abandonment to the other crimes you've committed this week." She gingerly passed Simon to Davey while making little kissy noises.

Annoyed, Kirby responded, "No one's been abandoned, Frannie."

Davey got right into changing Simon's very pungent diaper. He was naturally excited over his exploits with Tilda and couldn't help commanding everyone's attention.

"First thing, you all, Tilly believes her Acer does the writing. Pulling stories out of her rich subconscious. Cool, huh? So let me tell you what I did about the evil wall . . . "

Charles immediately interrupted, "That's fantastic news! Save it for tonight during dinner."

Charles desperately hoped he'd take the hint. Trooper Fran was all ears and was unaware of their involvement with Tilda. But Davey was hyped and blabbed on.

"As I was saying, I did some Acer voodoo and exercised the evil in the wall." He gave Simon's butt a couple of swipes with a moist Pampers baby wipe.

"My Boy! God, I love him!" cried out Kirby, "But will he ever learn to keep his big mouth shut?"

Ignoring her, Davey wrapped up the soiled diaper and continued, justly proud of his accomplishment. "Then, we turned the wolfsbane back into a poisonous plant, no longer under the wall's power! So, all's good in that department."

"Like I just said, Davey, let's discuss later," said Charles staring, unblinking at Davey.

"There's more! I made a quick scan of her emails, no way anyone else is working with her. Get this, she's ready to bail on Timothy, at least that's what she said . . . " his voice trailed off, finally aware by their stares that something was amiss.

As much as Kirby and Charles may have prayed for Trooper Forget to be comatose, Trooper Forget's quizzical looks meant she smelled something was afoot. If Detective White and Kirby were involved, it had to be wholly illegitimate. Plus, she loathed being left out of anything.

"What in God's name are you all up to? Davey babbling about an evil wall and wolfsbane? What the hell, someone better to tell me what is going on right now or shit's going to fly!"

There was the expected, awkward silence and furtive glances at one another. Quietly, they relocated to safer places away from Trooper Fran, who was taking deep breaths and ready to explode.

Charles finally broke the deafening silence.

"Trooper Forget, honestly, we were just yesterday talking about getting your help."

Davey at last caught on and attempted lame amends for his blabbing. "They were, really! I heard them talking about telling you something."

Charles was resigned—it was now or never—to enlist Trooper Forget. It wasn't going to be the conciliatory talk of saving Tilda he had planned to have with Trooper Fran over wine and dinner at an expensive restaurant.

"If I tell you everything, I mean absolutely everything, will you help us do a good, unselfish deed?" he asked.

"Law enforcement professional to professional, I positively do not want to be involved in your shenanigans. Better tell me what's going on and maybe I'll leave without busting all of you!"

"Okay, I'll tell you everything if you'll say yes to helping us," said Charles, as if he had some negotiation advantage.

"Fuck no! No fucking way!"

"Is that really no, Frannie? Coming from the most yes girl in the twelfth grade at Middlebury High?" snapped Kirby, informing everyone something they didn't need to know, but was cool to hear.

"Well, I couldn't possibly break the record you set before me!" growled Trooper Forget.

"Kiss my ass, you stuck-up snot. Slapping a speeding ticket on Charlie was ultra lowlife. Don't you know how cops help each other? It's like a major theme of fuckin' TV, Frannie!" Kirby shot back.

"Enough, ladies! Both of you, please, this is important!" Charles put his palms together as if he was making a little prayer (which they all thought was hugely silly for Charles, supposedly a hardened NYPD detective). "You two, please cool down."

Kirby glanced expectantly at the shop door, "We need Sam right away. Maybe he can better explain Tilly's fucked-up situation."

"Right! I have better things to do," said Trooper Forget. Casting her head about, "Where the hell's my gear?" referring to her holster belt and firearm, which were sitting on Sam's battered filing cabinet beside the TV set. She grabbed the unbalanced and weighted belt, heavy with firearm and ammo.

In the awkward process of flinging the belt around her shoulder, she abruptly swung about to face the shop door—precisely as it was vigorously booted open by Sam.

Her head and nose collided flatly into the heavy, swinging door. The Subaru parts Sam was lugging scattered to the floor and a flood of blood spewed out Trooper Forget's nose.

"Oh, baby, I'm sorry! Sorry! Sorry!" Sam cried out.

* * * * * *

It took ten minutes using ice cubes wrapped in towels to slow the stream of blood out of her nose. Trooper Forget ended up in Sam's green banker chair with her booted feet propped on his desk, wet towel on her face, and tissues stuffed into her nose. Noone knew what to say or where to look, so they filled in the awkward time by repeatedly pestering her by asking how she felt.

Sam kept trying to push on her a fist full of capsules, "Fran, you can't overdose on Tylenol. Two is not enough. Four is better, believe me!"

After things had quieted, Charles decided to give Trooper Forget another, more earnest try. And he would hereafter call her Fran, rather than Trooper Forget in an attempt to take the edge off their relationship.

"Fran, you know Tilly Duclos?"

She removed the towel from her face and whispered so as not to further disturb her swelling nose. "That's a joke, isn't it? Faded red '92 Subaru, plate GBT 814? A menace on our highways. A threat to the safety and well-being of men, women, children, and all forms of Vermont's natural wildlife. Currently, has an extension for emissions repair."

She snake-eyed Sam, who was consumed with being attentive to her discomfort.

"I'm working on Tilly's repairs, Fran. Really, I am."

She twisted around to give him a chilling look, "You've got another week's grace. After that, only some God-like intervention will keep me from getting her permanently off our roads."

Much to Kirby's wry amusement, Charles huddled yet closer to Fran and became fawningly sympathetic.

"Fran, you'll be fine in a few days, maybe have some minor discoloration. Now that you're feeling better, we wholeheartedly agree, working together we can get Tilly out of the driver's seat."

"The snake becomes nice when he needs something," Fran uttered, rewrapping the towel.

"I'll explain our predicament. Tilly has been sending queries to literary agents—"

"It's a submission for representation to literary agents by wanna-be writers," clarified Kirby.

"She's been ignored—"

"One could say disrespected," chirped Kirby. Charles gave her a look.

"In her angry, unbalanced mind and controlled by an imaginary brother, she's sending literary agents maple syrup samples—" he was still too slow for Kirby.

"Maple syrup samples laced with wolfsbane!" declared Kirby.

Trooper Forget, still holding her palm and a towel to her nose, muttered, "I'm advising you, everyone here, anything said may be used in a court of law." Then, she tried to slide out of the chair.

"Fran, just listen to the man!" Sam put his hand on her shoulder, keeping her from getting up.

Charles went on, "She's put four female literary agents and two innocent male companions into New York City hospitals. Thank God, they've all recovered. I'm here making an unofficial investigation and, if needed, will pass everything I've learned to your people."

"So, you've been lying to me all this time! Fishing! You dick! And you, too, Kirby Clark. I should arrest you both! Withholding evidence of a crime, accessory to misconduct."

"Fran, let me finish! The other day, if Sam hadn't alerted us, fifty-six wolfsbane-laced samples would have gone out to literary agents."

Kirby exclaimed, "Frannie, imagine fifty-six poisoned maple syrup samples mailed from our little fucking Bristol post office! Think how the shit would fly if we hadn't done what we did!" She threw out her arms as if reading a headline in the sky, "Bristol Vermont, Poisoning Capital of America!"

"That's what the post office thing was about?" Nasal mumbling from Trooper Fran. "Sam Piper, you backstabber, you knew all about this and didn't tell me!"

"You were busy," Sam pleaded.

By this time, everyone understood Sam and Trooper Fran had some undisclosed, personal relationship. This was being unartfully exposed by the too-familiar manner he was holding the ice bag to the side of her face while his arm was awkwardly wrapped around her chest and hoisting her left breasts.

Charles stepped in, "Fran, Tilly's mental illness created an imaginary brother, Timothy. Davey just confirmed that the fantasy brother is the one who persuaded her to act against literary agents. We've discovered all the paraphernalia in her barn."

"So, you're a psychiatrist, too, Detective White? Let me get this straight: Tilly Duclos is doing murderous acts against literary agents and you want me to help. Are you all out of your fucking minds!"

"Frannie, shut up and listen to the man!" bellowed Kirby, while dramatically buffing herself on the forehead in the "What, am I stupid?" response.

"Putting her in the system would just be cruel. Nine times out of ten it doesn't end well. Often, they become indigent, their property is confiscated, and they get marginal, if any, real care," said Charles.

After nudging Sam away from her, Trooper Fran regained composure and softly spoke through her face wrappings.

"Yeah, you're breaking my heart. Attempted murder is a felony crime. I don't give a bird shit on a post if you think I'm going to help you do anything—except help put her away!"

That kind of put a stop to everything. Everyone, except Fran sighed.

"I'm thirsty," said Kirby, finally.

Sliding a straw into an apple juice container for Simon, Davey asked, "By the way, who cuts the grass, does the snowplowing? Have you noticed the farmhouse is sliding off its foundation?"

They shared a moment of perplexity, then focused on Sam. He was collecting an odd assortment of different-sized glasses.

"I've been keeping up the best I can," said Sam. "Last year, I had to replace her front door or she'd freeze. That was a job for a professional, but I somehow did it, and it closed and opened. But friends, it's killing me, I can't do another winter for her. She needs to go into a real home with aids and medication."

Sam found the bottle of Bushmills Single Malt Irish whiskey squirreled away under his desk.

"Working together, we can make the rest of her life bearable in a decent environment, a place where she can't hurt anyone," said Charles.

"Notice Kirby, Fran, he said work together," reiterated Sam as he poured healthy shots for everyone.

Charles eyed Fran and spoke candidly, "We rid her of Timothy and she'll be free. Davey seems to be sure she has no confederates so there's no Internet conspiracy."

"Come on, Fran, we'll get her into treatment," said Sam. "And," as an afterthought, "off our roads, too."

"If KC and I buy her farm at a fair price, along with any other assets and her Social Security, she'll live in a decent home that will meet her needs," explained Charles to Fran who was checking her nose pads for fresh blood spotting.

"She'll teach yen-yang, whatever that game is," said Davey, now bouncing Simon on a knee.

"Yeah, that's going to be a big hit in the old folks' home," said Sam, making Charles guffaw.

Fran muttered from under the iced towel, "You two are that serious? Kirby, buying a place together with him? That's wack, or you're both pathetically lonely."

"Let's just stay away from personal stuff and stop straying from our subject," said Sam, trying to rein in the conversation.

"Trooper Fran, I'm NYPD. There's not much I can do. But you know everyone in the county—the Forgets are well-connected throughout the state. How can we convince you to go to your family to help us get her into a secure facility, not a cell."

"We're relying on you to do the decent thing, Frannie." Kirby carried on, trying not to exhibit her growing exasperation.

"Fuck that! Stop repeating yourselves. I'm not doing it! Let New York State or Vermont put her away," she snapped, unsoftened by their mushy pleas.

"Ah, well, there's a nasty rub to us doing nothing, Fran," said Charles. "No matter what evidence the D.A. has, her defense attorney is going to rip their case apart. He'll plead, 'Find that crazy brother who's done these horrific crimes! Let this innocent, fragile lady live un-besmirched by unsubstantiated, evil deeds done by her brother!'"

"You're telling us, if they can't prove the brother doesn't exist, she'll go free?" Aghast, Kirby staggered against Sam's metal filing cabinets.

"Can't prove a negative. Jury's not going to put her away. Happens all the time," agreed Sam.

Fran looked up from the face towel and eyed each conspirator. She gently rolled her knotted head about, shuffled her boots on the dusty floor between the curved oak legs of the banker's chair, and exhaled several huffs and puffs. All were reminded of Barney Fife, a comparison she would loathe, so they kept mum.

"Charles and Sammy are, I hate to agree, correct. No jury in Vermont or New York will do shit. She'll be freed, back tormenting us within weeks," said Fran, followed by a regretful sigh.

Was the tide was turning with Trooper Fran.

"There's insufficient time to do this properly. Find a real estate agent, get appraisals, put it on the market?" She was weakening.

"No other way. My captain will order me to turn everything over to the D.A. next time we speak. Both states will come to the same conclusion, it will be better for the other state to handle this hot potato. You can be certain there will be a hellacious public fight between Albany and Montpelier."

"I'm listening," said Fran, who, despite being obnoxious and nasty, was very smart.

"They'll both realize they haven't a case against her. Except perhaps, for mailing Timothy's packages." Charles took a deep breath, "This is no cakewalk for me, Fran. If NYPD finds out what I'm orchestrating, I'm toast."

Kirby, in a calm, civilized, and woman-to-woman manner, came nearer to Fran's mummy-wrapped face.

"Fran, the maple sugar industry in Vermont is going to get clobbered. We'll lose hundreds of jobs; money will flee the state. Worse, Canadian producers are going to skin us alive! We're talking about our state's reputation and its most recognized commercial asset!"

"Well, actually more people know us for the fall foliage, mumbled Davey to Charles.

"Can it, Davey!" shot Kirby.

Fran adjusted the bloody-nose cloth. Everyone stared at her, making her very uncomfortable. "Cut me some slack. I'm thinking about it, okay? I'm thinking."

"Come on, Fran. Do this humane act for her. You don't want things to continue with Duclos for another decade, do you?" appealed Sam.

"Yeah, fuck it. I'll make a few calls. What more can I do to jeopardize all the work I've done to make a decent life? And you, detective New York City shyster, fair market value for her farm. Not a cent less!"

"Alright!" Davey cried out and did a knuckle rap with Sam.

"Let's think positively about the future, okay?" said Sam, all lovey-dovey, their foreheads briefly touching.

"Ooooooh" was spontaneously mouthed by everyone, seeing the cat was now publicly out of the bag about the Fran and Sam relationship.

Sam said, "I'd kiss you, but you have a string of clotted blood that's . . . yeah, it's sliding out your nose. Take this cloth. Catch it quickly!"

Davey mouthed off, "Looks like a used tampon. Yuck!"

Kirby popped him on the back of his head.

"Mom! Leave me alone."

"Then, watch your mouth, big shot," she growled.

"We're all exhausted. Fran, you deserve gold stars. Let's call it quits for today," said Charles.

"Hey, we're a goodie-two-shoes SWAT team!" said Davey, passing Simon to Kirby and letting Mister Fritz out of prison. Davey collapsed the cage and began collecting toys. Mister Fritz went right to the pile of bloody tissues on the floor and grabbed a mouthful before Charles could get to him.

Fran lowered the bloodied nose cloth, "No, Davey, it's a felonious conspiracy. And David Clark, don't forget to renew your expiring driver's license."

That drew looks of surprise from everyone.

"Well, damn, you all. I had to figure out whose child I was sitting for!"

Davey looked up from collecting the cow toys and solemnly repeated: "*Felonious conspiracy.* It has an awesome ring, doesn't it? We're conspirators! I love it!" Davey threw a fist into the air, way too much like Che Guevara.

Charles grimaced. *Fuck me.*

Trooper Fran pulled herself together. The gun belt was carefully slung over her shoulder and Sam's arm supported her as they gingerly moved toward the door. Then they abruptly stopped—when she remembered something important.

"Charlie, I wish you'd explained this to me earlier. Like at the post office with Boucher."

"Yeah, I was dumb. Now, we know you'd understand," said Charles, being as contrite as he could.

"That's the problem. I reported the incident and your speeding ticket to my field station commander. I hope it doesn't get to your boss." She hunched her shoulders, "Sorry."

"Don't worry about it. We're wrapping it up. We can make it disappear."

"Alright, big shot detective, call me tomorrow. Tell me exactly what you want me to do then."

CHAPTER 52

Do not be so open-minded
that your brains fall out

That evening, Davey and Simon returned to Davey's apartment. Simon's mom had a night off the pole and planned to take him to an outing the next day with her parents in St. Johnsbury.

Having no desire to cook, Kirby got DoorDash delivery from Kentucky Fried Chicken: mashed potatoes, coleslaw, and a greasy half bucket, although KFC calls it "moist." They settled down to eat and drank a bottle of Cava sparkling wine while watching the news.

Charles kept busy flipping back and forth from several stations, editing their viewing into news highlights. Eventually, they migrated upstairs, showered, and had a stress-relieving encounter without messing up the sheets or even getting sweaty. Afterward, they decided to read for a while in bed.

Kirby finished the final four pages of *Breakfast with Buddha*. She closed the jacket and with a sigh rested it flat on her chest.

"I'm glad I read this. Not to freak you out, Charlie, but I'm attached to the idea that humankind may exist simultaneously in multiple levels of reality and different time spheres. My spiritual doppelganger is a French prostitute living with Napoleon. I trust you won't be jealous of a complex, stubby man who publicly passes gas at the dinner table," she said glancing over at him.

"Charming," said Charles, not looking up from *Landon Mayer's Guide to Flies.*

"My great-granny was a disciple of Madama Blavatsky, the spiritualist. She was big in Vermont at the turn of the century."

"The spiritualist, Madama Blavatsky? She's lightyears away in the metaphysical universe from your Buddha guy." He kept reading.

"I disagree, *mon cher.* Reincarnation is an element in almost all religions. Don't get me wrong, I'm not keen on the Buddhist cycles of reincarnation. I don't want to return as a butterfly on my path to divine nature."

Charles put down his book. "Thought you were going to drift off. Not sleepy?"

"Charlie, did you know many believe those who die, who never gained enlightenment, are propelled into a different existence? Their life gets picked up where it left off in another time? Cosmic strings woven into the fabric of their existence will forever connect them to their prior life. Sometimes, they have a notion of their past station; sometimes they don't. I think that's kind of cool, don't you?"

He gave her a quizzical look.

"No shit, Charlie! I didn't make that up! There are all sorts of tenets of reincarnation like that, that intersect in many belief systems."

"Well, it explains ghosts and sightings of dead people coming back for visits," offered Charlie, now sitting up. "It's reassuring the cosmos may allow the misfortunate a second chance for enlightenment when they missed what would have been their natural destiny. With that treasured insight, I'm done reading." He snapped shut his book.

Kirby rotated to her side to face him. "If a Creator deems life precious, that says to me no life will be frivolously squandered. Which is a very reverent way to emphasize humanity is to be venerated."

"If you say so, it must be," he said with a twinkle.

"That does create a conflict with abortion, doesn't it?" she said uneasily. "Of course, if you haven't been dropped, you haven't had a life to revisit."

"Jesus, Kirby, you country hicks. Humans are born, not 'dropped.' Life is complicated and so can be death," he reflected, "there are some things not worth arguing about. Especially with daughters."

"Or lovers. Charlie, I come with a pile of existential dilemmas from four semesters of Comparative Religion. I've got to explore backups since I'm likely doomed as a Christian."

"Nah. You may not practice Christianity but you do the best you can to live by it. G. K. Chesterton, or someone like that, wrote: 'Do not be so open-minded that your brains fall out.'"

"I like that. That's a good one for my Davey. Good night, Charlie. Love you."

Charles gave her words a brief consideration, recognizing it was the first time she had defined their relationship as one of love. "I know you do. I love you, too."

With that, they each turned off their bedside lamps. Kirby was soon asleep, but Charlie had a hard time getting to sleep—but not from existential questions looping through his brain. Trooper Fran Forget had taken a big step toward saving Tilda Duclos, which was great, and a commitment she could live up to without risking her career. But how was Mahoney going to respond if he discovered Trooper Forget's family was involved and that he and Kirby were angling for the felon's farm with her assistance?

Might everything they've accomplished and their lofty goal get tossed? And he disgraced?

* * * * * *

In the morning, after coffee and letting Mister Fritz out to expand the brown spots on the grass, Charles opened the flash drive with Tilda's files. In the latest version of *Final Love,* there were a slew of stream-of-consciousness sex scenes with some Roman centurion. Was Tilda a nymphomaniac? Before or after schizophrenia came into play? Or simply an oversexed senior? With the advent of online pornography, sex flourished within all age groups. He looked at her search history, but there were no pornographic sites.

Perhaps the library preinstalled adult site-blocking software?

He opened her emails and perused her in- and out-boxes—only rejections for *Final Love* from publishers and agents. Hallelujah! Tilda *was* working alone! Outside of the four agents from the guild rejecting her query and thus getting maple syrup samples, there was no indication syrup was sent to anyone else. Their next move would determine Tilda's future: a rest home or a cell. Either way, the repercussions would travel through Charles' career, Kirby's work at VAMP, and have a huge impact on Davey and Simon. Trooper Francine Forget will not be impacted much as she was insulated by layers of family.

In the two-plus years since losing Mary, Charles had abandoned prayer. He had little faith the Almighty had a yen to alter earthly outcomes. But this morning he stepped outside to the terrace, took in the crisp morning air, gazed up into the bright blue sky with its cottony white clouds, and implored: *Please don't let me fuck this up!*

* * * * * *

That evening, they met Davey and Simon at Olive Garden for dinner. Simon was big on the salty bread sticks and Kirby on the unlimited salad bowl. Charles and Davey surfed and turfed.

Charles, between bites of steak, spontaneously asked Kirby, "Do you have an attorney we can trust all of this to?"

"As far as you can trust any bottom feeder."

"Come on, Mom, Uncle John isn't that bad," said Davey, catching narrowing eyes from Mom.

"AKA Johnnie Lawsuit. My ex's brother did our divorce. Our eighteen years of marriage, or sixteen years of agony, earned me alimony of $1500 a month until I remarry." She glared at her son, making him squirm.

Charles got the impression when push had come to shove in their divorce, Davey may have taken a side, the wrong side.

"Don't look at me. I don't know anything about it," Davey's eyes rolled over to the salad bar for distraction.

"You better not. Don't worry, Charlie. Cohabitation doesn't count. A simple, honest split my greedy husband didn't want. He had a girlfriend on the side, and I didn't take to sharing. I hear the skank split from him anyway. Get this—one afternoon when I was at work, he tried to steal my furniture and guns! Can you believe it?"

Charles thought she had finished, looked at his cooling steak.

"Worse, he pilfered through my fishing gear, grabbing my best stuff. Then, he stole two of my Paul Schmookler presentation flies that were expensively framed and hung in the bathroom. The bum got part-time control of my Teddi, too. I'm just waiting for him to fuck up, 'scuse my language. Be late on the alimony once and then he'll get to know my dragon lady side."

She eyed Davey, giving him the indication that that was a message for his dad. Kirby had finally finished rattling off things of woe, her shopping list of misery from her ex—or so Charles thought.

"KC, some things, you know, water under the bridge. Also, we can't walk into a bank and simply apply for a joint mortgage and not explain what we're up to with Tilly. If we're going to buy the farm as partners, we need a banker willing to bend some rules."

"Got a great banker, no sweat. I trust you, Charlie—but I'm still going to keep track of my flies. And Davey, you should note how calm and collected Charlie is. You don't hear him shooting off his mouth, even if he's got a lot to brag about," she said, making them both laugh.

Davey sat up, "Mom, is it legal for Uncle Herb to do banking stuff for both of you? Isn't that a conflict of interest?" Kirby moaned and leaned into her palm on the table, momentarily hiding her eyes.

"Charlie, shockingly, my former has honest, good-hearted, accomplished brothers. A slick lawyer, a sensible banker, and a practical accountant. Whereas I ended up marrying the duckweed outdoors brother who sells used cars on the side. Fact is, they don't trust him any more than I do. He's sold them more overpriced, crappy cars over the years than Rat's Salvage in Colchester."

"Thanks, man, for looking out for me," said Charles, reaching to Davey for a knuckle tap.

"Divide and conquer, you two? Look out, Davey, you're on thin ice," said Kirby, grumbling.

Davey had decided to go back to his apartment with Simon after dinner, only an hour's drive. Simon's mom was taking him to a neighbor's birthday party the next morning. That little guy kept quite busy.

* * * * * *

Later that night, Kirby and Charles were downstairs on the sofa in front of the TV with the sound off and Mister Fritz lounging between them. Two empty glasses and an empty bottle of wine were resting on the low cocktail table in front of them. Kirby was wearing jean shorts with frilly, worn strands and an untucked blue herringbone long-sleeve shirt. Charles was musing on how enticing she was, even in her ex-husband's shirt. He dawdled with the TV remote.

"What do you want to watch?" he asked.

"I don't care what we watch."

"You're kidding."

"Nope, I'm not. I'm falling asleep. That was a nice wine."

He pondered, reminiscing on Mary's command of the remote.

"If we get this property, you'd want me to do all the work around the house?" he casually asked.

"You're wondering if I am a little miss homemaker in an apron, cooking brownies while you get to do the good stuff any self-respecting Vermont woman likes to do? How do you expect me to stay in shape if I'm not shoveling snow, carrying firewood, or pushing my car out of snow drifts?"

"Well, that's refreshing. So, you'll not be asking me to fix this or that?"

"Look, Charlie, darling. I don't want to deflate your masculinity but asking my man to fix something is not in my vocabulary."

Charles pondered the situation while scratching the recent grey growth on his chin. He wanted to cover all the entertainment bases.

"What about watching pornography on the computer?"

"When we're alone like tonight, that's one thing, but never with my son or grandson upstairs. In that case, if you're amorous and need relief, we'll take a drive. I'll thrill you in the car."

He took a moment to think about the options.

"I'd like to know what you *really* like. You know, sexual stuff you've kept hidden."

"What do you mean, *really* like?"

"Straight sex, oral, anal, lesbian action? Why waste time figuring things out?"

"Charlie, whatever floats your boat. We're almost halfway there already, aren't we?"

"That's true. Cool." Remote still in hand, he checked a few stations. "Sometimes a little subjugation might be fun, too," he probed.

"Sure, I'm up for experimentation. No pain, vomit, scat. Not interested in having a safe word.'"

"Absolutely, out of the question," wasn't his bag either.

She thought it over for a minute, decided to give it a trial run.

"Get over there, big daddy. On all fours like the dog you are," she ordered, then gave herself a loud swat against her exposed thigh as an incentivizing sound effect for him.

"What? KC, I'm not talking about *me!*"

She stared unblinking at him, then motioned with a finger to a place on the carpet.

"Really? You want me to? Honestly? Right now?"

"Crawl, crawl, you useless dog, to the kitchen!" she taunted.

He did. Across the carpet to the tiled kitchen entry, then turned to face her. *What's next?*

"Do the dishes."

"That's not quite what I had in mind."

She burst out laughing so hard, she slid off the sofa and knocked Mister Fritz off his spot. Inconvenienced, Mister Fritz trotted to his more placid bed in the kitchen. Kirby couldn't stop laughing and Charles didn't know what to do.

CHAPTER 53

Timmy Gardner passed away . . .

Charles' plan to rescue Tilda Wilcox Duclos from Timothy's domination had to happen quickly as the wheels of misguided justice had caught up to him. JJ, his charming trainee and devoted friend at the precinct, texted him something was ready to explode in the Glass Palace and an order to return to New York City from Captain Mahoney was imminent.

For Charles, he'd passed the point of no return. It was make-or-break time for the felonious conspiracy, and Charles decided he wouldn't leave until it was done. He'd have to stop answering his phone. As a get-around, he'd call the Glass Palace's direct line after hours when Bookus and Mahoney were off duty and leave a voice message. He'd mention things like he had no signal, his laptop was acting up, and a dead battery. Then, he'd drop a cryptic message regarding the status of the investigation, and that he wanted to take a vacation leave after wrapping up the case.

Trooper Fran Forget's facial disfigurement was a blessing for Tilda's rescue scheme. It allowed Fran to be on leave with pay, which gave her time to cajole her well-connected family into helping, and time for Kirby and Charles to conspire with her. Everyone of importance had to know and understand Tilda's pathetic predicament. It was subtly understood they'd have a debt owed to them by an NYPD detective.

Fortunately, Trooper Fran still didn't know Charles was set to retire within months.

In Charles' investigation of Tilda's situation, there was little on record. The Wilcoxes, Tilda's grandparents, had a mountain of state and county records, mostly from The Dewy Drop Inn period. Of more interest was uncovering information on Tilda's mom, Rose Wilcox Duclos, who had corresponded with a New York State adoption agency. Decades later, Tilda Duclos had spent considerable effort to uncover the whereabouts of a child in foster services in the early 1960s.

With all of Tilda's messes and her fractured life, Charles began to sense there was a link to another person—a link that, if true, would be astounding serendipity. No, it would be more like a train wreck or a bizarre freeway pileup where no one saw each other in the snow storm.

Charles had a final bit of research to do in the online county records. He searched the *Addison County Independent* newspaper for Tilda Duclos from 1955 to 1999 and found only illustrious local people with the last name of Duclos mentioned. All were incredibly successful and important members of the community: William James Duclos, III, a heavy equipment retailer, an accomplished snowmobiler, and a renowned maple sugar cooker; John Frye Duclos, a master carpenter and house builder extraordinaire; and Jennifer C. Duclos, four-time county fair winner for the best apple pie in Addison County. But the only mention of a Tilda or Tilly Duclos were in minor blurbs concerning Presley Public Library fundraising, and the sale of The Dewy Drop Inn.

Charles was about to fold up the laptop when he remembered the conversation with Head Librarian Reddy about the 1976 Bicentennial celebration. In a buried back page of the *Addison County Independent*, after the happy hoopla and smashing color photos of the Bicentennial celebrations, he uncovered in the Police Blotter section the final spike to Tilda Duclos' mental state and the cause for decades of anguish. The short paragraph explained everything:

"Ten-year-old Timmy Gardner suffered a fatal wound to his neck and a mutilated right wrist while igniting a powerful firework, commonly known as a "cherry bomb." The fireworks (sic) had been placed on a landmark stone wall at the family's vacation home in Lincoln. Reportedly, the firework was mishandled and exploded prematurely in his hand, unleashing a barrage of stone shrapnel. The fatal injury, a severed carotid artery, was caused by stone shards shooting into the youth's neck. The explosion also removed two fingers. Timmy Gardner passed away before his parents and a neighbor could rush him to Middlebury Hospital. Authorities are investigating the tragic accident."

No google map location was needed; Detective White knew where it had happened. He crawled into bed, snuggled up to KC, and decided not to tell anyone. No need to create more drama about Tilda's life.

* * * * * *

"Romance Agents & Writers Guild. Pamela speaking. How may I help you?"

"Hello, Pamela. This is Detective White, NYPD. I tried speaking with you and Jeffery at Brooklyn Hospital Center the morning you were hospitalized. I don't expect you to remember."

"I'm sorry, I hardly remembered a thing until days later. I'm at work and can't discuss it at all."

She glanced over at MJ. Thank God she had run out of tissues.

"I'd like you to call me back. It's very important."

"Have you found who poisoned us?"

"Can you keep a secret?" asked Charles.

"No, but I want to know what's going on anyway."

"Would you be interested in representing the culprit if they wrote a nonfictional account of the crime?"

"Oh, my God! Yes, of course!" Pamela whispered.

"Again, can you keep a secret?"

"Yes, of course! Mum's the word. I promise on a stack of Bibles!"

"Call me back when you can speak confidentially. Agreed?"

"Use the number that's showing on my cell?"

"Yes."

"Detective White, correct? Call you tonight, yes?"

"Correct. Say, any time after six-thirty but before seven." He disconnected.

* * * * * *

It was hot dog and burger night with Davey tending the grill, Charles making potato salad, and Kirby playing with Simon and Mister Fritz.

"KC, you invited Sam and Fran, but they weren't sure. Experience tells me that's a no," said Charles. "Davey, hold off on more burgers."

"All felonious conspirators are on for tomorrow?" asked Davey, pantomiming with an exaggerated punch to the gut.

"All aboard!" Charles said, adding some wine vinegar to the potato salad.

Charles heard Beethoven and hastened to his cell phone, which displayed New York City's 212 area code.

"Good evening, Pamela."

"Hello, Detective White. First, is this really a possibility—me representing the criminals who poisoned us?"

"That's affirmative. But it's going to take some finagling, and you're going to have to do exactly what I ask. Is that too much?"

"No, not at all. Agents are familiar with dealing with all sorts of limitations and restrictions. It's part of the negotiations, the process of getting published and out to market."

"There's not a lot of wiggle room on the negotiation side. You either take it or I approach Phylis Cartwell, who might be a better choice for my client's career."

"No, of course. You set the conditions. I do have a teensy, itty-bitty problem with MJ and the Romance Agents & Writers Guild."

"How's that?"

"My new arrangement with MJ is she gets first pick at new queries."

"Queries from unknowns?"

"Correct. She looks at everything. If there's a query idea that has a slight chance of being marketable, she'll feel out the situation and may sign the author. Frankly, it's never happened before."

"But she has first dibs?" clarified Charles.

"Yes."

"Are you at a computer, and can you access the guild's email submissions files?"

"Yes, I'm home and I have access to any files at the guild."

"I want you to look at submissions to the guild."

Long silence.

"Right now?"

"Yes, right now!" He was getting cranky watching Davey, Simon, and Kirby too frequently taste-test his unfinished potato salad.

"Okay, keep your shirt on." Pamela hummed a little ditty for a minute, "I'm in and have submissions from at least four years back. There are 67,000 in total."

"Look for any query from Tillysoldfarm@gmail or *Final Love*."

"Let's try query: Final Love."

Several deep breaths later, Charles could hear her typing.

"Good God. This emailer has hit us over a dozen times in the last three months."

"Has to be her. Read it."

"Let's see: '*Final Love* is a novel that will outsell the Bible.' Seems it's about a possessed stone wall and the tender love between—Detective White, this is just not worth responding to. MJ didn't respond and I didn't either. You want me to take this fruitcake on as a client? Are you for real?"

Pamela's sigh could be heard all the way to Vermont and to Kirby in the kitchen.

"Pamela, you're not representing her ability to write. You're representing a participant in a heinous crime that for humanitarian reasons will never be prosecuted."

"Alright, alright! I get it—hold on, what do you mean will never be prosecuted?"

"We'll get to that later. You now have a query that MJ can reject. Forward it or redirect it to her and have her reject it. You'll scoop it up before she figures what's what."

"That'll be easy for me to do. Is this query really from the criminals who made us sick?"

"You're not asking me to break confidentiality and professional ethics, are you?"

"'Course not. Can you give me a hint of why it actually happened to us and the others?"

"Sure. Think about this: six innocent New Yorkers are hospitalized because an unhinged geriatric librarian and her nonexistent, malicious brother seek revenge on callous literary agents who don't write thank you notes in response to their queries."

"Let me get this straight. The brother is the evil one, and he doesn't exist. The spinster sets out to poison me because I didn't respond to her moronic queries?"

"That's right. Although ultimately, it was probably MJ who is responsible," said Charles hesitantly.

"Damn straight. The maple syrup came addressed to her, and she gave it to me."

"That's correct," said Charlie.

"Is she ever going to be brought to justice?"

"Who? Sidel?"

"No! The lady who sent the poison!"

"Unlikely."

"And so, what happens to her?"

"With your help, we'll get her into a facility that will take care of her."

"Just to be clear, her story is the actual maple syrup crime? She's going to write her side, and I'm going edit, ghostwrite, and be her agent?"

"Pamela, I haven't any idea what she's going to write. I assume it'll be gibberish. But you'll be improving a pathetic, miserable life for someone who has no place to turn. You'll have to measure the value of that on your own."

"Detective White, I get your suggested narrative and the potential for a personal heartwarming read, but that may not be transferrable to a marketable book. I don't see a rosy ending."

"That's happening in a week. Hold tight for the denouement."

"Really? Okay. Do you have a working title?"

"How about: *Vermont's Sweetest Killers: The True Story of Tilda and Timothy?*"

"Too long, but we have time. It's not necessary to get bogged down with the title at this stage."

"Agreed."

"So, what do you get out of this?"

"That's complicated. The best outcome is that I get to be with someone I love."

"The lady who poisoned us?" He heard Pamela gasp and then choking noises. "I'm alright, I'm alright."

"Jesus, no, not her. Don't get me wrong though, she's endearing in inexplicable ways."

"That's all you're getting out of all your work?" Pamela asked with a hint of disbelief.

"No, there's more. Remember, mum's the word. I'll be in touch."

* * * * * *

"Trooper Forget?"

"Speaking."

"It's me."

"Me who?"

"Detective Charles White, NYPD."

"Oh, sorry, Charlie. How did you get this number?"

"Sam."

"Gotcha."

"How's the recovery?"

"Don't ask."

"Come on. How you feeling?"

"For a little ray of sunshine, they've given me more medical time off with pay because I was on duty at the time. I can't be out in public looking like this."

"That's nice!"

"You asked me to find how much the Duclos' farm is worth and her financials."

"You got it, baby!" he said, aping Kojak.

"Really, Charlie, take the lollypop out of your mouth."

"Just the facts, ma'am." Charles heard a big sigh.

"Lucky for you, Uncle Ray is President of the Ripton Credit Union. You owe him big time."

"I will do my best to make it all worthwhile."

Fran cleared her throat: "Less than a year ago, Tilda applied for a home equity loan. There are no mortgages or liens on the property. Despite all the equity in the property, her application was so incomprehensible, they decided to say she couldn't carry any additional expense as an excuse. But they did an appraisal. Ray says the value hasn't changed enough to merit a new one. I'm texting you the old figure right now."

He immediately heard Fran's text come in and took a quick peek.

"Got it. More than I figured, but still doable for us."

"Lest I forget," added Fran, "there's also a problem of delinquent property taxes. The county's mercifully not moved on it yet."

He nodded his head, responding, "That's no big deal."

"What are you going to do?" asked Fran.

"KC and I will make an all-cash offer to Tilly. I will suggest her attorney set up an investment package watched over by a guardian or some institution. KC caught a TV ad about The Oaks, a retirement home on the lake that might be good for Tilly. They could draw on her assets as needed through that responsible party. That's not in my skill set, so we'll rely on Ray."

"You're doing all this and, down the line, someone is going to ask if you're her legal guardian," warned Fran.

"Maybe a family member of yours can intercede as a representative of the state due to the emergency situation?" Charles couldn't resist crossing his fingers as that was a big bridge for Fran to cross.

"Hmmm. We'll have to see about that one, Charlie."

There were a few seconds of awkward silence.

"You ready to face Tilly again? It's going to be your show, just like before. Any questions?"

"Charlie, for crying out loud! It isn't like I haven't already done enough for you jailbirds. But, yes, for the old crow's sake, I know what to do," said Fran, confidently enough to satisfy Charles.

"You're being great, Fran. I'm genuinely impressed by how you're stepping up. You know, professionally, you'd make it on any force anywhere. You'd move right up the ladder and I'd be working for you in no time," said Charles, slathering it on.

"Thanks. Maybe you're not such a badass NYPD guy after all."

"I knew you were okay when I looked at the speeding ticket you wrote."

"What do you mean?"

"The mistakes."

"Mistakes? What mistakes?"

"Never mind. Are you ready for our next step? I mean, really ready?"

"Yes, Charlie. I'm all ready. We don't need to go over it again!"

"I'm concerned about the clothes for Davey's part. We're relying on Tilly to make a great leap of faith. That's crucial to the—"

"For fuck's sake, Charlie, you and Kirby will get it sorted! Give me a break and get off my phone. Sam's calling."

** * * * * **

"This is Alice Cooper, The Oaks Retirement Home of Burlington. How may I help you?"

"Hi, this is Kirby Clark. I'm involved with an elderly woman who needs permanent care."

"That's what we do."

"She's in her late-70s, physically fit, healthy—but has mental issues that make it hard for her to function responsibly in the general public."

"I see. Has she been diagnosed?"

"Not that I know of, but if The Oaks were to accept her, I'm sure you'd take care of that aspect of her health." Kirby closed her eyes and had fingers crossed on her loose hand. A little prayer ran through her mind.

"Yes, that's true. But we initially need to know something about our prospective guests. There'll be additional charges if she needs continual supervision or frequent travel to appointments."

"Let's cross that bridge when we get to it. Financially, how does it work?"

"You understand, we're private so we're under no obligation to accept anyone."

"Understood."

"Does she receive Social Security, and what type of assets does she have?"

Glancing down at a notepad, Kirby rattled off Tilda's Social Security income, savings, and investment income based on what Fran was able to weasel out of her uncle Ray at the credit union. This was all totaled into a cash lump sum they believed Tilda would have when they closed on the farm.

"Well, Kirby, she easily exceeds our asset requirements. We suggest her cash go into a managed fund by a trustee investment firm. At her age, I suspect there will be a drawdown on the funds as her needs change. But in any case, once she's in, she's in, and we'll take care of her until God takes her."

"I'm not sure about her relationship with God, but she is a writer. She has to have Internet service and a telephone."

"She can have all that, of course. Oh, but we do can block gambling sites and have a safe search setting for pornography that residents can override if they like."

Kirby had a mental hiccup, "Not a problem, block them both. Do you currently have room for her?"

"For sure. With her income, we can provide a selection of several wonderful suites: different sizes of bath and shower, a balcony with a lake or mountain view, her own refrigerator, and even a state-of-the-art entertainment center. She'd have her choice."

"I'll be dropping by to take some snaps of the available suites if that's okay?"

"It'll be nice to see you again. I graduated high school two years after you. It was great to watch you on the ice. Those were some times!"

"Thanks, I appreciate that. That skating was long ago."

"Well, anyway, tell your elderly friend we have wonderful activities. We've just snatched Slim Littlejohn, a talented Zumba instructor and activities manager, from a competitor. He'll take them in our new air-conditioned van to fairs, tractor pulls, senior coupon days—you name it. We also have birthday parties for all our residents. She'll have lots to write about."

"I've seen what you have posted online. Looks perfect for my friend. I'll be in touch."

CHAPTER 54

I didn't do it, and I know nothing about it

It was a cool, breezy morning. Tilda and Timothy were lazing on the porch. Tilda was in her rocker knitting yet another insanely colored scarf. Timothy had appeared doing his James Dean in the cuffed jeans, red cowboy boots, white T-shirt with cigs tucked in the sleeve, a red paisley bandana around his neck, a golden straw cowboy hat, and aviator sunglasses. He held a striking pose for Tilda to admire: one arm braced against the peeling paint of the rotting porch column. He gazed out at the fruited plains while fiddling with a yellow stalk of straw in his mouth.

"Well, nice to see you, stranger. You've missed a lot over the last few days while Slobberu's been at Sam's. I wish you'd let me know before you disappear. Then, I wouldn't have to tell you everything."

"I got distracted by important business in Boston with the mayor." He adjusted his straw hat and took a deep breath to indicate he was going to tell her something important, "We're letting them foul Disregards get more time to enjoy their petty, meaningless lives. That's not good, Sis."

"Oops, I almost forgot! Did I tell you Acer sent a young man over to upgrade our computer? He upgraded the system and was able to purge the evil spirit out of the wall!"

"No, you didn't tell me! I don't have to care about that fucking wall? I'm good with that."

"Timothy, you sure we're doing the right thing with the Disregards? I kinda appreciate having visitors so I can talk about writing. Frankly, I don't want others to know how mean we are."

"Here you go again! Doubting Thomas!" he said, lifting his hat to toss around his mullet.

"You ought to cut that stupid ponytail. It looks sloppy and queer."

"It's called a mullet, not a ponytail. Ponytails are for girls and are tied with little bows in the back."

"Makes you look like a weirdo, a purse-snatcher, or a goofy criminal."

"I've been called worse, and done worse, too."

Tilda looked up from her knitting to observe a cloud of dust rising by the main road. Someone had turned down the driveway!

"I'm getting my ass out of here," said Timothy, disappearing in a puff.

* * * * * *

A green Vermont State Trooper cruiser came into sight over the rise, drove up to the house, whipped around, and jerked to a stop beside the porch. State Trooper Francine Forget got out, adjusted her circular flat-brimmed hat, sauntered over to the porch, and planted a boot on the first step.

"Good day, Ms. Duclos."

"I didn't do it, and I know nothing about it."

"Subaru, red '92 GBT 814?"

"Slobberu's at Sam's getting fixed. He's doing the emissions inspection, too, so bugger off. Ooh, good Lord Almighty, what did you do to your face?"

"I had a fight with a door at Sam's garage while inspecting your dismantled Subaru. I'm well aware it's dreadful looking."

"That's an understatement. It's all black-and-blue, both sides down to your cheeks. Does it hurt? Looks like it really hurts. Do you take Advil? I might have some."

"Ms. Duclos, it'll be fine. Try to ignore it as I am trying to do."

"It's your face, do what you want with it. I'm just trying to help."

"I have to inspect your barn."

"Why?"

"Contraband."

"Contraband?"

"Cigarettes from South Carolina. You're trafficking in untaxed cigarettes, aren't you?"

"What?"

"Cigarettes lacking the Vermont State tax stamp, meaning the state taxes haven't been paid."

"No, I don't do anything like that."

"We can do this the hard way or the easy way. You can make me get a search warrant or you can walk me over to the barn, slide open those big doors, and say: 'Officer Forget, have a party!'"

"I say, let's have a party." Tilda dropped her knitting in progress, put on her yellow barn galoshes, and slogged to the barn with Trooper Forget trailing.

After sliding open the doors, Trooper Forget couldn't avoid stumbling into the sorting table. She studied the apple press, sniffed into the black plastic bags holding the crushed wolfsbane, and inspected the open maple syrup sample box along with all Tilda's production utensils.

"What have you been up to, Ms. Duclos?" ventured Trooper Forget.

"Nothin.' That's all-Timothy's doings. Just like I said, no cigarettes anywhere."

"Timothy's in some deep crap. First, I see illegal tampering with a sealed product. These maple syrup bottles are being opened. You're doing something to them and you're resealing with that wax you've dripped all over the table."

Trooper Forget held up a sample bottle by the screw top, gave it a shake in front of Tilda's beady eyes.

"Again, Tilda Duclos, what in the hell are you up to?"

"This is all Timothy's doing. He's a crazy son of a bitch! I know nothing about this." Tilda was panicking.

"I believe you because I'm certain you'd rather spend the rest of your life writing sappy love stories in a nice retirement home with a view of Lake Champlain. Rather than spending the . . . let's see, for how many years are they going to put you away?"

Trooper Forget took out her official notepad and started writing figures. "Looks like you're in for about forty years. That'll be at our uncomfortable and deadly cold, Northwest State Correctional Facility."

"Good Lord! Timothy done it! I'm innocent!"

"Nice lady like you, I know you're not going to take flight to Mexico. So, let's get this brother of yours under control. Where's he now? In the house?"

"No, he's gone for the day. Walked out of here a few minutes ago."

"He was just here? He's walking where?" Trooper Forget was incredulous.

"Maybe he's gone to pick up Slobberu at Sam's? Or gone back to Boston?" suggested Tilda.

"Alright, what does Timothy look like? Color of his hair, color of his eyes? Does he have a beard? What's he wearing today? How tall is he? You tell me right now exactly, Ms. Duclos, or there will be hell to pay!"

Tilda recoiled, "Good Lord, my Timothy wouldn't have a beard. He doesn't even have to shave! Peachy white skin—"

"Ms. Duclos, you're hesitating! Better stop wasting the state's time or our sweet deal is off!"

"Let's see . . . let me think. Clean face with blondish hair, sweet blue eyes. You know, he's a handsome James Dean type, same size and slim."

"Clothes, what's he wearing today? What's he wear every day?"

"What he usually wears is . . . ah . . . fresh, clean blue jeans with big, high cuffs so as he grows he can roll them down over his favorite red cowboy boots. Ah, let's see, a crisp white T-shirt with a Marlboro pack tucked in a sleeve. He always ties that red paisley bandana around his neck like Gene Autry. He just loves his straw cowboy hat and those flyboy sunglasses."

"That's a pretty incomplete description, Duclos. I don't think I've got enough, let's take a ride to the station."

"Oh, no! I can't go! Let's see, I almost forgot. Recently, he has his blondish hair in a big ugly mullet. I just hate that style. I tell him that, but he insists on wearing it. It's like a goofy ponytail but without the tie in the back."

"Okay, okay, I know what a mullet is. Here's what I'm gonna do. And I usually don't do this, but I'm a kind, a really kind, gentle woman in my heart."

"Me, too. I'm as kind as can be, and I write beautiful loving stories!"

"Here's my card. I'm writing my personal number right here. You call me when Timothy shows up. I mean quick like! None of this, 'Ooooh, I want to have a few words alone with my brother first.'"

"Okay. I promise to call you!"

"You're going to say to me, 'Please come right away! He causes me so much trouble! You need to put that crazy man away!' Aren't you?"

"Yes, ma'am."

"When I find this brother, Timothy, you're never going to have anything to do with him again because, like you've just now told me, we're going to put him away for good. Is that clear?"

"Yes, ma'am."

"Now, let's go over it again. If this felon brother pops up in your mind, you're gonna do what?"

"I'm going to call this police woman, so go away!" Tilda stamped her foot for emphasis.

"I'm not sure that's quite convincing enough," Trooper Forget wanted it in blood.

Tilda shrieked, causing some veins to pop out on her face, "Get out of my life, Timothy! I'm not talking to you anymore!" She repeatedly stamped her feet, raising a cloud of dust from the barn's straw-strewn floor.

"Okay, okay, calm down! I think we have an agreement, don't we, Ms. Duclos?"

"Yes, Officer, we do. I swear!"

"I'm packing up this illegal paraphernalia and taking it to our evidence room so we got all the goods on this felon, Timothy."

"Lordy, please do!"

"I'll see you later—when he shows up and you call. Don't forget Trooper Forget. You've got my number right on that card!"

"Yes ma'am!"

Tilda scurried back to the farmhouse. Trooper Forget backed up the cruiser to the open double barn doors and quickly cleared the table's contents into the cruiser's trunk. She closed the barn doors, jumped into the cruiser, and sped down Tilda's driveway. When she hit the tarmac, she called Charles.

"It was all there like you said. I've got everything in my trunk except the Ball jar. I left it on the table. It didn't have a tight lid, and I can't have that shit rolling around in my trunk. But I'm sure it's wolfsbane she's processed."

"That's great! About the jar of wolfsbane—ah, never mind. KC's here. You're on speaker. How'd everything else go?"

"I put the fear of the long arm of the law in her. She's ready to do battle with Timothy, wants him gone forever."

"Fantastic work, Fran!"

"I had my phone recording our conversation, so when I can pull over, I will auto-transcribe Timothy's description and text it to you. He wears a blond mullet, which she loathes. Can you get that? Anyway, when's the big event going to happen?"

"Sam's getting her Subaru together. He needs another day or so, then we're good to go."

Kirby shouted from across the room, "Except for what to do with Simon."

"Good God, aren't there babysitters in Vermont?" whispered Fran.

"We'll find someone," said Charles, holding out for a miracle.

CHAPTER 55

Everyone should get their slate cleaned once in a while

While Kirby vacuumed inside the condo, Charles sat outside on a faded green plastic lawn chair working on his laptop. Davey was settled on the grass nearby watching Simon struggle to put together a plastic learning toy. Various-sized rings were required to slip over a cone in the correct sequence. Mister Fritz watched every ring get placed, hoping one would drop for him to steal.

Davey began picking up Simon's toys; time to go inside. He glanced over at Charles.

"What are you working on, old man?"

"Cross-checking with RTCC to see if we have any new suspicious deaths or illnesses in the Tristate area that match our profile."

"What's RTCC?" asked Davey.

"Real Time Crime Center. Computerized data bank with files of priors and current investigations. Big Brother is watching if you're a miscreant. Stay cool, Davey."

Davey pondered the opportunity for an instant, "Can you see if I have anything in there, and if so, fix this travesty on my Constitutional rights?"

"I will not do that, no," said Charles, mindful of Mary's old refrain for him to "fix this." He hadn't thought once about Mary since becoming close to Kirby.

"That's not nice. Everyone should get their slate cleaned once in a while, don't you think?"

"No."

"What if I said I wouldn't help any longer with your Tilly scheme? Unless you, you know, cleaned up anything in that un-American RTCC file you might have on me?"

"Hmmm. I'd have to shoot you, put a gun in your hand like it was a suicide. Case closed."

"Bullshit!" Davey decided not to pursue the situation further; he actually didn't know Charlie that well—he might not be kidding. "In that case, what are we doing tomorrow?"

"We've got to buy Timothy's getup for you. Hate to think what red cowboy boots are going to cost."

"Charlie, what are you two plotting? You're making me nervous," said Kirby, coming out of the house.

"Mom, cool it! We're not talking about you. Eleven, medium. I get to keep the boots, yes?"

Kirby and Charles exchanged glances and responded in unison, "I don't think so."

"So, Davey, about this mullet hair thing."

"Fuck off! I'm not getting a mullet haircut! Final answer!" He strutted off, carrying Simon's toys into the townhouse. Simon and Mister Fritz stopped playing and stared at Charles and Kirby. *What happened?*

* * * * * *

Charles discovered the only red cowboy boots available in Burlington proper were in ladies' or children's sizes. They had to travel to Richmond to *Raddy's Outdoor Hut and Clothing Emporium* to find a men's size to fit Davey. The shop, situated within eyesight of the Winooski River and its tempting rapids, had everything they needed. Unfortunately, there was no time to cast a line or two.

The shop staff was busy outfitting a party of five out-of-shape Best Buy store managers who had been awarded a vacation fishing trip to Canada. They were selecting the cheapest gear. Kirby knew they could save 15 percent by buying the same gear in Canada because of the strong dollar and lower prices for the same made-in-China crap. Smarter yet, splurge and buy quality made-in-USA gear that would last a lifetime. Maybe a savvy salesperson would eventually reel them into that option. *Don't hold your breath*, reflected Kirby.

Gratefully, Kirby and Charles were left alone to rummage through the aisles at their own pace. They purchased a pair of bright red cowboy boots with stitching of a wrangler roping a steer for a staggering $875.00. Also, a red paisley bandana, a tan woven cowboy hat, and blue jeans with legs longer than Davey's.

The also shop had a well-equipped men's casual clothing collection in the golf section. Not surprisingly, Kirby wanted to put Charles into something new.

"You didn't bring any kick-around duds, did you? I mean, really Charles, let's splurge and get you out of those New York City detective rags!"

"These rags have to cover my office-on-the-go, so don't knock my functional attire. And I don't do that golf thing, so nothing with stupid logos. Unless it's a jumping fish."

They walked out of the shop with a complete Timothy setup for Davey. For Charles, two polo shirts, blue cargo shorts, black jeans, three boxer underwear, and three pairs of socks. All were added to his growing

Vermont expense on the department Visa card. He'd have to pay back any charges that smelled of personal, nondepartmental usage or accounting would go ape.

They sat in the parking lot mulling over their largest problem.

"That mullet haircut. If Timothy's her creation, why is she putting him in such a bizarre hairstyle? Fran said Tilly hates it. You think she gets tired of him pushing her around and can't do anything about it since she made him up! That's insane!" exclaimed Kirby.

"It's just another piece in the schizophrenia puzzle," said Charles.

"She gets back at him with some piddly little irritant," Kirby laughed.

"We can use that nugget of disdain, KC. But we still need the mullet for Davey."

"I got it! Burlington, UVM Theatrical Department!" blurted Kirby.

* * * * * *

Charles scared up, so to speak, a blond mullet wig from UVM's Department of Theater. He barged into a rehearsal of *Our Town* in the Royal Tyler Theater and announced to flabbergasted students and a shocked stage director: "I detect the burning of a controlled substance. How many of you have the required physician's prescription."

Charles parted his jacket, revealing the badge clipped to his belt and the holstered firearm. Within minutes, he had a blond mullet hairpiece from the student prop master. The mullet had been used in a reinterpretation of *The Barber of Seville*. After one week of performances, it had never been cleaned because it would never be used again. The prop master revealed that the audience decided the avant-garde interpretation of the Shakespearean classic, using the mullet and contemporary gangland clothing, was a disaster.

* * * * * *

They stopped at the Smoke & Vape shop on the way back. Kirby went inside to the plexiglass-enclosed counter, which had groupings of drilled air holes in the plastic, creating a rash of snowflake designs. Behind the plexiglass, a weary counterman was perched on a stool drinking coffee through a straw out of a Slurpee cup. He had a clear plastic air tube running up his chest that then split into each nostril. The tube was connected to a humming portable oxygen concentrator set on the floor.

He had been watching a TV mounted over the entrance. Every few seconds it flipped from *The Outlaw Josey Wales* to a split-screen feed of four security cameras. Two feeds showed the two aisles and Kirby at the counter. The other two were outside cameras covering the entrance and parking lot. In the parking lot feed, the 'Vette was stopped in three parking spaces and its dual exhaust was puffing clouds of condensation.

"That's how they park when they're going to rob me," he said smiling.

"Not today, not us."

"Kirby Clark, I recognize you from the rink. You're as pretty as ever."

"Oh, hi! Good times they were. Time flies."

"'Time flies like an arrow, fruit flies like a banana.' Groucho—one of my favorites," he said.

"My Dad announces at the yearly family get together: 'I'm not crazy about reality, but it's still the only place to get a decent meal.'"

"Yeah, that's a good one. Never thought you'd be a smoker."

"Not for me. They're a prop for a photo shoot. Don't even need the smokes. Just the box."

"Only need a box? I just tossed a Marlboro box in the trash. I hate selling them coffin nails."

He found the empty box in the trash and gave it to her. "No charge, my treat."

"Thank you. Hope you're getting along, okay," she said, mindful of what a drag it must be to be coupled to a machine.

"You're a sweetheart. Could be worse; could be home alone watching TV. This way, I'm making a little inheritance for my grandkids. Good luck with the shoot."

Back in the car with Charles, Kirby told him, "The counterman remembered me. It was kind of sad. He had oxygen piping going into his nose; I'm guessing emphysema. He gave me an empty cigarette box from the trash, and it's the very brand we need: Marlboro! That's a sign isn't it, we're doing something right?"

"You bet! Let's go out to dinner and celebrate. Tomorrow's the do or die day," said Charles.

"Do we make it shockingly expensive?" she asked, raising her eyebrows.

"Why not?"

"Take me to Hen of the Wood. I think asparagus is in season and their remoulade sauce is to die for. We'll need reservations."

CHAPTER 56

Head for the hills, boy!

The following morning, the felonious conspirators assembled at Sam's Garage. Trooper Francine Forget in the green-and-gold state cruiser followed Charles and Kirby through her community profit center, the blinking yellow light speed trap. At the garage, they were relieved to find Tilda's Slobberu off the rack and idling smoothly with a new head gasket. All ready to roll!

Davey whizzed in minutes later in his Honda, dumped Simon on Kirby, and disappeared into the garage toilet. He reappeared in blue jeans with cuffs rolled up to expose as much of the new red cowboy boots as possible, a pristine white T-shirt with the Marlboro cigarette pack (stuffed with toilet paper to hold its shape) tucked in a rolled sleeve, and the red paisley bandana knotted around his neck. The flyboy sunglasses finished the imagined Timothy look.

"I'm not putting this nasty mullet on until the very last second. It's dirty and stinky as hell!" he said, vigorously shaking the blondish hairpiece at arm's length. "I feel like such a clown, you making me do this," he grouched to an indifferent Charles and Kirby, both occupied with their personal angst.

Sam was quietly sipping coffee, wondering if he hadn't adjusted Slobberu's timing belt a little too tight lest it snap and trash the valves.

Having come up short for a babysitter, little Simon would be tucked in a canvas Tula Toddler backpack carrier where he'd be bound to granny's back for hours. *Get used to the term "grounded"—it will follow you until you're in your twenties*, mentally counseled Kirby. Mister Fritz was going to have to be leashed but allowed to come along. If he misbehaved, he'd be left in Sam's car.

Still grossly marred with black raccoon eyes and frightful dark-blue streaks from the door collision, Fran was nervously rambling and pacing about the office. Charles felt compelled to comfort her.

"Fran! You're starting to look pretty good. A few more days you'll—"

"Fuck off, White. You're aware this amateur psycho-manipulation carries severe consequences for all of us."

"What's she going to do, sue us for making her crazy?" offered Sam.

Kirby interrupted, "Get a grip on your anxieties, Frannie!"

"I'm trying to be responsible," Fran responded.

"*Alea itacta es,*" said Sam Piper, "That's all I got out of four years with the nuns."

"What does that mean?" asked Davey.

"The die is cast or, in our case, it's too fuckin' late." Charles looked Sam's way. "Make the call, Sam."

Everyone stopped what they were doing and held their breath. Curtain time. Sam picked up the desk phone and punched the senior-sized buttons.

"Good morning, Tilly . . . That's right. She's all ready . . . Sure, we'll settle after your next Social Security check comes in. No problem. I also did the emissions . . . No, no need to walk down here." Sam took a deep breath, "Your brother, Timothy came by and picked up your car. He's on his way to you right now. Left a minute ago."

Sam slammed down the phone.

"What'd she say?" asked Kirby.

"I hung up before she could speak."

"Here goes my life," said Davey, putting on the mullet hairpiece.

Kirby helped tuck in the edges. She inspected the fit of the odd hairpiece, smelt her fingers, and went to sanitize her hands.

"Davey, just stick to the plan. Everything will be fine," counseled Charles.

Minutes later, Davey made the turn off the main road onto Tilda's gravel drive. He rolled to a stop but kept Slobberu idling. Right behind, Sam arrived with everyone in his rusted green Subaru wagon and parked where the Williams Dairy's white fencing ended. Charles, and Kirby with Simon, quickly unloaded. Mister Fritz was on the leash, and as long as he behaved, Sam agreed to be responsible for their little friend. A stone's throw up the road, Trooper Forget's cruiser dawdled half on the road, half on the grass. Trooper Forget was prepared, but twitchy.

Charles alerted everyone to keep their eyes open for the minefield of cow pies ahead of them. Climbing the fence, with Simon on Kirby's back in the carrier, they followed the once-evil stone wall down to the barn. At a low spot, where the top rows of stones had slipped off, they stopped. They were parallel to the barn, but still had a clear view of the farmhouse several hundred feet away.

Unknown to the felonious conspirators, they were where Moo Moo had earlier breached the wall, and which the local hires had poorly rebuilt.

Waiting impatiently, and driven mad by the itchy mullet hairpiece, Davey called Charles, "Hey, old man, I'm not getting any younger out here!"

Charles called Fran, "You ready?"

"Yes, I'm fuckin' ready, Charlie!" Getting supporting nods from Kirby and Sam, Charles made the call to Davey.

"Red Subaru, you're cleared to the farmhouse."

"Roger that. Subaru GBT 814 rolling."

"Davey, I can't call Fran until you're certain Tilly sees you, so stay on speakerphone. We need to hear everything."

"Roger that."

Mashing the gas pedal, Davey sped down the gravel driveway, kicking up a mountain of dust. As he flew over the rise, his hand mistakenly hit the horn, adding more drama than necessary. A hundred feet or so from the farmhouse, he slammed on the brakes and fishtailed Slobberu to a stop. Afraid she was going to stall, Davey had to rev Slobberu's refreshed motor, adding more chaos.

Had he stopped far enough from the porch where Tilda's bleary eyesight would have him out of focus? He turned off Slobberu and got out of the car.

"Davey, you see us on the other side of the wall, catty-corner to the barn?"

They waved at him, and he acknowledged by tipping his straw cowboy hat. Mister Fritz, not willing to miss the show, leaped atop the wall and, when he recognized Davey, came up with an inconsequential huff. Davey expected Tilda to come flying out the door any second, yelling at him as before, but the farmhouse stayed ominously quiet. He awkwardly leaned against Slobberu's hood, wondering if they had crashed and burned.

"Nothing's happening, Charlie. No sign of her, and I'm checking every window," he groaned into the cell phone.

"Davey, take your hat off for a minute so she'll see the mullet."

"Maybe he should honk the horn again or something," suggested Sam.

"Wait. Give her time," said Charles.

A minute passed. Then another ten. A herd of cows they had spooked when coming into the pasture began returning. Enormous horse flies and no-see-ums were becoming a problem. The heat was unbearable.

"I'm thirsty, Charlie," announced Kirby.

"Have one of Simon's juices," replied Charles.

"I have beer back in the shop. Two cold six-packs. I could shoot back," offered Sam.

* * * * * *

Meanwhile, at the top of the drive, and purely by coincidence, Slim Littlejohn, all color coordinated in red gym clothes and in new red Pegasus Nike's, was on his way home from teaching a morning Zumba class. He crept to a stop alongside Trooper Fran's cruiser and unfortunately startled her.

"Morning, Officer. Having motor trouble—damn lady, what happened to your face?"

She glowered at him. "I ran into a door. Is there any compelling reason you've stopped here and are asking me a stupid question?"

"No, ma'am, only wanted to be neighborly. Thought a pretty lady like you might need a . . ."

"I suggest you move along before I demand your license and registration."

"Yes, ma'am. Are you sure I can't help? I'm a big strong guy; the ladies like me."

"You're really wanting me to get out and find something wrong with that truck and give you a citation?"

Slim didn't connect to what she said, because he was tuned into some la-la land fantasy: *For a state trooper, she's kinda cute. She's got a nice rack up front, and I bet she's sitting on a big soft butt. Maybe a hookup later tonight? I'll just step out all lazy-like and engage in some charming . . .*

After a few unbearable seconds without a response, and hearing his door unlock and open, Fran had had enough. She reflexively jerked out her Smith & Wesson automatic and brought it up so Slim was looking into the black hole of the barrel. Trooper Fran portrayed perfectly a whacked-out officer with a gun.

"I said get lost, asshole! I'm busy! Can't you take a fucking hint?"

That worked. Slim Littlejohn sped off, his ankles shaking in his Nike's while dribbling urine in his crimson sweats.

Firearm still in hand, Fran remembered an important detail when meeting the peaceful public at large. She pulled the magazine and began snapping out the bullets onto her lap.

Can't have a loaded firearm around civilians unless you're going to shoot 'em. Missed my chance, I could of practiced on that jerk.

* * * * * *

Davey remained posed on the hood of Tilda's Slobberu. He was going batty from relentless attacks by horse flies and the itch from the mullet. Just as he was on the verge of throwing the mullet to the ground and stomping it to death, a curtain moved on the second-floor window.

"Wow, I see her! She's peeking out," Davey's excited voice screeched over the cell.

"Play the hat, obscure your face. And keep that phone up in your pocket so we can hear."

"What if she starts coming over to me? We didn't cover that!" Davey was panicking.

"Hang on. She's got to believe you're Timothy. Let's see if she'll call Trooper Fran on her own."

The inside door creaked open and Tilda appeared. She hesitantly opened the screen door and stepped onto the porch. She was in her traditional morning getup, the long crazy-colored scarf, dirty sweat pants, an open frilly blouse knotted at the waist over a socially concerned but illegible T-shirt, and her classic yellow galoshes.

She cupped her hands to her mouth and shouted: "What do you want? Go away!" And then, "Wait a minute." She remained by the screen door squinting at Davey, unsure of what she was seeing.

Charles made the call to Fran: "Fran, you're on! High speed!"

On the tarmac, Trooper Fran hit the switches for pursuit lights and siren, made a skidding turn into Tilda's drive, and put the pedal to the metal. All the bullets rolled off her lap and scattered onto the floor.

"10-4. I'm on the driveway. Copy that."

Amazed, Sam said, "I think it might be working!"

Davey took off the hat, gave Tilda a clear view of the mullet for a second, cycled it on and off, then shouted back at her

"It's me! I'm Timothy, your brother!"

"Oh, my God, Timothy!"

"That's me!" said Davey, unsure of what else he could get away with.

Tilda began flailing her arms, "I warned you that mullet would turn you into a criminal! Now the law is after you! You gotta run, run, brother!" And then, as an afterthought, "Head for the hills, boy!"

"I see you, Fran. Go faster," said Charles, as the green cruiser appeared, leading a storm of dust clouds over the driveway.

Trooper Forget had the cruiser fly the rise, yanked the wheel hard over, and spun in front of the Slobberu. Davey lunged to safety on the hood. She leaped out of the cruiser, unholstered her firearm, and screamed, "Timothy Duclos, get off that hood and put your hands up high where I can see them! No tricks or I'll shoot!"

Davey quickly obeyed as commanded. She holstered the firearm, spun him around like a top, and slammed him against the fender. She jerked the cowboy hat off and on, giving Tilda another view of the mullet, then cuffed him.

"No, no! Don't hurt my boy!" screamed Tilda, coming off the porch and striding toward them.

Charles, on the phone, "Fran, you've got to get her back to the porch!"

Trooper Fran turned to Tilda and lifted her arm like she was stopping traffic, "Hold it! You better get your ass right back on that porch, Tilda Duclos!" Which stopped her. "Timothy's a criminal, and I'm arresting him. Don't interfere or I'll drag you to that icy cell I warned you about!"

Tilda hesitated, then slowly retreated. She had remembered Trooper Forget's terrifying description of where she'd be living—if she didn't honor their agreement.

"Timothy Duclos, I'm putting you in prison for a long, long time so you can't hurt your innocent sister. Do you understand your rights as I just read to you?" Trooper Forget shouted her lines loud enough for Tilda and everyone halfway to Middlebury to hear.

Davey whispered, "What rights you just read me?"

"Just say what you're supposed to say, idiot!"

Davey twisted around and shouted in Tilda's direction, "Officer, I swear I'll never come around and bother my sister ever, ever again."

Fran and Davey had gone off script; they were improvising. Fran opened the cruiser's back door, placed a palm on Davey's head, and shoved him inside.

Hunching down on the far side of the wall, Charles, Sam, and Kirby with Simon on her back slurping apple juice, did an exuberant high five.

"Yes!" Kirby glowed.

"So far so good," said Charles prematurely.

"Uh-oh," Sam saw impending trouble.

Undeterred, Tilda again stepped off the porch. She extended her long yellow scarf and wrapped it tightly to cover her head and shoulders. This time, she turned toward the barn. Hunching low to the ground, she began a peculiar shuffle across the yard. She'd go a dozen or so paces, then readjust the scarf over her head, furtively look about, and continue her sneak toward the barn.

"She thinks that scarf is making her invisible. That's so sad I want to cry," said Kirby.

"When people go off their rockers," mumbled Charles, "they're unpredictable."

"That's batshit crazy," said Sam, firing up an old cigar butt while attempting to unravel Mister Fritz's leash that had become entangled around his ankle.

After reaching the halfway point between the farmhouse and barn, Tilda bundled the scarf into a ball and sprinted the last few yards to the front of the barn. This maneuver took her out of their sight. They heard a barn door noisily slide on its rusty guides and the same sound as it was closed.

Trooper Fran rang in, "Suspect has entered the barn and closed the door behind her. What should we do, Charlie?" she asked, bracing herself on the open back door of the cruiser.

Davey was hunched low in the back seat of the cruiser, "Please take these cuffs off me, Fran!"

Charles buzzed in, "Fran, leave the Subaru. Take Davey to Sam's, have him change clothes. Both of you get back here ASAP."

Kirby groaned, "Fran's flipped her out. What the fuck, don't Vermont officers get sensitivity training?"

* * * * * *

Almost half an hour had passed, and the party at the wall was uncomfortable and ruffled. The wind had died, horse flies were attacking in waves, and cow pie stench filled the hot and humid atmosphere.

Davey, now in his own clothes, and Fran arrived at the wall after leaving the cruiser on the main road.

"You could have brought something to drink," said Kirby wishfully. "Charlie, if it's going to be a long time, Sam has two six-packs . . ."

Sam followed up, " . . . in the office fridge. Ice cold, two six-packs of Yuengling Black & Tan. Just sitting there."

More minutes dragged by. More horse flies and no-see-um attacks.

"You have any hard stuff back at the garage?" Kirby pointedly asked Sam.

To get out of the sun, they settled down with their backs pressed against the wall and took turns watching for Tilda. The herd of Holsteins, spooked earlier, was indifferently returning. A few fearlessly meandered right next to them. Everyone was bored, hot, and depressed, except Simon who was in Moo Moo heaven and had been transferred onto Davey's back.

Kirby said, "I'm really thirsty. When I'm thirsty, I get pissy," she glared at Charles.

"Me, too," said Sam, wiping his chin, and glancing at Charles, "I get hungry, too."

Fran, having nothing else to do, reloaded her Smith & Wesson magazine with shells from her belt and advised Charles, "We can't do this all day. What if she's hurting herself and we're twiddling our thumbs out here? We'll be walking home counting mailboxes."

"Cool it, Fran," counseled Sam, preparing to fire up a chewed-up cigar.

They heard the grinding of the sliding barn door, and Tilda reappeared, shuffling back toward the farmhouse. "Look, you all. She's come out!" said Davey, jumping up from the grass.

"She's got something in her scarf," said Sam.

"What'll we do, Charlie?" Kirby was beginning to panic.

"We stop her. Everyone call her!"

Charles cupped his hands together and hollered, "Tilly Duclos, look here! We're over here!"

All joined in shouting and waving, but she didn't respond until Fran stuck two fingers to her lips and let loose an unladylike blast. Tilda paused, bewildered. Where did that come from? Fran's second blast turned her to face them at the wall.

"Over here, Tilly! Come here!" The felonious conspirators were bouncing around like ballgame fans after a home run.

Perplexed with all the waving hands and hooting, she ambled over to them.

"What's she got in her hands?" whispered Sam.

"It's the Ball jar of wolfsbane," gasped Trooper Fran, "Damn, I shouldn't have left it."

Tilda stopped a few yards from the wall. She had wrapped the scarf tightly around the Ball jar as if cradling an infant.

"What's all this hullabaloo? Why are you here?"

CHAPTER 57

She'd have to tame them one by one—no, maybe several at a time

Charles took a step closer to the wall, "We've come to visit and have a serious talk, Tilda." Nodding heads agreed.

"I don't want to talk to you." She eyed Kirby, "You're out of luck. Timothy's gone."

"That's right. He's gone," said Kirby softly, recognizing her fragile state.

"Sam Piper, did you beat up that nazi, police girl at the garage? Just look at her face; I don't think that came from a door! And she said Timothy isn't coming back. Is that true, Sam?"

Before Sam could answer, Trooper Fran stepped in, "No, Sam didn't beat me up. And yes, I did collide with a door. Ms. Duclos, believe me, Timothy is permanently jailed. He's not coming back," Fran said in a surprising show of emotional calm.

Tilda responded with a puzzled look that evolved into a stiff upper lip. A standoff was developing.

"If Timothy's gone, I've got no one," she proclaimed, then twisted the Ball jar lid open, "You'll just have to watch me die!" and smacked her lips in preparation for a gulp.

"Whoa, whoa, don't drink it, Tilly! It's not wolfsbane!" shouted Charles, rapidly waving his hands and getting her to stop. Sam and Trooper Forget were poised to throw themselves over the wall.

"What?"

"It's urine. She peed in your jar," he said with a nod to Kirby who, from the surly look on her face, didn't appreciate being pointed out. Tilda hesitated, then carefully removed the lid. Sam was bemused. Davey gawked, *Mom peed in the jar?*

She dumped a little of the yellow liquid out and took a closer sniff. "Where'd you find asparagus this time of year?" She eyed Kirby with an uplifted chin. Kirby sighed.

"I don't want to drink it, then," and dumped all the wolfsbane to the ground, followed by the Ball jar and top.

"Good idea," said Charles, relieved.

"Why would you drink wolfsbane?" asked Davey, passing an apple juice to a fussing Simon, aware Kirby might be going for it if he didn't get the juice to him quickly.

"I don't want to live any longer. I've failed Timothy and my little friend. Terribly failed them."

"That Timothy was sending you right into a cold prison cell," chimed in Trooper Fran.

Davey stepped in and surprised everyone, "Hold on, Ms. Duclos. First of all, *Final Love* isn't finished. You can't just leave it undone. It's not fair to your readers who need your guidance and help!"

"He's right. And we have an offer to get you in a more favorable environment for your writing," said Charles. "You'd move into a nice suite near the water at a place called The Oaks. Show her the suites, Kirby."

Kirby clambered over the wall, acknowledging its past evil history by saying, "We don't have to worry about this possessed wall anymore; it's been exorcised by the Acer expert."

"Well, frankly, I did it," said Tilda. "I had to push the Esc key or nothing would have happened."

Charles gave Davey a thumbs up.

Kirby held up the cell phone so Tilda could see the images. She squinted at the small screen as Kirby scrolled through the suites. Many had balconies and views of the Green Mountains, others of Lake Champlain, along with a few shots of smaller single-room units.

"Don't have my glasses, can't see too clearly. But I can see enough to know I don't want to be near dangerous waters. So, forget it."

"Here's a suite with a view of the Green Mountains," Kirby was prepared.

"You're going to be with friends, travel to town events and tractor pulls! Maybe do some snowmobiling!" remarked Sam.

"Sam Piper! You know I don't do any of that stuff. Waste of time!"

"Tilly, we've been together a long time. Believe me, you'll like living there," answered Sam.

"So, what now? I've overcome the evil in the wall, but my brother Timothy is gone." Her head slumped; she began stroking under her eyes trying not to cry. "Without him, I have no future."

"That's not true, Tilly. A move to The Oaks will find you many new friends," said Charles.

"Just between us, I did think there was something awfully wrong with that boy. But now, I'm all alone and I don't know what to do."

Before Charles could step into the conversation, Sam climbed over the wall and snuggled up to Tilda.

Tilda looked closely into his eyes, "Sam, I know you do so much for me. I have so little money and little to offer."

"Tilly, our friend, Charles, is a good, honest man, and he likes you a lot. Just between us, you need to sell this run-down farm to this New York City Flatlander. You'll take him to the cleaners, and you'll never have to think about money again."

Kirby chipped in, "You'll have Internet and your computer booted up the day you move in. Someone else will cook and clean for you."

"Well, let's just forget it. I can't afford that kind of place."

"That's what they're saying, you could—if you sold this place," slipped in Fran, pointing her trigger finger at Charles and Kirby.

Sam continued, "Tilly, dear, you know how hard I work to keep The Lost Pine Farm going for you. Last winter, I plowed your driveway over a dozen times and shoveled so many paths to your porch, my back hurts just remembering it. Tilly, the siding is falling off on the house and the barn! Unless someone invests a ton of money, they're both going to collapse, and you'll be homeless."

"That doesn't sound good."

"You ought to move on their offer. Tilly, it's a hell of a good deal for you," said Fran.

"I haven't heard any offer yet."

"How much were you thinking The Lost Pine Farm was worth?" asked Kirby.

Tilda rubbed her nose and messed with the scarf while studying the farmhouse and barn. She saw the siding popping off and how the paint was eroded to bare wood. She knew the well was for shit and the electrical outlets sparked way too often. She was aware the house was slipping off its foundation because the floors were sloped and the windows wouldn't go up or down. Those things a buyer might not find until way too late.

"I have to think about it," said Tilda. No one moved, still hoping she'd get to a price.

Now that Timothy was gone, might as well hear their offer. Or better, set a price that'll make me richer than Scrooge. If they want it, make 'em pay for it.

Tilda thought back to the years at The Dewy Drop Inn and Mama Rose's method of sizing up a customer's ability to pay extra for one of their better, jazzier suites, even though they were all identical.

I paid $32,000 for it. Let's see, at 5 percent every year—well, maybe not averaging 5 percent, but just to round everything off.

Astonishingly adept at numbers, Tilda arrived at a figure: "I wouldn't part with my piece of heaven for under $162,000. Take it or leave it, no negotiations!"

"We'll pay you more. You'll be in a suite with a balcony and high-speed Internet by the end of next week." Charles followed up with, "Let's shake on it, Tilly. Just like we did before." He extended a hand over the wall.

The unassailable wall that had meant so much to Tilda in her literary pursuit had only been scaled twice: once by Moo Moo, who paid dearly for her transgression, and the second by Charles when he shook her hand at the fish pit. She knew his destiny was still in limbo, but now the evil wall was only a stack of old stones and could do no harm. Then again, it could always rise again? There was a risk there.

Unfortunately, with all the excitement and pressure of the day, her hands began to tremble, and her excitable heart beat faster, making her dizzy. Unable to calm the building stress, previously controlled by reaching for the Altoid tin or seeking Timothy's soothing support—she caved.

"I'll have to talk to Timothy. He does all my legal stuff."

That sent Fran ballistic. In an amazing athletic leap, she vaulted over the wall, dropped in front of Tilda, and began snapping her fingers as a hypnotist does to awaken a patient.

"For screaming Jesus, Tilly! Don't you remember Timothy's in jail and can't bother you anymore!"

Fran's crass and unsympathetic action was a saving act for Tilda and the felonious conspirators. What would have happened had Tilda reached out for brother Timothy? If she conjured his return, all that they had done would be undone. But Tilda was more confused than ever. Her swaying head telegraphed she was not going to make a decision. Kirby clamored over the wall, followed by Davey with Simon on his back.

Kirby elbowed Fran aside.

"Tilly, dearest, when I took these shots at The Oaks, I met these handsome, lonely men. They're in a couple of these shots. Look."

"What shots?"

She turned her iPhone screen back to Tilda.

Kirby crunched her shoulders and began a silly banter. "I said, wow, Tilly is gonna like this place with so many men! I was impressed by how good looking they were in their tight, athletic shorts. I couldn't say if they do that yen-yang thing you seem to enjoy, but you could ask."

Charles grumbled. Sam tried not to guffaw. Fran noisily cleared her throat. Puzzled at first, Davey made a good guess as to what yen-yang meant. Tilda studied the images of the senior men on the sun-filled terrace overlooking Lake Champlain. Kirby had been selective, shooting only the most virile, appealing men.

Turning from the iPhone, Tilda drifted into an absorbing fantasy. Leaving the wall, past the green pasture and meandering cows, to a fresh Acer screen and a new title page of a Tilda Wilcox Duclos novel: *Final Love II, The Mistress.*

All those handsome sex-starved men wanted to keep her for themselves. She'd have to tame them one by one—no, maybe several at a time . . .

It was a rich fantasy ready to soar off her keyboard. Tilda sighed and peered listlessly at her yellow galoshes. She was unprepared; not ready to separate from what *was*.

Sam and Kirby had failed, and she was going to muddle back to the farmhouse. Fran, having no notion of what else to do, gave up and slumped against Sam's back. Davey, in a fierce battle, was swatting horse flies away from Simon.

Silently observing from the other side of the wall, Charles read Tilda's expressionless face. She was missing everything; her mind was busy elsewhere. In her detached state, it was unkind and selfish of them to continue. He had to step in.

As Charles went to straddle the wall, he became aware of a freakish, luminous gathering of snowy flakes coalescing into a swirling mini-cyclone above the conspirators and Tilda. When the amorphous assemblage had collected, it spiraled downward to engulf them. Fully contained within the light-warping cocoon, Tilda and the conspirators' movements slowed until they were inanimate. They were suspended in an otherworldly phenomenon, a static state existing outside Charles' time.

From the engulfing assemblage, an effervescent, shimmering orb the size of a basketball, rose from the swirling mass. It glided to a place above the stone wall by Charles where it paused, and after a few seconds, violently imploded. The orb compressed into a small, pulsing black dot.

This unearthly compression, contained within the pulsing dot, had to be liberated. And it was—suddenly blasting out in a cascade of sparks so dazzling Charles had to shield his eyes. An otherworldly transformation had occurred.

Seated on the stone wall, only an arm's length from Charles, was Tilda Duclos' child friend, Timmy Gardner. On his lap rested a golden straw cowboy hat. He wore a checkered western-style shirt with scalloped, twin snap pockets His blue jeans had cuffs rolled high to show off blazing red cowboy boots. Around his neck, a paisley bandana had been tucked under his shirt in a vain attempt to stem a red torrent, now dried black, that had snaked down his pale neck over a half-century before. Where two fingers had been severed, a strip torn from a colorful summer dress had been fashioned into a crude, ineffective bandage.

Breathless from the mind-bending engagement with the unearthly phenomena, Charles had to steady himself against the wall to keep from falling to the ground.

Timmy Gardner's eyes were riveted on Tilly and her inanimate friends. After a short reflection, he smiled and rolled his head about; perhaps hoping she might see him. Or an innocent, uncontrollable response to memories of the happy times they shared?

Sadly—it was already time for him to leave.

From above, again, the luminous mass re-formed. Timmy stretched out a pale hand and waved goodbye to Tilly in an overdue farewell. Unable to move or speak, Charles watched as the ethereal cloud, fully reconstituted, coalesced around Timmy.

A second transformation had been set into motion. Not unlike how he had arrived, Timmy's apparition shattered into a dazzling display of sparks and luminescence—and disappeared. In his place, a new figure materialized. Not sitting, but leaning against the wall, was an old man. His frame was bent from a lifetime in the saddle, his face a river of connecting wrinkles that bespoke of a rugged outdoor past, decades of relentless sun, and freezing nights spent by a smoky campfire.

Whereas Timmy's eyes had been bright blue and sparkling white, his were red and tired. He wore a tattered leather vest over a soiled western-style shirt with frayed, scalloped pockets. A string tie with a chipped onyx clasp held a weathered hat to the nape of his neck. His hair appeared grimy and unwashed and on his hip in a scruffy leather holster, was a tarnished revolver.

Timmy had been replaced by a grizzly, time-weary cowpoke. His tired eyes drilled into Charles until, in a raspy but harmonious voice, a cluster of words instantly resounded into Charles' consciousness. When finished with his channeling, the tired cowpoke stepped away from the wall, spanked the dust from his faded, patched jeans, and drew several deep breaths as if he could taste the humid and rich farm air.

Bemused, he looked at Tilda. She and the conspirators, remained unresponsive in their timeless space. The cowpoke put two fingers together, touched his chapped lips, and threw her an admiring kiss. Finished with his mission, he flattened his scraggly hair with a calloused palm, found the brim of his dusty hat, and settled it onto his head.

He turned to face Charles. Their eyes met again. In the traditional Western see-you-later-pal sequence, he dipped his hat, and respectfully nodded to Charles.

The ethereal traveler, having been obliged to be part of Tilda's past, began to dissolve. Like an antique projector consuming the end of its carbon filament, he lost his glow and disappeared.

Charles slid over the wall as Tilda and the conspirators, all oblivious to the apparitions and unaware having lost an infinitesimal speck of universal time, were coming alive as if nothing had occurred. They were unaware of how transcendental Charles' universe had become and had no notion of what they had missed. Fully reanimated, they reflexively stepped back when Charles suddenly appeared in front of Tilda.

He took ahold of Tilda's frail arms. "Timmy Gardner, in the red cowboy boots, was here. He came to say goodbye."

Tilda snapped awake, "You saw my Timmy Gardner? Where?"

"Right there." Charles pointed to the spot on the wall. Tilda looked to where a half-century before, she had been destroyed. Her eyes swelled with tears.

"Tilly, I can't explain it, but in the mystery of our existence, his life continued. He wants you to know he's had the life he wanted. He wants you to know that."

"Oh, my God! Are you sure?" she tightly clutched his arms.

"Yes, for sure. He wants you to continue to bring your words of comfort to others."

She closed her eyes and took deep breaths. Her voice crackled, "If I leave, how will I know Timmy has really forgiven me?"

"He was your friend; you made him happy for those summers. He loved you so much he would bravely climb the wall against the will of his parents, to feed the fish with you at the pit."

"We had so much fun."

"He came back to tell you it's time for you to live without being wounded by his past."

Charles gestured at the old wall. "This collection of ancient stone has had a purpose for centuries, long before Timmy and you were here. It'll go back to how it was used before: defining property, and lives on each side."

Tilda gave her nose a wipe with her crazy scarf, exhaled as if purging her body of some dark cloud, and nodded her head in agreement. She wrapped her arms tightly around Charles. Her teary eyes traveled to her ramshackle barn, the farmhouse in dire disrepair, the old stone wall she detested, and finally to the expectant faces of her friends.

"If you'll feed my fish at the pit, I'd . . . I'd like to go to that place; the one Kirby showed me. The one with the view of the mountains and those lovely men."

With that decision, the felonious conspirators congratulated her for being so brave and for doing the smart thing—which likely left her confused about what exactly she had agreed to do. Bashfully releasing Charles, she hugged Kirby, then Sam, and apprehensively, Trooper Fran.

Davey, with Simon on his back, was crestfallen; after all, he was the principal player in Charles' theater. Tilda reached to him, "You were deceitful, but my Acer did need fixing. You were very nice to me . . . and who is this little angel on your back?"

Simon, flopping around in his canvas carrier, couldn't have cared less who hugged whom. He had been too busy sucking down his final box of apple juice and hosing down Dad through the canvas carrier. Besides, he had grown bored wondering why the boy in the red boots stayed on the wall when there were all those big beautiful cows to round up.

* * * * * *

At Sam's garage later that afternoon, the felonious conspirators and Tilda had a small celebration with Chinese takeout. For some reason, Tilda wanted nothing to do with the chow mein side dish. Afterward, when all of Sam's Black & Tans had been drunk and the bourbon bottle was empty, Charles and Kirby brought Tilda and Slobberu back to The Lost Pine Farm. After kicking off her galoshes on the porch, Tilda was led by Kirby upstairs and settled into her bed.

As the day closed, the felonious conspirators were emotionally drained, drunk and gloriously satisfied. They had kept Tilda from jail, arranged for her to live a more comfortable existence at The Oaks, and thwarted an insidious and punishing mental illness that had plagued her most of her life. It hadn't been cured, only thwarted. And finally, Detective Charles White and Kirby F. Clark were going to buy a farm.

CHAPTER 58

Now, you're making sense

Charles was on the sofa sipping a merlot while Mister Fritz was asleep between his legs. Kirby sat on a big cushion on the floor between the sofa and cocktail table. She twirled an almost-empty glass of the same and was contemplating opening another bottle. Charles had only briefly confided his confounding experience at the wall.

She was waiting for the saga to continue.

He pulled himself up on the sofa. "I should have told you earlier. In the *Addison Independent* Police Blotter, I discovered Timmy Gardner, a ten-year-old child, was killed on the Fourth of July, 1976. A firecracker blew off two of his fingers and flying stone slivers severed the carotid artery in his neck. He was Tilly's neighbor, her little friend. She raced him to the hospital but he died. I'm sorry, I held back the story from you; but it was unnecessary to our plan."

"That's okay, it wouldn't have changed anything."

"Today, I know it has more relevance to what Tilly had been dealing with."

"Nothing would have changed except I'd have been more upset."

"When you hear all of this, you'll think I'm nuts or that I had some flashback from the 'shrooms I may or may not have taken in college. I have to tell you everything, anyway," said Charles, as if opening a confessional.

He described how a swirling, light-bending mass had encapsulated Tilda and the conspirators. This led to their time-stopping freeze, an orb that floated over to the wall to explode and materialize little Timmy Gardner. He had a dried, bloody bandana around his neck and a hand was bandaged with strips torn from a dress. Both lent a macabre horror to Charles' surreal encounter. The actualization of Timmy Gardner was the first part of two transformations that had kept Charles bewildered, stupefied, on the other side of the wall.

Kirby interrupted, "These facts of the accident, you found them in the newspaper from 1976?"

"That's correct. The hocus-pocus part is—was, uniquely my experience," said Charles.

He went on to tell how Timmy waved goodbye to Tilda and ignited a second transformation. In Timmy's place, an old-as-the-hills cowpoke appeared in clothes he must have lived in for decades. A tarnished revolver was jammed in a leather side holster that hung from his hip.

"I intuitively knew he wanted me to see him as a cowpoke, not a cowboy. There's got to be some distinction between a cowpoke and a cowboy," said Charles wondering out loud.

"Difference is easy to imagine. One pokes cattle to move them along and the other is a gunslinging buckeroo, shooting innocent Indians. Go, go on." said Kirby.

"So, I'm beside this phantom and ready to collapse. The old cowpoke, probably eighty or more years old, looks at me. His chapped lips barely move, and words come tumbling into my head. When he's done with me, I realize it's what I'm supposed to message to Tilda.

"Astounding."

"After fucking with my mind, he turns from me and blows Tilly a kiss! And get this, he tips his hat to me, like *adios, amigo*, and then he fuckin' dissolves! Gone!"

"We've seen that a million times in movies!" said Kirby.

"I've got to get all of these thoughts swarming around in my, so I climb over the wall. That must have triggered you guys, because all of a sudden, you're awake—like nothing had happened!" Charles slugged down the last of his wine. "Come on, KC, tell me, what's not to believe about all that!" He laughed at how absurd it sounded.

Perplexed, Kirby said, "Damn, Charlie gotta tell you, when you were convincing Tilly, I thought, 'When did you become so sensitive?'"

"The old cowpoke had told me exactly what to say. Wasn't me."

He put the empty glass down on the coffee table. "Little Timmy Gardner was infatuated with becoming a cowboy or cowpoke. I remember the picture on Tilly's dresser, the boy was wearing a cowboy play suite."

"It tells us why Tilly created Timothy, a brother with that outdoorsy, cowboy look," said Kirby.

"Timothy Duclos was a creation that reflected her deep affection for Timmy Gardner and, at the same time, solved her need for companionship and family. I imagine her Timothy persona became frustrated and angry. He pushed her into revenging literary agents who were standing in their way."

Be right back." Kirby scrambled up from the floor and within a minute returned from the kitchen with an uncorked bottle of wine.

"Anyway, everyone thought you'd made up that little story about seeing Timmy to convince Tilly."

"You shouldn't discuss this with them."

"To assuage your existential turmoil, I have two reasonable explanations. Remember, Timothy was as real as rain to her; we know he was a psychotic creation. We've become so intertwined with Tilly; might you have been susceptible to her hallucinations? She only wanted to hear Timmy had become what he longed to be—a cowboy or cowpoke. That old cowpoke, the messenger, was another convincing creation to help her unburden and set herself free. And you convince her to do just that."

"Tilly's imagination made this up to absolve herself of Timmy Gardner's accident? That's your explanation, KC? That all this occurred between Tilly and me—us alone? It did not. I was dealing with influences from other times and places. That I'm sure of."

"You won't get an argument from me. You know where my head's at," Kirby said loading up the wine glasses.

"We have to find a better interpretation; not me as part of Tilly's psychotic imagination. No, this was all Timmy's doing."

"And how's that going to work?" asked Kirby, unconvinced.

Charles took a sip of wine and, before he could speak, had an epiphany.

"KC, if we're having to go down that rabbit hole to explain this, then we'll have to accept multiple levels of being, interactions with the departed, movements between time dimensions—fuck! These are all the unhinged tenets of after-life nutcases that I've always been very skeptical of."

Kirby added, "That's not so farfetched, Charlie."

"So, if the cowpoke was eighty years old back in 1976, he could have been a turn-of-the-century cowpoke. He looked and acted from that era. Timmy Gardner had his accident; the cowpoke died the same time. They connected spiritually. Timmy was too young to express what he wanted to say to Tilly."

"I'm with you so far," said Kirby.

"For God's sake, think about it; he was a mere child but he must have known Tilly's life was one of pain because of her love and affection for him."

"We can't assume her mental illness was caused by Timmy's accident," said Kirby, too clinically.

"Okay. I don't mean he caused her mental illness, but the accident contributed to her breakdown. So, Timmy wanted to make amends, and he needed a suitable vessel with the maturity to speak to Tilly. Ergo, the cowpoke. After all these years, we finally come along, creating an emotional distress in Tilly that becomes an opportunity for them to connect."

Kirby became very analytical, "We have to assume one's past is an indelible event and, in our scenario, is accessible in the afterlife. We have to accept that, to make your hypothesis work."

Charles carried on, "If we assume the cowpoke's willing to speak to Tilly, all of this makes sense. Maybe the old guy's spirit recognized something special in Timmy that he had as a child."

"You're applying earthly human emotions and interactions to those existing on the 'other side.' Sure, you're comfortable with that, Charlie?"

"Well, that's all we got, isn't it? Our perspective from here and now."

"Damn Charlie, was it Tilly's mental illness that enabled this reunion? Is being mentally ill a faculty for paranormal contact?"

Charles braced his head with an open palm, "Let's hope we don't get the chance to find out. But there's the bright side: Timmy got to live his cowboy's life."

"Unfortunately, vicariously. And, he had to get there the hard way," responded Kirby shaking her head in recognition of the painful truth.

"Now you're making sense," said Charles.

They sat back, and let all their lingering thoughts settle.

"You said you had another explanation for this insanity?"

"Yes. Charlie, ask the big question: did Timmy have to ask permission from someone or something to come back?"

"You're not taking me to Buddha or some other religion, are you?"

"What the hell, Charlie, accept it as you want. Existence may be a boundless realm, full of possibilities in all the physical, ethereal, and time dimensions. I'm not capable of understanding the mashed potatoes of our cosmic and temporal existence. But I readily accept existing in the continual graces of a limitless presence—even if it will always be a mysterious puzzle. If what happened to you fits another piece to that puzzle, and also reinforces my belief, I'm good. And if that presence may, in circumstances, intercede to give us a second chance, then yeah, Charlie, I'll go that 'wishful thinking' way."

Charles reached out and dragged her atop him, "You're so fucking smart."

CHAPTER 59

No, you idiot. What are you, fucking brain-dead?

Over the following week the felonious conspirators worked tirelessly to prepare Tilda for her new life at The Oaks. Concerned she might have cold feet at the last moment, at least one of the conspirators would drop in on her every day. Most often it was Charles and Kirby; they'd bring her a dinner or snack and a new supply of Dr Pepper. They got nowhere suggesting three cans of Dr Pepper every day were not essential for good health.

As far as Charles' NYPD responsibilities, he was either in the doghouse or on the firing line. He'd call in the middle of the night and leave a message on Mahoney's office line stating the case had become stressful and he needed another week of R&R. Yes, he was in the process of resolving the maple syrup poisonings. He'd have a complete report as soon as he could get back to N YC.

Ironically, it was visits from Davey and Simon Tilda most enjoyed. Their visits were held on the front porch where she would reprise an episode from *Bewitched* or *Little House on the Prairie* to the glee and joy of Simon who could not have understood a word. One day, they walked down to the fish pit where Tilda let Simon feed her trout fresh hamburger. Soon the trip to the pit became a habit. In many ways, Tilda began to bloom.

Surprisingly, the least of Charles' and Kirby's problems was the sale of The Lost Pine Farm and arranging Tilda Duclos' financials. Dealing with the legalities were uncomplicated after Tilda assigned a limited power of attorney to Sam Piper. Trooper Francine's family had relationships with every element needed in a real estate transaction, so the closing and documentation went smoothly.

The sensible and recently reelected county judge, the Honorable Justice Alice S. Eskew, agreed to interview Tilda Wilcox Duclos via laptop. Tilda sat on her porch with Kirby Clark, Trooper Francine Forget, Sam Piper (who was assigned limited Power of Attorney by Tilda), Postmaster Boucher, and Detective Charles White. Davey held the laptop, keeping them all in the shot, but panning over and zooming in to whomever was answering Justice Eskew's question. Justice Eskew grasped the favorable intentions of the felonious conspirators. A desperate plea made by Susan Williams of Williams Dairy was hard to ignore: "Please, Judge Eskew, please get that crazy hag in a rest home!"

Briefed by Charles and Kirby about the maple syrup investigation and the necessity of distancing Vermont from the New York City crisis, Judge Eskew threw up her hands. "Enough, enough! I don't need to know any more! Send everything to my clerk. She'll make it happen."

In one sweep of judicial largess (or bureaucratic indifference), approved documents setting up Tilda's guardianship with the most respected county bank were accomplished in two days. The real paper shuffling rested with the Addison probate court clerk. Fortunately, she was familiar with the well-established The Oaks Retirement Home. She arm-twisted The Oaks' management to provisionally accept an incomplete background check on Ms. Duclos. Surprisingly, Tilda had enough resources to live at The Oaks in their best unit without the cash from the sale of the farm to Charles and Kirby!

Before The Lost Pine Farm purchase could be closed, the bank demanded holding everything Charles owned in escrow while their mortgage applications went through the system. To Charles' discomfort, Kirby was unable to secure her share of the loan in time for the closing date, so the closing was temporarily delayed.

Consequently, it was Charles' personal property: the New York City condo, savings, investments, and the Corvette—that held the deal together. Kirby's participation would be recognized when her banker, that is, former brother-in-law, could write a mortgage in both their names. When Kirby's share was received, or if they decided on unequal participation, the deed and title would be transferred. Charles' surplus assets being held would then be returned to him.

* * * * * *

Three hundred and fifty miles away, the shit was flying in Mahoney's office. Nasty tidbits of circumstantial evidence were being dutifully collected by a spiteful Sergeant Bookus.

"As far as I can make out, Inspector, Detective White and his cohort, Kirby Clark, are in some shady relationship with this Vermont State Trooper, Francine Forget. Forget's the one who reported about White and the mayhem in the Bristol Post Office. I don't understand the details, but she's now part of their scam. White's girlfriend, Clark, has gotten their pal, a local garage mechanic, Sam Piper, power of attorney for the farm sale. I mean, seriously, that says a lot."

"You think White's got something this stupid going on when he's set to retire in a few months?" Mahoney was incredulous.

"Inspector, I'm just laying out what I've discovered. Trooper Forget comes from a very interesting family and White has researched them. He's also hacked into the loony lady's—excuse me, Tilda Duclos' computer. He must have broken into her residence."

"Go on, Sergeant."

"Everything about the original thrust of the investigation and his official duties have been compromised with his divorcee, Kirby Clark. The Middlebury librarian they interviewed says she believed the Clark woman was with law enforcement. The same misrepresentation occurred at the Bolton Post Office."

"Well, I suspected she was tagging along, but representing her as a law official, that's unrealistically dumb of White," said Mahoney.

"He's committed everything he's got into the purchase of the old lady's farm, which obviously is being facilitated by Forget's shady family."

"He's scamming the old lady out of her property? Do you think he's fabricated this whole story to make this swindle happen? Leaving us nowhere near finding the perpetrators?"

"Yes, boss. I do," he said smugly.

"Our investigation has gone nowhere," reflected Mahoney.

"Well, we've given him a nice holiday and provided him a fuck buddy."

"Let's keep it clean, Sergeant."

"Sir, you've no reason to believe anything in the RTCC reports and he's withholding information. That in itself is reason for disciplinarian action."

"Call White right now. Get him on this phone," Mahoney pointed to his desk landline.

Sergeant Bookus went back to his desk and made the call to Charles on a circa 1970 Bakelite phone, an antique phone he sequestered from supply. He intended to take it home when he'd gotten reassigned and far away from Mahoney. No answer. Called again. No answer.

He swiveled to peer in at Mahoney, impatiently waiting in the Glass Palace to be connected. "He's not answering, Inspector."

"Alright, fuck it! I've got a meeting at the mayor's office. Keep calling until you get him. Tell him I want him at my desk—tonight!"

* * * * * *

Several hours later, Inspector Mahoney returned to find Sergeant Bookus with his phone at his ear pretending like it was ringing.

"Still not answering, sir."

"Get me that Vermont colonel on the phone. We've got to end all this before I have to burn White for thirty years of service and put him in jail. I'm done with this nonsense."

"Should I alert the union, get a representative to sit in, make sure we do this right when we have him?"

"No, you idiot. What are you, fucking brain-dead?"

"No, sir, just going through a divorce."

"Another one? That explains a lot, Sergeant."

* * * * * *

Kirby and Charles were walking Mister Fritz on a leash around the condo's grounds. Kirby couldn't help but notice Charles' phone had rung continually. He finally had put it on vibrate mode. After half an hour of being on vibrate, he turned off the phone altogether.

"What's going on, Charles?"

"It's Sergeant Bookus. Best ignore him."

CHAPTER 60

The only paper I use today is toilet paper—I'm not big on that either

On the day of the big move, the felonious conspirators were fired up and ready to empty the farmhouse. Davey set the foldable playpen, the prison, on Tilda's porch, and so as to not have to deal with Simon *and* Mister Fritz, they were both sent to prison.

By midafternoon, however, the rented U-Haul truck, backed up to the porch, was still empty. It would have to be returned to the Burlington depot by nightfall, even if never loaded or emptied.

Under the little amount of sunlight that managed to slip through the grimy louvered blinds that were opened for the first time in decades, Charles, Kirby, Davey, Sam, and The Oaks' admissions representative, an attractive African American woman, Alice Cooper—found it necessary to zigzag like Liberty ships to avoid the "wealth" Tilly refused to leave: collapsed boxes, newspapers, mailed promotions, old magazines, and crap tossed out of cars by uncaring Flatlanders.

Tilda was planted on a pile of *House Beautiful* magazines from the 1960s, sipping Trader Joe's spiced chai tea. "There has to be space for my collections!" she began anew. On her lap rested the beloved Acer.

"There isn't room in your new suite, Tilly darling," said Kirby flatly.

Charles stepped in, "Remember when we first met, you wouldn't reach across your wall? You were brave and your hand went over that wall. We shook and became friends. Just the other day, we made a new agreement about moving to The Oaks. You haven't regretted either, have you?"

Tilda was quietly contemplating her answer.

"Let's make a new agreement: you'll be happy at The Oaks or you come back. No questions asked."

"You and your agreements, huh? I thought we were going to yen-yang. Big disappointment you turned out to be."

Kirby and Sam rolled their eyes.

Alice Cooper had had decades of experience bargaining with the elderly. "Say we move everything in your bedroom today. You'll sleep in the new suite in your own bed. We'll move everything else when you're settled."

"What? I don't want to sleep in my old damn bed! I want the new one with the big yellow duvet!"

"I understand. We'll leave the old bed, and you can sleep tonight under that yellow duvet on your brand-new Sealy Posturepedic bed."

"Oh? A Sealy bed? Like the TV ads? Where the pretty girl floats down onto the nice soft bed?" Her eyes seemed to light up as she re-enacted with outstretched arms, the floating down aspect of the ad.

"That's right! Exactly like the ones in the ads. So, Tilda dear, what furniture is needed for you to get through just tonight?"

"That's easy. Why didn't you ask me before? I must have the mirror, the one on the stand by my bed. I look into it and I see myself as a young girl again. And my mother's armoire. Can't forget that."

"Okay, good going, Tilda! Let's load up, right now," hastened Alice.

Kirby found a fitting metaphor, "Tilly, think of it like putting a sheet of paper in a typewriter. A clean sheet to start a new novel."

"I have a computer; I don't put in sheets of paper. Girl, you need an upgrade. The only paper I use today is toilet paper—I'm not big on that either."

* * * * * *

Soon, Tilda was riding to The Oaks Retirement Home, crammed in the U-Haul cab between Charles and Sam who drove. Simon rode with Davey in his Honda and was accompanied by Mister Fritz. Kirby finally got to spin the tires in Charles' Corvette, after agreeing to pick up Subway sandwiches.

Tilda carried on an animated and very sane description of how things used to be as they motored past her old haunts. At The Oaks, they unloaded and, with Alice directing, moved Tilda's things to her suite.

Kirby arrived at The Oaks an hour later. Charles' pride and joy was unbent and unscratched.

"I got lost—wink, wink," said Kirby, beaming as she climbed out of the 'Vette with deli sandwiches and drinks. For Charles, it was a flimsy explanation for why she was gone for so long. He knew she had run the crap out of it by the ticking and creaking sounds it made cooling down.

Tilda stayed in her rocker and waited patiently as they set up her room. She was resolute about how the standing mirror was to be placed by the bed. This led Charles to advise her to "cool it" about the yen-yang expectations at her new home.

Alice suggested, "Let's take a short rest, Tilda. You've had a long day, and I know you want to try out the new bed with the pretty yellow duvet."

"You see how my yellow galoshes will perfectly match the duvet!"

"Tilda, darling, you don't want to wear your galoshes to bed, do you?" asked Alice anxiously.

"What? Do you think I'm crazy? To bed? No, but I always wear them in the shower to get them clean."

When they had a private minute, Alice whispered to Kirby, "Don't worry, I'll get her into a bath by tomorrow."

* * * * * *

Not quite ready to split for home, Charles, Sam, and Davey were lingering in The Oaks parking lot drinking Black & Tan beer. It had been a day of waiting, less than an hour of work. Simon was napping in the Honda car seat and Kirby was inside with Alice trying to fill out a medical report on Tilda, a monumental task.

Sam fired up a cigar butt he had been carrying around in his top shirt pocket, the pocket with the big brown stain, and was leaning against the U-Haul's orange fender. Mister Fritz had found an unhealthy-looking rubber ball somewhere on the grounds and was pestering Charles to play fetch. After the morning hiccup, everything had gone smoothly, and they were content to have a reflective moment to revel in what they had accomplished in the last week.

"I like this beer, Mr. Sam," said Davey, polishing off his bottle.

"Yeah, my boy in PA got me hooked on it. You can't find the B & T everywhere, though," said Sam, as he watched two Vermont State Trooper cruisers ominously turn into The Oaks' parking lot.

They stopped behind Charles' Corvette, effectively blocking it from leaving. Four burly troopers exited the two cruisers: three men and an Amazonian woman, all in their fanciful green and gray uniforms with so many yellow stripes and pocket trimmings they could have been a marching band.

"What'd you do now, Davey?" asked Sam.

Charles stepped up to meet Trooper Sergeant Willow who was clearly in command. His jacket stripes and name tag said all that. Charles knew the shit had hit the fan; no need to make a fuss. The die was cast.

"How may I help you, Sergeant Willow?"

"Detective Charles White?"

"Correct."

"You carrying?"

"I am."

"Please surrender it to Officer Greenfield." The female officer took Charles' SIG Sauer and holster.

"We're to deliver you to the Walmart parking lot in Glen Falls, New York, to rendezvous with someone from your office. Sorry, that's all I know, Detective."

Alerted by The Oaks' staff at a window in Tilda's building, Kirby came running outside and latched onto Charles, pulling him aside before the officers could react. Understanding, they respectfully stood back a few paces.

"What the hell's happened, Charlie? What's going on?"

"I'll find out when I get delivered. This is extreme, even for Mahoney."

"What's the worst case?" her eyes began to well up with tears.

"The worst is what we talked about."

"You'd lose everything; we'd lose everything."

"Maybe Mahoney will see it our way, and not go further than a simple reprimand."

"Charlie, if they think you're a dirty cop, they could take everything from you! But most of all, your good name and years of service. They'll try to ruin you! Ruin us, Charlie! Those fuckers!"

"I knew it might happen. We got busted."

"Yes, but we did a good thing! That matters!"

"KC, saving Tilly and giving her a better life has changed me. Remember me telling you about cutting grass and when the Smiths came out to talk to me?"

"I do. The murdered couple," she said nodding her head.

"I took my three dollars and didn't follow-up getting them help the way I should have. I feel what we've accomplished with Tilly has untied a knot inside me—maybe, we can get a second chance for our oversights and selfish misdeeds."

"You idiot, it's called forgiveness!" They kissed for so long, everyone grew uncomfortable. Trooper Fran said, "Why don't you two get a room."

"KC, I love you, but you can't be dragged down with me. We've done what we had to do, and I don't regret a second of it. Especially finding and loving you."

"I'm right with you, Charlie."

"Give it a few days. If you don't hear from me, find a criminal attorney and tell everything. Until then, say nothing, do nothing. I'll call as soon as I know for sure, what's going on."

They hugged and kissed again, then separated. Charles rejoined the Vermont troopers who were growing impatient. Officer Greenfield stepped forward, "Detective, I have to cuff you. Orders." She snapped the shiny stainless-steel cuffs on one of his wrists.

"For the ride? Seriously?"

She glanced at her superior, Sergeant Willow. His eyes wandered up to the darkening sky. She took the cuffs off. Charles dug into his jacket pocket, found the Corvette's fob, and tossed it to Kirby. "Take care of her, KC."

He then winked, leaving her even more unsettled.

What the hell is that all about? A fucking wink about his car!

Charles was directed to the cruiser's rear bench seat by Officer Greenfield. She got in up front, shotgun next to Sergeant Willow, who had slid behind the wheel.

Greenfield turned and said to Charles through the grill opening in the plastic divider. "Detective, I apologize. This is bullshit. We know it's only about sending a message."

Sergeant Willow added, "Before you buckle up, there's a cooler on the floor. Help yourself to the water, but the Yahoos are Greenfield's. She might make you leave a buck."

"No, Sergeant. Detective White is my guest, and he may even have the other half of my tuna sandwich in the tin foil."

"Really? You told me you were saving it for me," said Sergeant Willow, making Charles smile.

As the cruiser crept away from the felonious conspirators, Charles was looking rather grim in the rear seat. Davey rambunctiously began throwing a fist into the air chanting: "Let him go! Let him go! Power to the People! Power to the People . . . !"

Sam looked at Kirby. "He'll grow out of it," he said confidently.

Kirby, with Mister Fritz wrapped under one arm and waving goodbye to Charles, managed to blurt, "He'd better."

* * * * * *

They headed south. The second cruiser peeled off once they had left the Burlington area. Turns out, both troopers were fishers and as they merrily cruised along, all had beaucoup opportunities to tell stories. By the time they approached Glen Falls, no one had anything more to lie about, and Sergeant Willow used the car radio to check in.

"Hey there. We're on schedule. Five minutes out from the 'mart's south corner."

A familiar voice came over the speaker, "Copy that. See you in five."

It was dusk as they drove into the huge Walmart parking lot that was glaringly illuminated with ghostly sodium vapor lights. Sergeant Willow quickly spotted the black Chevy Blazer parked in the southwest corner with the interior lights on and a blond female, head down. Had to be reading a book.

Charles was gratified to see Officer Jeanie Jones, had been sent to fetch him. JJ slid out of his old Chevy, the one he used every day for the past six years, and gave him an unrestrained hug.

"Wow, had I known this was what AWOL gets me, I'd do it more often."

"In your dreams," retorted JJ.

Officer Greenfield handed Detective White's clip holster and firearm to JJ. She passed it to Charles. He reached into the Chevy and placed it on the center console between the seats atop JJ's reading material, John Sandford's *Silent Prey*.

JJ made an exaggerated, comic, up-and-down inspection of Officer Greenfield's uniform. "That's some fancy getup they put you in. I especially favor the yellow pant stripe." JJ stifled a laugh.

This, Greenfield had heard way too often. "Yeah, we fuckin' hate 'em. I see you're allowed to travel in civies."

"I'm out of my officials as soon as I can find a phone booth," said JJ.

"You two, have a safe ride back to Gotham," Greenfield said, bemused.

"You bet," answered White. "Hey, I'll remember our ride and the Yahoo. Thank you both."

The Vermont troopers drove off the way they had come, but now returning like they wanted to get home, have a beer and watch TV.

"You want me to drive? You've been on the road, what, six hours already?" offered Charles.

"Hell no! I picked up this piece of crap yesterday from the motor pool. Don't know how the fuck you drove it."

Charles got in the front seat next to her, "I haven't missed it."

"I had an overnight with an old hug who trains horses in Saratoga Springs. That put me only an hour away from Glen Falls. Yes, if you must know, I'm all relaxed and quite happy."

"That's nice. So, I got you an unrecorded vacation day!"

"Speaking of being all relaxed, Charles, you've found someone new who has pushed you into this kerfuffle?"

"Oh, yeah, big time."

"Those fuckin' bitches. They'll screw your life up any way they can," said JJ, making him laugh.

"She's something good, JJ."

"That's nice, happy for you Charles. Meanwhile, some dick, whose name you'll have to pry out of me, decided to fuck up your assignment. 'Assignment.' That's what they're calling it so you can be held to dereliction of duty and fraud, rather than simply being a drunk cop on vacation. Which suits you better."

"The optics of my trip look pretty bad, I got that. In particular, who's after me besides Mahoney?"

"I give up. You've pried it out of me. That shit bag, Bookus. He's begging to get away from being Mahoney's butt boy."

"What has he done?"

"Besides arranging this trip for you? We've got four hours for me to tell you everything. Sit back, listen, and we'll plan your defense."

* * * * * *

They drove to New York City at a monotonous, sane speed. JJ was not confident Charles' street-abused city ride was safe at any speed—especially one over sixty-five. The trip took a painful five hours but they got to New York on one tank of regular because JJ wisely had filled up earlier and peed in Glen Falls.

"I was told to bring you to Mahoney's office, but as it's going on midnight, I'm guessing he's in the sack somewhere."

"Fuck him. I'm not sleeping on a precinct cot."

"Drop me home and you'll have this car to show up in bright and early tomorrow," concluded JJ.

They drove to her apartment in Hell's Kitchen where there was a drunk street person on her stoop.

JJ didn't hesitate, "Get up, creep! Get off my stoop and take that bottle with you." He did as told and wandered off.

After a hug, Charles acknowledged he owed her, "big time."

She reminded him to take his firearm between the seats. "Whatever happens, don't be a stranger, okay?" Charles slid in, waved a thumbs up, and pulled away from the curb. In the mirror, he saw her blow him a kiss.

* * * * * *

Getting hijacked and leaving Vermont in handcuffs wasn't the way Charles had assumed he'd return to the 7th Precinct. He had stuck his neck out too far and was on the way to getting it lopped off.

We'll see; it's all a fucking word game from here on.

Arriving home, he noted that they had begun erecting scaffolding on the facade for the brick repointing. He put the Chevy SUV in the

Corvette's parking spot. Collecting his mail from the stuffed mailbox, he piled the junk mail on the floor then dropped it all into the trash chute.

Walking through his apartment, he still marveled at the inspiring and spectacular view of the lighted Statute of Liberty. His friend, Mrs. Wilson, had gone into the refrigerator, cleaned out all the spoiled food and tossed the sour milk. Nice, thoughtful lady.

Never having gotten a line wet or tried out his Dog Puke Golden Stone knockoff was his only regret from the Vermont trip. He hoped Kirby could stay the course. No matter what happened to him, she had to walk away clean. He had several scotches and zapped a four-pack of frozen White Castle cheeseburgers he had saved for emergencies. He ended the night in his familiar, very comfortable bed missing Kirby's fragrance and warmness, and wishing he had his book on tying flies to read. He soon fell asleep.

CHAPTER 61

Cap, why did you authorize this moron to dig into my laptop?

The next morning, Charles paid a quick visit to Mrs. Wilson. She was saddened to learn she was going to be without her cherished walking companion, Mister Fritz. He told her he had a new girlfriend and had decided to indefinitely extend his vacation in Vermont.

* * * * * *

Charles dropped the Chevy at the motor pool for an oil change, bypassed his old desk, and went right to Mahoney's Glass Palace. Sergeant Bookus was engaged in a conversation on the phone, as he had been weeks earlier when Charles had been tasked to Vermont. This time, Bookus saw Charles coming down the hall and purposefully buried himself in the stacks of files and documents on his desk, carefully avoiding Charles' chilling stare. Before they could exchange words, Mahoney saw Charles through the glass partition and waved him inside.

"Good morning, Inspector Mahoney." Charles used 'Inspector Mahoney,' not the friendlier 'Captain Mahoney' of the good old days.

Mahoney looked around Charles to Bookus at his desk, "Bookus, come in here. Sit, Detective."

He pointed to the sturdy brown leather chairs facing his desk. "You enjoyed the limo ride back to reality?"

"That was unnecessary. Had I known you were so antsy, I would have called you sooner."

Sergeant Bookus dropped into the other chair carrying a bulging file that he had mashed together. Charles controlled his compulsion to grab Mahoney's glass Christmas globe, which had a picture of his kids floating around in snowflakes if one shook it hard enough, and pound it into Bookus' puffy face.

"Detective White, I have a disturbing amount of information indicating you have neglected your duties. When I sent you to Vermont—"

Sergeant Bookus interrupted, "Inspector, I recommend we record this meeting. May I?"

Bookus placed a small hand-sized recorder on Mahoney's desk, held his finger over the record button, and glanced at Mahoney for approval.

"Put that away, Sergeant. White, you start."

"It was my understanding that once I had put to bed the case in the fashion you directed, were I to want more time in Vermont, that time would be taken out of my unused vacation days. I admit, I was unable to stay in touch with this idiot because of the lack of signal in rural Vermont and bad batteries that wouldn't take a charge."

"That really is a lame excuse for disappearing for weeks, even if your assignment parlayed into vacation time and accumulated sick leave. Bookus, tell me what Detective White is truly accused of."

Bookus cleared his throat and opened the massive paper file on his lap. "On August second, Detective White, while on an official assignment as authorized by Inspector Mahoney—"

"Sergeant Bookus, just tell us what you've found. Pretend it's a college outline with bullet points, not your long-winded bullshit."

"Yes, sir. Detective White began a personal relationship with a suspect, at the least a person of interest, Ms. Kirby F. Clark. She accompanied him throughout his investigation, and at times he represented her as having an official capacity in the investigation. This misrepresentation occurred repeatedly. In an interview with Burlington P.O. Manager Donald Picard, and later postman Nathan Alberts, Clark questioned Bolton Post Office Manager T. S. Frasier. Frasier remembers Ms. Clark asking him questions. In the Presley Public Library in Middlebury, Head Librarian Alexandre Reddy remembers being grilled by Ms. Clark, leaving her upset and unable to sleep that night."

"Hold it, Sergeant. What say you, Detective?"

"That is a moronic mischaracterization of my investigation. Mahoney, for fuck's sake, you sent me to meet with VAMP, the Vermont maple syrup collective. Kirby Clark is their Director of Promotions. She fortunately had the time to help us out; all was approved by her boss. As a local, she knew the postmaster in Burlington, Donald Picard—"

Bookus interrupted, "Oh big effing deal!"

Charles continued, "Without Ms. Clark's assistance, I would never have been able to get access to the surveillance videos without creating miles of paperwork and delays. Without her help, the FBI and U.S. Postal Inspection Service would have, for certain, become instantly involved."

What! That last utterance made Mahoney sit up in his leather-covered swivel seat: *Without her help, the FBI and U.S. Postal Inspection Service would have, for certain, become instantly involved.*

He hadn't really thought of it that way, but now, clear as day, Inspector Mahoney saw he had been reckless in his handling of an interstate postal-based, multiple murder attempt. It screamed to be handed over to the feds; at a minimum, the FBI and U.S. Postal Inspector should have been alerted. He could face the proverbial firing squad and reassignment to some obscure New York State hamlet where he'd take charge of two ticket writers on scooters and one toothless, near to retirement, canine.

"Well, that's only one situation," continued Bookus. Mahoney had tuned out Bookus' drone; he was engrossed with foreseeing his career sliding down a toilet.

"I'm not finished, Bookus," snapped White. "Access to the Williams Dairy property came about because Ms. Clark was close friends with the owner. She directed us to the source of the wolfsbane used in the crimes."

Bookus jumped in, "Yeah, right, White. Did you give her a badge, too? Inspector, we have information on his NYPD laptop that came from the old lady's private emails." Bookus pointed an accusatory finger at White, "You hacked into the loony lady's computer, didn't you? You broke into her residence, didn't you? When you saw all her antiques, is that when you and Clark decided to scam her?"

"Cool it, Sergeant," said Mahoney. "What's that about, White?"

"First of all, Cap, why did you authorize this moron to dig into my laptop?"

Mahoney shrugged.

Charles leaned forward in his chair to be closer to Mahoney. "Be that as it may, information from Duclos' computer came from a tech to whom she willingly gave access. He upgraded her browser, removed a dangerous virus, and then pointedly asked if he could share her information, to which she agreed. I can get a written deposition from him and Ms. Duclos. Furthermore, Bookus, you flaming asshole, she has no valuable antiques."

"Cool it, White," admonished Mahoney.

Bookus continued, "I've looked into his spending on his department-issued credit card. He's spending close to $400 a week on gas! Bet he's filling up her car on our dime, too! But, happily, since he's been shacking up with Clark, there is no hotel bills! Maybe traveling officers should be asked to overnight with girls or boys they pick up? Think of the money we'd save!"

"I don't think we'll consider that option for stretching department funds," said Mahoney dryly.

"He's been charging booze at the state liquor stores, and bought a pile of expensive clothing. Get this, a pair of $875 red cowboy boots!"

White was steaming, "Bookus, I ought to wring your fucking neck! I've never had anyone question my receipts. They haven't been turned in yet! And, before submitting them, the cowboy boots, liquor, everything, would be charged back to me even though they were used in the assignment. You dickhead."

"Let's continue less emotionally. What else, Sergeant?" Mahoney had become more than a little detached as the FBI and U.S. Postal Inspection Service consequences were still worming around in his head.

Bookus wouldn't let up, "White's logged onto every official crime data site he can access in the field, looking into the Forget family. Francine Forget's the Vermont state trooper who facilitated the sale of the Duclos property to White through her family connections. No outside real estate agents were involved, no advertising, no counteroffers!"

"Hold on, Sergeant. Just because Trooper Forget comes from an interesting family, that doesn't mean she's bent."

"In this case, I disagree, sir. He's committed his savings and assets to the purchase of the loony woman's farm, all fraudulently facilitated by Trooper Forget's shady family. Why would she do that unless there was some payoff?"

"Bookus, you douche bag. I'm going to tell Trooper Forget what you've accused her of, and she's going to come down here and beat the crap out of you," said Charles laughing.

That got Bookus to jump out of his seat and get into Charles' face. "Screw you, White! Everything about this investigation has been compromised because of this slut divorcee and your lack of professionalism!"

"Calm down, you two. You seriously think, Sergeant, he's fabricated this bizarre narrative about this loon to make some scam happen?"

"We're talking about withholding official information from the chain of command. That in itself, is reason for a disciplinarian hearing. At the very least, he should have all his assets frozen until Internal Affairs can determine the depth of his crimes!"

Detective White knew when to keep his mouth shut. Bookus had had his word. Now, it was up to Mahoney.

"How much has White shelled out to make this alleged scam work? What's the farm costing him?"

"Looks like $425,000."

"Dollars? What the hell, Bookus! Does this farm have oil on it?"

Detective White maintained his silence, hoping it was going his way.

"No, sir. None that I can determine."

"What the fuck!" Mahoney tapped a Bic on his Mac keyboard, his nervous tick. Then as an afterthought, "Do we know its worth before White bought it?"

"I saw it somewhere here in the papers prepared by a bank for the loan application. The banker involved is the brother-in-law of Ms. Clark. Chancy that, huh?"

No reaction from Mahoney or Detective White.

Bookus separated a stapled cache of a few pages. "Yes, sir, here it is!"

"And what was the appraisal?"

"It came to $375,000."

Mahoney couldn't refrain from a jaw-dropping exclamation, "So he's scamming this mentally ill woman by paying her $50,000 more than it's worth?"

"I guess I could have gotten the figures wrong. But that doesn't change anything."

"No Bookus, no, no, no. Detective White may stray and get into a heap of shit, but he isn't totally stupid! At least, I don't think you are. Are you stupid, White?"

"No, sir, not stupid. But I have pulled some real boners, sir."

"Meanwhile, with all this jerking off, we're nowhere near passing a tit of information to the Vermont DA so they can make an arrest!" Mahoney was red in the face.

"Cap, that's not necessarily correct. I've isolated any NYPD involvement—"

Charles was replying when Mahoney snapped like a desiccated pretzel. He sprung up from his chair, and pointed to the door:

"Fuck you both! Get the hell out of my office. Bookus, you need a day off and a lobotomy. Detective White, you've got until five today to have a complete report on my desk. Then, I'll decide whether we need an investigation by Internal Affairs and a disciplinary hearing with the commission. A report here on my desk by five o'clock today! Got it!"

"Yes, sir."

✱ ✱ ✱ ✱ ✱ ✱

It was five-thirty and Mahoney had just finished eating. On his desk was an open can of Dr. Brown's Cel-Ray Soda, several pieces of crust leftovers from a pastrami-on-rye sandwich, and three squished mustard packets—all from Katz's Deli.

"That was an outstanding sandwich. Thank you, Charles. In no way will it affect my decision on your precarious future." He burped and put his hand to his mouth, way too late to be polite.

"Understood," said Charles, seated in the brown leather chair he had occupied eight hours earlier, sipping a Dr. Brown's Cel-Ray. He had bought a sandwich for himself at Katz's but had eaten it there.

"I read your chaotic, mindless report. An embarrassment to a man of your experience and ability. What you've done makes no fucking sense." He tapped his favored Bic pen on a pile of Post-it notes and Charles' hastily written report.

"That's one way to look at it, but I only had a few hours to prepare it," he answered.

"Alright, Charles, the whole shebang on our villains—and make it the honest-to-God truth."

Mahoney clumped the messy sandwich papers and used condiment packets together and tossed them, along with Charles' report, into his wastepaper basket.

"You can't handle the truth," said Charles, stifling a smile.

"Fuck you, wise ass. Out with it."

"I have a permanent relationship with Kirby Clark. Happened naturally over the first two days. Got to know her and her family, and we've decided we have a future together."

Mahoney exhaled exasperatedly, "Romeo, more about the crime, if you don't mind."

"When I understood Tilda Duclos' motivation to poison literary agents, I had to confront our classic dilemma: choosing between right and wrong. Right would be stopping her, but wrong would be punishing her. Her crimes were orchestrated by her imaginary brother—the Timothy character in my RTCC reports. Her background speaks to an underage rape, a lost child, undiagnosed mental incapacity, and anything else that can go wrong in a woman's life. In an ironic way, she's a victim, too."

Mahoney now was tapping the Bic impatiently on the Mac keyboard.

"I grew fond of Tilda Duclos. She's a trip, to put it mildly. I decided her interest and our state would be best served with her in a care home—not in a state-run facility for the criminally insane. With us buying the farm at a fair price, she would have the funds to get proper psychological care in a private rest home. Sir, writing is Tilda Wilcox Duclos' thing, not killing people."

"Oh, what a tangled web we weave when first we practice to deceive," sighed Mahoney, dropping the overused Bic and downing the last of his soda.

"Great Scott! My God, Mahoney. I didn't know you knew, much less could recite, one line of Sir Walter's poetry."

"I was an English lit major until the Marines. That's why I understand crazy people, and show you and Bookus so much patience. Wrap it up, White."

"I've neutralized her ability to start any sort of new criminal activity, and she is now residing in a facility that meets her psychological and physical needs. All this is now done without expense to New York or Vermont. She's old, fragile, and harmless. That's all of it, Captain."

"You're trying to make me cry. Is she at this moment in New York State or elsewhere?"

"Elsewhere."

"That's a relief. What do you suggest we do?"

"Nothing."

"You're serious? Explain."

"It's far too complicated for a bureaucratic mind."

"Figured you'd say something endearing, as there are so few months left to make your life miserable. Knowing that I may have to contain your cluster fuck, give me a simple rundown of the people this charade has bumped into. You know, something for my memoirs."

"We've worked with an overly cooperative judge, a reasonable banker, an old-fashioned country lawyer, even a U.S. postal person—plus a fleet of sympathetic secretaries in several elected public officers. All stuck their necks out to get our mentally ill suspect into a healthy environment where she could live and die peacefully."

"You're thinking all these innocent, well-meaning people will get hurt if this implodes?"

"You bet. Besides them, the maple sugar collective wants this to disappear. Why shouldn't they? They had nothing to do with the crime. Trust me, Vermont doesn't want to hear about poisoned maple syrup."

Inspector Mahoney made an odd grumbling sound. Charles decided to go for the kill.

"It'll be a hell of a story if it gets out, Captain. Duclos' pathetic situation will not escape the media; they'll be sure to spell your name right."

"That is exactly what I had advised you, I did not want to happen."

Charles had no answer for that, so kept his mouth shut.

"Essentially, you'll let this fester on my watch as another unsolved case when you know that's a total falsehood."

"I know for a fact, that Vermont State is not going to charge Ms. Duclos for poisoning six New Yorkers."

"And what about those injured New Yorkers?"

"They're alive. Going further has no benefit."

"Is she immobilized? I mean seriously, Charles, made harmless?"

"All done."

"Okay. In this situation, how do you suggest we proceed?"

"Captain, I strongly recommend a General MacArthur."

"I see. We let six New Yorkers' pain and suffering . . . *just fade away?*"

"Yes, Cap. For fuck's sake, an imaginary brother compelled her to commit the crimes. He can never be found, and there's no hard evidence either way, making a prosecution impossible. She has no recorded psychological issues, no medical history. It's a minefield for any district attorney, ours or theirs. And if New York were to somehow be saddled with her, a trial would be costly beyond our combined imaginations."

"You sound sure, Charles."

"Captain, are you going to keep me here all day going around and around? I'm trying to reassure you, there's nothing you can do!"

Alright, I get it!. Anything you may have done, or has been done, was on your own, and solely by your initiative."

"Absolutely, Captain."

Charles watched patiently while Mahoney took another slug on his soda and started up again with the tapping of his Bic against the Mac keyboard.

Why don't you put that fucking pen down and do anything else less irritating—scratch your ass for all I care.

"Rewrite that bullshit report into a professional document. Add an admission of culpability, including your inability to bring home the bacon, and I'll close the case."

"Understood. Consider it done."

"You have checked in and are back on duty, Detective White?"

"Correct. But I'd like to do one more trip north to wrap things up."
Liar, liar, pants on fire.

"Hmmm. I don't think so," said Mahoney without a millisecond of consideration. "By the way, my new buddy, Colonel Hanover, Director of Vermont State Police, sent me an email. You have a judgment and warrant filed against you for some $860.00. An unpaid speeding violation, busting a light, and a complaint of sassing a state trooper. All written in Bristol, Vermont. Someone's lost no time throwing the book at you up there."

"Fuck me!"

"Honestly, White, before I kick your ass out the door . . . confess: did you fish up there?"

"I swear, Captain. I haven't gotten a line wet."

"Hmmm. I have a few more months to torture you before you retire. Bring JJ current on cases you've worked on that are coming up for trial. We want her up to speed so she can appear in your stead."

"Will do." Charles placed his empty soda can on the side table next to his chair and stood. "Cap, I hate saying this, but I appreciate your integrity and fairness."

"Sure, you do. Stay away from my office, Detective White. And don't pull any more shit."

"I'll be good, I promise."

Charles was almost out the door before getting one last order from Mahoney who was pointing at the side table. "Don't forget that soda can."

CHAPTER 62

Slippery . . . phone sex?

Charles sat on the leatherette sofa in his condo looking out at the Statue of Liberty as the sun slowly faded. All the lights had come on and the ferries to New Jerry were crisscrossing the Hudson. A private twin-engine prop aircraft, much like Davey's Aerostar, came down the river followed by a helicopter with its side utility door open. He could see a long lens and a camera crew working inside; a cherry photo assignment, filming a new pristine, private aircraft with the dusk view of New York City and the harbor as a background. Or a snippet for a feature film or TV series?

Charles picked up his cell and speed dialed. "Hey, sweetie!"

"Well, it's about time, Charlie! You've kept me chewing nails for, what, twenty-four hours?" Kirby was driving her Jeep Cherokee loaded with dog food from Petco.

"I'm aware it's been forever. But I didn't want to jinx a good outcome by making assumptions that you'd hang on to. Wanted to make sure it was all over and we were good before calling you."

"Yeah, last time I saw you, you winked at me. Some reassurance."

"I couldn't say it, but when they nabbed me, and I was to be dragged back to Mahoney, I realized I couldn't lose anything, except maybe you. That's why I winked to let you know, it was all right."

"I take a wink as a pretty weak reassurance."

"You were worried they'd take everything, make it look like I was a crook."

"Yeah, that's the general idea. Everything was going to hell pretty quickly," Kirby said.

"Here's the scoop: we went to contract on the farm for cash, using all my assets as collateral, until we could get a mortgage written in Vermont. We don't have a title or deed on the farm. Our banker has everything in his pocket, and no way is your brother-in-law going to give all that money up to New York State without a long expensive battle. Since my pension is safe, locked in my union contract, they can't touch anything I own."

"Ah, I understand! It's all held out of state, frozen in an uncompleted transaction. You are a fox!"

"I've got to work tomorrow and put one last Tilly item to bed. But I'll be arriving tomorrow night in Burlington on the nine o'clock Greyhound from New York City. Think you can pick up this fox? I've got the whole weekend."

"Sure, but I'm using my Jeep to get you. It's slippery out."

"Slippery . . . like phone sex?"

* * * * * *

Charles parked the department's Chevy SUV illegally on the cross street in front of the building's side entrance with flashers blasting and the "On Duty" sign propped against the windshield. In the lobby, the young Hispanic doorman in a natty gray suit buzzed Martha Jane Sidel's apartment and world headquarters of the Romance Agents & Writers Guild.

"There's a Detective White here to see Ms. Sidel," he announced, gesturing to the twin elevator bank.

Pamela Gadfrey met him at the door, a large bundle of manila files balanced in her hands. She was more appealing than Charles had envisioned. His reasoning was based on her working with someone as unpleasant as Martha Jane Sidel, and that she could still be suffering from the wolfsbane.

"I finally get to see you in person, Detective White, after all this time. May I hug you?"

"Yes, indeed." They shared a short but mutually meaningful hug. She managed to keep a hold of the files and papers in her arms.

"How's our writer?" Pamela whispered.

"Writing."

"Excellent. Come in and meet MJ."

They walked into what had been the living room before MJ had it reconfigured into a larger office. There were two new desks.

"That's my desk and Silvia Martinez's. We share it since she's not here every day."

MJ was at her desk on the phone. She glanced up at Detective White and pointed a finger to a seat across from her. He remained standing until she ended the call.

"Officer White, I presume?"

"It's Detective White."

"I heard from your office no arrests are being made in our dreadful poisonings, even though you're aware who poisoned us. I frankly, don't know what to make of that, knowing this criminal is still out there, ready to strike at me again."

"No, that's not going to happen."

That seemed to alert MJ the conversation was not going her way, but she wasn't going to back down.

"Why aren't you going to arrest anyone?"

"There are stringent confidentiality regs because there's a mental health issue."

"That's absurd. So, we won't know who caused all this mayhem?"

"We know who committed the crime, and we know who was responsible," said Charles, going to the bank of windows behind MJ's desk. The windows looked across the street into a new apartment building and a bedroom with open floor to ceiling curtains. A young woman, with a white towel wrapped around her hair in a pink bathrobe, was making up the bed.

Charles had savored meeting Martha Jane Sidel for over a month and now reflected on whether it was going to be worthwhile, or only a spiteful exercise. He turned from the view to face her. She had risen from the desk and had both hands jammed into her hips, ready for a confrontation.

"Well, don't you think I have a right to know who did it?" she snapped.

"Do you recall being met on the street by a rather disheveled elderly woman? About twenty-five years ago?"

"What the hell are you talking about? I can't remember that far back."

"At the time, you were so upset, you filed a police report of the incident. You wanted to deal with her quickly if she ever showed up again."

"You're out of your mind!"

"You've been a big problem to everyone, MJ Sidel. A boatload of problems. Six New Yorkers were put into critical, life-threatening conditions because you are, how can I put it—a nasty, self-centered bitch!"

"Those are slanderous accusations! White, I'm going to report you immediately to your superiors." She pointed to the door, "Get the hell out!"

"Your mother is Tilda Wilcox Duclos. Your grandmother, Rose Wilcox, sent Tilda, a naive, confused seventeen-year-old, to have you in Troy, New York. You were placed for adoption because Tilda had no options, no one to turn to."

"Fuck off! Get out of my office!" screamed Sidel.

"Years later, she came to you begging for forgiveness. To a hot-shot romance writer on the rise, full of self-importance and financial success, you couldn't accept that the pathetic woman confronting you was your mother. You pushed her away like garbage."

"What are you, insane? That crazy woman, she couldn't have been my mother!" stammered MJ.

"You know damn good and well she was." Charles turned to Pamela standing nearby, mouth agape.

"I'm weary from having to deal with the worst in people. It's one of the things that has made my job so sad—and why I'm ready to leave it."

He turned and went for the door. The clutch of files Pamela held tightly to her chest tumbled to the floor. She glowered at MJ who was having to steady herself against the desk.

"You, MJ! Did you cause all this? All this pain and sickness because you abandoned your mother! Are you for fucking real?"

She kicked at the clump of files on the floor, further scattering them about the room and roared, "You asshole! Hold the elevator, I'm coming!"

MJ cried out, "Why should I have believed her? Why?"

They stepped into the elevator going down, already occupied by an elderly woman and her white tutu-trimmed poodle in her arms. MJ was right behind, but the elevator's doors closed in her face as she shouted: "Stop, wait! I'm so sorry, I'm so sorry! I'll send her money!"

As they descended to the lobby, the woman with the poodle said cautiously, "Well, that was certainly interesting! She runs an office out of her apartment, and I don't think that's kosher with our bylaws."

Neither Charles nor Pamela spoke until they were on the Third Avenue sidewalk.

"I'm going home, smoke some weed, order Chinese, and get super drunk with Jeffery. You care to join us?"

"Good idea, another time. I've got a dog to catch."

CHAPTER 63

With that name, how can it be a love story?

It was the onset of winter; the time of icy snow interspersed with ugly, freezing rain. Weeks before, Charles' Corvette had been retired to the barn and hooked to a battery trickle charge. Charles and Kirby drove in the red Jeep to The Oaks Retirement Home after buying two bundles of flowers and a vase at the Bristol Grand Union.

Kirby wore a red down parka that made her look like a big tomato. It covered her colorful paint-splattered clothes she wore when she worked on the farm. Charles looked like an NYPD detective, even with the new wardrobe Kirby had been buying for him.

At the visitors' check-in desk, they were told Tilda was becoming popular during the dining hour. Curiously, an ever-expanding number of male octogenarians were gravitating to her table to dine with her.

They found Tilda in her suite, hunched over the Acer.

"Hey, Tilly," said Kirby.

"I hear they're taking good care of you," Charles said, setting the vase of flowers on her desk.

"Maybe they are. I don't listen to them too much."

"You look quite healthy, Tilly. They're feeding you good stuff?" Kirby asked as they pulled up two seats next to her.

"That's still undetermined. They're letting me drink only one Dr Pepper a day, which is, I think, very, very ill-advised. At least, I can smoke weed whenever I want if I go out on the balcony," she said.

"They tell me you have visitors all the time," said Charles.

"I see my old neighbor, Slim Littlejohn. He takes us to Costco after begging for money. Or do you mean the old farts who hang out when I let 'em? They just want to see my undies."

Charles and Kirby held their breath; fortunately, nothing else about undies was said.

"How's the writing coming?" asked Charles.

"Can't you see? I'm trying to do it right now while you're yakking?"

"That's why we're here. You have an offer."

"We're finished with the sale of the farm. I don't want it back. You bought it, it's yours!"

"No, that's all settled. These are papers from Pamela Gadfrey of Gadfrey Literary Agency. She's a well-respected literary agent you queried for *Final Love*. She's one of the people who became very sick from the wolfsbane, so you should be very respectful toward her."

"I don't know anything about wolfsbane. Except Timothy went to prison and died because of it."

"He died in prison?" Charles and Kirby exchanged shrugs.

"Yep. Officer Forget and Sam Piper came by yesterday and told me all about it."

Surprises every minute from Tilda who had become popular with all kinds of visitors.

"I need to read to you the contract. It's important, and if you're going ahead with Pamela, she needs your signature."

"If you insist. Yes, get it over with!"

Charles read the letter out loud. Tilda impatiently fussed with her neatly manicured fingernails on the mouse pad and bounced her head left and right, signaling, let's go, let's go.

Dear Detective Charles White,

Thank you kindly for sending me the material based on the query submission of *Final Love* by Tilda Duclos. Your letter rekindled my interest in *Final Love* by suggesting the novel encompass the fascinating story of Tilda Duclos and her fantasy brother, Timothy.

I would cherish the opportunity to expand *Final Love* into a testament to her struggle with mental illness by becoming her exclusive agent, editor, and ghostwriter.

This agreement empowers me, with unfettered freedom, to edit and add to Ms. Duclos' work. It allows me to make decisions, generally reserved by the author, to make her story marketable. The division of earnings shall be as in recognized industry standards and finalized at a later date with the approval of her guardian.

If this is acceptable to Ms. Duclos, have her sign the enclosed documents with a witness.

Sincerely,

Pamela Jean Gadfrey

Founder & Agent, Gadfrey Romance Group

"So, that's it, Tilly," said Charles, putting the paper down in front of her.

"There's a typo. It should be 'fantastic brother' not 'fantasy brother.' And what is this 'mental illness' stuff?" asked Tilda skeptically.

"It's a hot topic in today's market. You know, it'll be good for sales," answered Kirby.

"Overall, Tilly, the agreement means you'll have an agent to represent your writings—if you want," said Charles.

"And take it to a publisher?"

"That's right. Pamela will do her best for you."

"You can expect she'll want to make a lot of changes to your work," said Kirby.

"What type of changes?"

"I'm sure she'll make changes in the text. Maybe change the title," offered Charles.

"Change the name from *Final Love*? To what?"

"Maybe *Killer Vine: The Story of Tilda and Timothy Duclos*," said Charles, looking skyward.

Tilda took a minute to think about it while they held their breath.

"With that name, how can it be a love story?"

"You'll just have to trust her and see," said Kirby.

"Whatever. That's okay by me. Make sure she spells my name right. It's French, and people try to pronounce the 's' when it's silent. You're just supposed to end with the 'o' sound. Just like that Trooper Francine Forget woman. For-jay. Same difference."

"Tilly, I have to read you the complete contract; you can sign it if it's to your satisfaction. Kirby and I will act as witnesses."

"Stop talking. Yak, yak, yak! Give me a pen for Christ's sake! You may be a stud, but you are un-godly slow."

While she stewed impatiently, he read each page aloud before letting her sign.

"Keep in mind, Pamela Gadfrey, your agent, will want to interview you to get to know you. Okay?"

"Yes, yes, yes. How can I forget? Drag my rocker over there before you leave—it's too heavy for me to move. Bring the folding table for my Acer, too."

They moved her rocker and table to where the sun was coming through the twin glass doors that opened onto the deck. Tilly could look out at the Green Mountains, watch the snow add a white dusting onto the deck, and work the Acer.

Preparing to leave, Charles kneeled down to her eye level.

"Tilly, did you know we found your daughter in New York City? The one you met on the street long ago."

Tilda's face became unsettled. "No, not that woman. She wasn't my child. My baby, my lovely child is still out there."

Charles and Kirby exchanged glances. Could there be a second child? No, this was a kinder way; hoping for something better to come out of that troubled time.

"I'd like to ask you another thing about what happened long ago. It may be upsetting, but I'd like to know," asked Charles.

"In that case, get it over with!"

"Tell me about your neighbor, young Timmy Gardner, and the accident."

They watched a tightness develop around her mouth. She fussed with her hair while incoherently mumbling.

"It might help if you speak out loud about it," said Kirby, resting a hand on her shoulder.

Tilda dropped her arms to her lap, exasperated.

"Oh, my little Timmy Gardner. He was small for his age, but the loveliest little boy. So sweet and happy, growing up like a wild bush. I'd watched him and his folks plant a summer garden year after year. You know they didn't live here full time."

"But they were here for the Bicentennial in 1976," said Charles.

"He was becoming such a nice young man. We fished at the pit together. I knew that could give people the wrong idea, but I thought of him as a younger brother."

Tears began to trail down her cheeks, which she swiped away with her palm.

"I saw him line those damn fireworks on the wall he had gotten from a school thug, I suppose. All the celebrations, all the excitement, he wanted to take part. He was so cute in his little straw cowboy hat and those red boots. You know, I yelled over and over again, "Don't do that or I'll call your folks.""

She paused, perhaps accepting it was better to unburden herself one last time to her friends.

"He lit one of them little red round things, but it rolled off. He grabbed it from the grass and set it right back on the wall. But it went off, making a big foul red cloud around his hand. Hundreds of little sharp pieces of stone, no bigger than my fingertip, flew out from the wall and hit him right here."

She reached over to Charles and touched him gently on the neck where the stone shards hit.

"There was so much blood, blood all over his clothes, blood on his little red boots. His papa and mama pressed his bandana tightly against his neck. I ripped a hem out of my dress, and we tied it around his bloody fingers. We couldn't stop the bleeding! We were all crying; I cried as I raced them to Middlebury Hospital. It was so horrible. I looked to the back seat, where he was crushed between his folks. His little blue eyes were open, but he had gone to sleep."

"We're sorry, Tilly. Real sorry," said Charles.

"I could never get the blood out where my little Timmy died. His folks left and never came back. Sold the land to the dairy. When Timothy visited, he didn't like seeing the old place, so he burned it down. End of story."

Tilda sniffled. Charles gave her his handkerchief. She wiped her nose and cleared the tears on her cheeks. "I don't want to talk about it anymore."

"Let's not." Charles took one of her trembling hands and gave it a gentle squeeze.

"Write about it. It'll make you feel better," suggested Kirby, giving her shoulder an affectionate rub.

In an abrupt, unpredictable reorientation, Tilda's horrific ordeal got put away, as if gone to a locked closet, the one reserved for unbearable memories.

"What the hell do you think I'm doing?"

"Okay. Understood. We just want to make sure you're happy," said Kirby.

"You *are* happy in your new home, aren't you, Tilly?" asked Charles, aware of his promise to her and the move into The Oaks.

"Yes, yes, yes, I'm just ecstatic! But I'm very busy, and we're in the twenty-first century and we do have phones. Call before you come to bother me," said Tilda, impatiently eyeing the blinking cursor on the screen under the title, *Final Love II*.

"We'll be dropping by every so often. And we'll remember to call," said Charles smiling.

As they reached the door, Tilda swiveled about and made a startling, emotional outburst that must have chiseled through decades of a disruptive, impossible-to-cure illness.

"I do love you both very much. I know and appreciate what you've done for me. You, Sam, Davey, and Simon—even the bitch, Nazi trooper Francine—you're all I've got. You are my family."

She turned to the waiting keyboard and the blinking cursor.

"Well . . . we'll see you soon, but we'll call first," said Kirby holding back tears.

They left The Oaks feeling heartened and wonderfully settled. For the first time, they knew how deeply appreciated they were. It had all been worthwhile. Everybody won.

* * * * * *

On their way home, they slowed by Bristol Falls. It would be another five months before the bathers and swimmers would return with picnics and teenager towel parties. The surrounding trees had dropped most of their yellow and red leaves, and the previous cold, clear waters of Bristol Falling Bra Falls had gained a tint of long-brewed iced tea. Through the gathering swirls of gently formed snowflakes, the peaceful scene marked a memorable time for Kirby and Charles.

"Charlie? Are we finally—ta-dah—case closed?"

"Yep. You did good, KC. We did good."

CHAPTER 64

Male No Single Visitors!
Door must remain open!

Charles was never going to get used to the dreary drive out of New York City to Vermont. He had already accumulated several New York Thruway speeding tickets. Without a green light from Albany, goodwill between New York state troopers and a retiring NYPD detective had limited sway. The speeding tickets were earned in a 2018 Subaru Charles purchased from Sam Piper. The Corvette didn't like ice and snow and would be immobilized in the barn on a battery charger until Spring came around.

This was one of his final days on the force. Charles was at his desk closing out files, preparing to turn over his desk keys to Detective Jeannie Jones, his anointed replacement. On his desk sat a Christmas advent calendar JJ had constructed for him. It had the little doors for each day to open, inside were different colored jelly beans. Most of the little doors had been opened, he was collecting the beans for Simon—although Mister Fritz loved them, too.

Beethoven's Fifth sounded. "Baby doll, what's happening?"

"Lots! We've got a rapidly shrinking construction list! Got about an inch of snow last night, but Sam came anyway with a log skidder. He pushed the whole house over two inches. We're now sitting on the original foundation boulders, all even-like. Charlie, I was so scared the whole house was going to collapse!"

"No problems with the electrical and water lines?"

"He found enough slack in both, and he disconnected the natural gas line. We'll be getting a new tank in a week."

"Awesome. We owe Sam."

"The Building Department approved our home-drawn reno plans. All the new windows can be now installed—get this—in one day! New insulation and sheetrock can go in when the windows are hung."

"Sweet! That's really good news."

It's going to be March before solar panels and the Musk's Powerwall will come, but that propane heater makes the place toasty so we can work."

"Excellent."

"The well drilling crew is bringing their rig tomorrow morning. He wants to get eight gallons-a-minute flow. Plumber's ready to do the hookups when we know exactly where the well is."

"Sounds good to me."

"Slobberu lives on. Davey visited Tilly; he told her his Honda died and she gave it to him."

"Well, I have mixed feelings about Davey keeping Slobberu."

"You can talk to him. I ran into Susan Williams at the top of the driveway in her black Suburban packed with kids and skis. They were on their way to try the first snow at Middlebury Snowbowl. She's wondering if we'd sell or lease our acreage on the other side of the road. I told her we would be willing to work something out. Whatever they need for pasture is okay by me. You approve?"

"Good move, KC. How's my tyke?"

"Davey has him hooked up to one of those spring chairs that's attached to the ceiling. He loves it. He's leap-frogging off the floor all day. We're calling him Birdman."

"Ah, after my Charlie Parker."

"Leaping off the floor all day. Birdman! Charlie? As in birds."

"Oh, sorry. Teddi and Mister Fritz getting along?"

"Right here at my feet. They're looking at me knowing I'm talking to you. I just learned my ex never got her spade. So, Mister Fritz is getting a little frisky."

"Don't, do not let it happen."

"As if he could reach her. Teddi's off to the vet tomorrow anyway. Meanwhile, Mister Fritz has been proudly showing up with dead squirrels. Two so far this week," said Kirby, followed by a sigh.

"Ah, shit. Well, he's a born ratter. How about our fish?"

"Love hamburgers. Unfortunately, Simon and I have given them names. I suspect you'll be dismayed."

"It's difficult to eat something with a name."

"Ha! You're not a Vermonter yet!"

Kirby shuffled a piece of paper. "Let's see, next bit of important info. The Oaks had to put a notice on Tilly's door: "No Single Male Visitors. Door must remain open with visitors." Other than that hiccup, she's peachy as can be."

They couldn't help but burst out laughing.

"KC, please tell me they won't kick her out, will they?"

"I checked. Charlie, they can't. It's in the contract. When are you coming back?"

"I'll drive up this Friday night. Can only stay for the weekend though. Realtor coming Monday."

"Can't wait. Really, really miss you. Mister Fritz and Teddi miss you, too."

"Maybe you can come down to the city while we sell the condo? Catch a show?"

"I've got Simon. Davey's gone round the clock at Fed Ex to make bucks for flight time with his buddy in the . . . Aerojet?"

"Aerostar. Jeez, I almost forgot. You'll love this. I got a long text from Pamela Gadfrey."

"Don't tell me. I pray she's not bolting," gasped Kirby.

"Au contraire. She's gotten the first four chapters of *Final Love II* read, and she's undecided if it's drivel or if she's discovered another William Carlos Williams."

"Fuck me! Really?"

"Honest to God, KC."

"I'm going to pee my pants," she, too, was having quite a laugh.

"Ah, can't wait to see what's going on. You're doing all the work. I feel guilty."

"I love doing it. It's not work. It's for us."

"Miss you. Love you."

"Charlie, make it easy on yourself. Get back to me as soon as you can."

"You bet."

The End

ACKNOWLEDGMENTS

My parents were avid readers and writers. My father, an architect, wrote about architecture. My mother, under the name Martha Melahn, wrote about everything else: cookbooks, romance novels, historical fiction. She was very encouraging towards my writing, offering insightful criticisms like, "You use too many semicolons." They were parents occupied with themselves but always had time for us seven children from two marriages. I miss them dearly.

My lovely wife, Randall, suffered through having to read first drafts, second drafts, etc., and was a sharp-eyed and patient reader. I can never thank her enough for making me keep the few sexual scenes tamer than tame so I can use my real name. Lest I forget, I can never thank her enough for being the most wonderful woman in the world and for being my mate for life. Our children are a blessing for so many reasons. If you have kids, more need not be written.

Along the path to getting into print, my most elegant and beautiful sisters, Bebe and Shelley, offered invaluable encouragement over the years of reading my scribbles. Bebe was especially helpful as she took on the arduous task of making several eagle-eyed edits on *Literary Agents Must Die!* and found enough mistakes to prove that I never should have matriculated from high school. I can't thank her enough for the time she labored on corrections and her wonderful support of all my keyboard adventures!

Important to getting the basic spelling and diction correct in early drafts, were the well-appreciated contributions by John Karam, a good friend from the Porsche Club whom I roped in to read *Literary Agents Must Die!* He microscopically checked every sentence and word. Wow, I never realized how often the spell-checker would mess up distinguishing "there" and "their." If you need someone to pull your work together, John's the man.

Among the others who helped with getting the manuscript up to snuff was Dannette Bock, an editing professional who did the final slap on my wrist and exposed so many idiotic mistakes in so many places. I can't thank her enough for getting my writing grammatically and structurally out of the eighth grade.

And finally, the prince o f them all, very special thanks to William Reiss; an esteemed literary agent with an extraordinary talent for words, tales, great ideas —and in my case, having incredible patience. Patience that allowed me to con him into looking at this wacky novel from the earliest draft to get his on-target advice and support over and over again with no intention of ever becoming my agent! That's dedication to the Arts! He's an exceptional man and a gift to the literary universe. William doesn't have to think twice about using maple syrup samples on his pancakes! And I'm thanking, too, his charming wife, Elizabeth, who never once uttered, " William, stop messing w ith Bo's insane story!" How I love them both!

ABOUT THE AUTHOR

I 'm not going to write what I've done, where I've been, or what has helped me be who I am. I've been blessed by a Creator that may be revealed on a wooden pew or a woven prayer mat. I couldn't care less where. I treasure my family, our country, people, fast cars, airplanes, boats, good food, political intrigue, military affairs—and I love writing about them all. I am in awe of our beautiful planet and the bewildering, infinite stars at night, and am thankful the Creator has shared it with me.